Safe Harbor

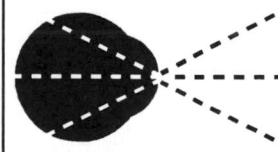

This Large Print Book carries the
Seal of Approval of N.A.V.H.

SAFE HARBOR

CHRISTINE FEEHAN

THORNDIKE PRESS

An imprint of Thomson Gale, a part of The Thomson Corporation

THOMSON

——✦——™

GALE

Detroit • New York • San Francisco • New Haven, Conn. • Waterville, Maine • London

THOMSON

GALE ™

LIBRARY OF CONGRESS CATALOGING-IN-PUBLICATION DATA

Feehan, Christine.
    Safe harbor / by Christine Feehan.
       p. cm. — (Drake sisters series ; #5) (Thorndike Press large print romance)
    ISBN-13: 978-1-4104-0334-6 (alk. paper)
    ISBN-10: 1-4104-0334-3 (alk. paper)
    1. Models (Persons) — Fiction. 2. Stalking victims — Fiction. 3. Sheriffs — Fiction. 4. Sisters — Fiction. 5. Witches — Fiction. 6. Large type books. I. Title.
    PS3606.E36S24 2008
    813'.6—dc22   2007036545

Published in 2008 by arrangement with The Berkley Publishing Group, a member of Penguin Group (USA) Inc.

Printed in the United States of America on permanent paper
10 9 8 7 6 5 4 3 2 1

*For Dianne Fetzer, my beloved sister,
whom I greatly admire and respect.
You are an amazing woman.
You've always known what you wanted
and gone after it courageously.
If anyone deserves a love story, it's you.*

FOR MY READERS

Be sure to write to Christine at Christine@ christinefeehan.com to get a FREE exclusive screen saver and join the PRIVATE e-mail list to receive an announcement when Christine's books are released.

ACKNOWLEDGMENTS

As always, I need to thank several people for their help with this book. Cheryl Wilson and Domini Selk for their patience and understanding. Special thanks to Cecilia Feehan for writing Joley's song to Hannah. To Anita, Kathi, Cheryl, Cecilia, Manda and Carol for their contributions, many thanks! Tina, for her unfailing support and help whenever I ask, and of course, Brian Feehan for his suggestions and talking over action scenes in the middle of the night — you all always inspire me to do better.

"ALL OF TIME"
HANNAH'S SONG FROM JOLEY

Verse 1:
When all has gone away
And you're alone out there
All you have to do is say
I need to hear that you care
I'll whisper or I'll yell
Whichever one you ask
I wish that I could tell
The feelings behind the mask

Chorus:
I'm knocking at your door
But it won't open for me
How can I be there
If you won't let me see
Won't you open for me
Won't you let me inside
I want to be able to see
All the feelings you hide

Verse 2:
When the world has walked out
And you're alone in the dark
When all you do is doubt
And try to find a spark
Call out my name, I'll be listening
Waiting for the wind to send
My name that you're whispering
Baby, I'll be there in the end

Chorus:
I'm knocking at your door
But it won't open for me
How can I be there
If you won't let me see
Won't you open for me
Won't you let me inside
I want to be able to see
All the feelings you hide

Bridge:
Don't be afraid
You don't have to fear
I'm by your side
For all of time
I'll never leave your side
I'm here for all of time
All of time

Chorus:
I'm knocking at your door
But it won't open for me
How can I be there
If you won't let me see
Won't you open for me
Won't you let me inside
I want to be able to see
All the feelings you hide

— Cecilia Feehan

1

"You want to tell me how the hell we got into this mess?" Jackson Deveau demanded as he whipped his arm around Jonas Harrington's waist and half dragged him toward the flimsy cover of an industrial garbage container. "We have a nice comfy job on the Mendocino coast and you decide you're bored out of your mind, which is pure bullshit by the way. You'd think getting shot once was enough for you."

If he could have answered, Jonas would have sworn at Jackson, but he only managed a glare as he forced his feet to keep moving. The pain was relentless, stabbing white-hot like a branding iron. He could feel the breath rattling in his lungs, bile rising and reality fading in and out. He had to stay on his feet. He sure as hell wasn't going to let Jackson haul him out on his back — he'd never hear the end of it. Jackson was right. They'd made new lives, lived good, found a home. What the hell had he been thinking?

Why wasn't it ever enough for him? Why did he have to keep going back, over and over, dragging Jackson and other men down into the muck and garbage of the world? He was no noble crusader, yet time and again he found himself with a gun in his hand, going after the bad guys. He was weary to death of his need to save the world. He didn't save anyone, he only got good men killed.

The alley was dark, the shadow of the surrounding buildings rising above the small lane, turning the edges black. They kept the garbage container between them and the street, where it seemed everyone with a gun and a knife was hunting them. Jackson propped him up against a wall that smelled of times Jonas didn't want to remember, where blood, death and urine all mixed together into one potent brew.

Jackson checked their ammo situation. "Can you focus enough to shoot, Jonas?"

That was Jackson, all business. He wanted the hell out of there and was going to make it happen. The men hunting them had no way of knowing they had a tiger by the tail. When Jackson used that particular tone of voice, men died, pure and simple.

They had to get past the entrance of the alley and it was blocked by the Russian mobsters. It had been a recon mission. Nothing more. They weren't supposed to be seen — damn it — they *hadn't* been seen — but it had all gone to hell fast, turning into a bloodbath.

They'd come to film what was supposed to be a few low-level Tarasov soldiers meeting with a couple of Nikitin's soldiers on the docks in San Francisco. An undercover agent had informed Gray and he wanted to know why the two rival families would be meeting. Jonas's first twinge of alarm came when he recognized the Gadiyan brothers among the participants. There was nothing low-level about them. Brothers-in-law to Boris and Petr Tarasov, they were definitely the upper echelon in the murderous crime family, enforcers reputed to be so bloody and violent that even men in the Tarasov family avoided them. And when Boris stepped out of the shadows with his brother, Petr, his nephew, Karl, close behind to ensure his safety, Jonas knew something big was going down. Karl was reputed to be far, far worse than the Gadiyan brothers.

Jonas and Jackson had looked at each other with their guts churning and hearts pounding because they were right in the middle of a hornet's nest with no way out. The group of Russian mobsters stood for a moment, all laughing together, and then Karl had grabbed one of the men they were conversing with and shoved him to his knees in front of his uncle. It looked to Jonas that all of the men were Tarasov soldiers. He couldn't identify the man Karl had singled out. His face was in the shadows and it all happened too fast. Petr calmly pulled out a gun and shot him in the head without a single word. The violence had been swift and ugly, with no warning at all.

Jonas and Jackson had gotten the murder on tape and were looking for a way out when another man walked onto the dock. He obviously was aware of the camera, his face hidden, a long bulky coat covering his body. Keeping his face averted, he talked briefly with the Tarasovs and then everything went to hell fast. Karl Tarasov had reacted instantly, sprinting toward the road, finding their car and driver and executing him without preamble. Bullets were flying as the Russians spread out and began to hunt Jonas and Jackson. Jonas took two hits, neither should have been serious, but he was losing enough blood to make the wounds fatal if he didn't get help fast. Jackson had two knife streaks across his belly and chest, injuries suffered as they fought their way off the docks into the alley. The mobsters wanted the film back.

No way were they getting it.

Jackson slapped a full clip into Jonas's gun and shoved the gun into his hand. "You're good to go." He slammed home a full magazine and shifted his weight onto the balls of his feet. "I'm going up top for a few, Jonas. You put another pressure bandage on the wound in your side, and no matter what, stay on your feet. I'm going to shake things up a bit in a few minutes and you've got to be ready to run."

Jonas nodded. Sweat dripped off his face and beaded on his body. Yeah. He was ready to run — and fall flat on his face — but he'd keep his feet and the gun and back Jackson in whatever crazy scheme he had. Because, in the end, he could always count on Jackson.

Jackson melted into the night soundlessly, the way he always did. He had come home with Jonas when they'd both been sick to death of living in the shadows — when Jonas just flat out missed the hell out of his adopted family. They'd joined the sheriff's department and lived a cushy life until Jonas had gotten himself shot on the job and became restless and edgy recuperating. His old boss, Duncan Gray, from a special ops team buried deep in the defense department, had come asking. Jackson would have given him a hard look and they would have stayed safe. But no, Duncan had known to come to Jonas, because Jonas fell for the "we need you" line every damn time.

It was a hell of a thing he'd done, pulling Jackson into this mess. And it wasn't the way he'd planned to die, a soft recon on Nikitin's rival mob to see who was coming and going and why. Nothing special, but here they were, shot to hell, and blood leaking out all over the place. Jonas opened the pressure bandage packet with his teeth and spit out the wrapper, slapping it in place before he could think too much about it.

Fire ripped through him, stabbing so deep his body shuddered in reaction. He had to hold himself up by gripping the garbage retainer hard — and wasn't that sanitary? Damn, he was in real trouble this time. He stood swaying, the only thing steady was his gun hand.

Reaching into his shirt pocket, he pulled out a photograph, the single one he carried, the one that mattered. He should have destroyed it. He could see his own face, the terrible raw truth caught on film. He was staring down at a woman and the love on his face, the stark hunger, was so evident it was a betrayal, there for everyone — even him — to see. His finger glided over the glossy paper, leaving a smear of blood. Hannah Drake. Supermodel. A woman with extraordinary, magical gifts. A woman so far out of reach he might as well try to pull the moon from the sky.

He heard footsteps and the whisper of clothing sliding against the wall. Ramming the photograph back in the pocket of his shirt, close to his heart, he shook his head to clear it. More sweat dripped into his eyes and he wiped it away. The hard-asses were coming in first, staying to the shadows but definitely advancing. The sweat stung his eyes, and blood ran steadily from his side down his leg, mingling with the rain that had begun to come down in a relentless pour. He steadied the gun and waited.

At the end of the alley, a man dropped and the first shot rang out almost simultaneously. Jackson was hell on wheels at that distance. Lying up on top of the roof, he could just pick them off if they were stupid enough to keep coming — and they were. Jonas took his time, waiting for a muzzle flash as one of them gave his position away by firing up at Jackson. Jonas squeezed and the count was two for them, but the entrance to the alley still looked a long way away when the stabbing fire was spreading through his body and his blood was leaking all over the ground.

Don't be such a pansy ass. You're not going to die in this dirty alley cut down by a few low-life rats. He spoke sternly to himself, hoping the pep talk would keep him from doing a face plant in the muck. The trouble was, these weren't just low-life rats, they were the real deal, trained in tactics just as he and Jackson had been, and they were going for the rooftop, too. He heard sounds in the building behind him — the building that should have been a warehouse empty of people.

The murder caught on that videotape tonight was worth a lot of lives. Jackson fired again and another body dropped. Jonas waited for the flash of return fire, but not a single bullet was fired. He groaned softly as realization hit him. They knew his position *exactly.* He should have moved the moment he'd fired. He was even further gone than he'd thought. He swallowed hard and stayed low, trying to be a part of the retainer, knowing he had to get out of there, but afraid his legs wouldn't hold. A wave of dizziness hit him hard, nearly putting him on the ground. He hung on grimly, breathing deeply, desperate to stay on his feet. Once he went down, he'd never be able to get back up.

Jackson came out of the shadows, blood dripping from his chest and arm, his face grim, eyes savage. He touched his knife and drew a line across his throat, indicating another kill — and that kill had come between Jackson and Jonas, which meant they were surrounded. He held up four fingers and directed Jonas's attention to two positions close and two behind them. He pointed up.

Jonas felt his heart skip a beat. No friggin' way was he going to climb a fire escape ladder three stories up. He doubted if he could have run the gauntlet, straight down the alley, but it looked a hell of a lot easier — and shorter — than three stories up. He took a breath, ignored the protest as a thousand dull knives sawed into his insides, and nodded his assent. It was their only chance to get away clean.

Jonas took a step away from the receptacle, following behind Jackson. One step and his body went ballistic on him, the pain crushing, robbing him of all ability to breathe. Shit. He was going to die in this damn alley, and worse, he was going to take Jackson with him — because Jackson would never leave him.

Enemies were closing in from every direction and there was just no way he could climb that ladder. They needed a miracle and they needed it fast. There was only one miracle that he could count on, and he knew she was waiting for his call. She always knew when he was in trouble. Jonas spent a lifetime protecting her, wanting her so badly he woke up night after night, sweating, her name echoing through his bedroom, his body hard and tight and so damned uncomfortable he sometimes wasn't sure he'd live through the night. But he refused to give in and claim her when he couldn't stop himself from taking jobs like the one he was on — because he was damned if he'd get her killed.

Still, he had no choice. She was his ace in the hole and he had no other option but to use her, if he wanted to survive. He reached out into the night and connected with a feminine mind. He knew her. He'd always known her. He could picture her in his mind standing on the captain's walk overlooking the sea, her platinum and gold spiral curls cascading down her long back all the way to her luscious butt, her face serious, gaze on the sea — waiting.

Hannah Drake. If he inhaled, he could

breathe her in. She would know he was in trouble. She always knew. And God help him, maybe that was what this was all about. Maybe he had wanted her attention — needed her attention — and this was the only way left to him. Could he be so fucking desperate that he would risk not only his life, but Jackson's as well? He didn't know what he was doing anymore.

Hannah. He knew he touched her mind, that she touched his. That she had known the moment the trouble had started and she had been waiting, steady as a rock, in her own way as reliable as Jackson. She waited only for a direction before striking. Now that she had one, all hell was really going to break loose. Hannah Drake, one of seven daughters born to the seventh daughter in a line of extraordinary women. Hannah Drake. Born to be his. Every harsh breath he drew into his lungs, every promise to stay on his feet, to stay alive, he gave for Hannah.

Jackson pointed back toward the building and Jonas swore under his breath. He took a tentative step back toward the shadows, bent over, stomach heaving, tossing up every scrap of anything he'd had to eat or drink in the last few hours. The terrible wrenching sent another wave of dizziness sweeping over him and jackhammers did a macabre tap dance, ripping through his skull. Sweat dripped and blood ran and reality retreated just a little more.

Jackson got an arm under his shoulder. "You need me to haul you out?"

They'd need Jackson's gun if they were going to make it. Jonas had to find a way to dig deep and stay on his feet, crossing the distance and climbing for freedom with two bullets in him, and a still-fresh wound from an earlier gunshot. He shook his head and took another step, leaning heavily on Jackson.

Hannah, baby. It's now or never. He sent the silent prayer into the night, because if there was ever a moment that he truly needed her unusual skills, it was now.

The wind answered, rising fast and furious. It blew down the alley with the force of a hurricane, howling and ripping strips of wood off the buildings. Debris swirled, rose into the air and flew in all directions. Cardboard and other trash hurtled through the air, slamming into anything in its path as the wind made its way to the back of the alley, where it curved and began to race in a horrifying circle around and around, faster and faster, building more speed and ferocity. The wind never touched either Jackson or Jonas; rather, it moved around them, creating a cocoon, building a shield where dirt and debris churned to form a barrier between them and the world.

Be safe. Two little words, wrapped up in silks and satin and soft colors.

"We've got to move," Jackson said.

Jonas forced his feet to keep shuffling, every step wrenching at his insides, the pain grinding through his body until he could only clench his teeth and try to breathe it away. His efforts didn't work. *Hannah. Baby. I don't think I'm going to make it home to you.*

The wind rose to a shriek of protest, throwing everything in its path into the air. Arms and legs tangled as men went down or slammed into the sides of the buildings along with the debris. Jonas could hear screams and grunts of pain as their enemies, caught out in the unnatural tornado, were tossed about in the fury of the wind.

Jonas stumbled, managed to catch himself, but pain and the waves of dizziness and nausea were his enemies now. His stomach heaved and the ground tilted. Blackness edged his vision. He stumbled again, and this time, he was certain he would go down, his legs turning to rubber. But before he could fall, he felt the pressure of the wind nearly lifting him, supporting him, wrapping him up in safe arms.

He let the wind take his weight and carry him to the ladder. Jackson stepped back to allow Jonas to go up first, all the while watching the alley and surrounding buildings, squinting against the force of the wind.

Jonas reached up toward the last rung of the ladder and white-hot pain burst through him, driving him to his knees. At once the wind caressed his face, a soft fanning, as if a small hand touched him with gentle fingers. All around him raged a virtual tornado, yet tendrils broke off from the spinning mass and seemed to lift him up in strong arms.

He let Jackson help him to his feet, buoyed by the wind, and he tried again, working with Hannah's windstorm, allowing the strong updrafts to aid him as he bent his knees and leapt to close the gap between him and the lowest rung. The metal struck the palms of his hands and he closed his fingers in a tight grip. The wind pushed and he reached for the next rung before his body could absorb the shock of taking his weight.

Somewhere far off, he heard someone's hoarse cry of agony. His throat seemed ripped raw and his side on fire, but he let the wind push and push until he was moving up the ladder to the roof. He crawled out onto the roof, praying he wouldn't have to get up again, knowing he had no choice.

Jackson dropped a hand on his shoulder as Jonas knelt on the roof, fighting for air. "You got another run in you?"

His ears were ringing so loudly, Jonas almost missed the thin whisper. Hell no. Did it look like it? He nodded and set his jaw, struggling back to his feet. The rain was relentless, pouring down on them, driven sideways by the wind, but still they seemed wrapped in a cocoon of protection.

Below, they heard shouts as a few of the braver men tried to follow them up the ladder. The wind built in strength, slamming into the building so hard more windows shattered and the fire escape rattled ominously. The ladder rocked with such force, the screws and bolts began to shake loose and drop toward the street below. The wind caught the small metal pieces and sent them hurtling like lethal missiles at the men attempting to scurry up the rungs.

Men screamed and let go of the ladder, jumping to the ground in an attempt to get away from the blast of bolts rocketing toward them. A few of the bolts drove deep into the wall and others into flesh and bone. The screams grew frantic.

"Damn, Hannah's royally pissed," Jackson

said. "I've never seen anything like this." He got his arm around Jonas and half lifted him to his feet.

Jonas had to agree. The wind was Hannah's favorite medium to work with and she could control it. And man, was she controlling it. He didn't want to think about how much of that anger might be directed toward him. He'd promised the Drake sisters he wouldn't do this kind of work anymore. They'd know he'd dragged Jackson right along with him, and telling them Jackson had insisted on coming along wouldn't do anything at all to get him off the hook.

He concentrated on his breathing, on counting steps, on anything but the pain as Jackson dragged him across the roof to the edge. Jonas knew what was coming. He was going to have to jump and land on the other rooftop, where they could climb down to the street and safety. Hannah would hold the Russian mobsters as long as she could, but only Sarah was in the country to aid her and Hannah's strength would eventually give out. She'd be all alone up on the captain's walk in the cold. He hated that — hated that he'd done that to her.

"Can you make it, Jonas?" Jackson asked, his voice harsh and clipped.

Jonas pictured Hannah standing on the captain's walk overlooking the sea. Tall. Beautiful. Her large blue eyes fierce as she concentrated, hands in the air, directing the wind as she chanted.

If he couldn't make it, he wouldn't get back to Hannah, and he hadn't once told her he loved her. Not once. Not even when she sat by his hospital bed giving up her strength for him to recover had he actually said the words. He'd thought them, dreamt of saying them, once he'd even started to, but he didn't want to chance losing her so he'd remained silent.

He protected people — it was what he did, who he was. Above all, he protected Hannah — even from himself. His emotions were always intense — his berserker rages — his need of her — the stark desire he felt when he thought of her. He had learned to shield his emotions from her almost from the time he was a boy, when he'd realized she was an empath and it hurt her to read people all the time. He'd been hiding his feelings for so long it was second nature to him, and no matter what the opportunity, he always fell back on the old excuse that his job would put her in danger.

It seemed pretty stupid now — especially when he called on her for help. He pulled his hand away from his side and looked at the thick blood covering his palm. Not bothering to answer Jackson, Jonas took a breath and leapt, the wind behind him, pushing hard so that his body was flung onto the other roof. He couldn't keep his feet or even begin to land gracefully. He went down hard, face first, the air driven from his lungs and pain burning through his body like a hot brand.

The dark closed in, fighting for supremacy, trying to drag him under. He wanted it — the peace of oblivion — but the wind whipping around him carried a feminine voice, soft, entreating, enticing. She whispered to him as the wind ruffled his hair and caressed his nape. *Come home to me. Come home.*

His gut clenched and he fought his way to his knees, his stomach heaving again. Jackson hooked a hand under his arm. "I'll carry you."

Off the roof. Down to the street. Jackson would do it, too, but Jonas wasn't going to take any more chances with his best friend's life. He shook his head and forced his body to the edge. He had nothing left but survival instinct and sheer will. He found the fire escape ladder and began his descent, every step jarring, his body screaming. The waves of dizziness and nausea began to blend together until he couldn't really tell them apart. His head felt light and the ground seemed far away, reality distancing itself farther and farther until he simply let go and floated.

Somewhere far away he thought he heard a woman's cry. Jackson echoed it and a hand caught the back of his shirt roughly, the sudden jar sending him right over the edge into the darkness. The last thing he heard was the sound of the wind rushing at him.

Hannah Drake stood on the captain's walk overlooking the dark, churning sea, arms raised as she drew the wind to her, channeled it and sent it racing across the night to Jonas Harrington. Fear and anger mixed together, two powerful emotions, thundering through her heart, racing through her bloodstream to make a high-octane brew, adding fuel to the power of the wind. Tiny pinpoints of light lit up the sky around her fingers as she continued to gather and direct the force to her bidding.

Far below her, sea spray rose into the air as waves crashed against rocks. The ocean heaved and rocked, spawning small cyclones, twisters racing across the surface, twin columns of whirling water raging right along with her.

Hannah.

She heard Jonas's voice in her head, the sound a caress, a soft brushing note that both warmed her and sent a chill through her body. It sounded too close to good-bye. Sheer terror swept through her. She couldn't imagine life without Jonas. What was wrong? She'd woken up with her heart pounding and his name on her lips. She'd known something terrible was happening, that his life was in danger. Sometimes, it seemed to her that his life was always in danger. "Oh, Jonas," she whispered aloud, "why do you feel the need to do these things?"

The wind snatched her question and flung it out over the sea. Her hands trembled and she bit her lip hard to maintain control. She had to get him home in one piece. Whatever he was up to, it was terrible. When he opened his mind to hers, when they connected, she caught only brief glimpses inside, as if he had compartmentalized his feelings and memories as hastily as possible. She saw pain and blood and felt his rage in a brief cataclysmic flash he cut off abruptly.

She needed direction to keep him safe, and she found and maintained it through Jackson. He was more open to a psychic connection when Jonas was too worried about her using her energy up. Jackson let her see the layout of the alley, the condition Jonas was in, the building they had to climb.

She sent a small acknowledgment, using warmth and color, knowing Jackson would understand, and once again lifted her arms. She commanded the five elements, earth, the most physical of all elements; fire, both powerful and frightening; air, always moving, her favorite, her constant companion and guide, providing visualization, concentration and the power of the four winds; water, the psychic mind; and of course, spirit, the binding force of the Universe itself.

Hannah, baby, it's now or never.

Hannah took a deep cleansing breath and harnessed the power of the wind, aiming and focusing, using her mind to draw the elements to aid her. She whispered a small prayer of thanks and opened herself to the universe and all the potential force she could gather to aid Jonas. The air above her thickened and darkened, clouds beginning to boil and bubble in an angry brew. Electricity flashed and sizzled along the edges of the heaviest clouds and the wind began to pick up even more, so that the cyclones out at sea grew taller and spun faster across the water.

Terror squeezed her heart and knotted her stomach. She couldn't imagine her life without Jonas in it. He was arrogant and bossy and always wanted his way, but he was also the most protective and caring man she'd ever met. How many years was this going to go on? How many times would he risk his life before it would be one time too many?

Be safe. She whispered it in her head, sent Jonas the message, wrapped it in soft, warm colors and hoped the simple request would convey so much more. The wind picked up on her fear — on her anger as she received another flash of sight from Jackson. The two men were going up a ladder and Jonas faltered. Her heart stuttered as she saw him go down.

Hannah. Baby. I don't think I'm going to make it home to you.

Her heart nearly stopped. For a moment there was a lull in the storm and then fury swept through her and she let it build, that terrible need for retribution that was a well inside her, bursting open, shattering every restraint she kept so carefully on herself. She built the wind to a ferocious pitch, a shattering fury that raced through the night to crash down like a hungry tornado in that backstreet alley so far away.

The gale chased hapless men with puny weapons that were useless against the forces of nature. The violent gusts smashed windows and sent glass raining down. Boards were picked up and thrown as if an unruly child threw a tantrum. Sweet angelic Hannah directed it all, her flashes of fury sending Jonas's enemies crashing to the ground, helpless under the onslaught of wind and rain and even icy hail.

In the midst of it all, she felt Jonas slip, move farther from her, pain knifing through him — through her, the connection beginning to tear. She sent a steady air-stream to lift him, the currents carrying him higher, shoving him up the side of the building to the roof and freedom. She teased at his face and neck with ruffles of a smaller breeze to try to keep him alert long enough for Jackson to get them both to safety.

She felt him gathering himself for one last huge effort and she sent one last blast of wind to coil around him and take him across one rooftop to the other. She felt the burst of tearing pain, an agony knocking her to her knees. She gasped, tears blurring her vision, running freely down her face. *Come home to me. Come home to me.* The plea was edged in reds and golds, blazing with light and need.

She felt his reaction, the struggle to his feet, the fight to keep dizziness from taking over — the determination that he would make it back in one piece. There was another burst of pain and he slipped even more, darkness edging her vision. Desperate, she sent the wind, a rush of air to wrap around him, and then the darkness took her, too.

2

Jonas blinked as he came up out of a sea of pain. "Son of a bitch, you're scary," he informed Jackson. "Where the hell did you get that look? Practicing in the mirror every day?"

Jackson grinned at him, but his eyes held worry. "Following you to hell and back. You're such a pansy, Harrington. Fainting like a girl. I had to carry your sorry ass all the way to the car."

"I knew you'd complain." Jonas inhaled and instantly frowned. "Not another hospital. You really must be pissed at me."

"You needed a few pints of blood."

Jonas refrained from replying when the doctor stepped into view, shoving a tray closer. This wasn't going to be fun.

Jackson ignored the doctor. "You have to figure out what the hell you're doing soon, Jonas, or you're going to get us both killed."

"No one asked you to come along," Jonas

snapped, knowing he was being completely thankless. He hated the truth when he heard it, especially when he knew exactly what Jackson was talking about. Not what — *whom.*

Jackson shook his head, eyes steady. "You can't save the world and you're going to have to come to terms with it. And you damn well need to fix things with Hannah."

"Mind your own damn business," Jonas snapped, knowing he didn't have the right, but unable to stop himself. He detested hospitals. He'd had his fill already and the wound wasn't that bad. He'd just bled like a pig and gotten a little low. He wanted to yank the needle out of his arm and go.

Jackson stared at him, his black eyes glittering with a coming storm. No one else was stupid enough to call down hell on themselves, no one but Jonas. When had he lost his mind? Jackson didn't deserve his crap.

"You made this my business, and don't try to pretend Hannah isn't the reason we're in this mess. If you'd deal with the woman, no one could talk you into anything like this crap mission. You'd stay in the safe zone, Jonas, and we both know it."

Jonas opened his mouth to deny the charge, but snapped it closed when Jackson looked at him steadily. The doctor doused his wound with some kind of fire-starting liquid that robbed him of thought and made him break out into a swcat all over again. He clenched his teeth and tried not to pass out.

"It's complicated," he said, when he could breathe again. The doctor gave him several shots and Jonas slipped a little farther back from reality. The edges around him blurred and darkened. "Hannah Drake is not like other women. She's different . . . special."

She was — *everything.* Magical. She was his — or she should be his. Why the hell wasn't she his?

"You're looking a little green," Jackson said. "Don't pass out on me again."

Jackson didn't miss much. He noticed every movement, every sound, watching the windows and doors and traffic on the street, and still saw that Jonas was swaying as the doctor began to suture the wounds closed.

"Hey! My side isn't numb," Jonas snapped, clenching his teeth and fists. If the doctor shoved the suture needle into his skin one more time, he was liable to pull out a gun and shoot the man.

"Hurry up, Doc, it doesn't have to be pretty," Jackson said, moving to the doorway and peering out.

Jonas noticed his hand was inside his jacket, where his gun was ready. The doctor gave Jonas another shot of anesthetic and Jonas pressed his lips together hard to keep from swearing. Jackson glanced back at him, looking less than sympathetic.

Jonas closed his eyes and thought about Hannah. Why hadn't he taken control of the situation before it ever got this far? He loved her. He couldn't remember a time when he hadn't loved her. It had just happened. He loved the way she smiled, the turn of her head, the flash of fire in her eyes, the little pout to her lower lip. It sucked how much he loved her. He was a man who always, *always*, wanted control, yet Hannah threw him off balance. There was no controlling Hannah. She was like the wind, unpredictable and fluid, slipping through his fingers every time before he could catch and hold her.

She made him angry when few others could get under his skin. She could soothe him with a touch. He was happy just looking at her — watching her — yet half the time he wanted to yank her over his knees and spank her beautifully shaped bottom. Hannah was complicated and he needed simple. She was brilliant and he was all brawn. She was ethereal, untouchable, the most beautiful woman he'd ever seen — magical even, and so out of his reach.

She was going to be furious with him for getting shot again. Especially as the last time had been only a few weeks earlier and he would have died without her. She'd nearly died herself trying to save him, sitting by his side for days on end, pouring her strength into him and leaving none for herself. He'd been too weak to push her away. He'd needed her there on so many levels, but it had been hell to watch her grow pale and fragile while he grew stronger.

Then afterward, how had he thanked her? Not the way she deserved, that was for sure. He'd been so edgy and restless, so moody. When the boss of his former special black ops team had come asking for help, he'd jumped at the chance rather than telling Hannah the truth about how badly she shook him up. He'd rather look death in the face like some defiant child. All because he loved her so much it was a torment and he knew he could never have her and keep his life the way it was. It wasn't that Hannah would object to the dangerous things he did — if she'd even have him — but he wasn't about to risk putting her in danger. Over the years, he'd made enough enemies that, sooner or later, one was bound to come after him — hell, it had already happened more than once.

He drew in a breath and tried not to wince. "Okay. You could be right. There's a chance she had something to do with it."

Jackson's eyebrow shot up. "A chance," he echoed.

Jonas scowled. "Keep it up. You'll be pulling every crap shift for the next ten months." It was an empty threat, but it was all he had left. He felt so damn tired and empty he just wanted to crawl in a hole and hide for a while, but he knew what was coming and there was no stopping it.

Jackson waited until the doctor had left the room before pulling up a chair and straddling it, facing both the door and the window. "I'm serious, Jonas. You're going to get yourself killed. You stepped right under that light in full view to take that shot. You had to have known you were exposed."

"Karl Tarasov, that son-of-a-bitch enforcer, put a fucking bullet in our driver's head, Jackson," Jonas snapped.

"It was an amateur move and you know it." Jackson was silent a moment. "Or suicidal." Again he fell silent, allowing the word to hang between them.

Jonas sighed and shook his head. "I'm

tired out, Jackson, not suicidal. I was just so pissed. He didn't have to kill the driver. Terry hadn't seen anything. Tarasov did it as a statement. So fuck them. I was just so angry."

"You have no business doing this kind of work, Jonas, I've told you that before. You just can't detach. We survived all these years because we stayed cool. You aren't responsible for Terry's death. He chose to drive the car. You weren't responsible for losing any of our men at any time." He sighed. Talking wasn't his forte and he'd been doing too much of it to keep Jonas on his feet. But this — this was important. Jonas was going to get himself killed. "You can't be emotional and survive, not in this business."

There were few men Jackson respected — Jonas was one of them. The man never stopped caring. It didn't matter if the bullets were flying and the jungle closed in, he'd come back for you. But life in the fast lane took a toll on men who cared and it was eating Jonas one small piece at a time.

Jonas shoved his fingers through his hair. Jackson was right. There was no way around it. "I know." But he'd never learned to turn it off. Hell yeah, he felt responsible. He couldn't sleep half the time, thinking about the boys, those young Rangers under his command, he'd brought home in caskets. There'd been too many of them, and of late, they'd haunted him both night and day.

"You're messed up, man. She's messed you up. You're going to have to resolve this thing that's between you or you're not going to make it. If you're waiting to get her out of your system, don't bother. I've known you for nearly fifteen years now and it hasn't happened yet. You were in love with her then and you're in even worse shape now. You don't have a shot in hell of making those feelings go away. Bottom line, bro, over the years you've gone crazier and crazier on me. You can't do that shit and work undercover."

Jonas swore under his breath. Jackson wasn't telling him anything he didn't already know. If he tried to deny he was that far gone, to claim that he could still hold it together, it would be a lie. He thought about Hannah every minute of every day. He dreamt about her at night when he could actually sleep. He often woke up dripping sweat, hard as a rock, his body on fire with need, the taste of her in his mouth, the scent of her in his lungs. It was getting worse, so much so that he was afraid to go to sleep at night. And when he saw her, he had to find something to push her away or he'd do something crazy like drag her into his arms and then it would just plain be the hell over. Because he didn't know how to be anything but what he was.

"You're damned lucky she hasn't gone and found another man, Jonas."

"Don't go there, Jackson."

Jackson's head went up alertly, his body going still, suddenly menacing. He stood up abruptly and signaled Jonas to silence, stalking once again to the door. "We've got company."

"You've got to be kidding me." He didn't bother to ask if Jackson was sure — the man's instincts had saved them repeatedly over the years. Jonas yanked the needle out of his arm and slid off the bed, looking around frantically for his shirt. It had been cut to ribbons, the material lying on the floor in a bloody heap. He grabbed his jacket, easing his arms into it. "What the hell did Duncan get us into? Karl Tarasov is not going to stop until he recovers the evidence. He isn't about to let his uncle go down for murder."

Jackson held up four fingers. "They'll be waiting outside as well. The Gadiyan brothers are cracking heads looking for us."

"Shit." Boris and Petr Tarasov headed the family of vicious mobsters renowned for their ability to launder money in any part of the world. Their criminal activities were legendary and they ruled by bloody force. Karl, Petr's son, and the Gadiyan brothers, in-laws, were their top enforcers. Having them on their trail wasn't promising.

Jonas instinctively started back toward the door, but Jackson stepped in front of him. "What we have on them is too important to lose. You want a shot at these men, we'll make a little noise and draw them to us, lead them out of here to keep them away from innocents, but we can't have a firefight in here."

Jonas knew better. Of course he wasn't about to put civilians in the line of fire, but he could feel anger rising, the way it had earlier — and it said volumes that Jackson felt he had to remind him.

What the hell had Gray sent them into? He knew it involved one or both of the very prominent Russian mob families operating out of San Francisco. The Tarasovs didn't bother to hide what they were, deliberately terrorizing their own people, taking bloody revenge if anyone crossed them. They'd been known to wipe out entire families. Boris and Petr Tarasov ruled their empire with fear.

Sergei Nikitin, their biggest rival, preferred

maintaining the appearance of a prominent businessman and jet-setter. He wanted acceptance and traveled with the rich and powerful, hiding his crimes behind his smooth smile, all the while handing out orders to kill anyone opposing him. The stakeout had been on the Tarasov family, and right now, Jonas was very worried because he'd stumbled into something much bigger than a couple of gangsters killing each other. Whatever it was, it wasn't good.

He swore softly as he yanked the thin blanket from the gurney, wrapped it around his arm and broke out the window as loudly as possible to draw the attention of the mobsters, wanting them to follow. Clearing out the jagged remains, Jonas quickly hoisted himself through, and stood to one side, covering Jackson as he followed.

They found themselves in a narrow strip of land between the hospital wings. It was a maze, mostly flat with dirt and concrete and once in a while grass, but the various angles of the massive complex could provide cover. They waited until they heard the shouts coming from the room they'd been in, and then, ducking low to avoid the windows, they ran fast, Jonas keeping pressure on his side to avoid leaving a blood trail.

A shout and one wild shot told them they were being pursued. As he wove his way around the buildings, Jonas tried to recall the details they'd filmed. It had all happened so fast. At first the men were talking and laughing. No one particularly special, not anyone from a rival family involved. And suddenly the Gadiyan brothers and Karl Tarasov had joined the small meeting. They'd been back in the shadows where Jonas couldn't see.

The men had instantly come to attention. And who wouldn't with that kind of clout around. When Boris and Petr Tarasov had showed up, everything still seemed ordinary — friendly. There had been no warning when Karl had yanked one man out of the group and Petr had shot him.

Jonas wished he could conjure up the details of the man who had come to warn the Russians. He'd walked up fast, his face covered and averted, hat pulled low, large dark glasses in place although it was very dark out. He had known the camera was on them — and that meant someone on the inside. They had a traitor in the defense department — someone paid by the Russian mob.

Had he captured the traitor's face? Jonas doubted it. He'd tried to, even panning down to pick up the shoes, but then all hell had broken loose. The group of men had all turned toward them, there had been a shout from behind the group, orders barked out in Russian. The men had started firing, pinning them down. Karl Tarasov made his way to their car to blow out their tires and kill their driver.

Something terrible had welled up in Jonas when he saw Karl shoot Terry in the head. He didn't even remember stepping out from behind cover, only the rage that had overwhelmed him. Less than half an hour earlier he'd been talking to Terry about his family, the mother he loved and supported, about his wife pregnant with their first child, the fun he had keeping up his driving skills, still able to do the work he loved without risking too much. Fortunately, Jonas had been in a dark shadow and Jackson had yanked him back as the bullets plowed into him.

Hell. Jonas wanted to hit something all over again. How many kids had he seen die? For nothing. For power or money or somebody else's ideology. His vision blurred and he touched his face, shocked when his fingers came away wet. He was too damned old for this. What was he doing?

Jackson dropped a hand on his shoulder, and they both halted, crouching low. "You can't save them all," he reminded him quietly.

Jonas didn't respond. Hell, no, he knew that, but he should have been watching out for Terry. He was weary of death and ugliness, of the mess people made of the world. And he was damned tired of running. "You sure on the count?"

"I saw four, but they aren't the ones behind us. I'm only hearing two and they aren't very quiet, definitely not Karl or the Gadiyan brothers. We've got two others circling around trying to get in front of us. I think the big guns are pulling out and leaving the expendables behind."

Jonas checked the loads in his gun. "Why would they do that?"

"They tore up the hospital. Someone had to have called the cops," Jackson said as they rounded a corner. He stopped running and signaled Jonas to keep going.

A bullet hit the wall behind them and plaster rained down on them. Both hit the ground rolling for cover. Jackson went to the left and managed to lie flat behind a low wall of bricks, and Jonas crawled his way through a thin hedge to crouch behind a small outcropping on a utility building.

"Did you see where it came from?" Jackson asked, his gaze coolly quartering the surrounding area.

"Nope. But I think he was above us from the angle of the shot." And that wasn't good. The shooter would have better vision.

"My thoughts exactly. Cover me." Jackson scooted fast along the brick wall, until he came to a small opening. "Ready?"

Jonas took his gun in a two-handed grip, finger on the trigger. "Go." He kept his eyes on the roof of the small utility building.

Jackson was up and over the wall, avoiding the opening, but diving into a hedge that lined the narrow walkway right beneath the building where they were certain the shooter hid.

Jonas kept his gun steady, finger taking up the slack. A flash of movement above their heads and he pulled the trigger, a steady, one-two-three barrage of shots. A body teetered for a moment and then tumbled from the roof, gun landing on the metal and sliding down to the ground.

Jonas kept his weapon trained on the shooter, moving up to check for a pulse even as gunfire erupted to his left. He saw Jackson roll and come up firing. The second man was caught in the throat and went over backward, blown off his feet to lie facedown in the dirt.

"We may have company," Jonas said.

"There are still two of them out there."

"I'll do a quick recon and make a call," Jackson said. "Can you identify either of them?"

"Definitely Boris Tarasov's soldiers," Jonas replied. "I've seen this one in the mug shots a dozen times. He's all over the war room next to Duncan's office."

With two of the mobsters and the worst of the bunch, the Gadiyans and Karl, still unaccounted for, Jonas wasn't taking any chances, sinking back into cover while Jackson went up onto the roof tops to try to make the call for backup. Duncan had a lot to answer for. Sending them in blind as if they were a couple of rookies was bull. More importantly, someone close to Duncan had betrayed them.

"I called it in," Jackson said, returning. "Duncan's sending a team to mop up and get us out of here. There's no sign of the other two. He said to stay out of sight."

"You mean stay away from his team?"

"That's what I understood."

Jonas muttered an obscenity and then crouched a distance from the bodies, sending out a silent call. *Hannah? You okay?* He knew what it cost her to expend so much energy.

A soft breeze kept leaves on the trees fluttering, but she didn't answer. His chest tightened. "So do you think she's all right?" Jonas asked. "I've tried connecting with her, but she isn't responding."

"Hannah?" Jackson was silent for a moment, turning his face up to the sky. "Yeah, she's all right. She's weak, but you knew she would be."

Hannah, answer me. Jonas despised the desperation he felt when he couldn't reach her. His adrenaline overloaded, heart beating too fast, too hard. Even his mouth went dry. Hannah had to be all right all the time or he just went to pieces, and for a man in his position, that was a death sentence. He definitely had to resolve this issue.

The wind swept over the building, this time more of a soft breeze. It rustled leaves on the trees and dropped down into the narrow lane where they crouched to ruffle his hair and touch his face as if soothing him. He heard his name, a soft sigh of a sound, a whisper teasing at the back of his mind. *Jonas. Come home to me.*

He glanced over his shoulder at Jackson. "Did you hear that?"

"Yeah, I heard it." Jackson stared over Jonas's head to the street, watching for their enemy while they waited for the man who had gotten them into so much trouble.

"How long have you known the Drake family?" he asked.

"I think I met them when I was around seven. My mother was very sick and I took over the household pretty early. It could get lonely and, when mom was bad, pretty scary for a kid, so I spent a lot of time in their home. The Drakes just let me come and go as I grew up. I used to climb in through a window when the front door was locked because I didn't want to bother going around to the back of the house, but they never said a word about it to me."

"And now the girls do the same thing," Jackson said.

Jackson was forcing conversation to keep him on his feet. Jonas knew Jackson rarely talked, not even to him. He didn't like physical contact, yet there he was, one hand on Jonas's sorry shoulder, the way he'd been doing all night, the way he did every time they went into battle together. "Yeah, they're my family and I'm not dragging them down into my world, especially Hannah."

Jackson flashed a small, humorless smile. "I hate to break it to you, bro, but she's already in your world, they all are."

Jonas shook his head and reached out again. *Hannah, are you alone tonight?* He hadn't felt the presence of any other energy like he normally would have if her sisters had helped provide the storm. *Where's Sarah?* Hannah needed someone with her after all the energy she'd used. He felt her touch, a small tentative brush . . . as if she was too tired to do more. *Are you still outside, on the captain's walk?* It was difficult maintaining the connection, the distance too far, and Hannah too weak. She was the stronger psychic and usually kept the bridge open between them.

Jonas felt anxiety creeping in. "I think she's still on the captain's walk, Jackson. She's alone and cold and weak. No one's there to help her. I've got to get back to her." She'd sacrificed tonight for him — for both men — and he wasn't about to leave her alone, drained of her energy. She needed to be inside, where it was warm, a cup of her special tea in her hands and Jonas watching over her through the rest of the night.

Hang in there, Hannah. I'll be there as soon as possible.

There was that gentle breeze again, so soft, brushing over his face like the touch of fingers. *I could use a little help tonight.*

That was a rare admission from Hannah, and his heart turned over. *I'm coming, baby, just give me a little time to wrap this up. Can you make it into the house?* He didn't want her lying in the biting cold, too weak to move. He was a four-hour drive away, not too far as the crow flew, but a long distance on winding roads.

I'll be waiting.

To Jonas's astonishment, Duncan arrived and shepherded them to his car while, behind them, his men moved out of the shadows to take control of the situation. Duncan drove them through the streets of the city back to his office, entering through a back way. It didn't take long to discover what they had captured on film. Duncan erupted into a barrage of swearing. Petr Tarasov murdered an undercover officer right in front of their eyes. It was the kind of evidence that could bring a death penalty conviction without too much trouble.

"We thought he was in solid with the Tarasovs." Duncan swore again and passed his hands over his face.

"No wonder Karl and the Gadiyans kept coming after us and then sent their soldiers when it got too hot. I'll bet they're already making tracks out of the country," Jonas said.

"Petr Tarasov is going to fry for this," Duncan snapped, fury in his voice.

The three watched in silence, a gasp of shock the only reaction until the man in the coat and hat walked up to Boris, the head of the crime family, and Boris turned his head to stare straight at the camera.

"Any ideas who tipped him off?" Duncan asked in a tight voice. "We'll need the guys in the lab to enhance this as much as possible. We need to find out who this son of a bitch is as soon as possible."

"He has to be one of yours. He must have tipped off Tarasov you had an agent undercover and then he got wind you sent someone in to film the low-level meeting. Only there was no meeting because the information your undercover fed you was his own setup. They got him there to kill him," Jonas said.

"We'll find the son of a bitch. He doesn't know who you are. No one does. I kept your names out of it on purpose."

"Because you suspected you had a leak," Jonas guessed, exchanging a long look with Jackson. He felt sick that he'd been standing there filming when another agent had been murdered in front of him. "At least you have enough to fry Petr Tarasov."

"Good job," Duncan added as an afterthought.

"Yeah, thanks," Jonas replied, working to

keep the sarcasm out of his voice. "I'm out of here."

"Sit down, Harrington, you're not going anywhere until we pick Petr Tarasov up and make absolute certain you're in the clear. I've lost two men and I'm not about to lose any more."

"Thanks for the concern, Duncan, but I'm not part of your team anymore and you sure as hell aren't tying me up tonight," Jonas protested. "I've got somewhere important to go."

"Not until this is cleared, Jonas," Duncan said. "Petr Tarasov murdered an agent and we've caught him red-handed. There's no way to dispute that tape. We've got a traitor in the department and I'm not taking chances with your life. And if that isn't good enough for you, Boris Tarasov believes in retribution. You killed several of his soldiers. He's going to want your head on a silver platter and I'm going to make damn sure he doesn't know who you are before I let you go home. Until we pick up Tarasov, you're going to be kept under wraps."

"Not happening," Jonas said. "I'm not part of the team anymore, Duncan. Obviously you knew you had a traitor or you wouldn't have gone outside the team for this recon. You suspected your undercover, the one who was killed, didn't you? And you wanted me to get evidence on him because you thought maybe he had a partner on your team."

"Something like that," Duncan said, his voice tight. "And I'm not chancing losing another agent. So unless you want this war to follow you right back to where you live, you're going to stay here under wraps until I make sure you're in the clear."

Jonas opened his mouth to protest, and then closed it. Damn it. He didn't want to stay but there was no way in hell that he'd risk bringing that bloodbath in the alley home to Sea Haven. There was no way he'd risk putting Hannah in danger.

"I need to make a phone call."

"That's not happening and you know it, Harrington. No calls, no e-mails, no text messages. We do this clean with nothing pointing back to you. We're taking you out the back way and stashing you until Tarasov is picked up and I'm satisfied he doesn't know your names."

"Who knew we were in the field?" Jonas asked.

"No one should have known. I asked you to help out as a personal favor and gave you Terry to drive. No other member of the team knew about the recon and I wanted to keep it that way. That's why I personally picked you up and got you out of there before the team moved in to deal with the bodies. The Russians play for keeps, Jonas."

"Hell, Duncan, I know that. And I'm sorry about your men." He didn't want to think too much about Terry or the fact that an agent had been murdered not fifty feet from him while he held a camera. The thought sickened him and he couldn't look at Jackson. Sometimes, like now, he was just so fucking soul weary he didn't know what to do. He needed Hannah or he was going to drown.

"I'm not adding you to the list of dead men," Duncan decreed, "so resign yourself, Harrington."

Jonas slumped back in the chair, pushing his hand through his hair. He was dirty, exhausted, covered in blood and hurting like hell now that the anesthesia was wearing off. He looked over at Jackson, shrugged his shoulders and gave in.

Hannah. I'm not making it back tonight.

3

Hannah. I'm not making it back tonight.

That was the last thing he'd said to her, followed by four long, mind-numbing, terrifying days of absolute silence. Damn Jonas Harrington to hell. She was through. She wasn't giving him another day — another hour — of her time. She'd wasted most of her life waiting for him, and if she meant so little to him, it was past time to make the break.

Just a few weeks earlier he had nearly died from a gunshot wound and nearly taken her with him, when she'd worked so desperately to save his life. What had the ungrateful jerk done to thank her? He'd gone out looking for trouble — and found it — again.

She had known the moment he was in trouble. She felt his pain, as if across a great distance, and knew immediately he was in San Francisco. Frightened out of her mind, she'd run to the captain's walk and sent the wind to aid him, but he hadn't come to her once the danger was over.

Hannah. I'm not making it back tonight. He hadn't even bothered to call her. Not to thank her, not even to make sure she was all right when he knew the toll the use of her gifts took on her. Not even just to reassure her that he was all right. Well, she wasn't going to be the one calling him. She'd had enough of looking like a fool.

She was heading to New York on another work assignment. She detested leaving, but she had a job to do, and this time, maybe she wouldn't come back. Maybe she'd have to just stay away from Sea Haven.

The thought made her eyes brim with tears and she stood on the captain's walk, three stories up above the endless waves, and stared down at the turbulent sea below. The water was beautiful in the moonlight; shades of black, deep blue and shimmering silver rippled across the surface. Spray leapt into the air with each rush of the waves crashing against the rocks below. She sighed and leaned her elbows against the railing as she watched the fog gathering in the distance, beginning to spread tendrils above the rhythmic waves. As always, the sea soothed her, tugging every drop of anger out of her, to leave her calm, but sad and wistful, aware that this time she had to act — she really did have to put distance between Jonas and herself.

"Jonas." She whispered the name to the sea, allowed the wind to carry the sound out over the water.

The sea whispered back, blowing vapor inland, long streaks of snow-white mist, so that it looked as if a comforter were being slowly pulled up over the bluff. The fog added an aura of mystery and ethereal beauty to the night. It crept over the sea and into the treetops, and began to surround her home. She always came here to find peace; this time she came to find the strength to leave.

She murmured softly to the wind and it rose in a swell, skipping over the water playfully, tossing droplets into the air so it appeared to be raining sparkling diamonds. She inhaled the scents of the sea. The swirls of fog danced in the slight breeze, layering over the surface of the water.

Hannah let the familiar sounds of the sea soothe her. This was her favorite place in the world. In all her extensive travels, she'd never found another spot she wanted to call home. She could breathe in Sea Haven, was comfortable with the camaraderie of the people in the small town. She liked that she knew everyone, that she could go to the grocery store and see familiar faces. There was comfort in Sea Haven, and the town was surrounded by the raw, powerful beauty of the ocean, which always gave her peace. The sea was constant, reliable, a source she could draw on in the worst of times.

She lifted her face to the sky, her breath rushing from her lungs when she saw three vapor trails beginning to form into solid circles around the moon. One glowed an eerie red, one a dull yellow and the last a dark, ominous black. Hannah snapped to attention, wariness replacing the dreamy relaxed expression the wind had given her. One hand went to her throat in a defensive gesture.

She was one of seven daughters born to the seventh daughter in the Drake family. Hers was a legacy of special gifts — or curses, depending upon how one viewed them. Hannah could call and send the wind, she could cast spells and had some small talent with herbs. She could move objects with her mind and read the mosaic in the entryway of the Drake home. Like her sisters, she could read tea leaves and, if touching others, often could even read their thoughts. She could also read the moon and sky, and right now they were giving her a blatant warning.

"Hannah!"

She frowned as the masculine voice drifted up to her from below, inside her house — the house that had been locked. She had even padlocked the gate again, binding the security device with a spell, but she knew it wouldn't matter — the heavy lock would be open and lying on the ground as it always was after Jonas touched it. She'd locked him out on purpose, angry that he hadn't called her, hurt that she didn't matter. He ignored her until he needed something and then he took her for granted.

She didn't bother to answer. He'd just keep yelling until she came down to him, or worse, he'd come up onto the captain's walk and give her a safety lecture. With another wary glance at the moon, she hurried from the deck into the house and down the stairs. If Jonas was in a bad enough mood, the moon might have been circled in the eerie yellow, but not with three rings. Something wasn't right.

Jonas emerged out of the shadows as she leapt off the bottom steps. He caught her around her waist, fingers biting deep as he lifted her clear and steadied her, setting her back on her feet. The moment of brief contact brought a searing heat, straight through her body to her bones. Jonas always had such a physical effect on her, when no one else ever managed to penetrate her deliberately haughty façade.

"You aren't supposed to be lifting me, Jonas," she reminded him, pulling away, keeping her face averted so he couldn't see the flush on her face. "You haven't been out of the hospital that long."

"Long enough," he replied, his cool, assessing eyes drifting over her from his superior height.

Her heart sank. They were both going to pretend the recent incident had never happened. Jonas wasn't going to tell her he'd been back working for his old team and she was too cowardly to demand answers from him. She had the sudden urge to cry. She'd sent him help, maybe even saved his life. His new wounds were recent — only four days old. The moment he'd put his hands on her, she'd been able to feel his pain — it wasn't like he could hide the information from her. But she wasn't going to help him heal this time. He could just suffer.

Hannah was tall, yet Jonas seemed to loom over her when he crowded her personal space, which was just about all the time. He always smelled of outdoors, fresh, like the sea and surrounding forest. He was tall, broad shouldered and heavily muscled, and he moved with grace and efficiency and complete confidence. He also saw far too much when he looked at her through those ice-blue eyes of his. No one saw her the way Jonas did, stripped of all her careful defenses and so vulnerable she ached when he was close. She absolutely would not let him see how much he hurt her. This time she'd go — and not come back. No fighting, simple dignity.

She stepped away, keeping her face averted. Irritation crossed his face and his eyes glittered at her, a sure danger sign.

"Your bags are packed and you're wearing makeup. You never wear makeup unless you're going somewhere."

"Hence the suitcases." She tried to slip past him, but Jonas trapped her against the banister and she was forced to halt. Hannah stared at his impressive chest and tried not to feel intimidated. He was so arrogant and with good reason. She couldn't stand up to him, she'd never been able to. And why did he choose this moment to show up? Why couldn't he have waited another hour? He always managed to find the exact moment when she felt the most vulnerable.

"Where are you going?" His fingers caught her chin, forcing her head up.

Her blue eyes flashed at him, letting him see her annoyance. "I told you last week. I have a job." And of course he wouldn't remember because she just wasn't that important to him.

"I told you not to go. You're supposed to be looking after me."

She was fairly certain her legs hadn't melted, but she felt dizzy being so close to him. She hated that he unbalanced her usual calm. Only Jonas could make her feel so combative and yet so needy at the same time. Her feelings for him were too complicated to sort out so she didn't bother to try.

"You're not in any danger, Jonas," she pointed out. "Only bored. You hate not working and you're so crabby no one else can stand being around you." *And you're working anyway, doing exactly what you promised you'd never do again.* She didn't say the words aloud — it wasn't part of the "pretend it never happened" game they always played — but she wanted to. She even had a sudden urge to just lift his shirt and examine his ribs. She knew there would be a fresh wound or two, but she remained silent like she always did, letting him walk right over her. His faint, answering smile made her heart turn over and she was angry with herself for her reaction.

"Unfortunately that could be true. All of your sisters have deserted me, not only going out of town, but the country. I'm going to starve. You know that, don't you? If you leave, I'm not going to get a decent meal and then how am I going to heal?"

"Sarah will be back from her trip with Damon tomorrow. She'll fix you dinner while I'm gone," Hannah said and pulled away from him. She detested that, as she stepped away, her body felt cold as if his had provided untold warmth and safety. She hated more that she was torn between wanting to laugh and cry. "You aren't going to starve."

"I like *your* cooking. And she doesn't give me hell the way you do. She just gets annoyed and tells me to go home."

Hannah didn't want to be charmed by him. Jonas was everything she could never be — adventurous, courageous, a man who lived his life confidently. "I should send you home, especially if you're going to give me a hard time." She should, and if she had any backbone at all, she would. She turned away from him, afraid he would read the hurt on her face as she hurried down the hall.

She felt his presence as he kept pace right behind her. It seemed sometimes that she'd always felt Jonas, as if he were a part of her, sharing her skin and her flesh and bones, crawling into her heart and stealing her soul. She blinked back tears, careful to keep her face averted as she made her way through the large house to the kitchen. She was so emotional lately, ever since Jonas had been shot and nearly killed a few weeks earlier. She had nightmares and spent most of the nights pacing or sitting up on the captain's walk watching the sea. She had to leave just to put some distance between them and get back her balance.

The last four days had been pure hell. She had waited for hours that first night, terrified for him. Then she'd cried for a day, waiting by the phone, not leaving the house. And finally she had to accept that he took her for granted, and that he wasn't going to call and reassure her — or thank her — or even acknowledge that she might be worried. She didn't matter; her feelings didn't matter; once he no longer needed her, she slipped from his mind. She swallowed hard, her eyes burning.

"Why are you insisting on going to New York? You don't even like New York. It's total bullshit, Hannah. And you can forget ignoring me like you do when you don't want to tell me things. We're going to talk." Jonas settled his fingers around her arm.

The action brought her attention instantly to his strength. That was what Jonas was all about — strength. He had it all and she had none. He never physically hurt her, not even when he was angry with her. And she could make him angry in a heartbeat — it was the only protection left to her.

As if reading her mind, he gave her a small, impatient shake. "Don't think you're going to drive me away with all your nonsense this time, Hannah. We have to settle this."

She sent him the haughty, over-the-shoulder look she'd perfected while dealing with his arrogance for years. "You mean you'll talk and I'm supposed to listen. I don't think there's anything at all to settle. I have a job and I'm going to New York. There isn't anything else to say." She couldn't talk to him. Once she said the things she needed to say, she'd lose him forever. There would be no going back, no hope at all. She'd have to accept that she was absolutely nothing to him.

"Really?" His hand transferred to the nape of her neck, his fingers brushing her skin intimately and sending a shiver of awareness through her body.

She was fairly certain he did it on purpose — that he knew her physical reaction to him

— but she couldn't be certain so she took the coward's way out and simply walked the few steps left to the kitchen. "I made you something to eat."

"But you're not eating." He made it a statement, clipped and harsh — accusing.

She took a breath and let it out, going straight to the stove to put on the tea kettle. Jonas stopped halfway across the room and she could feel his penetrating gaze on her, demanding an answer. "I have a show, Jonas."

He said something ugly under his breath and she stiffened. "I'm not doing this with you again, Jonas. I model. I have an assignment. You don't have to like what I do, but it's my job and I keep my word when I say I'll be there."

"I don't have to like it, Hannah, you're right about that, but considering what it does to you, *you* at least have to like it and you don't. Don't bother lying to me. I see liars every day in my line of work, and a child does a better job than you."

She waved her hand at the stove, too tired to argue with him and make tea at the same time, although the ritual often soothed her. The stove leapt to life, burning with a ring of tiny flames, the tea kettle whistling a demand instantly. She caught up the kettle and splashed water into a teapot, pressing her lips together to keep from telling him to leave. She didn't want him to leave, she wanted him to sit quietly and have tea with her. She *needed* him to sit quietly and talk with her. Before she left, she had to reassure herself he was unharmed.

She sneaked a quick glance. He looked a little pale, tired, lines etched into his face, but tough as nails. That was Jonas. Hard as a rock. He didn't need anybody, least of all her. She was fluff to him, nothing more. He'd always made that so clear. Her life was falling apart and he was like the sea, a constant, steady anchor she counted on.

"You just can't resist being the Barbie doll, can you," he said bitterly.

"Why do you have to do that, Jonas?" She turned, anger and hurt warring in her eyes. "I've never made fun of you being a sheriff. I could, you know. You're bossy and arrogant and you think you can control everyone and tell them what to do. I don't like that you risk your life, but you do that, too, and I never ask you not to do it." And she hadn't either. Her sisters had, but she had remained silent, praying he would give his promise, but supporting him in whatever choice he made. "I understand that it's who you are, who you have to be. Why can't you afford me the same courtesy?'

"You want me to be okay with you showing off your body to every nutcase in the world? It isn't going to happen, honey. You're extraordinary and you know it. No one looks like you, and your face and body are recognized everywhere, by everyone. I don't think there's a person in the world that doesn't know your face. You talk about taking risks. I risk my life to help other people. You risk yours so everyone can see just how good you look."

"Has it ever occurred to you just how utterly selfish you can be, Jonas?" She whirled around to face him, her back against the counter. She was a little shocked at the violence welling up in her. She had an urge to slap his handsome face.

Up close he always surprised her with his size. He was so perfectly proportioned she didn't always notice his height, but so close to her, he looked down on her, his shoulders wide and his chest a little intimidating.

He stepped even closer, so that his body crowded against hers, caging her, his heat warming her. "How am I being selfish by telling you a few truths, Hannah?"

"Go to hell, Jonas."

"Right back at you, baby."

She took a deep breath and let it out, the

air hissing between her teeth. "I guess on some level I've always known you didn't think very much of me, but I didn't realize just how much you despise who I am." She steeled herself to let him go — let her dreams go. "I want you to leave. And please respect the fact that I don't want to see you for a while, Jonas. I know you're part of our —"

"Shut up, Hannah. Just shut the hell up."

She stared up at him, shocked — stunned at the stark anger in his voice — the raw desire darkening his features, carved deep into every line on his face. Jonas caught her around the waist and jerked her body against his.

"You think I don't want to walk away?" He gave her a little shake. "You know damn well I can't. I can't breathe without you. I couldn't leave you even if I tried. I've accepted that you cast one of your damned spells and I'm lost — I'll always be lost. So if I'm a little angry with you when you take off your clothes for the world, then you can damn well put up with it."

For a moment she couldn't think or breathe. He had just insulted her beyond imagination, but . . . "What are you saying, Jonas? Are you trying to convince me that you're *interested* in me as a woman?" She felt behind her for the counter, afraid she might faint from sheer shock. There was a terrible buzzing in her ears and her breath caught in her lungs, refusing to move through her body. Her heart began to accelerate, racing as though it might burst through her chest. She began to tremble uncontrollably, her body shaking, toes and fingers tingling as she gasped, strangling, unable to get air.

"Oh, hell," Jonas muttered. Then louder and more commanding. "Breathe, Hannah."

"My sisters . . ." she croaked.

"They aren't here, baby, but I am and I'm not going to let anything happen. You know I'd walk through fire for you." Jonas pushed her head down. "You're just having a panic attack, honey, no biggie, you've had them before. Just relax and breathe. Do that little thing you do with counting."

How had he known about that? Her heart beat even faster. Her sisters had helped hide her condition for years, yet now, in front of Jonas, the one person she had worked so hard to keep it from, she was having a full-blown panic attack. And he knew. He even knew the small things she did to try to overcome the attacks.

Hannah sank to the floor, back against the counter, and drew up her knees, closing her eyes and forcing her mind away from terror. She tried to wave him off, wanting him to leave and not witness the utter humiliation of being such a coward. There was nothing to be terrified of — yet it happened all the time.

Jonas sat on the floor beside her, drawing up his own knees, his shoulder brushing hers. He pushed back her mass of curly hair with gentle fingers. "This is what was wrong in school, isn't it? All those years everyone thought you were so stuck up, you were hiding the fact that you had panic attacks."

His fingers slid around the nape of her neck. Strong. Sure. So like him. The slow massage distracted her as nothing else could have done. She leaned her head against the wall and let his fingers work their magic.

"It s-started the f-first day of kindergarten." She forced the words out, stuttering — the one thing she hated beyond all others. "I-I didn't want to go. I could have s-stayed home another couple of years, but M-Mom and Dad thought I should be in s-school because I could already read and do math at a fourth-grade level. So they insisted."

Her voice was so soft he had to strain to hear her. He bit back his first angry response. Attacking a decision her parents had made years earlier wasn't going to accomplish anything other than upset her further. Any communication with Hannah was tentative at best if she wasn't surrounded by her sisters. And if she was stuttering in front of him, she had to be really upset. It had taken too many years of frustration to discover Hannah's secret and the fact that her sisters helped her speak in public.

He took a deep breath and let it out, continuing with the slow massage on the nape of her neck, easing the tension and fear out of her. For the first time, she wasn't running from him and he was determined he wouldn't lose his opportunity. "I'm part of the family, aren't I? Why didn't you tell me?" He pushed the hurt away, far more comfortable with his temper. He'd been angry for a long time on her behalf — and at her.

"I-I was humiliated that I c-couldn't control it." She paused, drawing in a deep breath and forcing herself to stop the stuttering. Her sisters had helped a day or two earlier, and if she just stayed calm and talked slow, she'd be all right. "Someone like you, Jonas, someone so in c-control of everything could never understand what it's like to be so out of control — so afraid of everything. I don't think I've ever seen you afraid of anything or anyone."

She wasn't looking at him, and her voice, so small and forlorn, broke his heart. "Maybe not, Hannah, maybe I don't have a hope in hell of understanding what you go through, but shutting me out isn't going to help. I want to be there for you. I want you to trust me."

Hannah glanced at him, her eyes wide, tears swimming, but not falling. "I trust you, Jonas."

He shook his head. "No you don't. Not really. You thought I'd make fun of you, didn't you?"

She pressed a hand to her stomach. "I hate it. I hate you seeing me so — so — *cowardly.*"

"Is that how you see yourself? A coward?" He kept his voice gentle, when he wanted to throttle her. She was the last person on earth who was a coward. Why did she persist in seeing herself in such a negative light all the time?

"You know I am. You even called me a rabbit when you were in the hospital."

"I was drugged up and mad as hell. Someone shot me, Hannah, and you and your sisters were in danger. I knew you were giving me your strength. You sat there day after day getting pale and weaker as I grew stronger. It made me crazy. I still get crazy when I think too much about it."

He leaned close, framing her face with his hands, and told her the truth as he knew it. "I'm supposed to look after you. That's the way it works in my world. Maybe it's chauvinistic or whatever the political term is, but I like looking after you and your sisters. I don't want it to be the other way around, especially when I can see you fading away."

He ran the pad of his finger down her cheek, traced the shape of her lips and leaned in to brush the softest of kisses over her mouth.

Startled, her lashes lifted and her gaze collided with his. Her heart nearly stopped beating. One little touch and she was nearly in meltdown, forgiving everything, every insult, his overbearing, arrogant ways. Forgiving him for leaving her alone, frightened and angry for the last four days.

"Kiss me back, Hannah," he coaxed, an ache in his voice.

She heard his raw need and her body responded, even when her brain told her there was some mistake. His mouth was sheer magic — just as he was. Dark and sensual and so soft when everything else about him was hard. No one kissed like

Jonas, she was absolutely sure of it, his tongue sliding along hers until she was lost in his taste and scent and his pure masculine sensuality.

His hand cupped her face, thumb sliding over her skin, his body moving closer, arms tightening with possession. He was gentle, tender even, and she felt cherished — wanted and cherished.

Jonas lifted his head and looked at her, into her large blue eyes. A man could get lost there, trapped for all time — and he had. He didn't even care. He didn't want to escape. Her lashes were blond, but thick and curly and so damned feminine it made him ache inside. Her skin was the softest thing he'd ever touched. She was so soft, so fragile. And the look on her face, she looked frightened of him, but she wanted him. He saw it there, right along with the fear.

He could deal with her fear. He just had to go slow, not letting her see he wanted to devour her, share her skin, lock himself inside her until all the troubles of the world dropped away and he found peace again. He just had to stay in control — and wasn't he famous for control?

He traced her classic bone structure with the pads of his fingers, trying to absorb her into his own skin. No one had bone structure the way she did — it was one of the things that made her so famous and sought after. Her skin was every bit as soft as it looked, so flawless he was always amazed to see the sprinkling of light freckles across her small, straight nose. Her mouth was lush, made for kissing, made to bring a man straight to his knees, to bring him more pleasure than he ever deserved. He'd had enough fantasies about her mouth to fill a library.

He shifted his weight, and brought his head the scant few inches separating them to take her mouth again. What had he been thinking about control? The minute he sank into her dark heat, his tongue stroking along hers, taking her sweetness, tasting her, he knew all control was going to be lost fast. He needed more, needed her skin against his, her body wrapped tightly around his. He had known all along it would be like this, nothing ever enough until he had all of her — until every last inch of her belonged to him.

She trembled, somewhere between desire and fear. He stopped the hand inching up beneath her shirt and pulled back to look at her again.

Hannah took a deep breath and flashed him a tentative smile. "Come with me to

New York," she invited, her gaze shy — hopeful — the invitation unexpected. "Come to the fashion show and see what I do."

Everything in him went still. He drew away from her, putting space between them because he sure as hell couldn't touch her now and he wanted — no needed — to do just that and it would be disastrous. Hannah was an empath and they had suddenly gotten into very dangerous territory. "I can't go to something like that." He winced at the sudden harshness in his voice, but damn it all, she'd shocked him. She'd never so much as suggested he accompany her. He didn't dare appear in public with her. Duncan was certain no one had leaked his name, but Jonas wouldn't take a chance with her life.

Her face closed down, hope retreating. She nodded. "I understand."

"No, you don't. I want you to stay home, Hannah. There is no reason for you to go. Stay here where you belong." *With me. Stay with me. Save me. Be my everything.*

"I have a job."

It was a tired argument and they both knew it. She sighed and shook her head, her long spiral curls spilling in all directions. Something about the way she looked so defeated tore at his heart.

"Hannah, I'd go with you, but I can't." There was an unconscious ache in his voice. He knew he should sound tough and angry and let her think it was all about her exposing her body, but the regret was there and she was too quick on the uptake to ignore it. He shouldn't have come here so tired and worn out and needing her, but now it was too late.

Suspicion leapt into her expression and she clamped both hands to his chest, one palm over his heart before there was a damned thing he could do about it. He felt her spirit move against his. If anyone had asked him, he would have denied the connection, but with Hannah the sensation was always strong. He threw up mind blocks as quickly as he could, a practice he'd started years earlier when he realized she could "read" him at will, but Hannah was too fast. She tore through his mind before his shields could go up and exposed his darkest secrets. Her hands slipped down his shirt to the wound in his side. The throbbing stopped instantly, even as her face grew paler.

Jonas caught her hands and took them off him. Healing his wounds wasn't something he wanted from her. She'd done it once and had grown so fragile she still wasn't completely recovered.

She sank back against the wall, hands dropping to her sides, staring at him with her big blue eyes, the silence lengthening between them, the tension rising until he wanted to bang his head against the wall in frustration.

"Jonas . . ."

He held up his hand. "Don't. Just don't, Hannah. We're not talking about this."

Her eyes glittered at him. Flames crackled in the fireplace that hadn't been there before. The burners on the stove leapt into rings of fire, glowing red-hot, and he knew he was in trouble. "We're going to talk about it, Jonas. You *promised* us."

"I didn't promise. I said I was no longer working for the defense department and I'm not — wasn't."

"You're doing undercover work, you liar, and it's dangerous as hell." Her voice hissed out at him, a whip of anger only Hannah could wield against him. She could flay him raw with her disappointment and her fear. And she was afraid. She reeked of fear, the emotion pouring out of her as if a dam had opened wide.

"I've been going crazy, Hannah, and they asked me to do a little job for them."

She was silent a moment, her blue eyes

staring straight into his. "That's not the truth. Tell me the truth."

He sighed and raked his fingers through his hair in agitation. "Look, honey, I can't always tell you even when I want to."

"That's why you keep disappearing. What is this all about, Jonas? You seemed past all that, taking the sheriff's job, living in Sea Haven. You were happy again. It took you so long after you came back." It was true, his aura was nearly black at times, and when she touched him, even a small brief brush of her hand against him, the empath in her recoiled from the heavy darkness in him.

What could he tell her? His existence had been one long life filled with death and destruction, the seamier side of life, the dregs, the drug lords, terrorists and mobsters. He had retreated to Sea Haven needing to change his life before he drowned in the blood and gore and violence he never seemed able to walk away from. How could he tell her she had to save him? That would scare her to death, but it was the truth. Sometimes it just got too much to sit by and not do something real, like put his life on the line, and he needed her to pull him back from the edge of that precipice.

How could he explain how truly crazy he could be? When he'd seen Terry killed, he'd leapt into plain sight, with no cover, and begun firing at the attackers in a blind haze, somewhere between ice and white-hot rage, wanting to take all of them down. Hannah would run away and he couldn't blame her. Hell, half the time he couldn't understand why he did any of the things he did. He only knew that when he was with her, when he could see her and smell her and breathe her in, his life had sanity and meaning.

He needed to be like Jackson, able to switch off all emotion and get the job done, but he'd never mastered that art. He worried about his men, about his deputies, about the people he protected. Hell. He even worried about the families of the men he killed. He couldn't turn it off — he never had been able to — and he was damned good at what he did, so his old boss was always ready to hand him another job.

"Jonas," Hannah repeated gently, her fingers brushing his face. "What's wrong?"

There was desperation in his eyes, he looked driven, in pain — not physical — pure emotional pain, his heart beating too fast, his body almost rigid. He was holding on to her too tight, his grip hurting her, when he was always — *always* — gentle with her.

4

Hannah didn't know what to say to ease Jonas's pain. She didn't even fully understand the desperation in him, but she saw he was at a breaking point and it shocked her. Jonas was a rock they all leaned on. Everyone. Every single person in Sea Haven. People up and down the coast. Deputies. Firemen. Jonas Harrington was the man to go to when there was trouble because he would find a way to get you out of it. For the first time, Hannah could see Jonas was in real trouble and not from a life-threatening wound.

"I don't understand what's going on, Jonas. Make me understand."

He closed his eyes, shutting out the sight of her, but there was no way to shut off his senses. She was everywhere, inside him, and there was no getting her out. "I'm just lost without you, Hannah." And God help him, it was true. He'd been falling for a long time, and dangerous job or not, she had to drag him back into the light, where he could breathe again. He opened his eyes and looked into hers and found himself trapped there.

Hannah knelt on the floor in front of him and framed his face with her hands. Her heart was pounding so hard she was afraid she was going to go into another panic attack. She was offering herself to him, and if he turned her down, there would be no recovering from the heartbreak. She would shatter. But finding a way to ease that look on his face, his eyes, that was all that mattered now — not her pride or her fear.

She leaned into him and pressed a kiss to the corner of his mouth. He went very still, his breath hitching. She kissed the other corner, this time sliding her hand around to the nape of his neck to just hold him there. Hannah nibbled on his chin, his lower lip, pressed more kisses along his jaw.

Jonas made a single sound and his fingers tunneled in her hair, pulling back her head, his mouth fastening on hers. He simply took what she was offering and damn the consequences. He had to have her. He'd always known Hannah was the only one for him. Every other woman paled for him beside her.

He could kiss her forever. The silken heat of her mouth and the sweet taste of her became a craving. Once, he'd thought if he kissed her, his need of her would go away, but now he knew kissing her forever was not going to be long enough. He kissed her again and again, leading her into deeper, much more erotic kisses. She followed willingly, kissing him back, her hands sliding under his shirt to touch his bare skin. His body jerked, hardened, shuddered with need, but he couldn't stop kissing her, his mouth taking hers, tongue probing deep, wanting her sighs, needing her to kiss him back with the same building desire, so strong, so raw, it tore out his heart.

He had to taste her skin, and his mouth wandered from hers, just a little, following the contour of her face. He used his teeth, a small scrape, felt her answering reaction and continued down her long, beautiful throat. He'd fantasized about her throat right along with her mouth. There probably wasn't a square inch of her he hadn't fantasized about and he was going to explore every centimeter.

Her body trembled against his and he forced himself to pull back, breathing deeply, pressing his forehead against hers, keeping her close to him.

"I'm afraid, Jonas," she admitted. "This could be a terrible mistake, one we can never take back."

He went still inside. He couldn't lose her now. He couldn't. He was going to shatter into a million pieces if he lost her and he'd never recover — never find all the pieces and be able to put himself back together. Hell, he was already so unraveled, Hannah was his last hope. He needed her desperately.

"I haven't slept in four days, Hannah. To tell you the truth, not in weeks. I can't stop my brain and I'm drowning." He wanted to shut up. It was pretty much guaranteed that whatever he said was going to scare her even more, but he couldn't let go of her and he couldn't take back the words. His hands were clamped around her arms, fingers pressing deep. Her mouth had slid him toward sweet oblivion until all he could think of was being deep inside her, of her body wrapped tightly around his.

He felt her gaze move over his face. Her heart beat so wildly he was afraid she'd hyperventilate again. Abruptly he stood, cementing the decision that had been made for both of them a long time ago. "How much time do you have before you leave for the airport?"

For a moment she couldn't speak. The enormity of what she was doing hit her hard. She already knew it would be impossible for someone like her to live with him. If she did this, how would she face him day after day when he came to her house? How would she survive if he avoided her?

"Jonas . . ." She trailed off, standing close to his heat, wanting him with every cell in her body. "If we do this, there's no going back. We won't be able to pretend it didn't happen. If it doesn't work out . . ."

His arm swept around her waist and he pulled her tight against him. He wasn't about to let go of her. He'd waited more than half of his life for her. Now that she was really looking at him, now that her eyes were saying yes and her body was soft and pliant and molded against his, he wasn't about to let her get away. And what the hell was he saying anyway? She'd always been his. *Always.* Throughout the years, when other men came near her, he'd warned them off immediately.

Jonas kept her locked against him, letting his body tell her what he needed. He'd had enough of words. He could say everything he needed to say to her with his hands — and his mouth — and all other parts of his anatomy.

Her body melted into his, but she still pulled her head back, the look in her eyes uncertain. "I don't know anything at all about sex, Jonas."

He grinned at her, laugh lines crinkling around his eyes. "I know enough to get us by, honey. You don't have to worry on that score." He couldn't help the hint of satisfaction in his tone at the thought that there'd been no other man. There was no other way to feel when he'd loved her since he'd first laid eyes on her and she threatened to turn him into a toad — frogs could be princes and he was no prince. "Sarah's not due home tonight, is she?"

"No. She and Damon are off somewhere, she'll be back tomorrow evening."

"So we have the house to ourselves?"

She nodded and he was kissing her again, finding her perfect mouth with his and losing himself in the erotic heat of her. He buried his fingers deep in her mass of silken hair, taking two fistfuls, holding her close to him as he absorbed the texture of a long curl, all the while exploring and taking the kiss deeper and deeper. He wanted to live here, with her, in her magic and mystery forever.

He could sense her growing desire, but there was also fear, uncertainty. Jonas brought her up closer against his body and buried his face in her neck. "I need you, Hannah. I never thought I'd ever be man enough to admit that to you, but I do. I need you in my life."

He was making her weak with his dominating mouth and the strength of his steely arms around her, but it was his words, low, wrenched from him, that stripped her of every defense. He needed her. Jonas, the strong one every person in Sea Haven depended on, needed *her.* In a way no man ever had. She felt the ripple of his muscles beneath his shirt and wanted to feel the texture of his skin. She wanted the heat of his body, and the feel of his hands moving over her, making her his. She wanted desperately to belong to Jonas Harrington.

Even if it was just for a night. She'd take that and the consequences be damned. Maybe in every other part of her life she was so screwed up, she didn't know what she wanted, but this was different. This — him — she wanted with every fiber of her being. She always had. He was part of her, so entwined with her life, her family, her very existence, that she couldn't imagine a world without him beside her.

Hannah took a breath, let it out, and made the commitment. "I've never been with anyone else, Jonas. I'm not experienced like all your other women."

His eyebrow shot up, a faint smile softening the hard edge to his mouth. "My other women? I don't have other women. It's been you and only you for a long time now." Years ago when Hannah had been so haughty and elusive and so beautiful it hurt to look at her, he'd tried to prove to himself he could get any woman he wanted. The problem was — once he got them — they weren't Hannah and he didn't want them. His "women" had been a string of one-night stands, transient relationships filled with temporarily satisfying but ultimately empty sex, after which he'd always lain in bed, hard as a rock, and fantasized about Hannah. Yeah. He wasn't proud of that, but he couldn't go back and relive those days.

"I'm just saying . . ." She broke off, blushing.

"Don't worry, honey. I might want to strip you naked and take you fast and hard, but there's a part of me that needs to just go slow and savor every single second I have with you." He pushed the hair from her neck and kissed her, gentle featherlight brushes of his lips, and then open-mouthed, his tongue swirling and his teeth finding intriguing little places to nip and taste.

He suddenly couldn't take not being skin to skin, and if he was going to do this right, he'd have to be patient. He wanted to make memories she could never get away from. He swung her into his arms and took her up the stairs to her bedroom. He didn't want her ever to crawl in her bed again without thinking about him — about them — and wishing for him.

He sat her, not on the bed, but on the top of the oak cabinet, wedging his body between her thighs. Bending, he tugged off her slippers, and let them drop to the floor. There was shy anxiety in her eyes, but he didn't give her time to think, leaning forward, his palm cradling her nape while he seduced her mouth, his tongue gliding with moist heat, teeth tugging at her full lower lip.

Hannah was everything to him. She always had been. He had wanted her when she was too young even to consider taking her. And he had dreamt of her when he was far from home in Afghanistan and Colombia. He ached for her day and night. Since the moment he'd returned home, he'd been in a constant state of arousal, and there hadn't been a damned thing he could do about it. Until now.

The moment he got close to her, he

needed to touch her skin. No one had skin like Hannah. He stroked his hand down her face, savoring the feel of living silk, hot and so soft he wanted to sink into her forever. He reveled in the dark wonder of her mouth crushed beneath his.

"You have no idea how badly I want you, Hannah." His hand shook as he slid his palm from her neck to her breast. At once her nipples peaked, hard and tight beneath his hand. Her breath hitched as she moistened her lower lip with her tongue. She looked so frightened, so adorable, so achingly beautiful, her eyes enormous and scared, but wanting him. He could see that so clearly, in spite of her nerves.

"Can you light some candles for us, baby?" he asked, striving to put her at ease. "Just a few, something that smells good. I love it when you do that."

He managed to get rid of his shoes while she turned her head to direct the flames. Six candles leapt to life, light flickering softly against the walls. She turned back to him as he was shrugging out of his shirt, revealing not only his heavy muscles, but the scars of the earlier bullet, two old knife wounds and the latest injuries.

Hannah made a small strangled sound of distress in her throat and her hands slid over his chest, teasing his flat nipples as she moved her palms toward the newest wounds. He hadn't known his nipples could be so sensitive. It was as if she'd sent a bolt of lightning directly to the head of his cock. His body jerked and thickened more, straining at the material of his jeans. He dropped his hands to his waistband, opening the denim and shoving them from his hips. Warmth invaded his most recent injuries, tingling as Hannah's hands manipulated healing energy.

He pushed the jeans from his hips and his cock sprung free, erect and hard and very thick. Hannah's gaze dropped lower and she blushed. He felt her tremble. He was larger than some, and maybe a little intimidating to a woman who had never had sex. He took a breath and fought down desire, so intense, so brutal it felt like a punch. With Hannah, it wasn't all about sex, and that's what was nearly killing him.

Love hurt. An old cliché, but he found it was true. It was a physical pain, not just the agonizing fist of lust centering in his groin, but the strain on his heart. He had given up on knowing real love. He had come to believe he couldn't have Hannah, and she was the only woman who could bring warmth to that cold place in his heart —

where part of him had lost all hope for humanity. Now she was bringing him back to life and his heart ached, a sharp, dagger-like pain that told him it wasn't going to be easy loving her, having her, belonging to her. He would never be free of her. Never whole again without her.

Because there was fear in her eyes, he leaned forward again and captured her lips, kissing her gently, so tenderly. He worked at stealing her heart to replace the one she'd taken from him. The flickering light from the candles spilled over her, lending her satin skin a glow. Jonas pushed the neckline of her blouse down to blaze a trail of kisses to the creamy swell of her breast.

When his hands came up to undo the buttons, hers covered his, stopping him. He kissed her again. "It's all right, baby. I know this is right, Hannah. Trust me." He wanted her to give her body over to him. Be his. Belong to him. Always and forever.

She swallowed and nodded, kissing him back, relaxing against him when he spent a few minutes indulging himself with the heat of her velvet mouth. She moaned softly and the sound went through his entire body. Her hands went to his shoulders, fingers digging into his muscle, as if anchoring herself, holding him tightly to her. He let the kiss deepen again, not wanting to lose her, his hands once more dropping to the buttons of her blouse. Instantly her hands were there to stop his.

Even with his body raging at him, his brain managed to figure out the problem. He rested his brow against hers, breathing through the desire, turning his fists over to rub her straining nipples with his knuckles, despite the restraints she tried to put on him. "I've always loved your breasts, Hannah. I know that jackass, Simpson, made you self-conscious about them, but you're perfect for me. I love the fact that you're spilling over into my hands, so soft and inviting. Hell, baby, you're so damned sexy I'm going to have an embarrassing accident if you don't let me touch you. I have to touch you. It's beyond wanting now."

Her eyes searched his and she must have seen the raw hunger blazing in his gaze. She swallowed and nodded, but kept her hands over his, just lightening her grip.

Jonas was careful with her. She was so thin, so fragile. He could feel her ribs and her hip bones, her tiny tucked-in waist, but her breasts had refused to lose their curves even when she all but starved herself at her agent's demand. They were full and soft and generous and Hannah tried to hide them from the world.

He slowly undid the buttons, feeling as if it was Christmas morning and he was unwrapping the gift he'd waited his entire life for. His fingers brushcd sensitive, creamy skin, making her shiver as the material parted and gaped open to reveal her full, lush breasts. His breath caught and held in his lungs.

"God, baby, you're beautiful. I couldn't even fantasize this and I've got a good imagination when it comes to you." He pushed her blouse from her shoulders, letting the material float to the ground as he unhooked her bra. Before she could protest, he captured her mouth again, drawing her tongue into the dark recesses of his mouth, his hands shaping her breasts possessively, stroking the nipples with his thumbs.

"I've got to have you on the bed, where I can look at you and feel you next to me." He didn't want to take a chance on freaking her out when she was so shy about her body. Who would have ever thought that someone as beautiful as Hannah could have such a poor and inaccurate image of her own body?

He was shaking as he lifted her and carried her to the bed, following her down, watching her hair spill across the pillow, her breasts thrust invitingly toward his mouth.

Her skin gleamed a luminous cream in the candlelight. His heart thudded in his chest, and his body reacted with another painful jerking and thickening. She was like a fever in his system, burning so hot he was afraid if he didn't have her, he might spontaneously combust, but if she said no, if she was too frightened, he would stop. He'd spend the next five years in a freaking ice shower, but he'd stop. Love did that to a man.

He knelt on the bed, hands tracing the satin skin, cupping her breasts, tracing her ribs and finding the low-riding jeans. "Lift up for me, sweetheart."

Her gaze locked with his; she did what he said and allowed him to slide her jeans and underwear from her too-slender hips, down her long, glorious legs. He tossed the clothing aside and lowered himself over her, blanketing her nude body with his, inch by slow devastating inch, until they were skin to skin. She was hot and so damned soft he thought his body would sink — would melt — right into hers.

She gave another breathy little moan that shook him right to his toes. Jonas gave in to temptation. She was offering him heaven, and he wanted her, wanted her to belong to him body and soul. She was inexperienced and he was . . . well . . . he knew exactly what he was doing.

He kissed her over and over, drowning in her taste, wondering if she tasted so sweet all over. Her skin held a fragrance that was addicting to him and he took his time, licking and nibbling over her chin and throat, down to her breasts. Her breath hitched when he blew warm air over her nipples. She shuddered when his tongue swirled and teased, flicking the hard peaks before his mouth closed over the inviting temptation.

Hannah gasped, her body arching, her breasts sensitive, the sensations clearly shocking her as he suckled, his mouth hot, teeth scraping over her skin, tugging on her nipple. Her breathing became labored, her breasts rising and falling rapidly. He lifted his head to look down at the feast, inhaling her scent and noting with satisfaction the marks of his possession. Her skin was sensitive and marked easily, small strawberry bites that only added to the rush of lust building past anything he'd ever known.

He licked at her nipples, watching her face, the dark flush spreading, her eyes glazing. He let his hand trail lower, feeling her muscles contract in her belly, and then bunch beneath his palm.

"Jonas," she whispered, in protest maybe, but he lowered his head again, taking her nipple between his teeth and rolling and tugging gently, his tongue rasping over the tip until she gasped and her hips lifted for him. He slid his hand up and between her thighs to the welcoming dampness. His heart lurched in his chest. His cock jerked hard, swelling until he thought he'd burst.

His eyes met hers. She looked so dazed and stunned and so absolutely sexy lying there with her fingers tangled in his hair, shy trust mingled with shock on her face. He cupped her mound, so hot his palm felt scorched as he licked her other nipple, keeping her gaze locked with his. Her head thrashed on the pillow.

He slid his finger inside the creamy heat and she cried out his name, her tight sheath clamping down on him as her muscles protested the invasion.

"It's all right, baby," he soothed her. "I've wanted you for so long I think I'm just going to have to take my time eating you up like candy. You'll like it, honey, I promise." He kissed her belly. "You have to trust me, just relax for me."

Hannah stared at his face, stamped deep with dark sensuality, his eyes just as dark with hunger and focused intent. Her fingers bit into the muscles bulging in his shoulders as she braced herself for the sensations rocking her body. She was lost in a storm of pleasure washing over her like a tidal wave. She needed him — needed something — the force building inside her like a hurricane. She was trembling and couldn't stop. Small whimpers escaped and she couldn't stop that either.

His mouth moved over her belly, tongue teasing her navel, teeth nipping, his hair dragging over sensitive skin. She gasped again, nearly coming off the bed when his hands parted her thighs. She watched his head dip lower and lower, below her hips, and she froze, unable to think. Only her body reacted.

"Jonas?" She couldn't lie still. Her lungs burned, starved for air, and she swore the junction between her legs was on fire.

"I've waited a lifetime for this, baby, just give me a minute here. I need this." His voice was edgy with dark hunger. "You're mine now, Hannah. And your body is mine." To worship. To play. To use. To love. He was a starving man, addicted before he ever had a taste.

His hands lifted her hips even as he lowered his head and his tongue took a long, slow swipe of her soft flesh. She moaned and then her breath stilled in her lungs and time ceased to exist as he began to do exactly as he promised — eat her like candy. His tongue pushed deep into her center, sending streaks of lightning zigzagging through her body. Involuntarily her hands fisted in the covers and her head thrashed back and forth wildly. He stroked and nipped, stabbed deep and drew moisture. He feasted and devoured.

Her body drew tighter and tighter, a fist of sensitive muscles bursting into life as his tongue licked and stroked and sucked. Deep inside, every hidden secret, every intimate reaction, was uncovered. He made her blind with pleasure, made her crazy, the fire raging so hot and so out of control she didn't know who she was. She heard herself, crying, begging, as he pushed her higher and higher.

"I can't control . . ." She needed to stop, to catch her breath. The pressure continued relentlessly, building through her body. She felt like she was on the verge of coming apart. His arms felt like bands of steel, holding her down, while his mouth found her clit and suckled. She screamed as her body seemed to fly up and shatter. Just shatter. She twisted and rocked, unable to think, unable to know if she was fighting him, or pleading with him for more.

The sensations were terrifying, wave after

wave, as his mouth pushed her up and into a second orgasm. Even as she screamed again, he rose up and over her, pulling her thighs apart. He looked so sensual — so *ravenous.*

"I can't, Jonas. It's too much."

"Yes, Hannah. It's what you want, what I want. Trust me to take you there and bring you back. Let me take you all the way."

She wasn't going to survive if there was any more pleasure. She would shatter into a million pieces and there'd be no putting her back together, but he looked sinfully sexy and she wanted whatever he could give, no matter how afraid she got. She swallowed fear, her gaze clinging to his. "I'm afraid of myself, not you, Jonas."

"I know, baby. You're doing fine. I'm not going to stop and let you catch your breath this time. I'm going to take you right over the edge with me."

His breathing was harsh, his teeth clenched, and then he moved. She felt the thick head of his erection pressing tightly against her entrance, now hot and slick with cream he'd drawn from her body. Then he was stretching her, the sensation nearly a burn as he pressed deep, driving through tight folds, forcing her muscles to accommodate him. He felt thick, too big, impossible to take inside her, and then he thrust hard and deep, tearing past the thin barrier, mingling pain with pleasure as the bundle of sensitive nerve endings screamed with need. He destroyed her control with that one hard thrust, and then began to take her out of reality and into mindless ecstasy.

Jonas tried to regain some semblance of control, but her body gripped his like a tight velvet fist, hot enough to scorch. He braced himself with a hand on either side of her shoulders, his body blanketing hers, and bent his head. His mouth took hers as he began a driving rhythm through the inner muscles so tight and reluctant, seizing him as he plunged deeper and deeper. She gasped, her hips bucking to meet each thrust. The powerful strokes drove her higher, closer to the release he wanted to give her, yet he kept her from getting there, forcing her to go all the way with him.

He tore his mouth from hers, breathing deeply, pistoning harder, feeling her muscles heating, melting into living silk, pulsing with life around him. She thrashed harder under him, somewhere between fighting him and yanking him closer. She murmured something, a small cry of alarm, her nails biting deep.

Hannah was unprepared for the painful

pleasure racking her body, the pressure building and building until she fought for breath. Each hard thrust sent her reeling and the edges of her vision blurred. Above her, Jonas looked the epitome of carnal sin, his hair damp, his face etched in lines of passion, his breath ragged as his body rode hers harder and deeper, so deep and hot she wanted — no, needed — to come apart.

He dragged her legs over his arms, his hips thrust even deeper so that her muscles pulsed around him, clasping him tightly, squeezing down until he uttered a hoarse cry and the world around her went black and then filled with colors. The explosion ripped through her body, a storm of such intensity she couldn't even cry out anymore. Multiple orgasms tore through her, one right after the other, swelling in strength, her body spasming around his.

Jonas couldn't hold on with her body rippling and pulsing around him like a hot, silken fist. His release came harsh and violent, unrelenting pleasure roaring up from his toes and pouring down from his head to center in his groin. Pulse after hot pulse jetting deep inside her, filling her, adding to the waves of her climax so that she clamped down hard on him, sending another shaft of lightning whipping through him. He collapsed over the top of her, his breathing ragged, his lungs burning and his body shaking. He wiped the sweat from his forehead and tried to calm the pounding of his heart. Nothing had ever been that good.

Jonas reluctantly withdrew and rolled off her, tugging the blanket around her. Hannah lay limply beside him, her eyes dazed, her slender body slack, but his hand on her abdomen confirmed the aftershocks still rippling through her. "Are you all right, baby?"

"I don't know." Her fingers found his. "Am I?"

He grinned. "Oh, yeah, baby. You're so fine they need to find a new word to describe you."

"That was a little scary." He'd taken her over. There was no going back. She'd think about him, his mouth, his hands, his body, every time she lay on her bed. Her body sang for him, came apart for him. "I wasn't aware I'd been missing anything so spectacular."

Jonas frowned and rolled over, his arm settling around her waist. "Just remember who you belong to, Hannah. I wouldn't want to have to shoot anyone — or strangle you."

She leaned over to kiss his shoulder. "Why am I the one to be strangled?"

"It's a much more personal death."

"You've been a cop too long." She dragged the blanket up higher to cover her breasts. "I can't move."

"You don't have to move. Just go to sleep. When we wake up, I'll show you some other very intriguing things we can do."

"There's more? There can't be more." She yawned and snuggled closer to him. "I have to catch a plane in the morning, Jonas. You know it's a four-hour drive to the airport."

"Take a later one."

"Mmm. Maybe." She could barely speak, let alone move, and the thought of a four-hour drive and an additional plane ride to the East Coast was daunting. And she needed a hot bath to soothe her sore body. "I think you beat me up."

Instantly he shifted, his arm going around her hips, his hand pushing the blanket from her body to inspect her. "I got a little carried away, Hannah. I should have been much more gentle your first time. Hang on, baby, I'll run you a bath." There were marks on her thighs, on her breasts and even on her belly. "And I'd better shave. You have whisker burn on your face."

And on the inside of her thighs, but she wasn't mentioning that.

"I'm not certain I can actually take a bath

right now," she admitted. "Let's just lie here and count the stars." She waved her hand and the candles flickered out. A second wave had the French doors opening to let the night in.

At once a breeze cooled her body and Jonas tugged her closer to keep her warm. It was amazing to feel at peace. For his body to be at rest. She belonged to him. She'd given herself to him and Hannah didn't ever do things by half-measure. She'd been frightened, but his loss of control hadn't driven her away. She'd accepted his physical needs the way she accepted his temper and arrogance.

He slipped his hand beneath the blanket and let his palm, fingers splayed wide, drift possessively over her body. *His.* He tasted her in his mouth, breathed her in his lungs, had spent time inside her hot silken sheath. If there were miracles, he was living one. She didn't protest his touch, but turned her head toward him, her gaze locking with his. He held her with his eyes, not wanting her to look away while he explored every square inch of incredible skin. Warm and soft like nothing else he'd ever experienced.

"I love that you're mine," he whispered and nuzzled the blanket from her breasts so he could enjoy the sight.

Deliberately he allowed his hand to move lower. He felt her stomach muscles clench as his fingers skimmed over her. She tensed when he cupped her mound so he rested his hand there, letting her get uscd to the feel of his possession. He wanted to touch her like this whenever he wanted. He wanted her open to him, loving him, giving herself to him, and more than anything, he wanted her to feel the same way back.

There was no "if" they were together. They were. He'd made that clear before making love to her, and he wanted her to realize he was a physical man. There would be touching — lots of it. Her curves, her body, belonged to him and his to her. It wasn't about groping her — it was about loving her. He needed her to feel the difference.

Her nipples had peaked in the cool night air and he bent his head to run his tongue over one of them. He felt the instant answering flood of warm liquid against his palm and he slid one finger inside her. She was as tight as ever, her muscles clenching, the hot silk ready for him. He rubbed his head against her soft skin, blinking back emotion that threatened to spill over.

Hannah was completely, utterly, relaxed under his hand and she never made a single move to reject his advances. She might be a little nervous, but she was open to whatever he chose to do. He chose to kiss her. He loved her mouth. He reveled in the taste of her, the response he drew from her.

When he lifted his head, she wrapped her arms around him and drew him back down beside her. "Go to sleep, Jonas. Right here, with me."

He rolled over, pulling her on top of him so that her warm body was sprawled across his. He wrapped her up with one arm and drew the blanket over both of them. "Like this, Hannah. Close, like this." His arm circled her waist and she snuggled into him, fitting her body over his, breasts pressed tightly against his skin, her head on his pillow.

Jonas fell asleep with his hand cupping her butt. Hannah lay on top of him, listening to his breathing, hyperaware of his hand. Her body still tingled, still sang. For a short time, when he was inside her, she had known exactly where she wanted to be. She loved his touch. He scared the hell out of her by forcing her to go far beyond where she ever thought she could, but she trusted Jonas with her body and had given him everything he'd demanded.

That was so Jonas. She stroked his hair

with small caresses. He was demanding. He always would be. But sometimes, he was so vulnerable and she realized she had power in the relationship as well. She hadn't expected that. He was as vulnerable to her as she was to him. He just acted arrogant and bossy, but deep down, where it counted, he didn't want to lose her either.

She had to go to New York, the contract had been signed a year ago, but then she'd tell Jonas the truth. She had already informed her agent she was getting out of the business. She hadn't taken any new jobs in months and was simply going to fulfill the contracts she'd signed and then she'd live in Sea Haven and hopefully be with Jonas and start a whole new life.

5

Jonas paced across the length of the living room in the Drake family home, all the while glaring at the television. "She's been gone a week and hasn't even bothered to call home, Sarah."

"She called, Jonas," Sarah reminded him with an exaggerated sigh. "You yelled at her and she hasn't called since."

"I wasn't yelling."

" 'Get the hell home' isn't yelling?"

"I don't think it's necessary for her to be there all week. And why does she have to attend the parties every night?"

"It's part of her job."

"Is that what she tells you? Look at those men. They're staring at her." He jabbed his finger at the screen, brows coming together in a fierce scowl.

Sarah curled her legs under her, settling back into the plush chair. "This is the grand finale of the biggest fashion show held in

New York every year. Hannah is a model. Of course they're looking at her; she's wearing a gown worth thousands of dollars. The whole idea is to show off the gown. She walks the runway, makes a few turns, people ooh and aah, and the designer is in for the season."

"They aren't looking at the gown," he denied. "They're looking at Hannah."

"No, Jonas," Sarah corrected gently, "*you're* looking at Hannah. They're there to see the latest designs."

Jonas made a sound of disgust as he stopped in the middle of the spacious room, his gaze glued to the television screen. Hannah, tall, thin and utterly gorgeous, walked with complete confidence down the runway, paused, one hand on her hip, a look of haughty disdain on her beautiful face, turned so that the lights picked up the shimmering colors in her gown before moving on to the pounding beat of the music.

"Why does she have to wear such outrageous makeup? Hell, Sarah, that gown is slashed to her navel and they've painted glitter or something all over her front so every man in the place is definitely not going to be looking at the dress. I can't even describe the dress and I'm looking right at her."

"Please don't tell me you're gawking at

my sister's breasts." Sarah massaged her throbbing temples.

"*Everyone* is looking at her breasts."

"Go home," Sarah said. "You're making me nervous pacing back and forth. And if you hit the counter one more time in the kitchen, it's going to break and I'm going to ban you from the house for a week."

He paused to glare at her. "You can't. I'm recovering from a gunshot wound and they won't let me work. I have nowhere else to go."

The large rambling house sat on a bluff overlooking the ocean. Earlier, Sarah had opened the blinds so that all the windows displayed the incredible view of the sea. She could hear the soothing waves and sit and sip tea while she watched the blue water shimmer, white caps teasing the surface. The anxiety she'd awakened with had eased until Jonas had arrived to watch the fashion show with her. He'd turned her into a bundle of nerves and her head was pounding. It was going to be a long evening if she didn't get rid of him.

Jonas was never a restful person, but in all the years she'd known him, he'd never quite given off the amount of tension that was pouring from him now. Sarah wasn't as sensitive as some of her other sisters, but the energy was still affecting her. She felt almost sick with apprehension.

She leaned her chin onto her hand and studied the way Jonas moved across the floor with quick, restless steps that made no sound. The man was light on his feet and even lighter on patience. "I have no sympathy for you. I can hardly believe you were ever an Army Ranger, Jonas. You're like a crazy person. I swear, you've got my stomach twisted up in knots."

And her stomach was in knots. There was so much pressure it was all she could do not to throw up. Sarah repressed the urge to yell at him. She wanted to watch Hannah's performance. She was proud of the fact that Hannah was one of the top models in the world. There were very few times any of the Drakes could support her by attending a show. Sarah wanted to at least be able to say she'd watched it on television.

"She wanted us all there," she murmured, her gaze glued to the screen. "It was so important to her. Libby's somewhere in the Amazon and no one knows where Elle is. She just disappears for weeks at a time," she added, referring to two of her younger sisters. "Joley's in Europe for her world tour, Kate's in England researching a book, and Abbey is in Australia doing something crazy with dolphins, leaving me to hold the fort."

"They all deserted me," Jonas said. "Every last one of them."

"You drove them away, you bonehead. Jonas, I think it's important for you to know your social skills are sadly lacking most of the time, and when you're injured, they're nonexistent."

He shrugged his wide shoulders, his gaze still on the television. He could see why Hannah's blond curls were famous. The natural spirals cascaded down her back, wild and untamed, adding to her allure. Her large blue eyes and flawless skin showed themselves to perfection on camera, which was why she was sought after by every cosmetic company. She had an enormous, exclusive contract with the leading corporation, but other businesses were always trying to steal her away.

The camera panned the audience and came back for a close-up of her face. Jonas's stomach muscles knotted, the tension in the room rising perceptibly.

"She's so beautiful," Sarah said. "Sometimes the camera can enhance a model's looks, but Hannah really looks like that."

"There's a lot more to Hannah than her looks," Jonas snapped.

Sarah pressed her fingers to the spot just above her eye that was beginning to throb. "I love you, Jonas, I really do, but go home. You hate these things and I don't know why you're bothering to watch."

"I'm torturing myself." Jonas began pacing again as Hannah walked off the runaway, her hips swaying and the gown nearly glowing. The knots loosened just a little and he let out his breath. "Why the hell does she have to do that?"

Sarah sighed. "Do what?"

"Expose herself like that. I don't like it."

"Jonas . . ." Sarah's brows came together as her temper began to rise.

"There's no way security can watch over her. You saw that crowd. How many people do you think are there? At least two thousand, probably a lot more," he answered himself, becoming agitated all over again. "Every damn time she goes out, I'm afraid for her. There are so many lunatics in the world, Sarah, and when a woman plasters herself all over every magazine in the world and is on television batting her eyelashes, you know damned well she's going to have trouble. She and Joley need to stay home, where I can keep my eye on them. I'm getting too old for this crap and Hannah's giving me gray hair."

Sarah frowned. Jonas was sweating. Jonas never sweat, not that she'd ever seen. He was definitely acting far more proprietary over Hannah than usual. She studied him a little suspiciously, trying to read the harsh lines in his face. "Has Hannah been getting more letters than normal and you haven't told me?"

"Do you even hear yourself? Is it normal to get letters from crackpots? No, there hasn't been an increase, but the letters she does get are creepy and there are way too many of them. And Joley gets worse. I swear, every nutcase in the world is fixated on that girl. I just want them where I can look out for them, not traveling halfway around the world."

Of course Jonas wanted to protect them all, it was in his nature. He'd started with his mother and now he couldn't help needing to see to their safety, Sarah assured herself. That's all it was.

She glanced out the bank of windows facing the ocean. The sea was growing a little wild, reflecting her frame of mind. She'd been out of sorts for hours now, and blaming Jonas's edgy mood. White caps foamed and droplets sprayed high into the air. The wind stirred up the sea, whirling small eddies like minicyclones across the surface.

Below, on the rocks, the waves crashed hard. Already dark gray fog crept in from the ocean, slowly blanketing the area. Sarah leaned forward to get a better look.

"Jonas, were we expecting a storm? I thought it was supposed to be a clear day. The wind is picking up and the fog's coming in."

He turned to look at the churning sea, more because of her wary tone than interest. "I didn't pay attention to the weather."

His gaze jumped back to the television as Hannah once again appeared, this time in a different outfit. The jeans were pencil thin, rhinestones tracking down the sides of the legs and sparkling in twin arcs across her rear, calling attention to the shape and the way the material lovingly cradled her bottom. The tank was short, not meeting the jeans riding low on Hannah's hips, exposing a band of smooth skin, her intriguing belly button and a shimmering gold chain dotted with rhinestones.

Jonas felt the surge of heat spreading through his body. He couldn't look at the woman without his body reacting. He spent half his life walking around with a hard-on for her and the other half wanting to fight every man who looked at her. He could still taste her in his mouth, feel the way she was all silky heat, her body wrapped around his. "Damn her anyway, Sarah. Why does she have to do this?"

Sarah rose and walked to the window, staring transfixed out to sea. "She does it because it's her job and she makes a lot of money at it, Jonas." She murmured the words absently, her mind on the growing turbulence outside. The weather and the angry ocean seemed to match Jonas's dark, edgy mood.

Jonas glanced at her, but his gaze was drawn back to Hannah, his stomach back in knots, muscles tight. He actually felt sick. "I want her the hell out of there." He shoved his hand through his hair. "I mean it, Sarah. I'm putting my foot down with her. This is the last show she does. She can just retire."

That pulled Sarah's attention back to him. "How are you going to do that?"

"I'm just going to tell her. She can live with it. I've had to put up with this crap for years."

"You want her to retire when she's at the peak of her modeling career? You are aware she's the most-sought-after runway model in the world right now and that modeling careers don't last very long?"

"I don't give a damn, and if you ask me, this one's lasted far too long. She hasn't liked it for a while, but she's too stubborn to admit it — or maybe she's plain afraid to admit it — afraid of the reaction. It can't be the money, she has enough for ten people."

"What does that mean?" Sarah demanded.

"She detests exposing her body to everyone, she always has. Look what they've done to her." He gestured toward the screen. "She's made herself into a pleaser and they want bones so she's given them bones. I hate that she shows her body to everyone like that, but you know what, Sarah? Hannah detests it more than I do."

"You've made yourself believe that to justify your attitude."

Jonas shook his head. "You have. I feel it every time I see her on a runway or on the cover of a magazine, or worse, on a television commercial. She's successful, but she hates every second of it."

"You don't know the first thing about Hannah," Sarah objected.

"No, *you* don't know the first thing about Hannah," Jonas countered. "All of you think you help her, but you don't, because you don't understand her."

Sarah glared at him. "You're really making me angry, Jonas. Why do you have to be such a jerk about Hannah? She's a wonderful model, she always has been."

"She *detests* going out in public. She's a model because all of you have done something she thinks is spectacular with your lives and it was expected of her to be spectacular as well. And don't tell me that isn't the truth, Sarah. How many times did I hear all of you telling her she's beautiful and should be a model when she was in school? It came up in every single conversation about her future. That and how brilliant she is, how she has a gift for languages and can speak fluently in a half a dozen, so of course she needs to travel. That's such a must when you're brilliant. Heaven forbid a Drake do something as mundane as stay at home and be a wife."

Sarah glanced at him sharply. "She is beautiful. And she's perfect for modeling. She gets to travel and yet someone is looking out for her, which we both know she needs. She's too shy to go on her own."

"She never wanted to go in the first place, Sarah. You all pushed her into it." He threw his hands into the air, his dark anger matching hers. "You turned her into a Barbie doll afraid to think for herself."

"That's bull, Jonas. Hannah wanted to be a model and travel. Remember, we're able to read one another fairly easily. I think we'd know if she hated it."

Jonas swung around, for the first time she could ever remember looming over her in an intimidating manner — and he was intimidating. He actually took an aggressive step toward her and his fingers were curled into two tight fists, his knuckles white. "Would you, Sarah? Are you so certain of that? Hannah is powerful, maybe much more than you ever conceived. She would never want any of you to think she wasn't happy. Surely you're aware she has an eating disorder. How long have you known that? Or didn't you? Was she successful in hiding that as well?"

Sarah opened her mouth to protest, and then closed it just as abruptly. Hannah did have an eating disorder. Libby had uncovered it only a few weeks earlier, but all of them should have known. Hannah was capable of hiding her true feelings from her sisters — at least all but Elle — maybe even Elle. Sarah frowned. In truth, she didn't even know for certain whether or not Elle could always read Hannah. Unfortunately, Jonas was right about Hannah's abilities. She was powerful and she did love her sisters enough to hide her feelings if she thought they'd be uncomfortable.

"That can't be true," she murmured aloud, suddenly anxious. Hannah's panic attacks had started in school and continued throughout her modeling career. She seldom gave interviews because one of the other Drake sisters had to help her overcome her nerves. Could she really want to stay home and not travel the world? Was it possible she detested her glamorous job?

"Come on, Sarah, you don't want it to be true. You all are so certain you know what's best for Hannah and you make certain she knows it, too. The only time Hannah is really herself is when she's messing with me because I've made her angry."

"You mean you hurt her," Sarah accused, beginning to lose her own temper, but angrier with herself than with him, because she was beginning to suspect he might be right — and that would mean they had all pushed Hannah into doing something she didn't want to do. It would be like Hannah to stay quiet even if she was miserable.

He shoved a hand through his hair, clearly agitated. "I don't mean to hurt her. I want her to stand up for herself, to be who she really is, not who she thinks we all want her to be. When I make her angry, believe me, the real Hannah comes out."

"She isn't like that."

"She's a pleaser. You know she is. She wants everyone around her to be happy. You all expect her to be successful, and not just moderately successful; the demand is for a high achiever. All of you are fantastic at what you do . . ."

"And so is she."

"But she detests it. She'd prefer to live quietly, to stay at home and just keep everyone happy."

Sarah shook her head.

"That idiot agent of hers tells her to lose weight and instead of telling him to go to hell because she's so afraid she won't be perfect enough for all of you to love, she starves herself. I kept thinking she'd finally be done with it and walk away, but she's killing herself, slowly maybe, but it amounts to the same thing. So I'm going to put a stop to it."

"I think you're wrong," Sarah said, but it was no longer the truth.

Jonas swore softly. "I should have stopped her from leaving."

"Nothing could have stopped her, Jonas, she made a commitment and Hannah always honors her commitments." Sarah turned her back on him, once more staring out the window at the sea. Far out, through the gray fog, she swore she saw twin columns of water, whirling cyclones, spinning across the surface. The water had gone dark and turbulent, much like she was feeling. "What happened to my calm, peaceful day, Jonas? I was going to curl up on the couch and watch my sister do her thing since I couldn't be there in person."

Jonas turned back to the television. "Did Hannah really ask you if you could go to the event?"

"Yes."

There was a long silence while three models came out together and walked the long runway, pausing to do a turn as they strutted, their attitude a performance in itself.

"She invited me as well."

Sarah stiffened, whirling to face him. "She did what?" A chill crept down her spine. Goose bumps rose on her arms.

Jonas turned to face her and, for the first time, allowed her to see how ravaged and drawn he was. "She's never done that before. She knows I hate it. Why would she ask me, knowing I'd be sarcastic and mean if I went with her?" There were shadows in his eyes. "I haven't slept in days, Sarah."

"Why didn't you tell me right away? For God's sake, Jonas, you're like us. You know you have your own gifts. If you feel something is wrong, you have to say so."

"I'm not like you, not really," he denied,

this time shoving both hands through his hair, leaving him more rumpled and distraught than before. "I just figure if anything is really wrong, you'll know. None of you have indicated there's a potential problem so I just ignored the feeling I had. I don't have any special powers, Sarah. I don't."

She flashed him a look of disbelief. "Why couldn't you sleep?"

He shrugged again, muscles rippling across his arms and back as he paced restlessly. The TV announcer began describing another gown by a famous European designer, once again drawing Jonas's attention so that he stopped and stared at the screen. Hannah moved into the bright lights to a thunderous applause, spiral curls in platinum and gold hanging to her waist, her famous blue eyes shadowed with glitter to match the gold threads gleaming through the dress.

"Sometimes when I look at her," he admitted, talking more to himself than to Sarah, "I can't breathe. I've felt that way since the first time I ever laid eyes on her." His fists dropped to his sides, but they were clenched tight, so tight his knuckles were white. A muscle jerked in his jaw and his mouth tightened as the camera once more panned the audience, the commentator gleefully announcing that everyone who was anyone was at Fashion Week in New York.

"She has a wicked sense of humor, if she ever lets it out," he added. "I sometimes stir her up just to see her retaliate."

The camera picked up glamorous stars and public figures, wealthy icons and hotel owners, as well as reporters and numerous identifiable people from the fashion industry. Movie stars and politicians, household names, people from the music industry were all represented and, along with them, their bodyguards. Sarah drew in her breath sharply, one hand going to her throat.

"Jonas," she whispered. "I think I saw Ilya Prakenskii in the crowd. Why would he be there? He's a Russian hit man, isn't he?"

Jonas's eyes gleamed like twin chips of ice. "That's his reputation, but no one has ever managed to pin anything on him. If he's there, he's guarding Sergei Nikitin."

"That man who was so fixated on Joley? I know he has a bad reputation as a mobster, but Nikitin seems so young to have risen to so much power so fast."

"He's definitely with the Russian mob." He glanced at her and then back to the screen. "You're afraid of Prakenskii. Has he contacted you since the incident with Aleksandr and Abbey?"

"You mean when he saved Aleksandr's life and we had to give him our word that we'd return a favor?" Sarah asked with a little shiver. "No. I'd hoped we'd never see him again. He's a very powerful man. Like Elle, he has tremendous gifts."

"What aren't you telling me?"

Sarah bit her lip. "He has a path to Joley's magic. He can touch her, talk to her, fight magic with magic — and he's powerful, Jonas. To save Aleksandr, we made a deal with the devil."

"I hope he's not the threat I feel."

"Why would he save Abbey's fiancé and then harm Hannah?"

"I've never understood half of what people do to one another," Jonas said, pushing his hand through his hair once again. And he didn't either. Why people were so cruel to one another, why money and power drove them to kill and betray, he would never understand — not in a million years. And how he himself had gotten so good at killing and figuring things out, his mind cool and clinical in a crisis when he was so emotional deep inside where no one saw — no one but Hannah.

All the while the commentator rattled on about New York Fashion Week being the biggest gala in years, the best collections, the fabulous designers. Jonas turned his attention back to the screen as the camera once more took in the crowd. He spotted the elusive Russian hit man, standing just to the back of Sergei Nikitin, the mobster. His stomach did another somersault, the knots tightening, his fist clenching. Was it possible Nikitin wanted retaliation against the Drakes? There was *something. Someone.* He just couldn't find the threat, but he felt it on the outer edges of his consciousness, whispering to him, digging at him, making him hyperaware.

Sarah watched Jonas, not the screen. His gaze was fixed, and his body was utterly still as if he were hunting. She hardly dared to take a breath, afraid of disturbing his concentration. He didn't believe he had paranormal talents, but the Drake sisters had always been aware of his abilities — just not exactly what they were. He was certainly in tune with them — and with danger. His face had the grim expression he often wore when he was investigating a particularly intense crime.

Sarah swallowed the lump in her throat, fighting to remain calm. Apprehension ate at her, so strong she could barely breathe. Was the familiar feeling the beginning of warnings, precognition kicking in — or was it empathy for whatever Jonas was feeling — because she was beginning to get the impression something terrible was about to happen.

"What's wrong?"

"Damn it, I don't know." His gaze went dark with anxiety. "She's in trouble, though. I know she is. I should have gone with her."

Sarah swallowed her alarm, forcing down panic. "Calm down, Jonas. I want you to sit down and take a few deep breaths."

"Go to hell, Sarah. I'm not some little kid. Hannah is — *everything* to me."

Sarah's heart jumped. Jonas had never admitted his feelings aloud for her sister. He didn't even seem to notice what he was saying, and with Jonas, that was a bad sign. The Drake sisters had been born with special gifts, talents they relied on and were an intrinsic part of their lives. They'd always known Jonas had the same rare abilities, just as fundamental to him as breathing, yet he didn't seem to fully comprehend how to develop and use his talents on demand. The abilities were there, forces to be reckoned with. Sarah could feel the energy pulsing through the room, emanating off him in waves as he tried to ferret out the danger to Hannah.

"The reason you're going to figure out

what's wrong is because she is everything to you. We can take a plane to New York and be there in a few hours. She's safe right now. She's surrounded by television cameras and celebrities. There must be a few hundred private bodyguards in that building along with massive security."

Jonas's gaze leapt back to the screen, shaking his head. "She's not safe," he repeated, his white teeth snapping together. "There's someone . . ." His voice trailed off and his attention slipped from Sarah wholly back to the screen. His eyes had gone cool and assessing, his body utterly still, all of his concentration centered on the crowd behind Hannah.

Sarah heard the boom of the ocean, a portent of trouble. Her heart pounded along with the waves. She was suddenly very, very frightened for her sister. She searched the crowd, trying to see what bothered Jonas. The cameras jumped from inside the show to outside, where a crowd pushed along the sidewalk hoping to catch a glimpse of one of the celebrities. There were so many movie stars inside and the fans had come out to see them.

A reporter focused on several small groups holding protests across the street, each outshouting the other. There was the inevitable animal rights group protesting the use of real animal fur for clothing. Sarah moved closer trying to catch a glimpse of faces. Hannah never modeled animal fur, but she had refused to represent or join or in any way have her name used in conjunction with the large and well-known group, as she'd researched it very carefully.

Evidence had come to light that the members "rescued" animals from sanctuaries where the animals were well cared for, but kept in cages. The reporters had dutifully filmed the rescues, never realizing the real story was that the animals were immediately euthanized as there was nowhere to put them and no way to feed and care for them once they were taken from the sanctuaries. Hannah had been vocal in her refusal to join after she had done extensive research and several other misdeeds had been uncovered, rocking the foundation of the group.

"They hate her," Sarah pointed out. "I recognize the man with the beard. He threatened Hannah when she talked the reporters into investigating."

"Yes," Jonas agreed. "It's a powerful group with many celebrities lending their names without knowing what really goes on. Hannah blew their organization's secrets wide open and they lost a great deal of support, but more importantly, respectability. That means they've lost funding."

"Did she get any letters from them recently?"

Jonas kept his gaze glued to the television screen. "She gets letters from everyone, and yes, specifically, there were letters calling her a bitch and saying she wasn't going to get away with trying to ruin their organization. I talked to the board members and they said they couldn't control fanatics and had no way of knowing who would try to intimidate anyone in their name. They said they were grateful to Hannah for finding the bad apples in their group."

"And you bought that?"

"Not for a minute." Jonas frowned as the camera panned the crowd and settled on a second group of protesters. Realizing the television camera was on them, the people held up signs, shaking them and shouting, calling the fashion show abhorrent and an abomination against all that was moral and right.

Sarah sighed. "Now he's going after the fashion industry? That's the Reverend RJ. I think RJ stands for reject from theology class. He's very charismatic and has been gathering a good-sized following. Elle told me about him. He's been under surveillance for some time because he's very inflammatory and his 'religion' is officially considered a cult. He's moved his followers into the mountains about two to three hours' drive from here."

"Yeah, the deputies have told me how uncooperative they are. They don't allow anyone onto their property. He's building a fortress up in the hills, but so far, he hasn't really done anything wrong and his followers keep to themselves."

"He's going to be a problem," Sarah said, staring at the man on television as he waved his arms and gestured wildly. "He's a long way from California."

"Free television time. He can look important and gather more followers," Jonas said. "I've never understood how educated people are taken in by con artists like the Reverend." He inhaled sharply. "Right there, to the left of the Reverend's little flock. That's Rudy."

"Rudy?"

"Rudy Venturi. He writes to Hannah nearly every day. I should have known that little pervert would go to her event. The idiots advertise months in advance and might as well shout to every whacko out there to come and get her."

"The idea is for people to come to the fashion show, Jonas."

"Well, they've come," he replied grimly, "and my gut is telling me Hannah is in trouble. Try her cell phone."

"She isn't going to have a cell phone on her in the middle of a fashion show," Sarah said, but she picked up the phone and began to punch in numbers. "What should I say?"

"You tell her I said to get the hell out of there now. Don't take any crap from her, Sarah." He stalked across the room, reaching for the phone. "Here, let me tell her."

Sarah hastily hung up. "She isn't going to listen to you when you're barking orders. Can't you just tell her you think she's in danger? If you start swearing at her, she's going to turn stubborn."

Jonas turned away from her, but not before she saw the shadows in his eyes. He was really worried. It had nothing to do with Hannah's lack of attire, something he harped on regularly, but this time, she could tell, he was thinking of little else but Hannah's safety. With her heart pounding, Sarah quickly left a message telling Hannah they thought she was in danger and to please have an escort take her out of the situation.

The New York Fashion Week was one of the biggest events of the year. Sarah doubted

Hannah would get the message at all, let alone comply. "Even if she does leave, Jonas, will that make her safer? Right now, she's in the middle of a large crowd. Maybe she's safer there."

"She'd be a hell of a lot safer with me." His gaze was back on the screen, his white teeth snapping together with impatience. "Why the hell are they showing all the protesters? I want to see the crowd pushing up against the ropes."

"Who does Hannah have for security?"

"Her idiot agent hired someone. I can't wait to tell him he's fired."

Sarah's eyebrow shot up. "You're going to fire Hannah's agent? Does she know?"

"Do I really give a damn?"

"Jonas, you're so arrogant. That's not going to get you anywhere with Hannah."

"Being nice hasn't gotten me anywhere."

Sarah nearly choked. "Nice? You've been nice to her?"

"Considering what I wanted to do, then yes, I was being nice. Stop distracting me. I need to figure this out. Who do we have in New York?"

She knew he was thinking out loud and refrained from answering. No one was in New York. None of her sisters were even in the country. She felt helpless to warn Hannah. She pressed her fingers hard against her temple trying to still the throbbing pain there. Maybe she was just allowing Jonas to freak her out. She wanted that to be the case, but she was so afraid it wasn't. She knew — *knew* — Hannah was in trouble. The knowledge was bone deep now and she was thousands of miles away without a way to warn her sister.

She looked at the television set, waiting for the commercial break to be over so she could look at her sister walking down the runway. Hannah would know. Sarah crossed her arms across her waist and hung tight. "She'll know, Jonas. Just like you — like me. She's going to know there's danger and she'll be careful."

Jonas flashed her a quick repressing glare. She was a security expert. The fashion show and the party that would be held afterward were a bodyguard's nightmare and she knew it. She'd done her time filling in as a bodyguard, and that many people crushed into one room with booze, dancing and wild music was going to be the worst possible scenario to keep a client safe.

"She knew before she left or she wouldn't have asked me to go with her," Jonas said. "And she still went. Damn her for that."

"Jonas, that isn't helping. Hannah has a

job to do. If she gives her word that she's going to be somewhere, she has to be there. Her word is every bit as important as yours is. People count on her. Having Hannah model their clothes can mean a successful season. It's huge to have her on board."

"I can't believe you're defending what she's done. Her life is in danger, Sarah. Can't you understand that? Her life. She's risking her life for a fucking fashion show. You tell me how that's not just plain insane?"

6

Hannah smiled and waved for what seemed like the thousandth time in ten minutes. She was at maximum overload and had signaled her agent, Greg Simpson, numerous times that she needed to leave. He was having none of it, deliberately ignoring her frantic motions. It had been difficult enough to do the show, let alone attend the party afterward, and Greg was aware of it. She had a good mind to spill his drink right down the front of him so he'd have to leave. She sent him a little warning buzz, but he just flashed her a quelling glance, turned his back on her, and continued talking to Edmond and Colese Bellingham, the up-and-coming designers of the season.

Hannah sighed, knowing he was angry with her for her decision to quit. She blew a quick kiss toward Sabrina, a model she genuinely liked. Sabrina smooched back and rolled her eyes, before turning her attention back to one of the many actors surrounding her who didn't have a chance in hell with her.

"Hannah, you look gorgeous tonight," Russ Craun greeted her and leaned in to give her a kiss, handing her a glass of sparkling liquid as he did so.

Hannah turned her head to ensure his lips landed on her cheek, glancing at her watch as she took the glass. Her sisters usually gave her a little boost to keep her from having a full-blown panic attack when she was working, but they'd all been out of town and she was very shaky.

Russ was a friend, a high-profile football player with a reputation for high jinks, yet she'd found him to be very sweet. He attended quite a few of the same parties and he always made an effort to talk to her without doing anything more than harmless flirting. More than once he'd come to her rescue when men were crowding too close around her.

"Russ! It's always so good to see you." She looked around him. "Who'd you bring with you tonight?" He usually dated young, pretty actresses who hung on his arm and stared adoringly up at him. They never lasted long, but they looked good in the magazines and kept his name on the front page of the newspapers.

"I came alone, hoping you didn't bring a date."

Hannah laughed. "You know I never bring a date." She took a small drink of the champagne and let the fire slide down her throat. She wasn't much of a drinker, but she needed something to get her through the next few minutes until she could extract herself from the crowd and get to the safety of her hotel room.

"Why is that?" Russ asked, taking her hand and leading her through the enormous room. The party was pulsing with life and music, the sound loud, the conversations pushing the noise level even higher. He opened the balcony doors and led her outside. "That's better."

Hannah nodded in agreement and stepped close to the railing. Setting her glass on the polished marble, she gripped the edge with both hands and threw her head back to inhale deeply. "Don't you love the night? The stars are like gems." She lifted her arms toward the moon, her long hair spilling around her, her face lifted to the darkened sky.

"Do you do that deliberately?" Russ asked. "The moonlight spills over you and puts you in the spotlight. Your hair turns platinum and gold and you look like the most beautiful woman in the world with soft, tempting skin and mysterious eyes and the most sinfully kissable lips I've ever seen."

Hannah blinked at him and then burst out laughing. "Tell me you don't use that line on your girlfriends. They couldn't possibly fall for it."

He grinned at her. "What woman wouldn't want to be told her lips are a sinful temptation?"

"That was my skin, my lips are sinfully soft," she pointed out.

"Hasn't your boyfriend ever told you that you're a sinful temptation?" he asked.

Hannah hesitated. The question always threw her. She didn't really have a boyfriend. She'd never really had a boyfriend. There was only one man she was interested in and he would eat her alive. She blushed thinking about it. He already had. But Jonas wanted someone very different and Hannah could never be that person. She'd tried. He hadn't noticed that she'd tried, but she had. Just looking at Jonas hurt. She touched her lips. She could still feel his kiss. A sizzling, dazzling moment that stopped her heart every time she thought about it.

Her body tingled, went warm at the thought of the other things Jonas Harrington had done. His hands on her, his mouth on her, his body filling hers, moving inside hers. She fought to keep from blushing, because the things Jonas had done would make anyone blush — but she couldn't say he was her boyfriend. They'd had great sex. Mind-blowing sex. The kind of sex she hadn't known existed, but as always, they'd fought and he had been furious and disappointed and cutting. No one could cut her down the way Jonas did. No, she couldn't say he was her boyfriend.

"Don't tell me you don't have a boyfriend," Russ said, crowding her close to the rail.

Hannah disliked most people touching her. She detested that odd little quirk in herself. She wanted to be friendly and easy the way Sabrina was, but any company started the beginnings of a panic attack and a crowd like this was devastating to her. It was humiliating to be a grown woman, successful at business, but be unable to control herself the way even a young child could.

"Why do you always make a try, Russ, when you know I'm going to say no to you?" she asked, holding her ground for pride's sake.

His grin widened, became devilish. "Two reasons, Hannah, my little temptress. First,

I might get lucky and you'll change your mind. And second, I love that trapped look you get on your face right before you decide to let me down gently." He reached around her, caging her body, as he picked up her glass and handed it to her. Raising his own, he winked. "To another rejection."

Hannah watched him take a drink, a small frown pulling at her mouth. "Don't be silly. You ask me out when you have a woman on your arm. You've never been serious."

"Of course I'm serious. Any man would be serious over a chance at you, Hannah. Who is your mystery man and why doesn't he ever come with you?"

Hannah touched the glass to her lips, but didn't actually drink, a trick many of the models used when attending major events. "This isn't his thing."

"You mean guarding you from other men isn't worth his time? Because if you belonged to me, I'd be right at your side, making sure men like me didn't come near you." He took another drink, tilting his head to study her face. "Maybe he doesn't deserve you."

Hannah shrugged and this time she did take another swallow. It burned all the way down, but she needed a little false confidence with this strange and unexpected conversation. Jonas would probably laugh if he knew she thought of him as hers. Worse, he'd be angry with her and accuse her of using him to keep other men at arm's length — and maybe she did. There had never been room for any other man. Jonas had occupied all of her thoughts from the moment she'd met him — and she feared it would always be that way — even long after he married someone else and settled down to have a family of his own. They'd had mind-blowing sex and he was going to marry someone else and she was going to end up an old strange lady with cats all around her.

It made her want to cry. The liquid in her drink began to bubble and she automatically put her hand over the rim of the glass. She had to stay in control and any thoughts of Jonas always stole her control. She could still hear her own soft cries as his tongue made a leisurely foray over every square inch of her body. She took another swallow and let the fire settle in her stomach.

"See, there you go." Russ brushed his fingers across her face as if wiping away her expression. "You look so sad. I don't like you looking sad, Hannah. Give me a shot. I wouldn't put that look on your face."

She forced a quick smile. "Russ, you're a flirt and a bit of a hound dog. I've never seen you with the same woman twice. I would last one night and you'd be on to the next one."

"Maybe I just need a good woman to straighten me out."

"You're fine the way you are, Russ. When you find the right woman, you'll want to settle down." She glanced at her watch, anxious that the growing fear in her was from the knowledge that the boost her sisters had given her to stave off the panic attacks was wearing off. They'd been too long out of the country and her anxiety level was rising faster than normal, her lungs fighting for air when she should have felt so much better outside away from the crowd.

To stay calm, she took another cautious sip of the champagne. She didn't touch alcohol very often, and the drink hit her already churning stomach hard. Heat and then cold swept through her. She was suddenly nauseated. Her heart reacted, racing as she turned away from Russ, handing him the glass as she did so.

Russ set the glasses on the rail and took her arm. "You look like you're dizzy. Are you okay? I can drive you to your hotel."

Hannah remained silent, assessing her body. She was a Drake and Drakes had special gifts. Her body violently objected to the drink all of a sudden. How strange. She pressed her hand against her mouth and tried to step back away from him. Russ tightened his hold as she swayed.

"Hannah? Are you ill?"

"Miss Drake. Lovely to see you again."

Hannah stiffened when she heard the distinctive Russian accent. She turned slowly to find Sergei Nikitin, the Russian mobster, smiling at her with shiny white teeth. He enjoyed the good things in life; his Italian suit and shoes cost as much as a small car. Everything he had, he had gotten through someone's suffering.

Hannah felt the evil in him when she was so close, and it didn't help the nausea churning in her stomach. She glanced past him and her gaze was caught and held by Ilya Prakenskii. For a moment she couldn't breathe, unable to look away from his cold, merciless eyes. He was reputed to be a hit man for Nikitin, and at one time had been trained by Russia's secret police. Strangely, Hannah couldn't feel anything — good or evil — when she was close to the man.

"Miss Drake." Ilya nodded his head, moving past Nikitin to take her elbow and remove her from Russ's hold. He drew her to him. "You look ill. Do you need help?"

Hannah swept back her hair with a shaky

hand. She felt dizzy and disoriented. She needed to lie down. She should have been afraid of Ilya, maybe she was, but he was strong and holding her up and she felt confused so she remained still, afraid if she tried to get away, she'd fall flat on her face. If she answered, she might get sick.

"Hannah?" Ilya asked again, his voice low, but commanding. He tipped her face up toward his, staring down into her eyes.

"I was just about to take her home," Russ said, frowning at the bodyguard's high-handed proprietary manner.

Hannah shook her head, one hand pressed to her stomach. Models didn't throw up at parties right after the biggest fashion show of the season in the United States. Desperate, she wiped the beads of sweat from her face and tried to step away from Ilya.

Ilya glanced over his shoulder to the two glasses sitting on the railing and a low hiss escaped between his teeth. As he reached for Hannah's glass, Russ stepped back to avoid his arm and knocked into the railing, sending both glasses crashing to the garden below.

"Stay put, Hannah," Ilya instructed. "If you want to get back to your hotel, we'll be more than happy to escort you."

Sergei Nikitin smiled again, looking more

the shark than ever. "Of course, Miss Drake, it would be an honor to see you to your hotel safely." He turned his attention to Russ. "You are the football player."

His accent had thickened, a bad sign, Hannah thought. She had to take charge or she'd end up obligating her family even more than they already were to the Russians, and she didn't want Nikitin anywhere near her sister Joley. She might be confused and disoriented and very, very sick to her stomach, but she held on to that much. Sergei Nikitin wasn't a good man and he had a bad habit of turning up wherever her sister was performing, looking for an introduction.

Hannah made a concentrated effort to step away from Ilya and reach for Russ's arm. Ilya moved without seeming to move. Glided. Or maybe his muscles just rippled. Whatever happened, he was suddenly and solidly between her and Russ. Ilya spoke in Russian to his boss.

Hannah frowned. She knew Russian and she could have sworn he ordered his boss to watch the rapist while he took care of her. *Rapist?* She must have misunderstood. Russ was her friend. And where was her agent? She needed to leave. It was all getting too complicated and she was definitely going to be sick all over the Russian mobster's body-guard.

Nikitin replied and Hannah's face lost all color. She felt herself going pale. He told Ilya to throw the bastard over the railing. She understood that with no problem. She didn't have the strength to fight against two men to save Russ and they certainly had the wrong idea about him. She'd been uneasy all night, but Russ didn't need to rape women. They threw themselves at him.

"He's my friend," she said, or thought she said. Her voice was strange — tinny — far away. What was wrong with her?

Ilya shook his head. "She understands Russian, Sergei. Be careful what you say, she might not realize you're amusing your-self."

Hannah would have relaxed, but Ilya seemed to be staring Russ down, his pierc-ing blue eyes locked on to the football player with lethal purpose. Russ was very arrogant and she'd seen him intimidate several men, but with Ilya, he either knew the man's reputation, or something in those ice cold eyes warned him off.

Russ shrugged his shoulders. "Hannah, I can see you're busy. I'll just tell your agent you're ready to go."

Hannah watched him go through the

double French doors, leaving her alone on the balcony with a mobster and his bodyguard.

"We must take her to her hotel where she's safe," Nikitin ordered.

Ilya shook his head. "I can help her. Give me a couple of minutes with her, Sergei. If her agent shows up, distract him while I see what I can do."

"Her sister must know we helped her," Nikitin reminded him.

Ilya didn't answer, simply wrapped his arm around Hannah's waist and half carried her to the far side of the balcony away from his boss. "That man is no friend of yours, Hannah. He drugged you. I'm going to rid your body of it, but it's going to burn like hell. Do you understand?"

She didn't understand any of it, but she knew Ilya Prakenskii had the same gifts the Drake sisters did. She knew how they worked and that he was capable of removing a drug from her body. She also knew he was a very dangerous man, and anytime one worked with psychic abilities, or magic, whatever term one used, there was vulnerability on both sides. The Drake family were already in debt to Ilya and he had a path straight back to Joley. She was one of the most powerful of the Drakes. She didn't want him knowing anything about her just in case she had to protect her sister.

Hannah shook her head. "No." It was very firm. She'd deal with the drug. She could push it out of her own system now that she knew what she was dealing with.

"Yes," he countered. "You're in no condition to try it yourself. You know these things can be tricky. Hold still. And the next time you accept a drink from a man, friend or not, use your gift to make certain there's nothing wrong with it."

No wonder the man set Joley's teeth on edge. Hannah was no amateur — and neither was Joley. Ilya might think he was more powerful, but the Drakes could take him if they had to — as long as they didn't open themselves up to his magic. She tried to pull away, to stand on her own so that she could reverse whatever was wrong with her, but she was too dizzy.

Ilya's hand settled on her stomach, his arm around her, clamping her in place. He was enormously strong and having him take her over with so many people within screaming distance kept her silent. She felt warmth flow from his palm, through her skin, and into her churning stomach. She didn't want this, but there was no way to stop the flow of power from him to her. She felt their spirits connect. She flinched away from him, catching glimpses of things she didn't want to ever see or know about — dark, ugly things that belonged buried.

She felt heat, her temperature rising. Worse, she felt him in her head. Instinctively she knew what he was after. Even while he was healing her body, he was searching for memories of Joley — of her power — her abilities. He wanted to know the precise strength. Frantic, Hannah shoved at him, raising her arms toward the wind.

Ilya caught her wrists and yanked her hands to her sides. "There is a price for everything. This is my price."

Hannah shook her head, furious. "You betray everything you're given and you don't deserve your gifts. Stay out of my head. I wouldn't trade my sister for my own life, my dignity or my virtue."

His hand slipped around her throat. "You know nothing about me."

Hannah stared at him, refusing to look away or be intimidated. If he wanted to throw her off the balcony for telling the truth, let him do it. She wasn't giving up Joley, not for anything. "I know I don't want you near my sister. Whatever game you're playing, know we will defend Joley with our lives — not just me, but every single Drake, man or woman, child or adult, alive today." It was the absolute truth and she let him see the reality in her eyes.

"I am familiar with danger, Miss Drake."

There was no doubt he was. She felt it in him, read it in his memories — terrible things — things she couldn't comprehend in her world. She'd grown up with loving parents, her family close, the village where she lived close-knit and protective. His life, from childhood, had been one of violence.

He frightened her. Not her normal panic over nothing, but truly, deep down to the bone frightened. She knew her sister drew men like a magnet. She was elusive and wild and screamed sex on stage. Hannah glanced at his boss. Sergei Nikitin had been pursuing Joley across three continents. Was that what Ilya was up to? Was he going to use his psychic talents to put Joley in Nikitin's very dirty hands?

"Let go of me," she demanded. The heat from his palm had turned scorching, searing through blood and bone and invading every tissue of her body, but she felt better, her head clear. There was no doubt she'd ingested a drug. After all the security lectures by Sarah, she felt stupid. She never drank, was always careful, and now, when she needed her wits about her, Ilya Prakenskii had not only witnessed her stupidity, but had to save her from it.

"I'll let go if you don't do anything stupid like call the wind."

Hannah threw back her head, eyes glittering, fairly shooting sparks at him as her temper began to rise. She always stayed in control — unless Jonas provoked her. Tempers weren't a good thing when one wielded power, but the bodyguard deserved everything he was about to get.

Tiny flickers of flame ran up her fingertips, over her hands to her wrists, where his fingers had settled into a viselike grip. He snatched his hands away as the flames flashed over him, hot enough to warn him off. He stepped back.

"Good party trick. You should have used it on your friend."

"Thanks for your help."

His cold eyes slid over her, his face without expression. "I can see how grateful you are."

"I am grateful. But I'm not stupid." Although she had been for accepting the drink in the first place. "I don't want you near Joley."

"Why are you so worried?"

She couldn't read him. Whether she was touching him, or standing close, she should have been able to read his thoughts and emotions, but he was a blank slate. The glimpses of violent memories were gone. She studied his face. He looked dangerous. It was in the set of his shoulders, the fluid way he moved and the direct, cold eyes.

"Why would you be worried about Joley?" Ilya dropped his voice until it was a low whisper, impossible for the sound to carry farther than her ear. "She's a spell-singer, isn't she?"

Hannah's heart lurched. She struggled to keep her face composed. She blinked. He noticed. He noticed everything. "I'm not certain what you mean." There were few spell-singers in the world, not legitimate ones, not like Joley. She could call on the power of the one perfect note that supposedly had been used to create the world. The forces of the world, of the universe itself, could be drawn to do her bidding. In the hands of someone like Sergei Nikitin, Joley would be a weapon of destruction. He had no way of controlling her, or holding her — unless Ilya Prakenskii had the same talent. Was that even possible?

She resisted the urge to wipe her hand over her face, certain she was beginning to sweat. Was Prakenskii strong enough to control Joley? The thought was terrifying.

"You look pale, Miss Drake," Nikitin said,

his smile solicitous. And false.

Hannah's muscles clenched. She felt trapped. She managed a smile, slipping into her professional mode. No one could look haughtier than Hannah Drake. She even put one hand on her hip and struck a pose, as she flashed her small disdainful smile. "I'm feeling much better, thank you, Mr. Nikitin. Did you enjoy the show?"

"I couldn't help but think none of the clothes would suit your sister. Joley has her own style. Don't you agree?"

She didn't want Nikitin even saying Joley's name. Without conscious thought, she stepped toward the rail, her hands moving up and out. Prakenskii glided forward, wrapping his arm around her waist, pinning one arm to her side, firmly catching her other arm and bringing her wrist to his face as if examining it.

"You aren't injured, are you?" he asked, his blue eyes like daggers. *You will be if you threaten him.*

The threat was clear in her head, as if he'd spoken the words out loud. He was telepathic, which she knew. Joley complained he often spoke to her. And now he was in Hannah's head as well. The situation was getting worse and worse. It was no wonder she'd seen three rings around the moon. It was no wonder she'd been afraid to come on this trip alone. She should have considered that Sergei Nikitin would show up at Fashion Week in New York. He was always where the action was. Few people knew him for what he was.

Hannah refused to engage in a telepathic conversation with Ilya. The more he knew of her, the more power he would wield — and he was definitely looking for information on Joley. All this time, she had thought Sergei Nikitin was interested in her sister. Joley's public image was wild, a party girl. Recently there had been a terrible scandal, pictures of Joley with her long dark hair, pressed up against a window nude with her mysterious lover draped all over her. Only Joley had dyed her hair dark after the pictures had been taken, and she'd allowed the scandal to hit her full force, when the pictures weren't of her at all. Nikitin's interest might not be in the party girl at all and that meant they had a huge problem.

"I'm flying to Madrid tomorrow to catch your sister's concert," Nikitin persisted, ignoring the fact that his bodyguard was holding Hannah captive.

"She's very good," Hannah said politely. "You'll enjoy it."

"I've missed few of her concerts," Nikitin

said. "She's a wonderful performer. There's something extraordinary about her voice."

Hannah stiffened. She couldn't help herself.

Ilya tightened his hold. *Don't react. He knows nothing of Joley beyond that she's beautiful.*

Could that be true? And even if it was, why would Ilya warn her? She had never been so confused in her life. She wasn't made for intrigue. She forced her body to relax. Ilya let go of her, but he didn't step away. She'd already seen how fast he was and she wasn't about to let him stop her again. It only made her appear weak.

"I agree with you, Mr. Nikitin," Hannah said, polite as a child, "but then I'm her sister so I'm prejudiced."

"We're staying at the same hotel, and we're having a party there in a couple of hours, just a few selected friends," Nikitin continued, "if you'd like to join us."

Hannah opened her mouth to say no. It was the last thing she wanted to do, party with Nikitin and his friends behind closed doors.

"What a generous invitation, Hannah," Greg said, coming through the French doors just as the Russian issued his invitation. "Mr. Nikitin. I believe we met in

Paris." He extended his hand and Nikitin took it.

"Of course." Sergei turned on the charm, his white teeth flashing, his head inclining graciously, royalty to peasant.

Hannah found it interesting how Greg nearly fawned over him. Nikitin wielded a lot of power with his money and connections. Few wanted to know if the rumors about him were true. He had money, more than he knew what to do with. He often threw that money behind a new designer and he more than once had helped build careers. His parties were famous and everyone wanted an invitation — with the exception of Hannah. She couldn't ignore the rumors because being close to Nikitin was enough to reveal the ugly way he made most of his money. He appeared suave and sophisticated, but he had his hand in everything from drugs to murder. No one had proved it, and Hannah sincerely doubted that anyone ever would. He knew too many politicians, too many of the rich and famous. No one wanted to know he was dirty.

"Greg." She was disgusted with the way the man was ready to sell his soul for an invitation. "We should go."

Nikitin glanced at his watch. "We have a couple more people to say hello to and then we can all go back to the hotel." His focus was entirely on Greg now.

"We'd love that," Greg agreed, taking Hannah's arm.

It was a sure sign he wanted to go. He knew as well as she did that the invitation hinged on her accompanying him. Hannah kept her smile in place. All she had to do was make it to the door. The balcony didn't feel safe anymore. Nowhere around Nikitin was safe. She could just go along with the plan, and as soon as they were outside, she could have the doorman hail a cab for her.

She stole a glance at Ilya. He looked the image of the perfect bodyguard, fading into the background, his eyes moving restlessly, watching the rooftops, the windows from the building across the street. It was fascinating really, how he saw everything, heard everything, was aware of things no one else even considered. He was fully aware she intended to bolt the moment she was out of the building. She waited for him to say something, but Ilya simply followed Nikitin and Greg, who kept hold of her arm, back into the room.

The noise was deafening and hit her hard. The crush of bodies gave her claustrophobia. The room had been packed before she'd gone out onto the balcony, but now there was hardly room to maneuver. People called out greetings and congratulations as they worked their way through the crowd. Greg's fingers slipped off her arm and she quickly moved away, heading toward the door and freedom.

"Hannah," Sabrina greeted her, catching both of her hands. "I can't believe you're still here. You look pale, hon, are you all right?"

"I'm leaving now. A quick appearance and then I'm gone," Hannah said.

"Your trademark. Do you think you can make it to the door? We should have brought a couple of really big bodyguards to get us through the crush."

Sabrina turned with Hannah and began to work her way through the crowd. "I was hoping someone important would ask me to another big event, but so far nobody important has bothered. I swear, Hannah, you don't even want it and you have this awesome career and I'm dying to be in your shoes and I can't get anywhere."

"That's not true, Sabrina." Hannah was trying to see over the mass of people, judging how far it was to the door.

She was tall, but there were just too many bodies and she couldn't see beyond the swarm of people crushing them. She glanced behind her. Nikitin and Ilya were following fast, the crowd parting for the bodyguard. Her agent hurried to keep up with them, determined not to be left behind. It was no wonder she suddenly felt sick with fear. They were trying to catch her before she got away.

Ilya called out to her, suddenly breaking away from the other two men and shoving partygoers out of his way. Hannah's heart lurched and she whipped her head around, nearly bumping into Sabrina as they tried to push their way forward.

"What's wrong?" Sabrina demanded, glancing over her shoulder. "Is that man chasing you?"

"Yes," Hannah admitted, too frightened to lie.

"Who is he?" Sabrina inserted her shoulder into a slim opening between two men and pushed her way through, dragging Hannah with her.

"Nikitin's bodyguard."

"Good grief, Hannah, why are you running? Everyone who's anyone will be at his party — unless you did something to Nikitin. You didn't, did you?" Sabrina risked another quick glance. "He's catching up, move faster. Did Nikitin make a pass at you?"

Hannah's heart thundered in her ears. With every step, terror gripped her harder. She walked faster, bumping into people as she threw quick, nervous glances over her shoulder.

Hannah! Stop right now!

The order was sharp and clear and pain burst through her head as she felt the lash of a holding spell. She broke it, whipping her head around toward the door. It was right there. Freedom. Two more steps and she would be outside, where she could call on the forces of nature to aid her. She collided with a large body and a hand gripped her arm to steady her.

"Why hasn't she gone back to the hotel?" Jonas demanded, pacing as he watched the television set. "You'd think she'd at least check her cell phone. She didn't even check her messages after the fashion show. She didn't need to attend the party. That's not part of her contract, is it?"

Sarah sank into a chair and stared at the screen. The party was in full swing, reporters interviewing designers and movie stars rather than the models. She caught a glimpse of a couple of the other runway models she knew by name, but Hannah had disappeared into the crowd. The entire scene was crazy. Loud music, outrageous clothes, too many famous people all vying for the camera. There was no way to find Hannah in the crush, unless a reporter wanted an interview and Hannah never gave interviews. Still, she watched, straining her eyes.

Jonas was so edgy he was affecting the Drake family home. The walls rippled with the tension filling the house. It seemed difficult to breathe, the air too thick. Sarah couldn't look away from the screen, afraid if she did, something horrible would happen.

"There's Sabrina." She sat up straighter, her eyes glued to the dark, sleek-haired woman as she pushed her way through the crowd. "She looks like she's talking to someone else, just out of the camera's view, Jonas. I'll bet that's Hannah and they're leaving."

The camera panned a wider view and Sarah caught a glimpse of Hannah. She appeared to be hurrying, her long hair flowing behind her, her face strained as she glanced back over her shoulder. Several feet behind her, Ilya Prakenskii shouldered his way through the mass, clearly chasing her. Sergei Nikitin and Hannah's agent followed in the bigger man's wake.

"Oh, God, in front of you, Hannah," Jonas

shouted, suddenly rushing toward the television. "In front of you, damn it, look in front of you. Oh, God, no! Hannah!"

He drew his gun, an automatic gesture, but there was nothing he could do as Hannah turned her head and the knife slashed across her face. He watched helplessly, the arc, the man's determination as he relentlessly kept driving the knife home. Her face. Her chest. Her abdomen. She brought up her arms, a pitiful defense against a madman. He kept slashing and stabbing, over and over, using his body strength with every swing.

Jonas heard a raw, torn cry of utter, absolute anguish, knew it had been ripped from his soul. He dropped to his knees, unable to stand, impotent to do anything to stop the assault. Behind him, Sarah screamed and screamed.

Blood sprayed over the elegantly dressed crowd and the arm kept pumping, slashing and driving. He heard Sarah vomiting, but he couldn't look away.

Ilya Prakenskii caught the assailant from behind, dragging him away from Hannah, controlling the knife hand, swinging hard so that the bloody blade formed an arc and was driven deep into the man's heart. Ilya dropped him, turning to try to catch Hannah before she hit the floor. The camera panned down, but Ilya's body blocked the shot, leaving only the sight of a river of blood soaking into long spiral curls while the reporter tried to regain his composure.

Jonas sank all the way to the floor, his mind numb, shock spreading. He glanced over at Sarah. She lay on the floor, every bit as still as Hannah had lain, pale, her breathing shallow, eyes rolled back in her head. He felt it then — the staggering weight of knowledge as the Drake sisters became aware of the enormity of the attack. He heard cries of anguish, of a sorrow so deep it matched his own.

He touched his face and knew tears ran down it unchecked. He was afraid he might never be able to stop. The door burst open and Jackson stood framed there, his face grim, his mouth set in hard lines. "Let's go."

7

Jonas had never prayed so much in his life. He stared blindly out the window of the plane, alternating between feeling numb and lost and then struck with a rage so hot it terrified him. He was afraid to speak — afraid the anger would burst out and consume everyone around him.

He pressed his fingertips hard against the pressure points around his eyes, hoping for some relief from the throbbing pain. Joley had had a private jet waiting at the airport for them and he knew the Drakes would be flying in from all over the world, but how could they get there in time to save her life?

Hannah. He breathed her name. *Don't you leave me.*

They'd always had a connection, as long as he could remember. The first time she'd walked onto the school grounds, skinny, pale, all blond hair with springy curls everywhere, he'd known she'd been born for him. He'd been a few years older and was ashamed for staring at such a little kid, although, at ten, he wasn't looking at her with sexual intent. It was more that he'd known she was the one almost from the time he'd been running to the Drakes, but seeing her there, at the school yard — he'd just known. The knowledge shocked him because it was so certain. From that moment she'd been a part of him — like breathing.

Of course she'd never looked at him. Hell. She'd never even talked to him — not at school anyway. He'd hated that. Once he'd learned about her anxiety attacks and shyness, he understood, but at the time, it had been crushing. He acted confident around her no matter what was going on in his life. Even then, he'd felt he had to prove he was tougher, and stronger, in order to be worthy of Hannah.

And deep in his heart, he'd known that was just impossible. He'd never be worthy of Hannah. No one was. She was so different. Gorgeous beyond belief, but so much more than that. Sweet. So damned sweet. Wanting to care for everyone. And where did that leave a man who lived most of his life in the shadows hunting bad guys?

He knew her. Inside and out. He knew

her. She was a homebody, not the world traveler everyone thought. She was comfortable in a pair of jeans and a flannel shirt, not the sophisticated elegant clothes she wore so well. But he still couldn't have someone so good that light shone around her, not when he was always living in the dark. *Be alive, baby, for me, be alive.*

"She's still alive," Sarah murmured, as if reading his mind. She sat next to him, her fiancé, Damon, holding her hand tightly while she concentrated with every ounce of her power to stay connected to Hannah. All of the Drakes were, Jonas knew. Sisters. Aunts. Their mother. Cousins. The family was enormous, as were their powers, and Jonas knew beyond a doubt, they were all focused on saving one person. "We're doing everything we can."

"Just hang on to her until we get there, Sarah. Once I'm with her, I can help."

"Why would someone do that to her?" Sarah asked, her voice strained with grief. "Why would someone want to hurt Hannah?"

Damon immediately swept his arm around her and leaned in to put his head close to hers as if helping to absorb the unrelenting sorrow.

Jonas could have told him it would do no

good. Sarah knew, as he did, that whoever had done this hadn't wanted to hurt Hannah — they wanted to destroy her. The attack had been shocking, stunning, on television, a message sent to millions. The attacker was dead and they might never know his true motives or if it was a random act of violent insanity. Some were just crazy. Out of their minds. He'd seen enough of it to last him a lifetime. Sometimes there was no reason at all for why people did such crazy things.

"How soon can Libby get here?" He kept his fingers pressed over his eyes, hiding his expression.

"Not soon enough," Sarah admitted. Her voice cracked. "This can't be happening. Not Hannah. She's so . . ." She shook her head, pressing her hand to her trembling lips. "I have to concentrate."

"Do you have her?"

Sarah stiffened. It was the question she was dreading. Jonas was shaken — shattered, raw grief etched deep into his face. He would believe they had a chance to save Hannah, if the Drakes were holding her in their keeping. Jonas believed in few things anymore — but he believed in their family and the powerful bond they shared. She couldn't lie to him — not to Jonas.

"I'm sorry," she said as gently as she could, when she really wanted to cry a river of tears. "She was too far gone to reach out to us. Ilya Prakenskii has her. She'd be dead without him, even now, and they've taken her to the operating room."

Jonas sat up straight. For the first time he dropped his hands from his face. "How do you know?"

"He talks to Joley and she relays the information to us. Joley . . ." She choked off a sob, pressing her face against Damon's shoulder. He instantly murmured in her ear.

"Sarah?" Jonas prompted.

"Joley begged him not to let Hannah die. She's terrified of Prakenskii, so you can understand how extreme the situation is for her to put herself in his debt." She was rambling because she was so frightened, but she couldn't seem to stop herself. She needed as much reassurance as Jonas. "Still, he did save Hannah's life. You saw him."

"I also saw him kill the man who stabbed her." He had done it so easily, so fast the move was barely captured on film, so quick and practiced and smooth, Jonas knew he had done it far too many times.

Ilya Prakenskii. There was a real puzzle. Jonas had tried to dig up information on him. Abbey Drake's fiancé, Aleksandr Volstov, had known Ilya from childhood. Prakenskii had been raised by the state and trained as a lethal weapon, but from there, the trail went muddy and no amount of prying had revealed what the man was really involved in. Aleksandr suspected Prakenskii's current job as a bodyguard for a mobster was only a front for something else, but if that was so, his cover was impeccable. Jonas, for all his contacts, hadn't managed to find out anything. Ilya Prakenskii was a wild card and he held Hannah's life in his hands.

Prakenskii might have been working for his government, or he may truly be Nikitin's man, but whatever he was, he was trained as a straight-up killer — and he held Hannah's life in his hands.

"He couldn't do anything else," Sarah said. "It happened so fast. He had to stop the man."

Jonas wasn't so certain a man like Prakenskii *had* to kill. He had a choice and he chose death for the attacker. Why? Retribution — or something far more sinister? Hell. Jonas didn't believe in anyone anymore — especially not the man who had saved Hannah's life. He had to force his mind to think. It was the only way to stay sane until he was with her. Once he was with her, the rest of the world could go to hell, for all he cared.

"Did you bring the files on the wack jobs?" he asked Jackson, who sat across the aisle from him.

The deputy snapped open the briefcase. "They're all here. Do you think the killer acted alone?" Jackson glanced sharply at Jonas. "Do you feel the threat is gone?"

Beside him, Sarah gave a small sound of distress. "Oh, God, Jonas." She choked off a sob. "Do you think more than one man could be involved? Hannah could still be in danger?"

He wanted to reassure her, to make it all better. Jonas Harrington, the white knight, savior of the world. Hell, he hadn't saved the one person most important to him.

Hannah.

Just that quick he could see her again, on TV, smiling as the cameras flashed, and the quick look over her shoulder as she moved swiftly through the crowd, the turn, the look of shock, of horror as the knife rose and fell.

The air in Jonas's lungs caught and just held there, burning until he thought he might pass out. He'd faced bullets and blood and death on a battlefield more times than he'd wanted to count. He'd watched his mother, a wonderful, sweet woman, slowly eaten alive from the inside out, suffering every moment of her existence and he hadn't thought — hadn't believed — that there could be more pain. More anger. Feeling — being — more damn helpless.

"Jonas." Jackson's voice was sharp and compelling. "Focus. Are you feeling the same threat to her? Was this a loner?"

He cleared his throat and tried to pull himself together. "It's impossible to tell. The danger to her is so strong, I can't tell whether it's because she's near death or because someone is still waiting to get to her."

Sarah reached into the briefcase and took a few of the photographs, shaking her head as she looked them over. "Why in the world would you even be looking at these people?" She held up two of the pictures. "I doubt an animal rights group would conspire to kill her and keep sending assassins. And even the Reverend with his moral group would have little to gain."

"They'd stay in the news. Who knows how twisted people think, Sarah," Damon responded, drawing her closer. He'd been a victim and had the scars and leg that rarely worked anymore to prove it. "There could be a dozen reasons, all perfectly logical in their mind. Anyone who does this kind of thing is seriously screwed up."

Jonas turned his head to stare sightlessly out the window again. Nothing made sense anymore. Anyone but Hannah. He had wasted so much time waiting for her to make the first move. Why had he done that? He took command of every situation, but not with her. *Because she was afraid of him.* He suppressed a groan. That was the true reason. She was a pleaser, wanting him happy, wanting her family happy, always giving of herself, but never taking. She wanted him happy, too, but not at the cost of herself. He walked on her. And she knew herself well enough to know she couldn't afford to be swallowed whole.

"She has a temper," he murmured aloud.

Sarah glanced at him. "Who?"

"Hannah. She has a temper. And when she's angry, she can wreak havoc."

"Which is why she rarely does anything other than small, annoying forms of retribution, like blowing your hats down the street," Sarah said.

"I overwhelm her, don't I?" Jonas asked. He knew the answer. He was always ordering her to do something. He rarely asked. Hell, he'd been so damned mean in the hospital to her, it was a wonder she hadn't taken a gun and shot him.

Sarah shook her head. "I honestly don't know. I'm beginning to realize I don't know Hannah very well, Jonas. I thought I did, but all the things I thought I knew about her, well, I think she simply gave me what she thought I wanted."

"She's so damned beautiful and smart. She can outthink me any day of the week." Jonas shoved both hands through his hair. "You'd think she had enough confidence for ten people. She looks like she does. She's all don't-touch-me, don't-ruffle-my hair, I'm-so-fucking-far-above-you-you'll-never-be-in-my-league attitude."

"She's so painfully shy she stutters, Jonas; that's not something that gives a woman confidence." She rubbed her cheek against Damon's shoulder. "We had to help her make public appearances."

Jonas closed his hands into two tight fists. That should have told them something, right there. If Hannah couldn't go out in public without her sisters helping her, didn't it occur to them that the strain on her would be too much? He didn't state the obvious. What would be the use? Sarah was coming to the realization on her own and it would hurt. She loved Hannah. She would blame herself for not realizing that Hannah had been unhappy. All of the Drakes would.

Hannah. Baby. I love you so much. So damned much. Did I even tell you? He couldn't remember. He'd given her everything he was, worshiped her with his body, but had he said the words? *Coward.* He'd been a fucking coward even when she'd given herself to him.

"Jonas." Jackson's low voice cut through the recriminations. "You're going to drive yourself insane. Look at these files. Do what you do best. If Prakenskii removed the threat to her, fine, but if it's more, if there's a group behind this, let's make certain she's safe when she wakes up."

Jackson hadn't said "if" she wakes up. Jonas clung to that as he took one of the files and opened it to stare at Rudy Venturi's baby face. "Not him. He's so fixated on her that he'd never share her. He's got a fantasy going in his mind with her." He passed the file to Sarah. "You read it, Sarah, see if you feel the same way." Sarah had a good mind and a talent for "feeling" things he couldn't get. He'd bet money the attack hadn't been a conspiracy involving Rudy, but he wasn't willing to take a chance with Hannah's life. No matter what Sarah said, Rudy would be interrogated, but he might be low on the list.

Jackson handed Jonas the next file opened, tapping it as Jonas took it. "This reads like trouble to me," Jackson said. "I don't like the letters he's written or the things he has to say. He has several of his 'flock' backing him up and their letters are even more fanatical than his. The Reverend believes Hannah, and models like her, are enticing young girls into perverted acts by showing off their bodies and promoting sexuality and promiscuity."

Jonas swore. "What a self-righteous son of a bitch. He's the one forcing young girls to perverted acts. He has a little harem he's collecting, girls off the street, runaways. And the men in his flock are no sheep — more like wolves. So far we haven't been able to catch him at anything, but we suspect he has one of the biggest drug-running operations around."

"Does Nikitin run drugs?" Sarah asked, handing back Rudy's file to Jackson.

"Nikitin has his hand in nearly everything, but Tarasov, his biggest competitor, runs most of the drugs in Russia," Jonas said. He didn't want to discuss Boris Tarasov, not after he'd seen the explosive material that had been on the film he and Jackson had turned over to their commander. Karl Tarasov and the Gadiyan brothers had managed to make it out of the country, but Petr had been quietly picked up trying to flee, and was being held at an undisclosed location. Jonas sure didn't want to know the location, but he did want to know who the traitor inside the defense department had been.

"Do any of these files have anything at all to do with either of the Russians?" Sarah persisted. "Maybe Nikitin was there for a reason."

"Nikitin has a reason for everything he does," Jonas agreed, "but neither man has ever threatened Hannah, or even communicated with her. And she doesn't know a thing about drugs so we can rule out the Russians. Nikitin often attends high-profile parties, particularly in the fashion and music industries. I think it's safe to say he went there to be seen rather than to see Hannah." But he wasn't ruling anything out altogether. Everyone was under suspicion, even Ilya — especially Ilya.

"I want a closer look at the Reverend, too," Jonas said. "Sarah, study this file and tell me if you get any vibes off of him." He put the folder in her lap.

"I can tell you he's creepy," Sarah said, her hand sliding over the papers. "And he's not opposed to violence — or money. He's fixated on Hannah and Joley, too."

"Great." Jonas rubbed his pounding temples.

Sarah drew in her breath. "He's got a wall of pictures and articles on our family. I can see it."

"You freak me out when you do that," Damon said. "I'm never going to get used to it. Are you sure, Sarah?"

She nodded. "To someone like the Reverend, my family would be the closest thing to Satan he could find on this earth. If he's discovered any of us can do the things we do, it might be reason enough for him to stir up his followers to violence."

"There was a brief moment a reporter interviewed him and he quoted something from the Bible about reaping what we sow," Damon offered. "He looked very pious."

"Self-righteous prick," Jonas snarled. "Put him at the top of the list."

"This one is on the Let Animals Live Free, the LALF group. They've made quite a few threats to Hannah since she turned them down when they asked her to be a spokesperson for them. They have big bucks and a reputation in shambles thanks to her and one of her investigative reporter friends. They have a reputation for violence, all in the name of animal rights, of course, and we know members of the group have threatened her many times." Jackson handed Jonas the file. "I think we need to look very closely at them. One of the men who turned evidence against them, Benjamin Larsen, disappeared last summer."

"He's the one who got rid of the animal bodies, and he was taking tiger parts and selling them on the black market." Jonas forced his mind to remember, to think of something other than Hannah, lying so close to death. He could hardly concentrate with the roaring in his ears and the protest pounding the hell out of his gut.

"Exactly. A very lucrative business nowadays. The skin, the body parts, they can be worth a fortune if someone knows what they're doing. LALF would protest an animal sanctuary, get an injunction, take the animals away and euthanize them as soon as the reporters left. LALF claims they never received a penny of the money from the death of the animals, but Larsen claimed the domestic animals were given to research centers and the big cats were parted out on the black market."

"That's just sick," Sarah said.

"How in the world did Hannah get involved?" Damon asked.

Jonas sighed. "When she was shaking hands with them, she picked up all kinds of images and she took it from there, asking a friend who was an investigative reporter to dig into it. The entire mess was discovered and it was a huge scandal. LALF weathered it, they have a lot of political clout. Politicians and celebrities like the image of saving wildlife and LALF is very good at getting publicity. They blamed it on a few overzealous members and hired a high-powered publicity firm to turn their image around. But Hannah's been getting letters ever since."

Hannah. She'd cried over the knowledge, the impressions she'd gotten when she'd shaken the director's hand. Jonas had found her on the beach with tears running down her face. It was one of the few times he'd dared to hold her. She fit into his body so perfectly, made for him, belonging there. He'd wanted to slay every dragon for her to keep her from crying any more tears.

She'd been soft and warm and all woman, her hair flowing around them like so much silk. The sea had erupted into stormy columns of white foam, crashing against the rocks in harmony with her wild storm of tears. The wind whirled around them, closing off the rest of the world, making him feel as if they were alone together, the sun setting in every shade of red and orange, a giant glowing ball pouring molten gold into the churning water. Everything had been beautiful and perfect and so right he ached every time he thought of it. Everything about Hannah was magical — even her tears.

Jonas turned away from Jackson, making sure to keep from touching him. He knew Jackson was a powerful psychic, his talent different from the Drakes. He always wondered if Jackson could read people, pick up thoughts from them, but Jackson preferred silence to talking. He rarely gave anything about himself away. He certainly never discussed his psychic gifts.

Jonas felt broken, unable to stop grieving for Hannah. He didn't need for Jackson to see him so torn up inside, to see the depth of his feeling and need for Hannah.

"So LALF goes in the prime suspect pile," Damon said.

"Let Sarah 'read' it," Jonas said.

"I'm almost afraid to," Sarah said and reluctantly removed the folder from Jonas's lap. Her hands trembled. "I'm picking up a lot of jumbled things. Most of them feel genuinely passionate about saving animals. Unfortunately you have a couple who are using the organization for their own ends, which is basically money and power. And yes, there is hatred for Hannah. I can feel it, but can't give you a name. It feels male and female, so more than one. It could be a conspiracy." She made a face. "I'm sorry, Jonas, there are just too many people to get a good reading and it's all impressions anyway."

"You're doing great, Sarah."

She looked pale and exhausted. Jonas hoped he didn't look that way — scraped raw and exposed and so damn vulnerable for everyone to see. He whipped out his dark glasses and pushed them onto his nose to hide his eyes, afraid they were as red as Sarah's. His throat burned, his eyes felt like they had sand ground into them. He was a mess when he was supposed to be the one the Drakes could count on.

Hannah. Baby. Don't you leave me. Maybe if he said it a million times, sent it out there into the universe, she'd somehow hear. She'd know all the things he should have told her. Like she was his sanity. She was pure magic. Everything he'd ever dreamed of — ever wanted. She was the woman who made him whole. She made him laugh, soothed him, made him angry, gave him a reason to come home in one piece. *Do you hear me, Hannah? Don't let go. Wait for me. Be with me.*

His heart even hurt. Physically hurt. How many times had he gone to a house and told the occupants a loved one had died? There had been pain on their faces, emotions so ravaged he'd left the house feeling sick — and gone to Hannah. She'd taken it all away for him. But this — nothing hurt like this. Hannah couldn't take this away — not ever. He would wake up with nightmares over this. He'd never get over the image of someone stabbing Hannah, a vicious, determined look on his face. He doubted he'd ever let her get five feet from him again.

"Why the hell didn't I stop her from going?"

"Don't, Jonas," Sarah said softly. "Don't even go there. Hannah signed a contract. She made a commitment. Even if she didn't want to go, she would have kept her word."

"Who's next?" Damon asked. "You have a lot of folders there."

Jackson reached into the briefcase. "Stay focused, Jonas."

Jonas felt the briefcase in his hands, knew he'd yanked it out of Jackson's possession. "You want me fucking focused?" He threw the case down the aisle and followed it up, kicking hard with his boot, then whirled around to slam his fist into the nearest empty chair.

Thunder crashed in his ears, his eyes burned, his throat raw. "What the hell is there without her? Tell me that, Jackson. Tell me what the fuck I'm going to do without her. Because I don't know." He looked up then, helpless, impotent, lost. "I stood there watching — *watching* — as that bastard carved her into pieces." He spread his hands. "What is it with me and the women I love?" He turned and stormed down the aisle to the back of the plane, leaving the others sitting in stunned silence.

"Damn it," Jackson said. "He's losing it, Sarah."

"This is so close to home for him. You know about his life, his mother, right? He can't take it when things are out of his control."

Damon squeezed her shoulder. "I've always been curious."

"Very wealthy parents. Left him a fortune and a beautiful estate. They were older when they had him and they always wanted children. He was adored by both of them. Father died when he was five, and by the time he was six or seven, his mother was already pretty much confined to bed. He totally took over running their household. Did the shopping, paid the bills, read to his mom, just as if he were all grown up. It was crazy."

She rubbed her temples. "I'm not explaining this very well. After she gave birth, her immune system failed for whatever reason. The doctors said it was a traumatic event and her body reacted, but no one really knows. From that point on she was very frail, but she refused, absolutely refused, to give in to illness. Jonas took on the responsibilities because that's his nature and he loved her — she belonged with him. She was his family. Eventually she got cancer. It was horribly painful, but she had a will of iron. It nearly killed him that he couldn't stop her suffering. He came to our house when it just got so bad he couldn't look at her or think about her anymore."

Damon glanced down the plane toward the bathroom. "Should you talk to him?"

"What can I say? He knows as well as I do that the chances of saving Hannah are very small. We were there. Watching. Hannah is his family. The love of his life. She's what makes him want to get up in the morning. They belong. He feels completely helpless, and for Jonas, there isn't anything much worse when it comes to someone he loves. All of this" — she gestured to the files — "won't matter if she dies."

She hit her head against the seat. "Why didn't he show these files to me before — when he was so nasty about her going to work. I would have backed him up."

She handed one to Damon. "Look at this. This is a woman who stalked Hannah for about ten months. A restraining order was issued and the woman went a little crazy and slashed up a collection of clothes Hannah modeled. How she got backstage no one knew, but Hannah wasn't in the building; she'd already left."

Jonas reappeared, taking the file from her hand and seating himself beside her. "I put her on high priority because she used a knife, was able to penetrate security, and she was recently released from prison. The designer prosecuted and she was incarcerated." Jackson put the file into Jonas's hands. "Her name is Susan Briggs, she's middle-aged, looks normal but is obviously ill."

"She's definitely not all there and she's capable of extreme violence. She hears voices, probably schizophrenic. Put her in the high probability stack." Sarah tried to keep her voice even when she wanted to throw her arms around him and comfort him. "You should have showed all these to me."

Jonas looked down at her and Sarah winced. She knew the files existed. Joley probably had more. She hadn't wanted to know because she didn't want to be like Jonas, afraid for them, angry with them, wanting them to stay home and be safe. Maybe she'd known all along it was like this, so many nutcases, attracted by the glamour of Hannah's job and her flawless beauty.

"Oh, Jonas, what that man did to her." Sarah pressed both hands over her face. "I can't bear it. Even if she lives . . ."

"She will live," Jonas said. "That's all that matters. You can't think about anything else." Because he couldn't. He couldn't allow his mind to go there again. He didn't know what he'd do if the worst happened.

"Hannah is so different, though. Fragile and gentle. How will she ever get over the trauma of this kind of an attack?"

Damon wrapped his arms around her. "Hannah is stronger than you think. She'll rise above it. You wait and see. She's a Drake through and through and she has all of us to help her. She'll get through this."

Sarah looked at Jonas. Instinctively she knew, if anyone was going to get Hannah through this, it would be Jonas — but who was going to get him through it? She'd never seen him so strained. Nothing to date had ever shaken Jonas's confidence in himself, but he'd been a wild man, out of control, scaring the hell out of her in the aftermath of Hannah's attack. He'd been crazy, tearing up the room, smashing things, his face so twisted with anguish she'd managed to set aside her own unrestrained grief to help Jackson rein him in. And she could still see — and feel — the wild rage smoldering in him now. He had once again brought it under control, but it could erupt with any provocation.

There was no doubt Jonas loved Hannah. There had never been a doubt in anyone's mind except Hannah's — but no one had known the force of that love, the deep, ingrained need he had of her. Sarah still found it hard to look at him — he was so ravaged. Jonas. Their rock. Shattered into so many shards. Holding himself together through sheer force of will.

"We need your sisters. Libby has to get here fast." Jonas raked both hands through his hair. "She's coming home, right?"

Sarah nodded. Libby was a healer. Jonas knew she could perform what virtually amounted to miracles. She'd saved his life with the help of all the other Drake sisters, but they weren't going to arrive in time for this one. None of them. If Ilya Prakenskii couldn't hold Hannah, she was lost to them. Jonas desperately needed to believe Sarah and her sisters could save Hannah, but she needed to believe Prakcnskii could.

"Tell me what you know about the bodyguard. Who is Sergei Nikitin and what exactly does Prakenskii do for him? And Jonas, this time, tell me the truth. I know you know more about him than you're letting on. I don't care if he's some big government secret, I have to know who he is. He's all we've got right now."

"It might take Abbey to get to anything of value on Prakenskii," Jonas said. "I'm telling you, I ran into a stone wall when I tried to find out about him. I used every connection I had in the defense department as well as the Army Rangers, and I got zilch on him. The guy isn't what he appears to be, and he's got layers of protection built in around his file."

Sarah was silent, her small teeth chewing on her bottom lip as she turned the information over in her mind. "What about Sergei Nikitin? What do you have on him?"

"He's an altogether different kind of fish — big fish. No one has ever been able to pin anything on him, not in his country or ours or in Europe. Interpol has been trying for several years. He emerged strong from a rather bloody turf war. The spoils were divided several ways until he suddenly came on the scene, and then after a very nasty battle between factions, Sergei Nikitin and Boris and Petr Tarasov were left standing. There are others, but not like them. The leftovers were divided between the two families and the rest is history. Both families are extremely violent, willing to kill and torture to prove their point, which basically is that no one had better mess with them — and no one does."

"Are they friends?"

"They do business together, but no, they posture at each other. There have been a few killings between the two factions, but for the most part, they leave one another alone."

"Do any of the models run drugs?" Jackson asked Sarah. "Has she ever mentioned she was worried about someone? She would pick that up working so close to them. Or maybe one of the designers. They're bringing in clothes and props from all over the world."

Sarah leaned her head back against Damon's shoulder. "She mentioned that it went on. Mostly the girls who used. She'd say they weren't going to make it in the business. Some of them started using to stay thin. It's a hazard of the business, like eating disorders. It's high pressure, Jonas."

Jonas took a deep breath. He didn't give a damn about the job or why one of them might choose to run drugs. He only cared about the fact that one of them may have inadvertently pulled Hannah into a dangerous situation.

"When Libby comes, if Hannah's still alive, she can make it all right again, can't she?" Jonas wasn't certain what he meant, but he had to ask, to be reassured. "Tell me she can do that."

"If Hannah's still alive, we'll seal ourselves together and bind her to us," Sarah said. "That's what we did to you, using Hannah's connection to you."

There was a small silence. "I don't know what that means. I'm connected to all of you." Jonas frowned and rubbed his head again.

Sarah pressed both hands to his head before he could stop her. Warmth flowed from her to him, removing the pounding headache.

Jonas jerked away. "What are you doing? Save your strength for Hannah."

"I know, I couldn't help it," Sarah admitted. "Yes, we're all connected to you, Jonas, but not like Hannah. Your link with her is one of the strongest I've ever seen. In our family, we develop strong connections with our partners. Mom and Dad have a tremendous link between them. We all joke and say it's forged in steel, but you and Hannah . . ." She trailed off.

"What about us?"

"This is going to sound stupid, but I think your souls are linked. You were nearly dead when we reached you, Jonas, when you were shot a few months ago. I certainly couldn't get to you and I don't think even Elle could. She tried, we all did. We united and reached for you, but it was Hannah who held you fast. She was certain it was Elle, but it wasn't. The rest of us knew it was her."

"How come she didn't know?"

"When we unite in a circle, our energy flows from one to the other. It's hard to tell us apart, and she was so distraught. Hannah's very distinctive to the rest of us."

"So if you form your circle of energy, you can save her life."

"Prakenskii is doing that. We can hold her once we're together."

"And the trauma and the scars?"

Sarah shrugged. "I have no idea what we can or can't do. We'll have to watch Libby. She has a tendency to go too far and Hannah will resist if she thinks any of us are being hurt in the process of healing her. Hannah's powers are strong, Jonas. If she fights us, we could all be in trouble. She's stronger than most of us and she always takes care of the rest of us."

"You let me worry about that. Hannah will cooperate."

Sarah glanced at him sharply. "What does that mean?"

"It means right now, she's in a weakened state and she's not going to have any choice. She can get worked up about it when she's one hundred percent. Until then she can live with a dictatorship."

"Don't go off the deep end," Sarah cautioned. She didn't know what Jonas was capable of with Hannah. He had hidden talents he rarely acknowledged, but he was confident he could enlist Hannah's cooperation and that was something even Sarah was uncertain of.

"Plane's about to land," Jackson said, gathering the files and stuffing them back into the briefcase. "There'll be a car waiting to take us to the hospital."

8

"Is she alive?" Jonas demanded as he approached the Russians in the waiting room. Beside him, Sarah leaned heavily on Damon.

Ilya Prakenskii nodded, staggered and reached out to steady himself by holding the wall. "She's been in surgery for hours, but they just brought her into recovery. She's in critical condition and very weak." He glanced at Sarah. "Your sisters had better get here soon."

"They're all on their way. Mom and Dad and my aunts as well."

"I don't like the feel here, Harrington. Hannah's agent is over there." Ilya indicated a slender man in a gray suit talking with the police. "He's pretty shaken up."

Sarah grabbed Jonas when he took an aggressive step toward the agent, and clung tightly as she felt the tremor run through his body. "Don't, Jonas. You're really upset and you might hurt him. I don't want to get thrown out of here."

She studied Prakenskii up close. He was a good-looking man in a tough sort of way. Right now lines etched deep in his face from the strain of holding Hannah to life. "Are you going to crash?" She'd seen her sister Libby, with that same gray tinge, her body trembling with exhaustion and her eyes sunken in. Prakenskii was showing classic signs of psychic overload. He'd spent far too much energy on keeping Hannah alive.

"If we're going to save her, you'll have to help," Prakenskii admitted, sinking back into the chair he'd risen from when they had approached. "She's so close to death I'm not certain we can give her enough time until your family gets here. I did what I could on scene, but there were so many wounds, too much blood loss, and she was already drifting away. I barely had the chance to link with her." He glanced up at Jonas. "She said your name, Harrington. Even with her throat sliced in two, she wanted you."

Jonas's heart clenched in response, a painful constriction that robbed the breath from his lungs. She'd called for him. Reached out. Needed him — and he hadn't been there. All this time he thought he could keep her out of danger, but it had found her anyway. Ironically, the danger had nothing to do with him. All those years wasted, all that time. He'd been such a martyr, staying away for her own good, and Hannah had gone to work, done her job and some nut had attacked her. He should have been with her. His name was the last thing — the *only* thing she'd said.

He swallowed hard and pushed away grief. "Have they given you any indication how long this could take?"

"She's been in there for hours. They've come out twice to say she's still alive." It was obviously a strain for Prakenskii to talk. "Just a few minutes ago they told us she was in recovery but . . ." He trailed off.

"But what?" Jonas demanded.

"They don't know what's keeping her alive. She lost so much blood they're worried about brain damage. None of them believe she'll make it beyond the next couple of hours."

"You're keeping her alive," Sarah said. "That's why she's not dead." She sank into the chair opposite him. "As the others arrive, it will lighten the load on you. Thank you for saving her for us. Let me help you. I can connect with you." She made the offer without hesitation. It gave Prakenskii a decided advantage if he chose to use it because, once connected with Sarah, he would have another path to follow to the Drakes' energy source, but that didn't matter now. The only thing that mattered was keeping Hannah alive.

He nodded and she was surprised — because if she opened herself and her magic to him — he had to do the same to her. Sarah settled back in the chair, facing him, and took a deep breath, allowing her mind to open, to reach and stretch and merge.

Prakenskii looked directly at her, his eyes flickering a deep blue-green. For a moment she was stunned by the vibrant color, as if the sea had come to stormy life, but then the color swirled and darkened and she was looking into empty, fathomless mirrors. There was no way to "read" him. Ilya Prakenskii remained a closed book and that was nearly impossible when they had linked together. She should have been able to read him the way she was certain he was reading her.

She could feel his exhaustion and strain. The fight to keep Hannah alive was taking a toll on his tremendous strength, although his physical appearance didn't reflect the dire situation. He was fighting with everything in him to keep her alive and his strength was definitely waning. She reached inside his mind looking for the path to her sister. Pain hit her, tearing through her mind and ripping through her body so that she was thrown back, away from Prakenskii.

Sarah gasped and doubled over. "She shouldn't be feeling anything at all. She's unconscious, isn't she?" She looked at Ilya. "Isn't she?"

"She appears unconscious, but she is closer to the surface than she should be because she's waiting for him." Ilya indicated Jonas.

Jonas's breath hitched in his lungs. That would be like Hannah. She wouldn't just go down easy, not if she had something to say.

"You've got to get in to her," Sarah said. "Make them let you, Jonas. She can't be in this kind of pain and survive. Go sit with her, and Mr. Prakenskii and I will hold her until the family gets here."

Jonas nodded and went to find the head nurse. It took a lot of persuasion as well as flashing his badge and mentioning danger several times, but he had always been a persuasive man and he found himself walking into the room where Hannah lay so still, surrounded by machines.

Jonas sank down onto the seat beside the bed. Hannah was swathed in bandages over most of her body. Her face was swollen and bluish from bruising. A single sheet covered her body. Beneath it she looked so thin and small, not at all the tall, imposing woman who was Hannah Drake. Her impossibly long lashes lay in twin crescents above her classic cheekbones, looking incongruous beside the bloodstained gauze.

His heart clenched so hard it felt like it was in a vise — an actual physical pain — and he pressed his hand hard against his chest as he lifted the sheet to inspect her body. She was wrapped like a mummy, from her neck down. He swallowed the bile rising as he noted she'd been slashed in the throat as well as her face, chest and abdomen. Her attacker had been every bit as vicious as he'd appeared on television. Jonas had hoped it had been the camera angle, but it was obvious the man had been determined to kill her.

His gut knotted into tight lumps and his throat burned raw. He sank into the chair that had been placed beside the bed and looked her over, looked for a place he could touch her skin — not the hideous thick gauze that seemed to be everywhere. Her hands and arms were bandaged right along with everything else. He knew she would have defensive wounds, he'd seen them enough times on victims, but for some reason he was unprepared for seeing them on Hannah.

Jonas swallowed several times as he carefully slid his hand under her bandaged one. Only the tips of her fingers protruded. He lifted her hand with great care and brought her fingers to his mouth. He had to kiss her, touch her, find a way to caress her. He needed skin-to-skin contact because he had to have tangible proof she was alive and would stay that way. Her breath seemed too shallow, her chest barely rising and falling beneath the thin sheet even with the ventilator.

"Hannah, baby, you're breaking my heart." Just looking at her hurt. He couldn't imagine anyone hurting her this way. What had she done that was such a crime? She was too beautiful with her flawless skin and her unusual hair and tall, elegant, so very classy figure, and her looks had drawn attention to her. Would someone really want to kill her because she was too beautiful? "Nothing makes sense," he murmured, listening to the machines doing her breathing for her.

He put his head down on the bed as the smells and sounds assailed his senses. His stomach lurched, protested. Hannah was hooked up to machines. His beloved Hannah with her laughter and her temper and her silly trick of knocking his hats off his head with the wind. He had a closet full of hats, and he provoked her on purpose sometimes, just to feel the touch of the wind. Her touch. Feminine and soft with her particular fragrance attached. Sometimes he imagined he felt her fingers caressing his face, tracing his jaw, and then the slap of the wind would remove his hat — but it was well worth that single heart-stopping moment.

"You know you have to live for me, Hannah," he said aloud, sitting back up. He kissed her fingertips, drew them one by one into the warmth of his mouth. He ached for her — for him. "I can't imagine my life without you in it," he whispered. "There'd be no purpose for me." He wasn't a poetic man, but he had to find a way to make her understand. It seemed so important to him that she understand what she meant to him. Everything good in his world was lying in that bed with a machine breathing for her.

He leaned closer. "Hannah? Can you hear me?" Her face was partially covered by the bandages and the sight of her lashes lying so thick against her pale skin made his eyes burn. "I should have told you a long time ago." He raked a hand through his hair and pressed several kisses into the mass of hair at the top of her head.

There were so many things he should have said — should have done. Time wasted. He couldn't think why now, only that he hadn't told her how much she meant to him. If he'd been so worried about her because of the things he'd done — and did — in his life, he should have quit. She was more important. He didn't have answers or questions. He could only pray because, in the end, she was all that really mattered.

Jonas. I knew you'd come. Too hard to talk out loud.

Her voice in his head shook him. He leaned closer to her, touching her hair, kissing her fingers, trying to let her know he was there and wouldn't leave. "I'm here, sweetheart. Right here with you. Can you hear me? I'm not going anywhere." She had a tube down her throat, a good reason why she couldn't talk out loud. Did she even know? "Do you remember what happened? You're in the hospital. You need to rest and just hang on until your family gets here."

Are you all right?

His heart turned over. That was just like Hannah, asking if he was all right when she was fighting for her life. "Scared. I'm scared,

Hannah. You've got to hold on until your family comes. Libby is on her way and so are the rest of them. Everyone's coming, Hannah, because you're important to us and we can't lose you. I can't lose you."

I needed to tell you I'm sorry.

His heart nearly stopped. "Sorry? You have nothing to be sorry about." He kissed her fingers again, pressed them to his mouth. "I'm the one who should have been here with you. Do you remember what happened?"

I remember being afraid and then there was pain, so much pain.

Her voice cracked and he felt the pain sweeping inside him as if there was so much she couldn't contain it in her fragile body.

"Rest, Hannah, go to sleep and let Prakenskii and Sarah hold you until your mother and sisters come. Just go to sleep. I'll be right here." He didn't want her to sleep, he wanted her to keep talking. It was terrifying that she hadn't opened her eyes and that he might be imagining the conversation because he needed to hear her voice.

Jonas nibbled at her fingertips. "I love you, Hannah. You hang on."

The sound of the machines answered him. If she'd been there, close enough to the surface of consciousness to talk to him, to be aware of his presence, she no longer was. He glanced anxiously toward the monitors. Her heart was still beating. They didn't expect her to live. The doctor had told him, his face sober, his eyes meeting, then sliding away from Jonas, as he had given the news. Jonas shook away the memory and the feeling of utter despair. The doctor didn't know the Drakes. He didn't know about magic and wonder and family unity. Hannah was a part of something extraordinary, and through her, so was he. She would live because the Drakes would save her.

He glanced out the glass partition to the room where Sarah and Damon waited with Prakenskii and Jackson. His gaze was caught on Sarah. The eldest of the Drake sisters, she was the one who ultimately had the last word. She was very athletic — he'd always admired her in school. Fast and sleek, she could run faster than most of the boys, and she had an uncanny knack for disappearing in plain sight. She was beautiful, with the Drake skin and huge eyes and a glossy mane of hair, yet she could just fade into the background when she wanted. She had worked security for a big company, breaking into buildings for clients and showing them all their weaknesses and then finding ways to improve the security. At times she acted as a bodyguard, and with her special talents, she was a darn good one.

Jonas both admired and loved her, and often sought her counsel when it came to cases of burglary. She had a good eye and a quick mind. She was engaged to Damon Wilder, a brilliant man whom Jonas respected. Right now, Sarah looked tired and drained with sorrow weighing her down. It seemed shocking, when she was such a strong, optimistic person, and it made him even more afraid for Hannah.

Throughout the long morning the older Drakes kept arriving, one by one, women crowding into the waiting room, murmuring softly, their faces stained with tears, hugging one another as they tried to give each other courage. Hannah's aunts and her mother, sitting, facing one another with Prakenskii and Sarah.

Hannah's parents came in to touch their daughter, shaking their heads when Jonas would have risen and reluctantly relinquished his place by her side. They hugged him, but neither spoke, and that left an empty, hollow feeling in the pit of his stomach. He had always counted on the Drakes' strength of family, their ability to pull anyone through. He'd been wounded, yet he'd survived. Surely they could bring

Hannah back from wherever she was.

Elle was the next of Hannah's sisters to arrive. The youngest of the Drake siblings. Her long bright red hair was pulled back in a ponytail. Her face was devoid of makeup and ravaged by tears. She looked so young, a woman with as much or more power than all of her sisters combined, as she was the one destined to pass on the gifts to her daughters. Jonas had always loved her as a baby sister. She was beautiful with her flashing green eyes, and her so-quick temper. She was quiet and kept to herself for the most part, although, like her sisters, she was protective and closed ranks — sometimes against him.

He had no idea what Elle did for a living. Like most of her sisters, she had above-average intelligence and a good education. Elle was good at everything from criminalistics to chemistry. She could easily pass for a twelve-year-old or a sultry siren depending on how she dressed and did her makeup. Jonas worried about her more than he did any of the other Drake sisters. She seemed lost and alone, and perhaps she was. There was no getting close to Elle. You could love her, but she only let you in so far.

He knew his best friend Jackson had some connection to her. Whatever lay between them, Jackson never discussed, but it was there, and sometimes Jonas wanted to warn Elle not to provoke Jackson so much. It was dangerous territory, but he remained silent because Elle just didn't invite confidences. Jonas only knew that whatever lay between them was dark and strong and bound to blow up in their faces someday.

Elle touched Ilya Prakenskii's shoulder in silent thanks and flicked a glance around the room until her gaze settled on Hannah through the glass partition. For a moment, grief was a terrible mask and she reached up her hand to touch the tears on her face. Her gaze collided with Jonas's, and briefly, they were locked together, their sorrow and fear holding them prisoners, then she blew him a kiss, breaking the spell. She sank gracefully on the floor in front of Sarah and lowered her head so it was impossible to see her face.

Jonas felt relief sweep through him. The aunts, he knew, held the same gifts as the Drake sisters, but he didn't know them as well. The sisters he believed in — the sisters he knew loved Hannah with everything in them.

Kate came next. Kate, a sweet-natured woman who laughed and loved and wrote bestselling murder mysteries. She was the quietest of the Drakes, preferring to stand on the sidelines and watch. Books were her best friends next to her sisters. He remembered her as a child, haunting the bookstores and libraries, always with a book in her hand and one in her backpack. She often entertained the family with stories. On holidays, when they were growing up, she would write plays for the sisters — and Jonas — to act out.

Kate rode horses and yet always looked immaculate, not a hair out of place, her makeup so perfect he wasn't always certain she wore it. Her fiancé, Matt Granite, was an ex–Army Ranger, right along with Jonas and Jackson. They'd formed a tight bond together and their friendship went way back. Jonas felt protective toward Kate and had been extremely happy Matt was her choice. Kate kissed Elle, hugged Sarah, cried with her mother and father before coming to stand with Matt in front of the glass. Kate waved at him through the glass and stared at Hannah with sad, red eyes and lines of strain around her mouth.

A chill went down Jonas's spine. Did they all feel that Hannah was so close to death that there was no hope? The idea of failure crept in unbidden but, once in his mind, refused to go away. The Drakes were gathering, but instead of appearing confident they were tense and subdued.

"Listen to me, baby," he whispered against the gauze covering Hannah's ear. "Do this for me. Hang on for me. You're everything to me, baby. They're all coming. I know you can feel them with you. Your mother and aunts are already here. So are Sarah, Elle and Kate. The men are here as well. Your father, Damon, Jackson and Matt. They're holding you close to them and I'm right here with you. Live for me, Hannah, live because our lives are better with you in them."

Abbey rushed in with her fiancé, Aleksandr Volstov, her dark wine-red hair wild, tears on her face as she flung herself into her mother's arms and then turned to look at Hannah. She pressed a hand to her mouth, nodded to Jonas, looking tired and worn. She took a seat on the floor very close to Kate, who reached for her hand.

Abbey had an affinity for the sea and all its creatures. She often reminded Jonas of a mermaid, with her dark red hair spread out on the water and her lithe body swimming strongly. She was a marine biologist, renowned for her work with dolphins, as well as having a talent for knowing the truth and a vast love of the sea. Abbey was the most serious of the Drakes, aside from Elle. She was careful with her speech, for good reason, but since Aleksandr had come back into her life, she laughed more. Jonas thought it was a good match and hoped to utilize Aleksandr's police skills eventually.

"Abbey's here, Hannah," he encouraged, pushing back her hair and wincing at the way her skin felt cool and clammy.

He wanted to yell at the Drakes to hurry. Get the planes moving faster, get everyone here. He could tell Hannah's sisters were joining with Sarah and Prakenskii as they became part of the circle in the waiting room, because with each sibling's arrival, Hannah's presence seemed closer, as if they were slowly bringing her back from a great distance.

Jonas felt Hannah's body jerk, and he swung his head first toward her in alarm, and then at the Drakes in their tight circle. Ilya Prakenskii played a huge part in the Drakes' mental connection to Hannah. Jonas knew that Hannah's reaction had come from Ilya. Jonas looked toward the door and Joley swept into the room. Joley, the most famous of all the Drakes. Wild, uninhibited Joley. She had a voice that could soothe or incite thousands. She never just walked. When she moved, she flowed, every curve exuding pure, unadulterated sex. Jonas sometimes felt sorry for her. She was born with an allure few could resist, but he felt sorrier for the man who would want to love her.

Joley was fiercely independent and very, very powerful in her magic. She was a joy and a presence. All of the sisters looked out for one another, but Joley had made real sacrifices to her reputation to protect Libby. If there was a favorite sister for him, Jonas knew it was Joley with her free spirit and outrageous looks. Like a brother, he often worried about her. She could stop traffic just walking down the street in a pair of jeans. Few were aware of how smart she was. Fewer still knew she held a third-degree black belt and had trained in Krav Maga or that she was a dead shot with a gun.

Jonas watched with curiosity as she moved into the room, her presence ratcheting up the tension visibly. She let out her breath and her gaze was immediately riveted to Prakenskii's. Energy crackled and the walls rippled. The women in the room froze. The men stiffened and came to attention, Jackson positioning his body protectively in front of Elle. She said something to him and Jackson's gaze slid over her, as cold as ice, and he merely shook his head.

Through it all, Ilya Prakenskii never blinked. Never looked away from Joley. There seemed to be a weird battle taking place and then Joley averted her gaze, color creeping up her neck and flooding her face. Tears shimmered in her eyes and not even the Russian could resist Joley with sorrow lining her face and tears on her lashes. He spoke, his voice a low murmur Jonas barely caught, something in Russian, but whatever he said, Joley nodded and sank down beside Elle, who took her hand.

"Libby should be coming any time," Jonas whispered to Hannah. "She was back investigating little lethal worms, or whatever they are, on the tree leaves on a farm in the Amazon." He brought her fingers back to his mouth. "She's so smart, Hannah, and there's not a mean bone in that girl's body. She'll pull you through. She won't let anything happen to you."

It was a prayer more than anything else and he recognized it as such. Libby Drake was a healer — a miracle worker. She'd saved her fiancé, Tyson Derrick, and she'd saved Jonas. Libby looked fragile, with her pale skin, slender body and blue-black hair, but she could lay her hands on someone and fix whatever was broken. The family —

the town — and especially Tyson watched over her, because it was too difficult for her to turn away people who needed help and the toll on her was tremendous.

Jonas knew she needed a man like Tyson in her life. He was capable of putting the brakes on Libby and guarding her. Ordinarily Jonas would have been standing shoulder to shoulder with him, but not this time. This time Jonas was prepared to get on his knees and beg her to save Hannah. It was selfish and wrong. He loved Libby and he knew healing Hannah would be a risk, but she *had* to keep Hannah alive — there simply was no other choice. He couldn't exist without Hannah.

He felt the change in everyone the moment Libby stepped through the waiting room door. Fear turned to cautious hope. It was a terrible burden they were all putting on her and Jonas knew Hannah wouldn't want that life-or-death responsibility on her sister — but it didn't matter to him. God help him — as much as he loved them all — none of them mattered to him the way Hannah did. He hated himself for that streak of selfishness, but he was honest enough to admit that he would risk all of them and himself to save Hannah.

He watched Libby through the glass. She

looked small and fragile, not at all the woman capable of gathering the strength of the others and using it to heal her sister. If she had been walking down a crowded street, no one would ever suspect the power she wielded. She greeted her parents and sisters, all the while holding tightly to Tyson's hand. Jonas suspected her fiancé was unhappy with what she was about to do, and he didn't blame him. If it was Hannah risking her life, he would have felt the same.

Ashamed, he put his head down on the mattress beside her. "I love you, Hannah. More than my life, more than any other. I know I won't be able to look in the mirror for a long time after this, but you have to live, baby. For all of us. Do you hear me? Take what Libby gives you and come back to us."

Jonas felt the gathering of power begin to ricochet off the walls. The waiting room took on a glow of many colors, a bright burst of yellows and oranges that filled the spaces around the older Drake women. He lifted his head to watch the power and energy in the form of various colors bounce off the walls. The women swayed slightly, their bodies graceful.

And then Hannah's sisters stood together,

their voices rising in a melodic chant. Joley threw off the colors of fire, red, orange and gold; Sarah had the colors of air, yellows and greens; Abbey's colors came from water, blue and sea green; Kate was earth, her colors browns and greens; Elle was surrounded by all the colors of the elements in various shades, representing them all. Lastly, Libby brought them all together in spirit, a white light with violet edges surrounding her, moving outward to encompass the others.

Jonas could feel the current of electricity and knew they were pulling energy from every source around them. Hannah's six sisters, her mother and her six aunts. Thirteen extraordinary women gathered in one place for one purpose — to heal Hannah.

Ilya Prakenskii stood, his body still swaying with the effort of holding Hannah. To Jonas's astonishment, vibrant colors glowed eerily around him as well. Vividly bright, they were more like Elle's with all the various colors, yet different, the shades off from the women's. Only the reds and golds and oranges matched Joley's exactly, so much so that the colors seemed to bleed into one another. Tiny sparks hissed and glowed in the air between them, adding to the gathering power.

Hospital personnel were uneasy, watching the scene with a caution born of the rising tension in the waiting room. The air was charged with it. Sitting beside Hannah's bed, Jonas refused to relinquish his place. If they were going to come in — and they were; nothing, not even security, would stop them — he was going to witness the healing. He had to believe Hannah would live. He had to walk out of the room believing she was going to live or he wasn't going to survive the night.

The hairs on his arms stood up as the women filed into the room, one at a time. The nurse protested, but no one paid attention and Hannah's mother imperiously waved her to silence. The Drake women surrounded the bed; Libby and one of the aunts Jonas recognized as Nanci rested their palms on Hannah while the others linked hands.

The effect was a dazzling light show, although the room wasn't bursting with light — Hannah's body was. It slid over her, around her, through her. Light played over her skin and pressed inward through her pores — or maybe it burst from inside her out. Jonas couldn't tell which came first. A dance of colors sparkled around her and Hannah's skin went from pasty white to luminous.

Jonas retained possession of her fingers and became aware of heat slowly driving out the clammy cold of her skin. Warmth pulsed through her in waves. He felt the stirring of her in his mind. A soft inquiry. Alarm. Hannah surfacing. Her long lashes fluttered and his heart nearly stopped. The chanting never wavered, but continued low and melodious.

He glanced at the heart monitor. The weak, erratic beat had strengthened to something much steadier and relief made him collapse back into his seat. He waited, but she didn't open her eyes.

"Enough, Libby," Tyson said. "You can come back tomorrow, but that's enough today. I mean it."

Libby's hands remained on Hannah, but the chanters stopped, their colors fading as they withdrew support. Mrs. Drake put her arm around Libby and physically pulled her away from her sister. "Tyson's right, Libby, we can't take any chances. She's better — stronger. That's all we can do today."

"She's going to live, Jonas," Sarah assured him when he would have protested.

Jonas wanted to snarl at Tyson, throw something at the machines as Libby was helped from the room. Her color was gone and she stumbled, obviously weak. The older Drakes helped Nanci as well, although she didn't look as quite as bad as Libby. Hannah didn't move. Other than that one flutter of her lashes, she hadn't improved.

Elle touched his hand. Kate kissed him. Abbey brushed her fingers over Hannah's and his joined hands. Joley stood beside the bed weeping.

"How could this happen, Jonas?"

"I don't know, honey. I honestly don't know."

"But you'll find out. You'll make certain whoever is responsible will never get near her again, right?"

"Prakenskii took the knife away from him, and in the struggle, her attacker was killed."

Joley lifted her tear-streaked face to look at the Russian. His face was gray, tired, carved with deep lines. "Thank you again. Did you know him? Recognize him? When you touched him, did you get a sense of why he would attack my sister?"

"I felt his fear. That only. It poured off of him."

Jonas frowned. "He fought you. I was watching the broadcast. He fought you and kept trying to go for her."

Joley made a small sound of distress — of protest. "I'm sorry, honey," Jonas said.

"This isn't something you need to hear. I'll talk with Prakenskii later. You're both exhausted. I'm going to stay with Hannah. Why don't you regroup?"

"I'll see you to your hotel," Ilya said, making it a statement. "Do you have your security people with you?"

She nodded. "You can't wade through the reporters."

"We'll get you out," he said firmly. "Come, Joley. You need to rest."

Jonas kissed and hugged her before turning her over with a small bit of reluctance to Ilya Prakenskii. The man had undoubtedly saved Hannah's life, yet Jonas feared his motives. He was the bodyguard of one of the most powerful Russian mobsters and was feared from Europe to the United States.

"Her signs look better," the nurse said when they were alone, distracting him from his speculative thoughts. It was quiet and there were no flashing colors or feel of power. After the impressive display he felt let down.

He glanced at the nurse in her blue scrubs and name tag, her hair pulled back. She looked neat and efficient. He hoped she was competent, too.

"What exactly did they do? There's a

definite change in her. It doesn't make sense, but she looks as if she could breathe on her own."

Jonas remained silent as the nurse consulted with the doctor, and over the next few hours, Hannah was allowed to breathe more and more on her own. It was a huge relief when they finally took her off the ventilator, the first sign that she might live.

Jonas brought Hannah's fingertips to his lips and bent forward until his head lay on the mattress beside her body. He had never been able to stand hospitals, not after his mother had been taken from her room, never to return. The sounds and smells were the same. The machines seemed alive when he closed his eyes and listened, as he had so many years ago. Praying. Praying for a miracle, just as he was doing now.

He had no feel for the passage of time. Sometimes he whispered to her, other times he slept. The nurse hovered close, watching over Hannah. He kept his head down and allowed himself to doze, drifting off until he was somewhere between sleeping and awake, somewhere his mother stared at him with pain-filled eyes and a man stabbed Hannah viciously with a knife while he stood behind a wall, pounding with his fists, trying to beat it down and get to them.

Jonas jerked awake, as a different nurse entered the room. He looked around for Hannah's regular nurse. He liked and trusted her.

The woman glanced at him and then averted her eyes, maybe, he thought, because he looked so damned distraught. He wanted Hannah to show dramatic signs of responding to the healing by the Drakes. Shouldn't she have sat up and demanded dinner or something? Ripped off the bandages and smiled at him? Instead she lay sleeping as if in a coma, her heart and lungs still being monitored.

He tried to breathe away the tightness in his chest, sending the nurse a false smile. "I thought Katherine was Hannah's night nurse." Was Katherine the right name? The nurse had introduced herself but he couldn't remember. He was so out of it — so upset.

"Katherine asked me to give her meds to her." The nurse didn't look at him as she walked around the bed, a syringe in her hand.

Jonas's radar suddenly went ballistic. He stood up, stretching in a deceptively lazy manner, sharp eyes drifting over the nurse, taking in the fact that her hands were unsteady. Her voice was a flat monotone, and at no time did she look directly at him. Doubt trickled down his spine — doubt and alarm.

"That's nice that you all help each other out. Katherine was supposed to be right back. Hannah isn't supposed to be left alone like this. What's the holdup?" He put censure into his voice. The name hadn't been Katherine. Kelley maybe, but definitely not Katherine. It had been on her badge. A "K" name.

The nurse didn't pause. Didn't look at him. "She had to use the bathroom, she'll be right back." She fussed with Hannah's line, giving him a quick, nervous smile as he began to walk around the bed toward her.

"What's that?" He indicated the syringe in her hand as he slowly stalked her.

"A painkiller," the woman answered. Her hands trembled as she fumbled with the line. The room was cool, but she was sweating.

"Wait a minute," Jonas rushed her, instincts guiding rather than his brain. "Stop what you're doing." He leapt the distance between them, inserting his body between the nurse and Hannah's IV. He grabbed her arm, missed, and as she turned, he caught her hair.

He heard her sob, a hiss of breath and a low cry of terror as she whipped around, kicking at him to get him off her. Before he could stop her, she shoved the needle into her own vein, squeezing the plunger, her eyes holding terror as she went to the floor. Jonas knelt beside her, but it was too late. Her breath came in ragged gasps, her eyes went opaque and then there was a horrifying silence.

9

Jonas slammed his hand against the wall right next to the detective's head. "Don't give me that bullshit, save it for a civilian. Who the hell are these people — what do you have on them so far?"

Detective Stewart sighed and gave in. "The attacker was a man named Albert Werner. He's an electrician, has a wife and kid. The cameras picked up a couple of shots of him outside during the fashion show. He was talking to the Reverend RJ at one point." Stewart handed Jonas a grainy photograph of a tall, well-built man talking to the Reverend with people obviously shouting protests in the background.

"What did the Reverend have to say?"

"Only that he was a troubled soul and seemed agitated. The Reverend invited him to be saved, or something to that effect, but the man refused. The Reverend's opinion seems to be that Ms. Drake reaped what she sowed."

Jonas swore, his teeth coming together with a vicious snap. "Did you find any connection between that fake Gospel spouter and Werner?"

"We're working on it. The perp did make a sizable donation to the animal rights group about a week ago." The detective handed Jonas another out-of-focus picture. Albert Werner stood with the animal rights group shouting at the reporters.

"What about the nurse who tried to kill her? Is she involved with either group?"

"She wasn't a nurse. She's a vet tech and her name is Annabelle Werner. She's the perp's wife."

"His wife? His wife came to the hospital and tried to finish the job? That doesn't make any sense. I don't remember their names from any of the threatening letters written to Hannah," Jonas said. "Did you find anything, a threat against her, a reason they'd hate her so much to do something like this?"

"Not yet. We went through the nutcase file and they aren't there."

"What about their kid? Did she have aspirations of becoming a model?"

"She's in a hospital for eating disorders, which might be a motive. Totally emaciated.

She's twelve. She has pictures of movie stars in her room, but not of Ms. Drake, but still, that could be the connection. Kid starves herself wanting to be a model just like Hannah Drake. Everyone knows the face and name. She's an easy target to blame."

"*Both* parents decide to kill Hannah? This is in retaliation for the kid?" It didn't wash. "Albert Werner couldn't have expected to get away with it. The cameras were on him. He had to know that. It was too public unless he wanted to make a statement. He attacked her like he wanted to destroy her, destroy her beauty — and then her life. The first blows weren't killing blows. They were all about disfigurement."

Just saying the words aloud brought up the stark images his mind just couldn't forget. His gut twisted. The knife slashing viciously, brutally, over and over, ripping Hannah to pieces. Bile rose. Sweat broke out. "The doctor said the first few strokes were deliberate and precise, but shallow, cutting across her face, neck, breasts, waist and stomach before he began stabbing deep enough to kill her." He fought back waves of nausea, trying to keep his voice, trying not to let it be personal, to think of the victim as Hannah — his Hannah. "I'd like to consult with a friend of mine, a psychiatrist, show him what you have on the attackers and ask his opinion, because it just doesn't add up for me."

It seemed more likely to him that they were programmed, maybe hypnotized or magic had been used — but how could he tell the detective that?

"Not for me either," Detective Stewart admitted. "Because if the husband is dead, the wife has to worry about who's going to watch over the kid. Why come to the hospital and risk killing her with you in the room? It doesn't make sense."

"Are you checking to see if the Werners belonged to the Reverend's little flock? Maybe the conversation was a little different than what the Reverend is telling you."

Stewart nodded. "Oh, I'm certain it was different. I've interviewed the Reverend a few times now, and I think the man is a crackpot — a charismatic one — but still a crackpot. He's been recruiting young girls off the street to take back home with him. Says he's trying to save them, but I'm not buying it."

"Why'd you pull him in for an interview?" Jonas asked curiously.

"There was an attack on a young prostitute. She's barely fifteen. Someone nearly beat her to death. Did just about anything they could to her. Her friends swear it was the Reverend. Of course he has an airtight alibi. Members of his church claim he was with them all night praying."

"But you don't believe it."

"Not for a minute. But the girl's too scared to talk. I think the Reverend can get his people to say or do just about anything for him. I think they give him their kids and their money. And if there's a connection between him and the Werners, it wouldn't surprise me. I think the Reverend could talk someone into murder as well."

"He's from our part of the country," Jonas admitted, "and we've been trying to nail him for a long time. He owns a lot of land and keeps it locked up tight. Once the girls are brought there, no one sees them again. Unfortunately he finds the kids no one is interested in, so he can get away with it. You think he might order one of his followers to do a slash job on Hannah?"

"He's capable," Stewart said. "And whoever went after the prostitute cut her up pretty bad — with a knife. Her face is never going to be the same."

"Can you work on her, see if she'll identify him?"

"She's already disappeared. The moment

she was out of the hospital, she was long gone."

"Do you think she ran, or someone grabbed her?"

Stewart shrugged. "She's a street rat, who knows? But even if her friends are wrong and it wasn't the Reverend, he's trouble. He's slick, though. He sure can suck you in when he's talking. He sounds very cool until he begins to rant fanatically about women and how they're the downfall of good men and he has to save them from themselves."

"So what do you have on Werner's wife?"

"Not much. She doesn't have so much as a parking ticket. Highly respected as a vet tech, fellow workers as well as the neighbors all liked her. She got the drug from work. They use it to euthanize animals. Everyone who knew them seemed genuinely shocked that either of the Werners would be involved in a killing. The husband doesn't really have much of a history either. Not anything to give me a heads-up on him. A few tickets, one fistfight."

Jonas tapped his fingers on the small end table in the waiting room, scowling as he concentrated. More and more it seemed as if the parents might have been programmed to kill. But why? And for whom? "Have you interviewed their daughter?"

"She's pretty broken up. I couldn't get much out of her. She knew of Hannah Drake and admired her, but the entire world knows Ms. Drake's face. I didn't notice she was overly fanatical about her, and like I said, when we searched the house, there were pictures of movie stars, not models, in her room. We found two magazines in the house with Ms. Drake in them, but that's not unusual either. Her face is on the cover of a lot of magazines."

The detective couldn't stop the quick, curious glances he kept sending toward Hannah through the glass. "I think Ms. Drake is pretty safe from the kid and there isn't any family left to come after her."

Fighting back the urge to deck Stewart, Jonas shoved his hands through his hair and followed the detective's gaze. To his astonishment, Hannah was looking back at him. His heart jumped. "Would you please keep me apprised of every aspect of the investigation? As soon as possible, we'll be moving Hannah closer to her home."

"I'll need to speak with her. The doctors this morning said she had improved dramatically."

"Not dramatically enough for you to speak to her. I'll let you know if she says anything or if she's able to be interviewed."

The detective nodded, and moved away, glancing once more back at Hannah as he did so.

Jonas muttered curses to himself as he walked back into the room, switching immediately to a smile. "You woke up, Hannah. You've been sleeping for a few days now. You scared the hell out of me." He sat in the chair, his heart pounding, trying to look casual and upbeat.

She looked a mummy, swathed in gauze from her hips to her cheeks. Her face, what little he could see of it, was swollen and bruised. Her skin was so white she seemed to fade into the bandages and sheets around her. Her gaze was locked on his face, and if he wasn't mistaken, there were tears close.

Jonas leaned forward and pressed his palm to the top of her head, providing contact and warmth. "Everything's all right, baby. All you have to do is lie there and get better. You're getting stronger." He would never get the sight of her like this out of his mind. Never forget the panic sweeping through him. He'd never get over the terrible bone-deep grief. He couldn't close his eyes without seeing the knife. The blood. He had never felt so helpless — so useless and impotent — in his life. He should have been there. *God in heaven. I should have been there.*

Jonas.

He heard the fear in her voice, the echo of it in his own mind. His gut clenched in reaction. He fought back his physical response and forced himself to smile at her in reassurance. "I know, honey. He can't hurt you now. No one is going to hurt you again. How are you feeling? Are you in pain?"

"My throat." *It hurts to talk. My throat is raw. I hurt everywhere. Even my mouth.*

The doctor had said her voice would never be the same. "The nurse can give you more pain meds."

No. I just want to go home. Take me home. I feel like a freak show. Everyone stares, even the nurses.

"We're going to move you to a private room, which we can much more easily guard. We'll get you out of here as soon as possible."

I can't remember very much.

He used his thumb to brush away a teardrop on her cheek. Her lashes were wet and spiky and so heart-breaking he wanted to gather her close and shelter her against everything and everyone. "You don't have to remember. We're all here with you and we're going to get you home."

"What do I look like?" She raised a bandaged hand and touched the swath of gauze around her face.

A shadow fell across them and Jonas turned just in time to see a man dressed as an orderly snap a picture of Hannah with his cell phone. Swearing, Jonas leapt up and caught the man as he was hurrying away. Yanking the phone from him, he dropped it on the floor and stomped on it.

"Hey! You can't do that."

"You're lucky I don't have you arrested." Jonas noted the name tag. "George Hodkins. I'm going after your job for this."

"It's worth a lot of money, man. I'm going to school and I need it."

"Go to hell." Jonas shoved him away and kicked the broken phone hard enough that it hit the wall. He signaled to the charge nurse, pushing the man toward her. "He's trying to profit by taking pictures of your patient. As soon as you take care of this, I'd like to get her moved to another room where we can protect her better."

The nurse scowled at the man. "Yes, of course, Mr. Harrington." She switched her attention to the orderly. "How dare you invade one of my patient's privacy?"

Jonas left them and returned to Hannah. That had been too easy. Had the man had a gun instead of a camera, he might have gotten a shot off. He couldn't protect Hannah here. He needed to get her someplace where he could control all movement around her. As soon as possible they had to transport her back home. Joley could provide a plane. He sank back into the chair beside her, his mind racing with details.

You can't get so upset, Jonas. There are going to be pictures. The horrible little rag magazines must be having a field day. She suppressed a sob, but not before he caught it in his mind as she turned her head away from him.

"Screw the reporters, Hannah. I can deal with them. We're making arrangements to get you home as soon as the hospital gives us the word. Your sisters and aunts are taking turns coming in to help speed your recovery throughout the day so no one gets worn out, but they can heal you much faster at home. We'll be out of here in no time." And he would be able to control the security around her much more easily.

The brisk tap on the door had Hannah cringing. Her agent, Greg Simpson, brushed past Jonas without a glance and leaned down to air kiss the top of Hannah's head. "They wouldn't let me in until today, Hannah. This is terrible. So terrible. Who would do such a brutal, unforgivable thing? The reporters won't leave me alone. I've had to give so many interviews, I'm losing my voice."

Hannah didn't turn her head back toward her agent, but lay very still, almost frozen. Jonas felt her heightened tension and distress and reached around Simpson to take her bandage-wrapped hand. She curled her fingers around his.

"Say no."

Simpson whirled around as if just noticing Jonas's presence. "What?" he asked stiffly, frowning at the hand-holding.

"You could say no to the press conferences. Tell them to go to hell. They're circling like vultures."

"Of course they are. Hannah is known and loved the world over. Everyone wants to know how she is — if she's going to live — if she can take her place in the fashion world again. It's big news. You must have seen all the flowers and cards and well-wishers."

Jonas felt a small tremor run through Hannah. "She's very loved," he admitted, wanting her to know he was aware of the adulation from around the world.

"So of course she needs to say a few words to reassure her fans. I can select the reporters who have been good to her, the caring ones . . ."

Hannah shuddered and made a small sound of dismay in his mind. She didn't turn her head or look at her agent.

Jonas stood up, forcing Simpson to back up a step. "So you're here to check on whether Hannah is up to a press conference. No, she's not. She won't be talking to reporters. And we're not bringing photographers into the room either."

"There's no need to get angry, Mister . . . Who are you anyway?"

"I'm Hannah's fiancé." When Hannah's mind reached out to his in shocked reaction, Jonas bent to bring her fingers to his mouth. *Don't worry, baby, I'm not going to carry you off yet. I'm just getting rid of this worm for you.*

For the first time, there was a ghost of a smile answering in his mind. *He is a bit of a worm. But he's the real deal when it comes to getting the jobs.*

He's a publicity hound.

"Hannah doesn't have a fiancé. I would have known about it."

"And somehow the news would have gotten leaked to the press."

"The press is part of Hannah's life." Simpson looked suddenly sad, mouth drooping, eyes like a lost puppy's. "Although I can't see how our Hannah will ever recover the incredible good looks that have made her into such a star. My God." Both hands fluttered, went to his face in distress. "He slashed her to ribbons."

Hannah's body jerked as if someone had shot her. Her reaction was physical as well as mental, pulling away from Jonas, refusing to look at either of them.

Simpson paced across the room, avoiding Jonas as he frowned and rubbed his palms up and down his chest. "I'll have to do damage control on the accounts. There're so many of them. The cosmetic company, the perfume. We were in negotiations for a major chain with a brand of clothing. I'll have to get someone geared up for a takeover or we'll lose it all. You have people counting on you. Have you spoken with the plastic surgeon yet? Was he able to put your face back together when they operated?"

"Get. The. Hell. Out." Jonas enunciated each word between clenched teeth.

"No. No. You don't understand. You think I'm not compassionate, but that's my job to put aside emotions and keep Hannah's business going. I'm responsible for cleaning up this mess."

"You're responsible for getting her into it," Jonas snarled, knowing he was being unfair. "She shouldn't have been there in the first place. Get the hell out of here and leave us alone."

"I'll be back, Hannah, when you're more yourself and we can talk about this," Simpson said as he backed out of the room.

"Damn little toad," Jonas hissed under his breath. He sank back into his chair. "All he's thinking about is his commission."

Hannah didn't turn her face back toward him. Her fingers opened and her hand slipped from his. His chest tightened and he forced back a wave of fear mixed with anger. His emotions were all over the place and he had to rein them in if he was going to do her any good. He straddled the chair and watched her for a moment, the stiff line of her body, her averted face.

"Are you worried about the things he said? Scars? Losing your career?" He hadn't worried about anything other than her life. He wanted her alive any way he could get her.

Aren't you?

He bit back his first answer and analyzed the voice in his head. The advantage of telepathy was that the voice carried emotion with it, and she was hurt, but mostly terribly frightened. And she was apprehensive about how she looked.

"You're not your body, Hannah. You never

have been to me. I don't know about the rest of the world, all I can tell you is that I love you — the person. The one who makes me laugh and makes me so angry I could shake her. You make me feel alive. You make me feel cherished. I never had that, you know. My home wasn't like yours. Now, when I come, you have tea and cookies and half the time a meal waiting just for me. You always make me feel important — and that I belong." He cleared his throat, feeling a little foolish spilling his guts to her when she wasn't looking at him. "You make me feel like a man should feel — well — when you aren't mixing me the hell up."

In spite of her fear, Hannah responded, turning back to him, her blue gaze colliding with his, and the impression of a small smile in his mind. *You mix me up, too. Thank you. It's frightening not knowing what I look like.*

"Can't Libby heal scar tissue?"

Do you think she's a miracle worker?

Her question hung there. Ridiculous. Poignant. Ludicrous. And then he felt the burst of her laughter breaking against the walls of his mind and he wanted to weep. The sound was soft and true and so perfectly Hannah — his Hannah. The one few others knew. He needed to hold her to him. His arms ached to gather her close, but he was afraid of hurting her.

Hannah reached up and brushed at his cheek. *You have tears in your eyes, Jonas. Don't look so sad. I'm sad enough for both of us.*

He swallowed the lump threatening to choke him and caught her hand, bringing it to his chest. Her fingertips were the only actual skin he could reach and he rubbed the pads of his own fingers back and forth over them, needing the contact with her. "Are you sad thinking you might have scars?"

She'd been so beautiful, astonishingly so. He could understand it and maybe it would upset him when he got over his fear of her being murdered right before his eyes — not this lifetime — or the next — but sometime.

I didn't know anyone could hate me so much. What could I have done that would make someone want to hurt me this way? I don't understand.

He brought her fingers to his mouth, kissing her, nibbling with his teeth, fighting back the waves of nausea and anger and stark, raw fear at the thought of a madman viciously stabbing her. "Nothing, Hannah. Absolutely nothing. He was mentally deranged. There's no explanation."

She swallowed hard and tested her voice.

"There has to be." Her voice was low and husky, still melodious, but a whisper of sound.

That little whisper traveled right down his spine and through his body, rocking him, the way only Hannah could. There was nothing sexy about lying in a hospital bed, covered in bandages, but her voice, her eyes, the whisper down his spine, brought his body to instant alert. "I'm so fucking glad you're alive, Hannah."

Hannah blinked at him, shocked by the burst of emotion pouring out of him when he was usually so reserved, so careful not to swamp her.

"I'm here." It was all she could think to say when he was so torn up. She could feel the pain in him and it surprised her that he allowed her to feel it.

He shook his head. "It was too close, Hannah. Too close. If Prakenskii hadn't been there . . ."

Her brows drew together. *I remember him now. He was chasing me. Through the crowd. I was afraid for Joley.* She made a sound of distress and looked up at him. *He asked me if she was a spell-singer.*

Jonas shook his head and glanced back toward the nurse. *I don't know what that is. What's the significance?* Because just the thought upset her. He could see she was becoming agitated and he forced air through his lungs in an effort to try to calm her down. "Relax, baby, nothing is going to happen to Joley. I've got round-the-clock guards on her. She's too upset about you to be mad at me, either, so that's a plus."

Hannah closed her eyes, already weak and worn out, her voice still that husky thread. "Strong." It was too much trouble to talk out loud so she switched back. *His magic is strong and ancient. He knows the old ways, the traditional ways.*

Jonas smoothed back her wild, springy curls. "Go to sleep, honey. Prakenskii kept you alive so I don't care if he's the devil right now. We'll deal with all that later."

Tenderness. Who would have thought he was so capable of such deep emotion? And he was beginning to worry about the fact that she couldn't talk. The knife had slashed across her throat. Was there even more damage than the doctor had first thought? Probably. Most likely. Even with the Drakes coming together to heal her, they were trying to keep her alive, not worry about the little things yet.

Jonas. Don't leave me alone here. I want to go home. I don't feel safe here.

He smiled around her fingertips. "You

don't have to worry about me leaving you alone, Hannah. I'm going to lock you up in a room at home." He felt her shudder, but it was more in his mind than anything else and he frowned. "You don't like the idea."

There was a small silence. He thought she might not answer him.

If I was outside, no one could have done this to me. I have little power indoors. I feel safe outside.

Jonas frowned. "Hannah, I don't think I'm understanding what you're saying."

That's all right. I don't know what I was saying.

Her voice was fading again as exhaustion took over, but Jonas wasn't so willing to let her go. She was lying. She knew what she was saying and it was important. "You can control the elements outside," he said. "And that makes you feel safe."

She didn't respond, but he felt her assent in his mind.

Jonas shook his head. "Hannah, are you telling me you don't feel safe indoors? Here? In the hospital?" He felt that same tightening in his gut right before his alarms shrieked at him. *She'd asked him to go to New York.* He hadn't listened then but he was damn sure going to listen now.

When you're with me.

"Do you still feel you're in danger?" They got the couple. The kid couldn't pose a threat. She was under sedation at the eating disorder clinic. It was natural, he reassured himself, for her to be fearful. She'd gone through a brutal, life-altering attack. Being afraid was simply that — not precognition. Still, his mouth had gone dry and his heart had accelerated.

What do you mean — couple?

Jonas swore under his breath. What kind of idiot was he? An amateur? She turned her head back toward him and opened her eyes. He felt the impact of that blue gaze all the way through his body, like an electrical jolt. She was not happy with him. She'd caught his thought just as if he'd spoken it out loud. He knew better around her, especially when she was speaking telepathically. He mentally kicked himself.

Jonas. What couple?

He kissed her fingers again, wishing he could scoop her up onto his lap and hold her close. "The man's wife tried to inject Beuthanasia into your IV." Her gaze never wavered. It was impossible to look away.

Did she say why she wanted me dead?

"She didn't say anything." At least it wasn't a lie. She'd know he was lying, she always knew. Hannah continued staring at him. "For God's sake," he snapped, exasperated. "It isn't important right now. I'm taking care of things."

She did blink then. Long lashes sweeping down, giving his body another jolt. Geez. She did it so easily to him. She always had. Even wrapped up like a mummy, she could make every cell in his body zing.

I'm hurt, Jonas, not mentally incapacitated. Tell me. I have the right to know and I'm not some fragile flower that's going to wilt or be crushed, so just tell me.

Fragile was exactly what she was. He touched her face with his fingertips, brushed at strands of her hair. "I think I have the right to protect you, Hannah. You took about ten years off of my life. I'm not hiding anything. The woman is dead. We have no idea what the motivation was, but we're looking into it. In the meantime, I'm staying right with you. There's no need to be afraid."

He hoped he was right. Prayed he was right.

There has to be a reason, Jonas. Did I know them? Had I slighted them in some way? Maybe they thought I was rude to them. Sometimes people try to talk to me when I'm going out to the car and I can't talk without stuttering so I just smile and wave.

His heart ached for her. He bent closer, his posture protective, loving. He didn't give a damn if the entire world knew she turned him inside out. "This wasn't your fault. Stop trying to make sense of it. There *is* no sense to it, Hannah." He used the pad of his thumb, stroked little caresses over her brow. "I love you, Hannah. You know that, don't you? You know I love you."

He felt her withdrawal, her mind pulling away from his. At once she was cautious. *You don't have to say that, Jonas. I don't want you to, not now, when I don't even know what I look like.*

"Now you're just pissing me off, woman. Do you think you're talking to that little rodent, Simpson? Why the hell did you keep him on as your agent?"

Hannah blinked at his shift to anger and then to Greg Simpson. *He's amazing in the fashion world. Really has a feel for the designers, who are going to make it and who aren't. He's abrasive and arrogant, but he's made the careers of some of the biggest names in the business. I would never have made it without him.*

Jonas wasn't altogether certain that was true, but what did he know about the fashion industry? Greg Simpson was a respected name in the business and he certainly brought in the deals for Hannah. Jonas had never really inquired too much about the kind of money Hannah made, but he knew it was a lot — more than he cared to think about. "Is he always like that?"

No. He's a shark during contract negotiations and the clients adore him. He knows exactly what to say to them. He wields a lot of power in the industry.

There was something more — something he wasn't getting. If Greg Simpson was such a hot agent, then it would stand to reason he'd be smart enough to treat his number one client with kid gloves, but he wasn't doing that. He was insulting and rude. He was giving press conferences when he should be shielding her. Something was very off. "Hannah. Did you tell him you were going to quit?"

She was silent, but he caught the sheen of tears in her eyes. His gut clenched and twisted into tight knots. Everything inside him went still and the cop took over.

"When did you tell him you were quitting?"

Hannah turned her face away. *It doesn't matter.*

"That's why he's been such a pompous little weasel. You wouldn't have put up with him if he always treated you like that. You told him you were quitting. You're his number one client and he gets a lot of mileage out of being the agent of number one. Damn it, Hannah, why didn't you tell me you quit?" He leaned over her, upset enough to catch her bandage-covered chin and tug until she looked at him. "When we were together, why didn't you tell me? You'd already quit, hadn't you?"

There was the smallest of nods. *I still had contracts to fulfill. I told him no more, that I wouldn't take any more.*

"When?" he demanded.

Do you remember when you walked in and Greg was on the speaker phone a few months ago? He suggested I get a breast reduction. There was painful embarrassment in her voice — in his mind. Shame even. *I don't always fit into the standard size made for runway models, and with the huge fashion shows coming up, apparently some of the designers complained.*

Jonas had been furious, he recalled. Hannah was already starving herself and Simpson was pushing her to lose even more weight. She was as thin as a rail, but she still had generous breasts — something not welcome in the fashion industry apparently.

That had been several months ago. "You actually told him then that you wanted out?" He was definitely going to look into a tie between the couple who had attacked her and Simpson, although it didn't make sense, but he was paranoid where she was concerned. Simpson stood to lose a lot of money if she quit.

I'd been in the business long enough. I'd made enough money to live comfortably wherever I wanted and I wasn't about to get a breast reduction.

"Thank God something brought you to your senses. Give me a timeline on this, Hannah. You told him — what was his reaction? When did he start getting nasty with you?"

Hannah's brows drew together. *What are you thinking? That Greg would want to hurt me because I told him I was quitting the business?*

"Of course not." It was exactly what the cop in him was thinking. Simpson was getting a lot of media coverage out of the attack, and what would it have been like to lose your most famous client? He could well imagine Simpson smoldering with rage and wanting to get back at her. Now, not only was there an outpouring of sympathy for him, but he would be even more sought after.

Jonas just couldn't get behind the fact that

a couple with no priors, no hint of mental illness, would develop a hate so deep they would attempt to kill Hannah in such a vicious manner. The attack had personal written all over it. It was dramatic, had been on television. *Inside Entertainment,* the popular celebrity gossip show, had advertised heavily that they would carry what they proclaimed as the party of the century — that every star was attending. That meant Albert Werner had *wanted* the attack to be caught on film. He had wanted the world to see it. He had known he was going to get caught and must have been prepared to end his life, just as his wife had.

And that brought the entire matter right back to psychic powers. Who had them and who stood to gain by forcing a couple to kill Hannah Drake? He was going to start digging for a connection with Simpson. The man would come out of this a media favorite. And, it had to be said, he had to look a little deeper at Prakenskii.

Jonas.

He nibbled on her fingers. "I'm right here, baby. Don't worry so much. You know me. I like everything neat and tidy." He glanced over his shoulder as he heard the Drakes arriving. "Your family is here for another healing session and then we're going to move you to another room."

Her fingers hooked his. *When can I go home?*

"Soon, honey. I promise. I'll get you home soon."

10

Hannah stood in the center of her room, shaking, bile rising in her throat. Around her, face up on the floor, were shards of the full-length mirror, replicating over and over a horrifying, monstrous image of her body. She looked like a crosspatch quilt, not real, someone sewn together.

She pressed her fingers to her eyes hard, stemming the flow of tears. She would not do this. She wouldn't. She was alive. Her sisters were healing her. Anyone else would be dead. *Dead.* She needed to be grateful for the miracle they'd handed her, not too vain to cope with the results. The slashes on her body would fade with time — much faster than normal. Libby was certain the Drake sisters could keep most of the scars from showing too much. She needed to be grateful.

"Hannah?" The knock on the door was soft. Hesitant. Persistent. "Honey, we heard a crash. Are you all right?"

Hannah swallowed hard and grabbed her robe, hastily covering her body. She didn't dare take a step with her feet bare. Glass was scattered all over the floor. Large, jagged pieces and small tiny shards. Ruined. Like her life. Like her face. Her body. *Everything.* "I'm fine, Sarah. I just dropped something. I'm just about to lie down."

"Let me in, honey. I'll help you pick it up. I heard something break."

"I've already got it." She needed Sarah to go away. They all had to leave her alone and give her some time. She was broken into a million pieces, just like the mirror, and she had to find a way to put herself back together. She had to find a way to believe in herself. She didn't want to be like this — scared and lost and feeling so alone.

Mostly she couldn't stand the deception anymore. She could feel her sisters' pity. Poor Hannah. Whatever will she do? We have to think for her. Figure her life out, now that she's ruined. The sympathy was killing her. She couldn't be in the same room with them, and they whispered. *Whispered.* As if she was on her death bed. Maybe that's the way all of them viewed her now. Hannah Drake, the model, certainly was. And who the hell was she now?

"Hannah?" Sarah knocked again. "Let me in."

"Sarah." Hannah's voice broke. She choked. "You've got to give me some space. I'm sorry, I just need time. Give me time."

There was a moment of silence. She could feel the weight of Sarah's hurt and sorrow crushing her — crushing both of them.

"Hannah, open the damn door."

There was nothing soft or hesitant about the command or the voice. Jonas didn't believe in coddling. He'd see her for the coward she was. He'd think it was vanity. Poor little Hannah, unable to stand not being the Barbie doll.

Immediately following Jonas's demand, she could hear her sisters whispering to him, furious that he would use that tone and maybe upset her. Protecting her, standing up for her and she so didn't deserve it. She hated that they wanted to protect her — that they felt it was necessary. All of them jumped him, demanding he back off and let them handle her. Because poor little broken Hannah needed to be handled.

She felt the insistent burn of tears. How utterly pathetic could she get, standing in the middle of her room with broken glass surrounding her — *mocking* her — and her sisters and Jonas crowding together outside her door whispering together. If it wasn't so wretchedly sad, she would laugh.

She'd managed to keep everyone at bay the first week home by simply staying in bed, but her refusal to eat had upset them all so much, and she could see she was wearing them out as they tried to heal her, so she'd made the effort to get up.

"Hannah. I'm not kidding around with you. Open the fucking door now." There was an edge to his voice, as if he were gritting his teeth and biting out each word. Her heart accelerated and her throat seemed to swell.

There were more whispers. She could have told her sisters all the demands in the world wouldn't work on Jonas. He was going to come in. There were no walls between Jonas and Hannah. He never allowed them unless he was the one erecting them. He simply smashed every barrier down. She closed her eyes. When he opened the door — and he would — her sisters would see the mess she'd made and the sympathy would pour from them with such force she would be overwhelmed and drowning instantly.

She wished she could just disappear. Instead, when she heard Jonas working the lock, she reached out to him. *Please don't let the others see in, Jonas.* It cost what little pride she had left, but she made the plea. Her sisters didn't need to see just how weak and useless she really was. Jonas already knew. Maybe they did, too, maybe that was why they always bailed her out, thought for her, directed her and babied her. She hadn't been able to bear the look on her mother's face so she asked her to leave along with the aunts. If one more person fussed over her, she might jump off the balcony.

"Sarah, Kate, just stay out," Jonas barked, holding the door closed. "I'm not going to hurt her. She's quite capable of putting me in my place if she needs to. Go away and let me talk to her alone."

"She's fragile, Jonas. Don't be such a bear with her." Kate's voice was low and anxious. "You can't just barge in on her and yell at her."

"Why would you think I'd do that?" Jonas asked.

"Maybe using the 'F' word was a clue," Kate said.

Hannah found the churning in her stomach easing a bit. Jonas was not going to treat her as if she might break apart any second — even if she already had.

Jonas slipped inside, shut the door and turned the lock. She stayed very still as he surveyed the damage. Her full-length antique free-standing mirror was shattered, only two small, jagged shards hanging from the frame. The glass was everywhere, scattered all over the floor, pieces even sticking up like small daggers, glittering like silver.

"Don't move, baby," he said. "Not one step."

"In spite of what everyone thinks, I'm not suicidal, just irrational." Her voice came out in a husky whisper, one the doctors said she would have to get used to. She kept her hand in front of her face. He'd seen her swathed in bandages, but she'd taken them off to look and the sight had been hideous. She didn't want to look in a mirror and she didn't want to see her reflection in his eyes. Most of all, she didn't want to see pity on his face.

Jonas stepped through the glass and caught her up, cradling her in his arms. "On the bed or out on the balcony?"

She blushed. Not just her face, her entire body. His breath was warm on her neck. Her robe had gaped open and he was staring down at the slashes standing out so raw and angry across her bare flesh. "Jonas. Don't look."

"Why the hell not?"

"Stop swearing at me. And you know why.

It's aw-awful." She closed her eyes. She would not stammer. She refused to be any more of a mess then she already was.

Jonas took her to the edge of the French doors and set her on her feet, his hands going to the front of her robe and sweeping it open before she could stop him. "I'm so fucking glad you're alive, do you really think I care what the stitches look like? I want to see if you're healing properly. The docs didn't want you to come home yet."

All the color drained from her face. She gasped. A single strangled cry escaped as she attempted to step back and jerk her robe closed, but he held the material apart ruthlessly.

"I don't know, baby," he mused, "it still looks painful." The pads of his fingers brushed the curve of her breast. "Has Libby taken a look at this? Because she needs to. It's very red. Could be infected."

Only a few short weeks earlier, Jonas had touched her breasts, his mouth had been right where his hands were, hot and hungry with need and desire. She expected to feel his revulsion and outrage, but instead, there was calm acceptance mixed with worry for her and approval of the rate her sisters were healing her. Not so fast that it drained all of their energy and left them unable to function, yet she was alive and the wounds were healing from the inside out.

But not where anyone could see.

She felt very vulnerable standing there naked, her robe held open while he inspected the wounds as clinically as if she was a broken statue glued together rather than a real flesh-and-blood woman. She didn't know which was actually worse. The wounds traveled from her face to her belly. Horrible deep slashes and punctures, shallow ones that ripped across her pale skin.

"What did Libby say about children?" His voice turned gruff. His fingertips drifted up to her throat, slid over the gashes there, traced a path along her breast, down her ribs to her stomach and finally to her abdomen, where he lay his palm, fingers splayed wide. "Can we still have children, Hannah?"

She blinked back tears at the rasping in his voice. His emotion didn't spill over to swamp her, but it was there, buried deep, and she heard it in his voice. "There is no 'we,' Jonas, there can't be."

"Don't give me a lot of bullshit right now, Hannah." He let go of her robe and transferred his grip to her arms, yanking her to him hard, bringing her body tightly against his. He buried his face in her neck. "I thought I had this under control. You're safe. Damn it, you're safe."

Jonas spoke out loud, needing to hear the words, but a tremor ran through him, the terrible rush of unspeakable terror as images filled his mind. He pressed his face tighter against her neck, crushing her in his arms, trying to hold her close enough — tight enough — to wipe out the inconceivable. He thought he was over that moment other than when it haunted his dreams. Each night he woke in a sweat, her name on his lips, bile in his throat and a gun in his hand. But seeing her body brought back every slash and brutal stab of the knife. He knew where every mark would be. How long, how deep — in utter horror he had watched the scene unfold on television until his mind had gone numb.

For one moment he couldn't breathe. He'd thought he was past it all, yet here he was clinging to her, needing comfort, instead of providing it for her. She was ragged. He'd expected that. He hadn't expected her withdrawal from him, or her denial of their relationship, but he should have. He had to shift back, get his feet under him and sort it all out.

Hannah stood frozen in his embrace, shocked beyond words — even of comfort — and it was her natural inclination to comfort others. Jonas was a rock. Always. He'd been so stoic in the hospital, it had never occurred to her that he'd been so terrified. Her hands went, of their own volition, to the nape of his neck, tunneling into his hair. "I'm all right, Jonas," she lied.

He lifted his head and pressed his brow to hers. "Not yet, honey, but you will be. And you didn't answer my question. What did Libby say about children?"

Hannah couldn't make herself deny she loved him, not when he was so shaken. "I can have children, Jonas, but . . ." She trailed off, both hands in his hair. He was trembling, his powerful body revealing the extent of his fears. Somehow, because he needed her to be strong, she found she could be. Maybe she could be all right again. Maybe she could find a way to believe in herself. Hannah Drake. Who was she? How did she define herself?

"I'm so glad, baby. It would have been okay. I would love a child we adopted, you know. I thought about that a lot, Hannah, so if Libby is worried that it could hurt you, or be dangerous, we'll go the adoption route."

She shook her head, tightening her fingers in his hair. He wasn't going to listen to her about ending their relationship. As far as he was concerned, they had crossed a bridge together and there was no going back. She honestly didn't know how she felt about it.

He pressed a kiss against the jagged wound splitting one side of her face in two. "You sit out on the balcony while I clean this up. I don't want you walking around barefoot."

"Please don't say anything to my sisters." She stepped away from him, drawing the robe tightly around her, careful to keep her back to the ocean. She could hear the helicopter circling overhead. "I wish the photographers would go away."

He grinned at her. "Well, you're doing wonders for the economy around here. Prices for rooms have tripled and even quadrupled in Sea Haven. Especially when it comes to rooms for the paparazzi. Everyone is trying to protect you in their own way. The Salt Bar and Grill where Trudy Garret works has put up a new sign. NO SHIRT, NO SHOES, NO SERVICE, NO PAPARAZZI, not that it seems to deter them. None of your sisters can step outside without being photographed."

"Hand me my blanket." She indicated the one at the foot of the bed.

Jonas crunched more glass under his feet as he caught the soft blanket up and handed it to her. Hannah draped it over her head like a cape with a hood, hiding her face in the folds.

She turned then, keeping to the shadows of one corner, but lifted her hand and brought in the wind from the sea. It rushed in, hard and fast, pushing at the helicopter so the pilot had no choice but to take it away from the house. "If I keep the wind blowing strong, they can't come at me from the air and I can get a little peace." She pushed her hair behind her ear and sank into the chair she'd put in the corner of the balcony where she could face the sea.

She found it endearing that the townspeople would seek to find ways to drive the photographers and reporters away. It was one of the things she loved about Sea Haven. While it was true that they knew one another's business, they were also open and friendly and supportive through every crisis or every wonderful event.

She glanced down to the beach and was shocked to see Joley and Elle striding along the sand in plain view of the cameras. Elle raised her hands as if in fun, gesturing wildly toward Joley, who turned and blew a kiss up toward Hannah. Hannah bit down on her lip. God only knew what her two younger sisters might do. It didn't take long to find out. The sand rose up in answer to Elle's graceful hands.

Hannah's wind took the grains of sand, whirling them into tight eddies that swayed in tall columns across the beach, slamming into camera lenses, pummeling the men and women trying so desperately to get a shot of Hannah's ruined face. The wind rose, blasting the particles harder so that they bit into flesh and covered hair, got into mouths and equipment, driving the intruders away.

Hannah shook her head as Joley and Elle joined hands, turned toward her and made a sweeping bow. Hannah couldn't help smiling. They were so outrageous. She gestured toward the bluff above them where cameras with zoom lenses focused relentlessly on the Drake house. The two girls looked at one another and the wind carried their laughter up to Hannah.

"What are they up to?" Jonas demanded, after first using a hand vac, dumping shards of the mirror into the wastebasket and coming out onto the balcony. "That's their witchy laugh, the one that always tells me they're up to no good."

"I have to agree," Hannah said.

"Usually you're right there in the middle of the trouble," he added. "The three of you inherited the trouble gene." He rested his hands on the railing and peered down at the two Drake women, who faced the north this time, toward the long cliffs out in the ocean where birds by the thousands rested above the waves and white sprays of foam. The birds lifted almost at the same time, filling the air with flapping wings widespread, wheeling in the air and heading straight toward the bluff. The sky darkened with the migration. The sound of gulls shrieking mixed with human cries of alarm as the birds dove down toward the photographers, driving them back. A veritable cloudburst of bird droppings landed on the cliffs, coating the cameras, people and cars in the vicinity.

Jonas leaned over the railing and whistled. "Wow! Buddy! Don't be looking up. Good one, Joley, perfect bull's-eye! Eww, that was just nasty, must taste like crap."

Hannah shook her head. "You're as bad as my sisters."

"Well, those nasty little rats can go take pictures of someone else." It felt good to find some humor in the situation. The Drakes had their own way of handling things and it was probably better than his way. He wanted to smash all the expensive equipment and feel the satisfaction of his fist hitting faces. Being an elected official —

the sheriff — it probably wasn't the best or most appropriate idea.

"I guess we should be worried about bird flu, although maybe if they all get it, everyone would have a little peace for a while."

"Elle will have that covered," Hannah said. "Let them vent. It's so much safer with pranks."

He turned to face her, studying her face hidden so carefully inside the blanket. "Like the hat trick you were always pulling. What did you want to do instead of robbing me of my hats?"

She shrugged. "I have a terrible temper, Jonas. Most of us do. Not Libby, of course, you'd have to be really awful to get her riled, but it's just safer to do funny or harmless things than vent with anger."

"So you were really angry with me," he persisted.

"Sometimes."

"What did you throw at the mirror?"

A knock at the door had him frowning and her sighing.

"Hannah, it's time for you to rest." Libby stuck her head in the room, eyes suspicious as she looked at Jonas. "You don't want to overtire her."

Hannah couldn't help glancing at the floor to see if the remains of the mirror were picked up. Not only had the glass disappeared, but Jonas had taken apart the frame and stowed it out of sight. She flashed him a grateful smile. "I'm just sitting here, Libby."

"Well, you can't overdo, hon. You should still be in the hospital." Libby made several gestures toward Jonas, trying to hint to him to leave.

He crossed his arms over his chest and leveled a look at her. "I'll make certain she doesn't overdo it," he assured.

Libby scowled at him. "Visitors tire her out, Jonas."

"Fortunately, I'm not a visitor," he returned smoothly, "I'm family."

Libby glanced at her watch. "I really think she needs to lie down and take a nap."

Jonas's eyebrow rose. "Really? What do you think, Hannah?"

It was an opportunity to get rid of him. On the other hand, Hannah was tired of being treated like a child and he was asking her opinion instead of making it for her. She was sick of everyone making her decisions.

"I'm not tired, Libby. When I am, I'll send Jonas away."

"Are you sure?"

Hannah nodded, afraid to trust her voice.

It was husky enough and she was suddenly close to tears. She had a vision of her sisters gathering downstairs. *Poor Hannah, we have to come up with a future for her.* Sometimes she thought she heard the house whisper it. She turned her face away and closed her eyes, sorrow tearing through her. Were there stages she needed to go through as a victim? Because right now, all she wanted to do was cry. She felt confused and apprehensive and wanted to be alone — although she would be terrified if no one else was in the house with her.

Libby hesitated, shot Jonas a warning glare and then went out, closing the door behind her. At once the whispers started up again.

"I tried, but he wouldn't leave," Libby said.

"She wasn't in tears, was she?"

That was Kate and the anxiety in her voice made Hannah wince. She glanced up at Jonas with a small moue and a slight shrug. "They think I can't cope."

"Show them you can."

Hannah sighed. "You see everything in black and white, Jonas."

He rested his hip on the railing. "Does that mean you can't cope? It's no big deal, Hannah. It was a vicious crime, it's natural to have to have recovery time."

She held up her hand. "I don't want to talk about it yet."

"Well, at least come over here and wave at Joley and Elle before they go ballistic on us. Joley's flapping her arms like a bird. Do you think she believes she can fly?"

Hannah peered over the railing. Her sisters were gesturing wildly, Joley doing exaggerated sign language and Elle writing in the sand. "What in the world are they doing now?"

"Trying to tell you something, obviously. Why doesn't Elle just use telepathy like a normal Drake?"

"Because I asked them all to stay out of my head. I don't want to risk catching their emotions or have them feeling mine."

"You talked to me."

"I was desperate. I didn't want them to see the broken mirror." She leaned over the balcony railing so far he wrapped his arm around her, blanket and all. "What is Elle writing?"

Far below on the beach, Elle was dragging a piece of driftwood through the wet sand, making three-foot-tall letters.

"That's an 'R' and a 'U,' " Jonas translated. "And why didn't you want your sisters to see the mirror?"

"It's getting difficult to be around them, Jonas. They . . . *reek* . . . of sympathy. Sometimes I think I'm drowning in it."

"Of course they're sympathetic, Hannah. They love you."

"I know that. Don't you think I know that? They'd walk through fire for me. I know how I'd feel if this had happened to one of them, but it didn't. It happened to me and I can't breathe with all the pity in this house."

"Compassion," he corrected, narrowing his eyes as he stared down at the dramatic writing below. "That's a double 'S' she's drawn there — or a snake. Maybe she's asking if I'm a snake. R U a snake? And they have compassion for you. They were all terrified, honey, just like I was, the way your parents and aunts were. It's natural they want to look after you."

"I know." Now she felt guilty. She was always guilty. She swam in guilt. She looked up at the sky and wished she could fly away.

Jonas tugged her closer to him, bringing her beneath his shoulder. "Your sisters have always smothered you, Hannah. They can't help themselves. Maybe you're just a little more sensitive to it right now. And that's all right. Tell them to give you some space." He glanced back to the beach. "Joley is standing on her head. She really has lost her mind."

Hannah looked down and sucked in her breath. "It's says 'Russian.' Elle's writing the word 'Russian.' Joley's wiping it out so if a photographer is still around no one can see. The Russian must be somewhere close."

"How would they know?"

"Joley would know. He did something to her — marked her in some way. She can feel him and sometimes he talked to her." Hannah waved her hands toward the beach below and the wind kicked up the sand, spreading it across the letters, effectively hiding the evidence. "I know he saved my life, Jonas, but what I don't know is why. He's too interested in Joley. At first I thought it was because he's a man and all men are interested in her."

Jonas kissed the top of her head. "Joley's sexy. I figured out pretty fast I was going to spend a lot of time beating up the boys in her school if I didn't put out a few warnings. And just for your information, Joley doesn't appeal to me at all that way. I've never wanted anyone but you."

"You're such a liar. You've always been a terrible flirt. And I remember the night you had an invasion of frogs and one of your little hussies came flying out your bedroom window."

"I *knew* you did that." He laughed, and tipped up her face.

Hannah pulled away from him before he could kiss her. She couldn't stand him looking at the ruin of her face. She couldn't stand to think of him seeing her body. Why hadn't she thought herself beautiful when she had the chance? She was always dieting and working out to get the right body for the runway instead of enjoying what she had. She'd never looked at herself and liked what she saw. Never. Not since she realized she couldn't talk in public and crowds made her panic. Not since she realized she wasn't anything like her beautiful, accomplished sisters.

"What's wrong, Hannah?"

She sank back into the chair. She was not about to tell him she was thinking he'd never see her as beautiful again. Would she ever stop whining to herself? She pushed her own personal grief aside and searched for something substantial, something real, to worry about. Something true so he wouldn't know she was so shallow.

She forced herself to meet his eyes and voiced a concern she'd had since the party in New York. "I'm worried about what Prakenskii might want with Joley. He and Nikitin both mentioned her right before . . . it . . . happened. And Prakenskii asked me if she was a spell-singer."

Jonas blinked. He wasn't exactly certain what spell-singing was. Joley had a voice that could have belonged to an angel or a devil. Either way she could mesmerize a crowd. But Hannah was worried; it wasn't that difficult to read her.

She pressed a hand to her head. "I was running from him. I felt so threatened. I kept thinking if I got outside, I'd be all right. I remember being afraid for Joley."

"Breathe, honey. Just take a breath and let it out. Libby said your memory might begin to return, but if it doesn't, it isn't a big deal. We're going to figure things out eventually. Give me a clue about spell-singing. What does that mean?"

"Sergei Nikitin has been following Joley around for a long time now, trying to get an introduction, trying to find a way to get to her."

"He wrote a couple of letters to her, but her manager intercepted them. Fortunately he always hands over letters to security, even though Nikitin has won some kind of celebrity status and pretends he's a legitimate businessman. He likes to be in the 'in' crowd and Joley is definitely 'in.' Anyone seen with her is written up in every tabloid around the world. She's news, baby, and Nikitin wants to rub shoulders with society. He thinks he can hide what he is that way."

"So far he's managed to do it," Hannah pointed out. "I think it's more than that, though, or why would Prakenskii ask me if she's a spell-singer?"

"You haven't explained to me just what that is yet."

"It's dangerous, Jonas. She could be potentially deadly. Sound can cause a lot of damage and it can even kill. Joley is capable of that, not to mention she can take a roomful of people — a stadium full of people — and get them to do what she wants."

Jonas was stunned. He sat there trying to keep his mouth from hanging open. He'd always accepted the things the Drakes could do as something good. Even with Hannah sending the wind to rescue him, she'd saved his life. He hadn't thought too much about the others, not quite so lucky, the ones who had been caught by her fury.

"Joley's too strong to be used that way."

"Is she, Jonas? I don't know, but Prakenskii was able to keep me from dying and I should have been dead. Libby might have been able to keep me alive for that long without aid, but I don't honestly know if she could have. It took strength and endurance and a lot of power. A *lot* of power. He's already marked Joley. And he wears her down, whispering to her at night. Only a handful of people in the world know what a spell-singer is and what they can do. Ilya Prakenskii knows and that night he and Nikitin wanted me to go back to the hotel with them. What do you think Joley would do if Nikitin put a gun to my head?"

Jonas went very still. "You don't think he could have arranged the attack on you and then had Prakenskii save your life so Joley would feel as if she owed him, do you?"

"Prakenskii doesn't talk much, but when he saved Aleksandr's life, he told us we owed him then. I imagine he feels this is a much larger debt."

"Could he be a spell-singer?" Because if Joley could mesmerize a stadium full of people into doing what she wanted, couldn't Ilya Prakenskii mesmerize a couple into murder?

"I see where you're going with it and I just don't think he could hide that from us. We've been in his head too much. One of us would have known."

Another small knock on the door had Jonas slipping his hand inside his jacket to grasp his gun.

Sarah stepped in with a wide, forced smile. "Hannah, I thought maybe you'd like something to eat. You really should keep up your strength."

"I should, too," Jonas reminded her, relaxing. "If you're bringing Hannah a tray, bring me one, too, please."

Sarah's gaze swept the room. She frowned. "Hannah? Where's your mirror?"

"I had a little run-in with it," Jonas said. "She loves me anyway, don't you, baby?" He crouched down beside Hannah and took her hand, looking up at Sarah with a wry smile. "Guess that earns me seven years of bad luck."

Kate poked her head in the door. "Hannah, you have a visitor. Ilya Prakenskii is here to see you."

A shiver slid down Hannah's spine. She couldn't hide her uneasiness from Jonas, not when he was so close and holding her hand.

"I'll go down," he said.

Hannah pulled her hand away, sick of being coddled. Yes, she was frightened, but Joley was *her* sister, her responsibility, and she wasn't going to send Jonas down while she cowered in her room.

"While you get dressed," he added. "Don't take all day."

"No." Sarah shook her head. "She doesn't need to go down. Stay here, Hannah. Kate and I can go with Jonas and see what he wants."

"No, I need Hannah to come with me. I want her impressions of anything Prakenskii says or does. She's the strongest empath among you."

"Elle and Libby are empathic and Elle is stronger than any of us," Sarah corrected.

"Libby is all about healing, Sarah," Jonas said, a bite of annoyance in his tone. "And Elle's volatile. If Prakenskii is here for something other than checking on Hannah, I don't want Elle starting a war. Keep Joley and Elle far away from him."

"Hannah can't go down," Sarah said. "I forbid it."

"Hannah." Jonas turned to her, his tone absolutely neutral, his gaze gentle. "You tell me what you want to do, baby. I'd prefer you there, but if you'd rather not — say the word."

"Jonas," Sarah hissed. "Stop pushing her. You're always pushing her. She's barely out of the hospital. She needs looking after."

Hannah moistened her suddenly dry lips with her tongue. Her heart pounded hard in her chest and little jackhammers tripped at her temples, but this needed to be done.

Not by Jonas or Sarah. But by her. She owed him a debt and more, she wanted to look into his eyes and read him the way she could most people, because if he presented a threat to Joley, they all needed to know.

"Jonas is right, Sarah. I want to see Prakenskii myself. I need to thank him for saving my life, and like Jonas, I want to see if I can read him. I spent a lot of time connected to him."

"And he has a path to your spirit, Hannah. To your soul. He knows who you are and what you can do."

"That's true," Hannah admitted, "but at the same time, I have a path to his spirit. He can't block all of us and I need to find out information."

"But . . ." Sarah protested.

"Get dressed, baby," Jonas said decisively. "We'll meet you downstairs." He held the door open. "Sarah? Kate? Let's go see what Prakenskii wants."

11

"Ilya, good to see you again." Jonas extended his hand toward the Russian.

Ilya rose from the chair where Libby had seated him and shook the sheriff's hand. He nodded to Kate and Sarah. "I had hoped to see Hannah."

"She'll be down in a few minutes," Jonas assured him. "She's doing much better."

"I was surprised they allowed her home. Another few days in the hospital would have been good for her," Prakenskii said.

"She needed to be home with us," Sarah said. "And Libby is a doctor. She makes certain Hannah is well cared for."

Jonas studied the Russian. In the hospital, he had been too consumed with Hannah to do anything but stay by her side and will her to live, but now he looked closely at the man who had saved her life. Ilya Prakenskii gave Jonas the impression of a caged tiger, quiet and watchful, power and lethal intent coiled and ready to spring with razor-sharp claws. It was impossible to try to read behind his piercing eyes. Ice cold, dagger sharp, Prakenskii's eyes revealed absolutely nothing, not even to a professional like Jonas.

"And it's easy to protect her here, on your own home turf," Prakenskii said, his voice casual. There was nothing casual about the sweep of his gaze as it went around the room, taking in every detail. He focused for a moment on the intricate mosaic tile at the entryway. A muscle ticked in his jaw and his gaze met Sarah's briefly before moving toward the entrance. A polite smile showed white teeth and nothing more as he rose. "There you are. It's good to see you up and around, Hannah."

She had dressed in a long flowing skirt and a long-sleeved blouse. Jonas closed his eyes briefly as she moved into the room. To him, she was beautiful — utterly — absolutely beautiful. The scars were jagged and vicious, bright red and raw, seaming her face and down her neck in angry patches, but it didn't matter. Hannah appeared ethereal to him, mysterious and sexy and the epitome of feminine courage. She had hidden from him — her sisters — reporters and photographers, but had refused to hide from a potential enemy. Her shoulders were straight, her hair streaming down in long spirals, and even without makeup, even with the horrible wounds still so fresh, she appeared elegant, graceful and welcoming.

Pride swelled in him and Jonas came to his feet, crossed instantly to her side and swept an arm around her waist, his gaze meeting Prakenskii's. It was both a warning and a declaration between men.

Prakenskii took Hannah's outstretched hand and bowed low. "You are healing nicely. Soon, there will be no evidence. Are you sleeping well? Sometimes, after these incidents, one has trouble."

To Jonas's surprise, Hannah told the truth. "I have trouble, but Jonas and Sarah both warned me I might, so I wasn't surprised or upset by it." She indicated his chair. "Please sit down. Would you care for some tea?"

"I'd like that, thank you."

Hannah waved her hand toward the kitchen and seated herself opposite Prakenskii. "It was quite unnecessary for you to come all this way to check on me, but I appreciate it." She smiled at the man, but her hand slid down Jonas's arm until her fingers were linked with his and she was squeezing so tight her knuckles were white.

"Of course I would want to know how you were doing," Prakenskii said. "When one develops such a connection, the interest is always there."

His accent put a twist to the words and his gaze remained steady on her face. Sarah stirred uncomfortably and Jonas felt a surge of power in the room. He couldn't tell where it came from, but Ilya Prakenskii swung his head alertly, a wolf catching the scent of prey. Jonas watched him closely and he could see everything shift and focus beneath that calm demeanor. Joley walked into the room. It seemed as though everyone held their breath. The tension ratcheted up another notch.

He knew. Did you see that, Hannah? He felt her before she came in.

Prakenskii's head swung back, just briefly, so that those piercing eyes could flick from Jonas to Hannah, and for the first time, there was surprise.

He knows. Hannah's husky voice slid into Jonas's mind. *He knows you're telepathic and it surprised him.*

It surprised me as well, Jonas admitted truthfully.

Prakenskii once again rose to his feet. "Joley. It is always a pleasure to see you."

She didn't offer her hand, but smiled and

inclined her head, queen to peasant, her dark brown eyes going almost black as her gaze swept the Russian from head to toe. "Don't stand, Prakenskii, it isn't necessary."

"It is, however, courteous," he said with a slight bow.

Joley blushed, the color sweeping up her neck into her face, and her eyes glittered, twin points of black obsidian. The floor shifted beneath their feet, lights flickered, curtains fluttered, even the walls undulated in sweeping waves as the room swelled with power. A picture above the fireplace fell. It stopped abruptly in midair and then, before it could hit the floor, rose leisurely to hang neatly back in place. Everyone in the room went still as they absorbed Prakenskii's obvious reprimand.

Hannah's hand slipped from Jonas's and she rose with her usual grace, crossing to Joley, slipping between Prakenskii and her sister to slide her arm around Joley's waist. "Thank you for dealing so efficiently with the reporters, Joley. You made me laugh and few things make me laugh these days."

"I enjoyed it, although nothing stops them for long. They've surrounded the place. The only reason the fence hasn't been torn down and trampled is because we have a security force guarding it."

The tea tray floated in with several steaming mugs and she directed it toward Prakenskii, as if every day of the week people saw floating trays. "The cookies are Libby's, so they're particularly good for you, along with tasting great. The honey is in the small creamer."

The Russian deftly plucked a mug and a cookie, lifting the cup toward Hannah in a salute as he reseated himself. He didn't outwardly appear in the least upset over his less than enthusiastic welcome from Joley, but the tension in the room remained. "The place is overrun not only with photographers and reporters, but also your fans. In the crowd it is impossible to tell who is friend or enemy."

Jonas leaned forward, snagging Hannah's hand and tugging until she sat beside him. He shifted slightly, enough to put his body in a position to defend Hannah should the need arise. He didn't trust Prakenskii, not with an aura of danger surrounding him and every single Drake sister on alert. He wished Sarah and Kate had kept Joley out of the mix. Joley and Prakenskii obviously rubbed each other the wrong way and he could see, quite clearly, that in spite of Prakenskii's expressionless features, a storm lurked below the surface when his gaze rested on her.

He's angry with Joley for some reason, Hannah confirmed, *but I can't tell why. Not just angry, Jonas, he's livid with her. I can catch glimpses of it, like a white-hot rage, and it isn't even buried all that well. I don't think he cares if I know or not.*

It was an unexpected complication. And Prakenskii's veiled warnings annoyed Jonas. "If you know something, just say it, straight out, Prakenskii. Why would you think an enemy would be in Sea Haven? They're dead."

Sarah gasped and Kate made a sound of distress. Libby frowned and missed taking a cup of tea from the tray as it passed her.

"I don't think it's necessary to discuss this in front of Hannah," Sarah intervened.

Hannah gripped Jonas's hand harder. They were doing it again, protecting her. Had she always been such a baby that they felt the need to wrap her up in cotton and shield her from every danger? Or was it the attack? Had it changed her sisters as much as it had changed her?

Jonas laid his other hand over hers, trapping her fingers and hiding the white knuckles from Prakenskii's sharp gaze. "Of course Hannah wants to know whether or not Ilya believes there is further danger to her. We all do."

"I don't think you believe for one moment that the danger to Hannah is past," Prakenskii said. "It read like a hit to me. And hits, as amateurish as that one was, are usually paid for and ordered by another individual hiding in the shadows. But you know that, Mr. Harrington."

"Jonas?" Hannah looked at him, forcing him to meet her inquiring gaze.

"Damn it, Hannah, don't look at me like that."

"Don't swear at her, Jonas," Libby snapped.

Both ignored her.

"It isn't over?"

"You didn't think it was either, so don't even go there. That couple were idiots. Like Prakenskii said, amateurs. Someone else had to be behind it. Why do you think you're not in the hospital right now? I needed you where you had protection around the clock."

"Did it occur to you that if I'm in danger, and you bring me here, so are my sisters?" Hannah hissed the words between her teeth at him, her bright hair crackling with electricity and the liquid in her tea mug boiling.

"Sarah is a security expert. Your sisters are

all psychic and they have enough powers to help. We can see what's coming at us here."

"I'm not going to put my sisters in jeopardy, Jonas, not for one minute. You should have told me immediately what you thought."

"I agree with Hannah," Prakenskii said, joining the fray without a qualm. "The others shouldn't be placed in harm's way. It only makes for more targets and therefore more suspects."

Joley threw her tea mug at him, her aim deadly accurate. Prakenskii waved his hand and the missile and liquid stopped in midair. He flashed her one, deadly look, his blue eyes darkening to a turbulent sea. He snapped something at her in Russian.

Hannah made a small strangled sound and Joley's breath was a hiss of warning.

What did he say to her? Did he just threaten her? "If you have something to say to Joley, Prakenskii, say it to everyone. If you're threatening her . . ."

He told her to stop being childish, Hannah reassured Jonas.

"Joley is perfectly capable of looking after herself with me, aren't you?" Prakenskii said.

"Absolutely," Joley acknowledged and waved her hand toward her tea mug. Liquid filled the cup and it floated back. "Don't worry, Jonas, I'll be fine." She snapped something back at Prakenskii in his language and then switched to English. "And for your information, Hannah is our sister. We're not about to cower in the corner while she's in danger, so go beat your chest somewhere else."

What did she say? Jonas asked.

She called him a few vile names.

"One of these days, Joley, I'm going to retaliate and then what are you going to do?" Prakenskii asked quietly, his gaze holding hers.

"Don't," Hannah intervened. "I need you to tell me what you think is going on, Prakenskii. Joley, please." *See, Jonas, he keeps directing the focus back toward Joley. What does he want from her? I'm afraid for her. Could this be about Joley?*

Jonas turned the idea over in his mind. It felt wrong to him. Everything so far felt wrong. He was missing the crucial piece of the puzzle that would snap everything into focus for him.

"Please accept my apologies, Hannah," Prakenskii said. "It was not my intention to upset you. I wanted to assure myself that you were doing better and to warn Mr. Harrington that I still feel a threat is imminent.

Unfortunately I can't tell where it's coming from or who it's directed toward."

"Why would you warn us?" Jonas asked bluntly.

Prakenskii sighed and put down the mug of tea. "Perhaps it is as simple as Hannah's sister is marrying one of the few men in the world I call friend." His gaze strayed to where Joley stood rigid against the wall. "Or perhaps I wanted to see, one more time, whether the reason I can no longer sleep at night is worth it."

Joley pressed tighter against the wall as if making herself small, yet there was defiance in every line of her body. "I don't owe you any explanation whatsoever."

"Then I call in one of the favors your family owes to me. It is not your personal debt, but a debt of honor your family owes to me."

Joley's face went pale. "For that? We owe you two lives, yet you'll give up one for a simple explanation of my behavior? You aren't the brightest bulb on the planet, are you?" Her melodic voice held the whip of insult and she tossed her head defiantly. "I thought you knew everything. You're not nearly as powerful as you want us all to believe you are."

"Too powerful to be goaded by a rude, ungrateful coward who is still a child playing at being an adult."

But her insults were getting to him. The balance in the room had shifted from the Drakes to Prakenskii and both Hannah and Jonas felt it. Hannah intervened again. "I'm the one who owes you, Mr. Prakenskii. If you would be so kind as to tell me what your favor entails, I'll do my best to help you."

"I would like an explanation —"

"Don't. Don't ask," Joley said. "Please don't ask."

"I gave you every opportunity to explain."

"You haunted me day and night, *tormented* me. Made me angry. It isn't your business. It's stupid using up a favor from our family for such a trivial thing."

"Trivial." He stood up, and his rage poured into the room, white-hot, just as Hannah had said, a volcano erupting, so that the walls bulged out, unable to contain the red and black energy bursting into the room. The ground shifted and shadows moved over the mosaic tiles. Feminine voices cried out in eerie warning, rising from the floor and the walls.

The Drake sisters leapt to their feet, and Jonas put his body between the women and the furious Russian. He looked at no one but Joley. The two of them stood, their gazes locked in a battle no one else was part of or could understand.

"Stop!" Hannah glared at them. "Please sit down, Mr. Prakenskii." When he didn't move, she stepped closer. "Ilya. Please."

Prakenskii slowly pulled his gaze from Joley's and took his seat. Joley shook her head as everyone else visibly relaxed and then she turned on her heel and left the room. The tension instantly lessened.

"Please accept my apologies once again, Hannah," the Russian said. "I should have been more careful. I rarely lose my temper. I have no excuse." He lifted the mug of tea to his mouth, blew to calm the boiling liquid and took a drink.

"I don't understand. Why are you so angry with Joley? Is she in some kind of danger?"

Hannah forced her mind open, reaching — stretching — to catch a glimpse of the truth in him. She felt a barrage of emotions, the intensity nearly overwhelming, but just as quickly, he shored up his defenses and became as cold as ice.

"Joley deliberately puts herself in danger."

Hannah sank back into the chair and glanced briefly up at Jonas. Prakenskii believed he was telling the truth. She caught that as well as the accompanying temper pushed down deep. "What do you mean?"

For a moment she could barely breathe. Was someone after her sister, the way someone had wanted her dead?

Sarah opened her mouth but Hannah held up an imperious hand, effectively stopping anything she might say. Hannah never took charge and it shocked her sisters.

Joley stepped back into the room, her dark eyes blazing. "You want to know about the pictures in the tabloid? Me with my latest lover?" She glared at Prakenskii, both hands on her hips, tossing her head so that her hair went flying in all directions. "It's publicity. The man is history already, so you don't need his name, but a photographer followed us to the house Tyson bought for Libby and caught us. Big deal."

Prakenskii never took his eyes off her face when Joley made her declaration. A long slow hiss escaped and he stood in one fluid movement, with all the grace and predatory menace and deadly threat of a fully grown tiger. "When one calls in a favor, you tell the truth. I demand the truth and the name of this man who had his hands and mouth all over you."

"What difference does it make who he is?" Joley's chin was up, her eyes throwing off sparks.

"I would not want to kill the wrong man."

"Whoa. Stop right there." Jonas jumped up. "You can't make threats like that."

"It is a matter of honor." There was no emotion in his voice whatsoever. Prakenskii shrugged as if a life didn't matter at all to him.

The Drakes looked at one another, puzzled, and then at Joley. She sucked in her breath. "Ilya," she began and then stopped, looking helplessly at Libby.

Ilya Prakenskii followed her gaze and frowned. "You owe me the truth and I've asked for it. One of you needs to provide it."

Hannah looked around at her sisters. "I do owe you a tremendous debt, we all do, but this is not my secret to tell. If it was, I would give you the information that you ask for, but I'm sorry, I can't."

Prakenskii looked around the room at their faces. "I have asked that a debt of honor be repaid. You are refusing me?"

Libby shook her head. "No, we're not." Color swept into her face, but she kept her gaze locked with his. "I was with Tyson at his house and someone wanted to harm him — us. The man took pictures of the two of us. I'm a doctor and I'm not used to tabloids and the terrible things they do to a person's life. Joley dyed her hair and took the heat, pretending the pictures were of her, so my reputation wouldn't be damaged," Libby said. "It was a generous and loving thing for her to do."

Prakenskii stood absolutely still in the middle of the room. His gaze rested on Joley's averted face. "It was dangerous. And she knows it was. Look at me." When she didn't, his voice hardened. "Look at me."

Joley lifted her gaze to his.

"You should have told me when I asked."

"It wasn't your business."

Hannah held up her hand. "Why does he keep saying you're doing something dangerous, Joley?"

Joley shrugged. "I don't know. He thinks I'm drawing all the crazies to me."

Hannah went pale and reached back for Jonas, unaware that she did so. "I know you have precog, Ilya. If Joley's in danger, come out and say so. Tell us where the danger is coming from."

"I have said so. And if I knew where it was coming from, I'd eliminate it," Prakenskii said. "I know you don't trust me, Hannah, none of you do, and it doesn't really matter, but whoever arranged the attack on you was making a point. It was brutal and vicious and direct. They tried to destroy your face and your body and then take your life. They'll come after you again. And Joley is drawing the same kind of attention, but why? You'll have to ask her." He spread his hands out.

He turned and headed toward the door. "I'm going to be in town awhile. I know you won't ask for my help, but you're going to get it anyway."

"Is Nikitin in town?" Jonas asked.

"Oh yes. Joley's here. The press is here. Nikitin is going to be right in the thick of things. He can do business from anywhere in the world, thanks to cell phones and computers."

"Why do you work for him?" Jonas asked.

Prakenskii shrugged. "Where else is a man like me going to find work?"

Joley's breath hissed out between her teeth. "Yeah, go crawling back and protect that worthless jerk. It isn't like you can change who you are."

Prakenskii paused at the door, his eyes glittering as they drifted over her furious face. "No, I can't. Any more than you can."

Jonas followed him outside. "Is Nikitin involved in the attack on Hannah?"

Prakenskii's eyes had gone as cold as ice. "If he was, he'd be dead. Despite what you think of me, the Drakes are under my protection. But I'm hearing rumors —

whispers — and so far I haven't been able to find out who put out the hit, but there is one." He gestured toward the crowd of people around the fence. "You have a problem here. Whoever it is will strike again and they'll do it differently this time. They got their media attention and they made their statement. Now they want her dead."

Jonas sent a long assessing look at the crush of people around the fence. Flowers, teddy bears and candles were everywhere. But he recognized a couple of the Reverend's close guardians and he spotted Rudy Venturi, a man who followed Hannah everywhere she went, right up front, clutching flowers in his hands.

"If I didn't tell you before, Prakenskii, thanks for saving her life. She told me she never would have made it without you."

Prakenskii stepped off the stairs and turned back, shaking his head, musing aloud. "It was a brutal attack, Harrington. Something's not right about it to me. That kind of hatred should be easy enough to spot." He paused and looked slowly around. "Whoever wants her dead — they're here. They're right here in her hometown and they're waiting for the chance to strike. I can feel them."

"Thanks. I'll find them."

"I don't doubt that you will — but will you be in time?"

Jonas's face hardened. "Oh, yeah. I'll be in time." He watched Prakenskii stride off, wondering just what game the man was playing — and what Joley was up to. He needed to talk to her and fast. The last thing he wanted was to add another complication to this mess.

He took a deep breath and let it out, Prakenskii's warning sinking in as he took another slow, careful look around the crowd. Jonas felt it, too. Prakenskii wasn't blowing smoke to make himself important, something evil lurked in the air.

Down near the gate, Matt Granite, Kate's fiancé, gestured for him. Matt was standing in front of Rudy Venturi. Rudy was small and slight, with bright, dyed hair pulled up into spikes, with a nondescript face. Without the hair it would be easy to miss him in a crowd. Jonas imagined most people did overlook him.

He took his time, sauntering down toward the man, not wanting to spook him. The last time they'd talked hadn't been pleasant. Jonas had interrogated him for hours after Hannah had received a threatening letter from him, calling her a stuck-up bitch — and the man had money. Lots and lots of money — money enough to hire a brutal and soul-destroying attack on Hannah. Had he been that angry over a perceived slight? Had he been so enraged that he paid for someone to slash her face and body to ribbons before the man used her as a punching bag with a knife clutched in his fist?

The images came back, vivid and sickening, so real he could count the splashes of blood spraying the room. His stomach twisted and heaved and he stumbled, his body breaking out in a sweat. He ruthlessly willed the images away and forced a smile when he stopped in front of Rudy, keeping his voice friendly.

"Are you Rudy Venturi? Hannah told me you come to all of her events." To his knowledge Hannah had never directly spoken to Venturi. Jonas had made it very clear — *ordered her* — to stay away from him. The man had a sizable trust fund, due to a car accident that left him without family and slightly brain damaged. He traveled extensively, mostly following Hannah from shoot to shoot.

Rudy nodded, clutching his flowers.

"The doctors have said she can't see anyone right now. She needs to rest," Jonas said, holding his hands out for the flowers. "Were you there when she was attacked?"

Rudy nodded as he reluctantly handed the huge bouquet to Jonas. "Sh-she should have h-had a bodyguard."

"I agree. That's why I'm here now. I'm not going to let anything happen to her," he added. "Did you see the man who stabbed her?"

Rudy pressed a hand to his mouth and nodded vigorously. "Th-there was so much b-blood. I thought she was d-dead and I wanted to d-die."

"No, she's very much alive. Did you see the man who attacked her talking to anyone else before the attack?"

Rudy slapped his hands on his thighs in agitation. "Yes! Yes. He kept sh-shaking his head back and forth. I saw him p-pull out the knife. The other man hit h-him on the back as he went up to the rope line. I t-tried to tell the policeman, but the p-preacher was yelling and the policeman went to talk to h-him instead."

"You really saw him, Rudy?" Jonas asked, working at keeping his voice calm and even. Rudy would never make a good witness, and he lived in an alternate world, but if he was telling the truth, it could be a big break for them. "You could really help Hannah if you could describe him for me."

Deliberately he stepped closer to the man,

creating a sense of urgency and camaraderie. "Here, come inside the fence and talk to me where no one else can hear you." He held the gate and watched as Rudy's chest expanded with importance and he walked onto the Drake property. "You do want to help her, don't you?"

"She's so nice. She always smiles at me. Everyone else looks right through me, but she sees me — and she smiles."

"I think she's nice, too," Jonas said. "It was good of you to bring her flowers." There were flowers all along the fence from well-wishers all over the world, but Jonas made a show of looking at the arrangement. "She really loves flowers."

Half the freaking world was sending flowers and it still hadn't occurred to Jonas to do so. All he wanted to do was hold her. Feel her. Touch her. Know she was safe. A man like Rudy Venturi knew enough to bring her flowers, but Jonas hadn't even thought of it.

"Rudy, you have to help her now. Try to remember everything you can about the man talking to Hannah's attacker."

"I don't have a new signed picture of her. She always gives me one, but she didn't this time in New York."

"Hannah gives you a picture?" He was going to shake her until her teeth rattled if that was true. She knew better than to get too close to the rope line. He'd warned her a year ago to stop signing autographs for people.

"Signed to me," Rudy continued. "It says, 'Wishing you the best, Hannah.' Every show she brings me a new one and she didn't."

Jonas clenched his teeth and bit back a curse. That was so like Hannah to smile and nod when he was discussing security and then do whatever the hell she wanted to do. "She probably had it with her and, when she was attacked, couldn't give it to you," he pointed out, keeping his voice even.

Rudy nodded and frowned a little. "But if I tell you what he looks like, you'll get me her photograph signed? It has to say, 'Wishing you the best, Hannah.' It has to say that, because she always gives me one."

He was going to do more than shake her. What the hell was she thinking? Rudy may have seemed harmless, but if she was going to single him out and make him feel special, she should have had a security guard do it for her. Jonas forced a smile. "I'll make certain it's signed, Rudy. Tell me what you remember."

Rudy scrunched up his face and made small noises, like a computer trying to access information when it was old and tired. "He was big."

Jonas waited, but Rudy looked happy with himself. "Big. Okay. I got that. What color of hair? Was it short or long?"

"Blond and short. Very short. And he looked mean. He smiled, but it wasn't real. It was the same kind of smile you have."

Jonas went still. Rudy might have suffered brain damage in the accident, and he appeared childlike, but he was still sharp, or maybe like a child, he could perceive the truth easier than an adult. "I'm sorry. I'm upset about what that man did to Hannah."

Rudy nodded. "Me, too." His brows came together as he studied Jonas's face. "I know you. You talked to me before. You weren't nice."

Jonas sighed. He'd been afraid Rudy would recognize him sooner or later. No, he hadn't been nice. He'd interrogated Rudy roughly, hammering away at him while the man became more and more confused and upset. "I'm careful of Hannah's safety and she had been getting some threatening letters."

Rudy hung his head. "I wrote to her."

"Yes, I read the letters. You wrote several." Rudy had called her some nasty names and the threat was more implied than stated.

Jonas had wanted to come across the table and smash him until he realized the man was so fixated on getting Hannah's picture that it superseded actually talking with Hannah. Or was Rudy clever enough to just appear dim and bumbling? Jonas had discovered killers were very manipulative and deceptive.

"I was angry because she didn't give me the picture. When she was in Australia, she didn't give me. She always gives me one."

"Yes, I know she does," Jonas said with as much patience as he could muster. "I'll get you one from her, signed the way you like it. What else do you remember? Did you hear anything they said? Did the man have scars? A tattoo?"

Rudy looked excited. "On his hand, right here." He rubbed his knuckles. "He had something on his hand. I'd never seen it before."

Jonas tried for several more minutes to extract information, but Rudy clearly knew nothing else. He was willing to make it up if Jonas wanted him to, for the picture, but he really didn't remember anything else.

"I'll see that she gets your flowers, Rudy, unless you want to leave them at the fence with everyone else's," Jonas offered.

Rudy took the flowers back and put them

in front of all the other arrangements, facing toward the windows of the Drake house. "She can see them here. Are you getting my picture now?"

"Yes. Would you mind standing back behind the fence now, so the security people won't be worried?"

Rudy walked back through the gate and pressed close. "You'll get it signed?"

Jonas nodded and hurried away, snagging Matt, who was patrolling the fence-line with a couple of the other men in the family and the security they'd hired.

"Have you seen Jackson around?"

Matt indicated up the hill. "He thought he saw a couple of reporters climbing the fence and went in that direction to check it out."

Jonas swore softly. "Why won't they all go home?"

"I don't think it's going to happen for a while," Matt said. "But the businesses in Sea Haven are flourishing. Every hotel is filled and the stores and cafés are making out like bandits. I think the prices are tripled."

"So I've heard." Jonas scraped his hand over his jaw. "Tell Jackson we need to review all the tapes again — the ones the stations shot of the crowd outside both the fashion show and the party."

"You think you got some new information?"

Jonas shrugged. "It's worth a shot."

12

The Drakes were waiting for him in the living room — all but Hannah. They knew he was angry by the line of his body. Sarah leapt up to intercept him as he started to the staircase, but he held up his hand to stop her, flashing her one, emotion-laden look.

"Don't," he warned.

She hesitated. "Tell us, Jonas."

He glanced over her head to Joley. "You take care of that one." He jerked his head toward her. "And I'll take care of Hannah." He cast one more furious look at Joley and hurried up the stairs to Hannah's room.

The door was closed and locked and this time he didn't bother knocking. The hell with it. He began working on the lock. Joley came up behind him with Sarah.

"You have to leave her alone, Jonas. It was too much for her, facing Prakenskii like that," Sarah said. "She needs to rest."

"And you need to mind your own business. Hannah's a grown woman. She's *my* woman." He made the declaration as he freed the lock, opened the door and stepped in, closing it on Sarah's furious face.

Hannah was pulling clothes from her dresser, tears streaming down her face as she stuffed them into the small sports bag she had open on the bed. He could see the fatigue and the dark circles around her eyes. His heart twisted in spite of his anger. Hannah was a woman of such contrasts. She appeared fragile and delicate, yet had a core of steel. She had panic attacks, yet courageously defended her sisters. She was shy, but made herself into a public icon.

He would never, as long as he lived, get over seeing her come into the room, head up, her face slashed deep and raw, but her eyes steady as she faced Prakenskii with such regal dignity. He knew it cost her pride. He knew she didn't want to be seen. But she had stood up to all of them and insisted on being treated as an adult. He had never been prouder of her. Yet here he was, about to chew her out. Again. He sighed.

She looked up, her wet eyelashes spiky, nearly breaking his heart. Her hand went defensively to her throat — where three deliberate slashes had been made, damaging her vocal cords for all time. He wanted to gather her into his arms and hold her close.

"Get out," she said. "You have to get out and leave me alone."

Fury swept through him. So much for good intentions. He slammed the door closed again, this time against Joley as she attempted to enter, and turned the lock, crossing the room in three swift strides.

"What the hell did you think you were doing, Hannah?" Jonas caught her by the shoulders and gave her a little shake. "Do you *like* playing with fire? I told you to stay away from Rudy Venturi. He may seem harmless, but he's living a fantasy and you don't know what could happen if his fantasy is disrupted."

"Jonas!" Sarah protested, from the other side of the door. "What are you doing?"

"I'm going to beat her, that's what I'm doing," Jonas snapped. "Why can't you, just once, go along with something I say, Hannah? That man is loony tunes and you're bringing him a signed photograph *personally?* I know what I'm talking about when I tell you about security, but no, you just have to defy me." His eyes darkened, blazed down at her upturned face as he gave her another shake, anger sweeping through him, building and building as the images of a knife slashing at her while he was thousands of miles away played in his head. "You do whatever everyone else tells you like some damned puppet, but me, you have to argue and defy me at every turn. Even if you're taking a chance with your life."

"Stop it, Jonas," Joley called, pounding on the door. "Stop it. You sound like you're going to hurt her."

"I'd never hurt her," Jonas declared, abruptly letting Hannah go. "Get the hell away from here, Joley. You, too, Sarah. This is between Hannah and me."

"I'm fine, Joley," Hannah assured her. "Leave us."

"Are you sure, Hannah?" Sarah asked. "You don't have to put up with him yelling at you."

"I don't interfere between you and Damon, Sarah," Jonas hissed. "Do us the same courtesy. Go away." He shoved both hands through his hair, waiting to hear the fading footsteps before he glared at Hannah. "Damn it. Why would you risk your safety like that?"

He stepped back away from her, his hands shaking as he paced across the room. His chest heaved as he tried to draw in air, as he tried to push away the images crowding in. There had been so much blood. Her long hair had been everywhere, but instead of platinum and gold, the spiral curls had been red. He could barely breathe and he actually staggered, reaching out blindly for anything to anchor him.

Hannah caught his arm. "Sit down, Jonas. You haven't slept in days."

"Weeks," he corrected and sank into the large chair by her fireplace. He wrapped his arms around her waist, burying his face against her stomach. His arms tightened, two steel bands, locking her to him, holding her as close as he could get her. A shudder went through his body. "Damn it, Hannah. You're killing me."

Hannah's fingers tunneled in his hair, made small soothing circles against his scalp in an effort to calm him. "It's all right, Jonas. I'm alive. It's going to be all right."

Kneeling, she rested her head against his, not certain she was telling the truth. She wasn't certain she'd survived. She was living, but she lived with terror and the realization that someone hated her enough to destroy her. She wasn't strong like her other sisters. She preferred the shelter of her home, of her town, the familiarity of things she'd grown up with. She had always felt safe in Sea Haven. Now she didn't know where safety was. Whoever hated her was here in Sea Haven and she couldn't risk them harming her sisters — or Jonas. She had to leave and she had to leave alone.

Jonas usually shielded her from the intensity of his emotions, but right now, he was too upset. She sensed in him that same desperation she remembered from so long ago, when he'd tried to hold his mother to him, tried to save her, tried to find a way to take away the pain in her. Jeanette Harrington's pain had been, like Hannah's, both physical and emotional. She didn't want to die and leave her son alone in the world. Hannah didn't know how to live. Jonas felt the responsibility for both of them — he always had — and right now, it was all mixed together with rage and grief.

In that moment she knew, with astonishing clarity, that her own uncertainty didn't matter to her. She felt the shudder that ran through Jonas's body and she had to find a way to take away his pain. She caught the images of the attack on her in his mind. The desperate need to get to her, the agony at the thought of losing her. The rage at himself for not being with her to protect her. She didn't find pity, or horror at the sight of her mutilated body, and that was an unexpected gift. But the love she found there, strong — intense — desperate almost — choked her. How could she leave him when she felt the same way?

"I'm angry with you, Hannah," he whispered, keeping his face buried in the warmth of her neck. "I'm really angry with you."

"I know." She cradled his head with her arms, holding him close. "It's all right. We'll get through this. I don't know how, but we will." She was grateful there were no witnesses to Jonas's panic. He was a strong, proud man, and falling apart in front of anyone — especially his family, whom he believed he needed to protect at all times — would be humiliating to him.

"You have to listen to me, Hannah, when it comes to issues of your safety. I can't function like this. The fear is paralyzing, demoralizing, I can't even breathe thinking about you like that. You have to at least do that for me. Give me that."

She pressed kisses to his forehead. "I wasn't doing it on purpose, Jonas. It wasn't defiance. I didn't feel a threat from Rudy — only loneliness. I know what that is. Sometimes, even surrounded by my sisters, I feel lonely."

"Because you think no one knows the real you," he said. "But I do. I see you, Hannah.

You've never been alone." But she hadn't seen him. She couldn't read him and she hadn't seen past his frustration and anger. He'd protected her from knowing his real feelings. She'd coped for so long, bombarded by the people around her, and he hadn't wanted to add to that burden. In the end he'd nearly lost his chances with her.

"Hannah." He tightened his hold on her. "Rudy Venturi is unstable. You felt sorry for him, but it didn't occur to you that in his mind he isn't a threat. You wouldn't feel it from him because he doesn't think what he does is wrong. If he decided he had to kill you to keep the bad men from getting to you, he wouldn't think it was wrong. He wouldn't feel evil or even threatening because his intent is to help you. You don't see everything like you think you do."

Hannah sighed. "I'm sorry, Jonas. I don't mean to make you so crazy. I did feel sorry for him. I didn't think handing him a photograph would be a big thing. I should have listened to you."

"All right," he murmured. "All right. Tell me about the Reverend. Did you talk to him as well?"

The switch in topics had her flinching. Hannah tried to pull back, but he kept his arms around her, lifting his head and looking down at her. "You did, didn't you?"

"He's here, just in the next county, practically a neighbor, and I thought if he could just see I wasn't trying to unduly influence young girls . . ."

Jonas closed his eyes and groaned. "Hannah, he's a couple of hours away. He doesn't have anything to do with you."

"Some of his followers were at nearly every show protesting. They were saying things specifically about me to the press. I just thought if he met me, he'd see I wasn't such a bad person."

"And what happened at that meeting you knew I'd say absolutely no to?"

Hannah took a deep breath and let it out, her gaze sliding away from his. "He made me angry, okay?" She did pull out of his arms and stood up, crossing the room with swift, long strides — runway strides — unconsciously graceful and sexy. She whirled around, her large eyes darkening with temper. "Honestly, Jonas, he was the most unreasonable man and very sleazy. I tried not to intrude and read his thoughts, but he was broadcasting so loudly and he was just disgusting — a pervert."

Jonas groaned and passed a hand over his face. "Don't tell me you called him on it? You didn't, did you, Hannah?"

She put her hands on her too-slender hips, her chin going up. "I certainly did. He stood there with his pompous, pious attitude, all smug in front of his little group of followers, and acted so self-important, telling me what I did was an abomination. It's not like I'm sleeping with designers. And I told him that."

The knots in Jonas's belly were becoming permanent. "You told him you knew he was sleeping with his young followers, too, didn't you?"

"Well, he is! Innocent girls who trust him. I pointed out that he was the one following the path of the devil." She pursed her lips. "And I might have given him a small demonstration of power when he got really nasty with me."

Jonas groaned, nearly tugging out his hair in exasperation. "No wonder he fixated on you. You should have stayed away from him. He would have gone after more exciting prey if you hadn't engaged with him."

"He's a pervert, Jonas, and you should lock him up."

"This is getting worse. You should have told me you'd confronted him." He suddenly frowned. "What made you decide to confront him? You never do that kind of thing. Why in the world would you start with the Reverend?"

She shrugged, looking suddenly wary. "Greg thought it would be a good idea if we buried the hatchet. He didn't think it was good media to have a preacher protesting every show. He thought if we got together, the Reverend would be reasonable."

Both could hear someone fumbling at the lock.

"Jonas, Hannah really needs to rest," Sarah called out. "I mean it, if you don't stop arguing with her, we're coming in and making you leave. Stop browbeating her."

"Go away," Hannah and Jonas shouted simultaneously.

Jonas curled his fingers into a tight fist and turned away from her. He was back to wanting to shake some sense into her. "You listened to Greg Simpson involving security matters and not me?"

"You're making this personal, Jonas." Hannah touched her throat as if it ached. "Greg is my agent . . ."

"Was." Jonas corrected. "If the bastard shows up here, I'm throwing him in jail."

Hannah closed her mouth abruptly on whatever she was going to say, a small shiver running through her. It was becoming difficult to breathe. Her chest felt tight and her lungs burned, starved for air. "I don't want to argue about this. I did what I thought was best for my career."

"Yeah, because your career was so much more important than your life."

Hannah hissed at him, her eyes glittering with sparks. "You're making me angry, Jonas. Is that what you want? You're angry at me so you're going to say mean things to get me upset? You don't have to remind me that I screwed up. I'm the one with my face hacked to pieces."

Sarah thrust open the door, their loud voices disturbing all the Drakes, giving Sarah what she thought was sufficient reason to interfere. Hannah waved her hand and the wind rushed in from the balcony and slammed the door closed before Sarah could step into the room.

"Don't you dare do that," Jonas snapped, stepping forward, crowding Hannah's space, stalking her across the room as she retreated. "Don't you play your 'poor me, I just got out of the hospital' trump card. Not over this. How many times did I tell you how to handle these nutcases? I've been in the business for years, Hannah. It's my job to know how to handle them, yet you're going to take the word of a layman over mine?"

"It wasn't like that, Jonas," Hannah protested, coming up against the wall. "And stop trying to intimidate me. It only makes me angry."

"Be angry then. Maybe you'll figure it out this time, baby, because I'm getting damned sick of always being last on your list. When I tell you something, do you think I'm making it up just to annoy you?"

Hannah bit down hard on her retort and realized that for the first time since she'd been attacked, she felt alive. Her blood was singing in her veins and her pulse was thundering in her ears. Jonas refused to treat her as if she was a fragile, delicate flower, too bruised to see the light of day. He was angry and he let her know. She felt *normal.* Jonas made her feel normal and it felt good. Just moments earlier she'd been close to a panic attack, but just like that he'd wiped it out.

"Sometimes, yes I do. You annoy me on purpose, especially when it comes to my job. You've always hated it and made fun of it. Greg managed my career. I had to believe he suggested what he thought was best."

Jonas went very still, his body crowding hers, so close her breasts brushed his chest and he was aware of her every breath. "Are you telling me Simpson suggested you give Venturi an autographed picture at every event he attended?"

She put her hand on his chest, fingers splayed wide, bracing herself for the storm. "I wanted to do something, and I asked him if he would see to it that Rudy received a picture from me. He said I should give it to him myself every time Rudy attended. He took photos a few times and had a couple of pieces written up about it. I did tell him I didn't want it used for publicity, but the articles had already been submitted."

Jonas swore again, biting the words off between his teeth, his fingers sliding through her hair to the nape of her neck. "You're in so much trouble, Hannah." There was both a warning and a drawling caress in his voice. "Why didn't it occur to you that I had your best interests at heart?"

"Maybe it was the 'Barbie doll' comment. Or the 'taking your clothes off for the entire world to see' accusation, or the million and one barbs you like to throw at me." She rubbed her throat again, wincing a little as the pad of her finger slid over the two deep slashes, still raw and red.

Jonas caught her hand and pulled it to his chest, capturing it there while he leaned in to brush the cuts with kisses. "Don't touch that. Is your throat hurting?" Her voice was even more of a whisper of sound.

"Inside. It feels torn and bruised."

"Then don't argue with me. I'm right anyway and you know it. You should have listened to me." Jonas pressed feather-light kisses along her throat, and up the curve of her chin. "Say it, Hannah. Say you should have listened to me."

She couldn't think very well with his body pressed so close to hers and his mouth running over her skin. She'd been so determined to keep him at arm's length. Whatever everyone else thought, she knew instinctively that danger surrounded her. It wasn't coming from one particular direction, but the wind told her. She remained outside as much as possible, hoping to determine her enemy, but the person's identity eluded her. She could only try to protect the people she loved. And she loved Jonas. She couldn't remember a time when she didn't.

"Jonas . . ." She inserted both hands between her and his chest, trying to get a little space. "You know this can't work." Just the thought of losing him made her cold inside, but even Jonas needed protection. He didn't think so, but she'd seen him vulnerable and in pain. Better he be angry with her and know the complete truth, than later despise her.

Swift impatience crossed his face. "Don't

even start, Hannah. You've pissed me off enough for one day."

"It can't work, Jonas. You think you see who I am, but you see who you want to see, just like my sisters do."

"Your sisters see who you deliberately project for them," he corrected. "I see *you*."

"I'm a coward, Jonas," she admitted, desperate to save him. "You'd love me for a while, and then when you realized what I really am, you'd grow to despise me."

He burst out laughing, bent forward and kissed the tip of her nose. "You might be a coward when it comes to admitting you love me, but you're no coward, baby."

"I am, though." Panic. It was coming back the way it always did. Full blown, attacking just as the man who had stabbed her had. Gripping her with tight fingers, until she fought for breath, until she couldn't think straight. It had gotten worse since she'd been stabbed. The walls closed in on her, and trapped as she was now, with Jonas's body blocking her from running, she had to reach deep to stay in control.

"Because you'd rather stay in Sea Haven than travel the world? Because you're a little shy in public? Or you stutter once in a while when you're around people you don't know? If you were a coward, Hannah, you wouldn't have tried to please your family by going out and pursuing a career you didn't even want — a very public career."

"I should have stood up for myself."

"Yes, you should have, but trying to please people you love doesn't make you a coward. Exasperating maybe, but no coward. And you've never had trouble standing up to me."

She looked down at the evidence of the cuts on her hands and arms. "Yes I do."

"No, you want to please me, just like you want to please your sisters, but you stand up and do whatever the hell you want to do when you want to do it. I'm getting gray hair, I ought to know."

Hannah frowned. Did she? She didn't know anymore. Her life had changed dramatically in seconds. She touched the terrible wounds on her face and neck, but avoided touching her breasts. She still saw every imperfection in her body, every extra pound, and now there were terrible, gaping wounds in her flesh. Jonas had cupped her breasts, looked at her as if she were the most beautiful woman in the world. She couldn't bear the memory of him looking at her so reverently, so lovingly.

Abruptly, she caught up her blanket, and took refuge on her balcony. Although the sun had already set and it would be difficult for a photographer to get a clear picture of her, she slid the blanket like a hood over her head to keep her face in the shadows.

Jonas followed her with a small frown. He had never been all that good with words when it came to Hannah. He was certain he could charm the birds out of the trees when it came to others, but Hannah turned him inside out and made him an idiot. He hated that she was hurting. Every instinct, body and mind, wanted to protect her, wanted to make it all better, but he had no idea how. He was fumbling his way, making mistakes and losing his temper.

Restlessly, he went to the railing to get a better look around them. There were no nearby buildings where anyone could lie on rooftops with rifles, but someone could get an angle from the bluff. The strong winds constantly shifting over the cliffs would make the shot extremely difficult, though. There were probably only a few dozen men in the world who could make that shot and he doubted if any of them had a grudge against Hannah.

"I'm safe up here. The wind would warn me."

Jonas looked out over the water, noting the rocks. Boats couldn't get too close and the waves were too strong and choppy. Again, it would be difficult to get a good shot.

He leaned one hip against the railing and looked down at Hannah's bent head. She still wasn't really looking at him, hiding her face in the blanket. He didn't want her hiding from him. She'd stood openly in front of Ilya Prakenskii, the wounds stark and raw on her pale face and neck, yet she hid from him. The lump in his throat was choking him and the wind was bringing in sea salt, burning his eyes.

"You know I'm not going to let you get away with this. What were you doing packing a bag?" He kept his gaze fixed on her face. She'd never been good at hiding her emotions from him.

Hannah pulled the blanket closer around her, obviously trying to shield her expression from him. "I just need a little space."

Jonas sat on the railing and swung one foot back and forth, letting silence lengthen and grow. The sea birds called to one another as they flew in lazy circles overhead, one occasionally darting down to disappear into the sea before popping back up with a fish on his way back to the rock where he'd perch for the night. The ocean tumbled and rolled, a thunderous music ebbing and swelling in the background.

He let out a sigh. "You're lying to me again, Hannah." He leaned forward to capture her elusive gaze with his. "Do you think I'm going to let you get away with it just because you have a scar or two?"

She touched the unsightly lines on her face again with her fingertips. "I'm not asking you to. It isn't your business, Jonas."

His eyebrow shot up. "Really? You're not my business?" He snorted derisively. "You've been my business since kindergarten. Why did you pack a bag, Hannah?"

Sparks leapt in her eyes and her white teeth snapped together with a bite of temper. "I'm protecting my sisters — and you." Angry with him, she blurted out the truth and was instantly sorry.

He should have known — should have guessed. Hannah who thought she was such a coward. There was a curious melting sensation in the region of his heart. He crouched down in front of her and framed her face with both hands, leaning in to brush his mouth over hers. The softest of contacts, barely there, just a whisper of his lips over hers.

Hannah pulled back, blinking away tears. "You can't do that anymore. Please, Jonas, just go."

He sank back on his heels, studying her distressed expression. "You know me better than that. Start talking, Hannah, and it had better make sense, because you and I both know, I'm not letting you walk out of here alone. You want to leave, we'll leave together, but you're not going anywhere alone."

"I can't be with you. I just can't. You have to accept that it's my decision."

"Not on your life, baby."

"Jonas. God. Why can't you just let it be? Look at me. I can't look at myself without feeling sick." The admission was made in her soft, husky voice, but the whisper of secrecy created an intimacy between them. "I can't bear for you to look at me like this. And I'd never, never want to be seen with you in public."

"Oh for God's sake." Exasperated, he glared at her. "Are you kidding me?"

"Jonas, you're very good looking and you're well known around here. You hold a political office. You ran for sheriff and you were elected. Can you see us side by side? Poor Jonas with his freak of a girlfriend."

"You aren't doing this, Hannah."

"It's the truth. I can't walk outside without photographers wanting to snap my picture and plaster it all over the gossip rags. With you, I'd be in all the newspapers. I do have some vanity and some pride."

"I'm not listening to this crap." He stood, for one moment looming over her, throwing a dark shadow across her face, his jaw set, his mouth in a hard line, then he simply scooped her up and cradled her against his chest, sitting in her chair, holding her on his lap, blanket and all. "You're so silly sometimes, Hannah, you make me crazy. I don't give a damn what people say. I never have."

He kissed the corner of her eye, pushing the blanket back, so he could rub his chin over the top of her silky curls and kiss her eyebrow, blaze a path to the corner of her mouth, skimming the angry red slashes with tiny butterfly kisses as he went. His mouth settled on hers with exquisite gentleness. Her lips were soft and full and trembled beneath his. Her answering kiss was tentative, reluctant, so he kept coaxing her, nibbling at her lower lip, teasing the seam of her mouth with his tongue, brushing his lips back and forth over hers, tugging with his teeth until she gave in and opened her mouth to his.

He poured everything he was into the kiss, giving her love and tenderness and support, mixing it with desire and heat and raw need. His palm settled around the nape of her neck, fingers finding the treasure of platinum and gold corkscrew curls, holding her still so he could explore her mouth. He was careful, gentle, never letting his passion have free rein, never allowing it to carry him away. Her chest and ribs and stomach were covered in wounds and he took care not to rub against her skin although holding her wasn't enough.

Hannah's mouth was warm and moist and tasted like she did, honey and spice and ultrafeminine. He could spend a lifetime kissing her. At first, she was passive, allowing him to kiss her, but as he coaxed, she began to come to life, breathing with him, tongue tangling with his, sending delicious little licks of electricity singing through his veins. With great care, he brought her closer, angled her mouth for a deeper, more satisfying kiss.

Her lips heated, softened, clung to his. His body turned to steel, hard and hot and so alive he could feel lightning arcing through his bloodstream and heard thunder in his ears. His palm cradled the nape of her neck, and he shifted her just a little so she would fit more comfortably in his lap. He had her trapped, but was careful to make her feel safe, not captured. Loving Hannah wasn't easy. She was always on the verge of taking flight, almost as if she was afraid of the intensity of passion he roused in her.

One hand slid down her spine, a slow journey of discovery, while his mouth tried to sate an ever growing desire. Lust was sharp and deep, mixing with love, so full he couldn't tell where one started and the other left off. Hannah was an explosive mixture of exotic, innocence and pure unadulterated sex. She moved and he was instantly riveted. It didn't take much. Even her new voice seemed erotic to him. Hannah fit with him. He'd known on some level even when they were kids, that she was *the one.* She was made for him. He kissed her again and again. Soft, gentle kisses, hard, hungry kisses, probing and exploring her heated, passionate mouth.

Hannah moved against him restlessly, her body in meltdown, her need of him shifting from mental to physical. His mouth seemed to be devouring her, yet she wanted more, wanted to be closer, wanted to feel the heat of his skin beneath her hands and mouth. She was so selfish. It was always about her. Her wants. Her needs. She was putting Jonas in danger, just as she was putting her sisters in danger by staying there. Abruptly she lifted her head, aching with wanting to hold him close, afraid she didn't have the necessary courage to let him go.

"Jonas . . ." She was going to have a panic attack. She was. Again. Right in front of him. She couldn't catch her breath. Couldn't think with the thundering beat of terror in her ears and fear pounding through her body. She hated the insidious weakness that crept up and pounced whenever she was certain she could be strong. It stole too much of her life away, it took her ability to function and reason.

"Don't say it, baby, please." He rested his head against hers. "Let it be for now." He dragged in a hard breath, trying to bring himself back to reality.

She was getting ready to bolt. Hannah was pulling back, away from him, and it had nothing at all to do with arguing. She was so determined to protect them all, she was making herself sick. And if she had one more panic attack and fell apart in front of him, he was going to pick her up and carry her off where no one else would ever find them, just like a caveman. It was going to happen.

Jonas pushed down his own panic and kissed her mouth and forehead, gently pulling back himself. He set her on her feet as he stood, holding out his hand to her, determined not to lose her. "I swear, Hannah, you're thinking so much, smoke is coming out of your ears. Just stop. Let's stay outside together until you're too tired and I'll lie down with you. If you're afraid of that, I'll go sit out there on the bluff again and spend another night in the cold."

Hannah hesitated, and then slowly stretched out her hand until her fingers lay in his palm. He tightened his hold instantly, not giving her time to change her mind. The air was cooler as the breeze blew in from the sea, bringing salt and mist and the taste of the ocean. He'd much rather lie beside her warm, soft body, even if it meant his own would be hard and painful, than spend another night worried while he sat on the bluff watching from a distance.

"I knew you were out there. It made me feel safe."

"You are safe with me." He wrapped her back in her blanket to shelter her from the heavier wind. When she sat down, he pulled his chair close to hers. Leaning forward, he framed her face with his hands and looked directly into her eyes, capturing her gaze so she couldn't look away. "I know you're scared, baby, but that's not being a coward. We have something special between us. You can't let this madman take it away."

Hannah couldn't help herself. In spite of

her resolve to protect him, she leaned close, putting her head on his shoulder, and snuggled into him. "I know we do, Jonas. I just don't know what to do about it." She pressed her lips against his neck and sat up again, pulling back.

"I do," he answered. "I know exactly what to do."

She wasn't touching that. Instead, Hannah drew her knees up and stared out over the ocean, where the sun had already sunk into its depths. Earlier, the sun, looking like a giant red beach ball, glowing with promise, rays streaking out with orange and red bolts as it tipped, had seemed to pour molten lava into the churning waves. The entire sky had been layered in bright, vivid color. The sunset was always so beautiful, but she loved this time of day, just as night and day met and passed, like two ships out over the sea.

The sky darkened slowly, as if a blanket was slowly drawn over it. Clouds drifted lazily and stars glittered like gems. The moon, in whatever stage it happened to be in, gleamed a beautiful silver, spilling its light across the dark waves. Peace reigned.

Jonas had deliberately kept her out here, out where she could breathe freely and without too much worry. He had noticed her quickened pulse, her labored lungs and the desperation building in her. She thought she'd been clever hiding it, she could always hide from everyone — but not Jonas.

Hannah rubbed her forehead. Her face itched and burned, but if she touched it, the sensation was worse. She felt revulsion in the pit of her stomach. She couldn't bear to look at her face in the mirror and she had no idea how much longer she could continue to face Jonas feeling so broken. She stretched out her hands to him for evidence. They were shaking.

Jonas caught both of them and brought them to his mouth, his lips tracing the slash marks. "Give yourself time, Hannah, but don't think you can shut me out. I'm not about to let you go."

"I'm trapped here now, Jonas. I can't go out in public. I can't remember what I might have done to make someone hate me so much. I can't make love to you ever again . . ." Her voice broke and she snatched her hands back, bringing the blanket up around her face to cover her sob. "I hate this — this self-pity. I promised myself I wouldn't do it, but I have to stay away from you. If I see you, Jonas, it's so much worse. I can't see you."

He felt raw inside, torn open with his guts spilling out. He dropped his face into his hands for a moment, trying to clear his brain, trying to allow himself to think clearly. He took a deep shuddering breath and straightened his shoulders. "You're confused, Hannah, and it's understandable. Fortunately for both of us, I'm not. You need me, whether you think so or not, and I know damn well I need you."

He waited until she looked up at him. "I do, Hannah. I never thought I'd look at a woman and know she's the reason the sun comes up in the morning, but you are."

"What if they hurt you? Or my sisters? Jonas, what if some madman takes a knife and comes at you in the dark? You just turn around and he's slashing you. Saying 'I'm sorry, I'm sorry,' but cutting you into little pieces. I couldn't bear that. I really couldn't. I'd rather give you up and have you stay alive — unhurt."

Jonas's head went up alertly. "What did he say?" He reached out and pulled her hands away from her face. "Look at me, Hannah. He said something to you?"

She frowned, trying to remember. "I'm so tired, Jonas, and I can't think straight when I'm tired." She glanced inside at the bed. "I'm afraid to lie down."

He tamped down impatience, his thumb sliding over the backs of her fingers, stroking her sensitive skin. "I am, too. Nightmares are no fun." He tugged her hand, determined to get her to lie down on the bed with him and rest. She was exhausted, sitting up night after night. Perhaps it had been a mistake bringing her home from the hospital so soon. At least there, they could have knocked her out so she could get some rest.

"Come on, baby, I'm not taking no for an answer and you're too tired to argue with me when you know you won't win." He tugged at her hand, taking her with him back inside her bedroom.

She went with him reluctantly, settling beside him, insisting he keep the French doors open. Jonas wrapped his arm around her waist and held her close. She was stiff at first, but slowly, as he nuzzled her neck and pressed kisses into her hair without attempting anything else, she relaxed against him, her body soft and feminine.

"I'm hurting my sisters. I hate it. I can feel them all the time now — except Elle. She stays away from me. She doesn't want to intrude on my privacy. But I feel so horrible because I can't go back to the other me."

She leaned into him more, fitting her body closely with his, brushing his groin with her bottom and sending an electrical current racing through his bloodstream. Jonas gritted his teeth and breathed.

"Can you feel them? The house is filled with grief and sympathy and confusion. I've done that, Jonas, and I don't know how to undo it."

He brushed kisses over her eyebrow and down along the savage wounds to the corner of her mouth and then to her throat. "You didn't do it, a man with a knife did it. We love each other, all of us, Hannah, and we'll be stronger when we come out of this. He can't destroy our family. Your sisters will give you whatever you need to cope with this, and they'll cope in their own way. They don't baby you because they think you can't handle it, they do so because they want to show you love."

"Why do I get so upset with them?"

There was desperation in her voice. Jonas shifted her against his chest, so that her head rested on his shoulder and he could wrap both arms around her. "Anger is a part of recovery and all of us are here, close to you. Someone hurt you, Hannah, traumatized you, you're going to be angry one moment and afraid the next. That's natural and we all expect it."

"I don't — didn't. I'm ashamed that I

can't stop hurting everyone."

His hand slid over her hair, tangled in the silky strands. "Go to sleep, baby, and let me worry tonight. Your sisters are gathering to aid you. I can feel the surge of power in the house. When you wake up, your wounds won't be quite so raw and hopefully you'll feel a little more at peace."

Hannah allowed her eyes to close as she inhaled, dragging Jonas's scent into her lungs. He felt, smelled and tasted so familiar to her. Safe. Strong. So Jonas — and he was right. She felt the rise of feminine power, strong and sure and loving, all directed toward her. Tears stung her eyes and wet her lashes. No matter how upset they were, her sisters reached out to her with love and healing.

"I love being a Drake," she whispered.

"I do, too," he answered and brushed another kiss along the nape of her neck.

13

Jonas came awake, fully alert. It had taken hours for him to drift off, too aware of Hannah beside him. Her sleep was fitful, her body moving constantly and her arms flailing as if defending herself. She cried once, breaking his heart. He lay in the darkness, stroking her hair and murmuring softly to her until she calmed. Now, he lay in the dark with the butt of his gun snug in his palm, his finger on the trigger, listening to her soft moans of distress, his stomach in knots.

Hannah, sweetheart, it's just a bad dream, he assured her, but he pulled his arm from around her warm, soft body and sat up with deliberate slowness, careful not to make a sound. His instincts were kicking in hard and maybe it wasn't a dream after all.

He put his hand over her mouth and leaned close to her. *Stay quiet. Tell me what you feel.*

Hannah's eye, so blue in the daytime, appeared dark and fathomless at night. She frowned beneath his palm and then he felt her reaching, her mind expanding, searching . . . A gasp escaped. *They're here. We have to get downstairs now.* There was urgency in her voice, in her mind, in the way she sat up and gripped his arm.

The doors to the balcony snapped closed without a sound, curtains flying at the rush. Jonas scowled, annoyance rushing across his face. "That wasn't necessary, Hannah. You could have accidentally made noise and alerted them that we're aware of their presence. Besides, I'm going out anyway to see who's coming at us. You go downstairs and call 911."

Hannah shook her head. "It wasn't me, Jonas, the house has gone into protection mode. We have to get downstairs right now." She was trembling.

Jonas helped her out of bed. They were both still wearing clothes, so he simply wrapped her sweater around her and ushered her toward the door. "I'll take you down with your sisters, baby, but I have to get outside."

Hannah slipped her hand into his. "No, you don't understand. You can't go outside."

Jonas let her pull him out of the room and

head down the hall in the dark. Below, in the living room as they came down the winding staircase, he could see candles flickering in a wide circle around the intricate mosaic on the floor in the entryway. A second circle enclosed the first, a wide pathway containing small dark smudges every so many inches.

Sarah reached out and hugged Hannah, drawing her into the center of the circle. Hannah kept possession of his hand, tugging until he stepped inside. The moment he did, Joley and Elle closed the circle behind them.

"Sit, Jonas," Sarah said, pointing to a spot at the top of the mosaic.

"Sweetheart, I have to go outside where I'm going to be the most help." He looked around the circle at the faces of the Drake sisters. In the candlelight, their beauty struck him, all different, all exotic. He could well believe they were ancient souls from a time long past with their hair down and their cool assessing eyes. Mostly what struck him was their lack of fear. Like Hannah, they were trembling, but it wasn't because they were afraid of the men creeping toward their home through the trees and shrubbery.

"The house will protect us now, Jonas," Sarah said. "You'll have to stay inside."

He hated it when their beliefs and rituals clashed with his territory. "The house didn't protect you last year when the men after your fiancé broke in here and nearly killed you," he pointed out. "I'm not taking any chances. Call the sheriff and get me some backup."

Hannah clung to him, refusing to let him go. "That was different, Jonas, we'd opened the house up to those men. We had the gates unlocked and the doors were welcoming. We put the house in protection mode when I came home from the hospital. Please sit down with us. You can't go outside."

Sarah shook her head. "In any case, the phone isn't working. We're on our own."

"More reason than ever for me to be outside where I can protect you."

Joley caught his other arm and Libby reached out, shaking her head. Kate and Abbey moved in behind him. Then Elle put her hand on him and he felt it — the shuddering of the grounds and the sudden shifting in the house as if it was awakening. His stomach lurched in protest and his heart accelerated as adrenaline flooded his body.

"What if Jackson comes? He always knows when you're in danger, Elle." He was suddenly very much afraid he didn't know what kind of power he was dealing with.

"The house will judge their intent toward us, not toward anyone else," Sarah assured him, "and act accordingly."

"The house would never harm Jackson," Elle answered calmly.

He looked around at the somber faces and sighed. He couldn't imagine a house protecting them, but he could protect them — all of them — even from inside if he had to. "Tell me you have a gun, Sarah."

"I have one as well," Joley said. "And yes, a permit to carry it, so don't ask."

Sarah seated herself in front of the mosaic and the sisters positioned themselves around the artfully crafted tiles. Jonas took his place between Hannah and Elle. Power swelled the moment the circle was complete and the floor continued to shift and move as if alive. The sisters locked hands and began to sway, chanting softly, the words more felt than heard, echoing through his mind. The sound was melodic and sweet, rising above the silence of the night in a whisper of dramatic notes until he thought he could see them gleaming in the darkness.

On the floor in front of him, the mosaic began to swirl with vapor, smoke rose, or rather fog, as if a breeze had come to clear out the gray mist and leave the mosaic tiles comprehensible to those looking. To his astonishment, he could see the grounds surrounding the house, as if the tiles were a camera screen, broken into pieces, but providing a picture of the outside world. He could see the fog hanging thick above and around the house, protecting it from prying eyes, but the grounds appeared crystal clear in the mosaic tiles.

Something moved stealthily through the shrubbery, working to gain access to the house itself. Shadows moved and the figures of several men crept forward. They were dressed in black and gray, blending into the night, their facial features distorted as if they wore masks beneath the hoods. Gloves and boots with tucked-in pants, along with the way they moved and carried their weapons, that told Jonas they were under attack by professionals.

His heart jumped and he tried to let loose of Elle's hand so he could reach for his gun again, but she held on to him tightly. He was sitting on his butt and it looked like at least five men were working their way through the brush to the house. What kind of lawman was he?

And then the bushes moved, roots erupting from the ground and lashing out like a whip with nine tails, sweeping fast toward one of the black-clad men. The lash struck him in the stomach hard, lifting him and sending him flying several feet to land sprawled out against the fence.

Jonas blinked and looked around at the circle of sober faces. Feminine. Soft. He thought of the Drakes as gentle and kind. Bringing harm to no one, yet none of them blinked or winced or looked away. The vibration beneath him continued and the wood creaked and groaned, alive and alert and waiting for the intruders to come too close.

The man who had been thrown climbed unsteadily to his feet, gripping the fence for leverage. He shouted and jerked his hand clear. Smoke rose from the wood where his glove had melted onto the fence. He hurried back up the slope, avoiding the brush where something had struck him, taking an alternate route that brought him into a grove of trees. He moved with much more confidence once in the mixture of redwoods, oaks, pines and spruce.

Jonas was afraid to take his eyes from the man in the mosaic as he gained footing through the labyrinth of trees. The tension built in the room. The chanting swelled, the words evoking protection against evil, and behind them, in the second circle, shadows lengthened and grew, forming insubstantial, transparent figures of women dressed in garb from centuries gone by. The floating figures positioned themselves in a tight circle around the Drakes and Jonas, as if anyone would have to get through them to get to the inner circle.

Jonas leaned forward to see the mosaic better when the intruder began to scale a tall, thick tree. Branches swept outward, long curving boughs providing a ladder for the man to climb. One branch reached toward the balcony on the second story. Joley's room. The man put his foot on the branch and began to ease across.

The tree shuddered, bark rippling. Needles shivered. The man stopped, looked around him apprehensively. There was a moment when Jonas counted his own heartbeats. One. Two. The branch dipped down hard and fast. The intruder's mouth opened wide with a scream as he clutched at several smaller branches to keep from falling. The thick limb rose fast, the smaller branches breaking, catapulting the intruder several feet into the air and over the bluff. He spun, arms and legs sprawled, like a windmill, before falling far below into the turbulent sea.

"Holy hell, Hannah."

"I know, it takes getting used to." She

leaned her body close to his, offering shelter, protection, without ever breaking the link with her sisters.

Sarah leaned down to blow on one of the dark candles in front of her, just outside the double circle. The light flickered bloodred and then was gone, sputtering into the wax.

Jonas turned his attention to two men scaling the walls of the house. At the same time two others were heading for the lower story. One of the two men scaling the building was extraordinarily strong and immediately outdistanced his partner as he went up the north side of the building next to the tower. He was using the corner to help propel himself upward. The mosaic glowed red-orange. Smoke puffed out from under each hand and foot until the man climbed faster and faster, finally leaping to gain the balcony. He stepped onto the solid surface and paused, bending over, breathing hard.

Around him, the wrought iron began to bend and reshape, the railing forming into what appeared to Jonas as an animal with a spiked tail and a spiraled horn. The man backed up, pulling out a gun, his gloves burned and still smoking from touching the side of the house. The animal reared up on hooves, rising above the intruder and then lowering its head. The man fired several rounds in rapid succession, but the animal pawed the ground and hurtled itself relentlessly forward. The intruder was fast, whipping to one side, grabbing the horn to give himself leverage in a desperate attempt to save his life. The tail struck, lashing around, piercing the man's stomach and lifting him into the air before dropping him onto the balcony floor.

Beside him, Hannah let out a small sound of distress. Instinctively, Jonas started to let go of hands in order to comfort her, but Elle and Hannah held on tightly, shaking their heads. He frowned as he watched, in the mosaic, the balcony floor slide open and the body drop to the ground below.

At least he'd have a body to work with. Someone he could identify. The big man had moved in a way he was certain he'd seen before.

As he watched, the brush and trees swayed, leaves rustling, and across the ground, vines shot out, wrapped the body up tightly as if in a carpet, and then rolled it toward the edge of the bluff.

"Stop!" Jonas called out. "Make it stop. I need that body. What if I can't recover it from the sea?"

The intruder slipped off the edge of the

cliff and dropped into the churning water below. Sarah leaned over and blew on the second candle. It sputtered, glowed red, and drips of wax beaded on the floor like bright blood spots before it flickered out.

The second climber had reached the balcony on the second floor over by the west-facing room — Elle's. The same trail of smoking palm and foot prints led up the side of the house. He swung over the wrought iron railing and landed in a crouch. Almost at once the floor jiggled under his feet. He looked down and the solid flooring had turned to a gel-like substance. He began to sink into it. As he did, the gel thickened and lengthened, slowly but surely encasing his body. He fired his automatic, round after round, into the gel, but it kept forming around him. He tried to thrash his way free, but the house ate him, inch by inch, absorbing him into the gel until he was completely inside, surrounded by the balcony itself.

Jonas felt his stomach lurch. "This is an illusion, right? Tell me it's an illusion, Hannah, because this is crazy." He clutched her hand tighter, suddenly afraid for all of them. If the house was alive, no one was safe. He wanted to grab all the women and get them out of there.

"Part illusion, part real. They believe it, so it's so," Elle said. "They came to kill us, Jonas. The house is made up of the spirits of our ancestors. Did you think they would lie idly by while we were under attack?"

'Cuz, yeah, didn't everybody's ancestors rise up and destroy enemies? "Fine then. Tell them to save me a body."

The balcony lurched and spit the intruder out into the tops of the tree branches. The branches swayed and sent the body to the sea below. Jonas swore as Sarah blew out the next candle.

The two men entering through the ground floor were at the windows now. One was at the kitchen window and one on the other side of the living room. Every instinct Jonas had insisted he draw his gun, but Elle and Hannah held his hands tight, keeping him locked within the circle. The hairs on his arms stood up, and the room crackled with energy and power. The floor continued shifting and the walls seemed to undulate. Behind them, the transparent, filmy figures swayed and danced, their arms extended, their hands linked.

Jonas could barely make himself stay sitting in the circle when he knew any moment the two men would break through the windows. He heard a scream, abruptly closed off, and the sound of gunfire. He peered at the mosaic just in time to see cracks forming in the ground and earth opening up along the kitchen where the intruder tried to get to the bank of windows. Every step he took produced an ever-widening crack. There was nothing to shoot at, only the yawning abyss staring at him. He finally ceased trying to gain the house and began to backpedal carefully, placing his feet lightly on the ground as he retreated.

Jonas switched his gaze to the last man in the mosaic, then realized the window the man was trying to gain entry through was just straight ahead of him. He watched in a kind of fascinated horror as the intruder used the butt of his gun to hit the glass and shatter it. Again he pulled at his hands, but Hannah and Elle hung on grimly.

All around him the chanting swelled, *Harm no one, harm no one.* What the hell did that mean? He was going to have to shoot the poor son of a bitch, but maybe that was a far better way to go than what the house of horrors had planned. This was a hell of a way for men to die, even if they deserved it. He still wasn't certain if it was real or an illusion.

The window shattered with a crash of glass, breaking into jagged shards that exploded inward into the house, paused in midair, reversed and stood poised in the darkness. Jonas found he was holding his breath. The intruder stuck his gun through the frame, finger beginning to tighten when the sharp spears hurtled forward. Blood sprayed, the man screamed wildly, yanking his arm back outside even as his finger squeezed and bullets bit into the side of the house.

Around them, the smoky figures writhed and moaned, as if absorbing the shock of the bullets. The intruder screamed again and the sound of footsteps faded as he retreated. Once again the ground shuddered and opened. The screams faded as the edges of the earth resealed. Jonas stared down into the mosaic and noted the other man had made it back to the fence, climbing over, leaving scorch marks behind.

"I'm not going to say I can at least collect DNA samples," he muttered, "because every time I open my mouth, the evidence disappears."

With a little sigh, he watched the droplets of blood absorb into the wood and the window reform. "I have to tell you, I've seen some freaky shit around you girls, but nothing like this. I have just one question. Have you told your fiancés about this? Because quite frankly it scares the hell out of me."

"You never have to be afraid, Jonas," Hannah assured. "The house judges intent."

"Hannah. Honey. Half the time my intent is to strangle you. And I don't doubt whoever ends up with Joley or Elle will want to do worse than that."

"Hey!" Elle objected and Joley punched his arm hard.

He glanced around at the wispy gray figures as they began to settle down, one by one merging into the shadows or the smudge marks on the floor. The tension in the room slowly eased and the shifting beneath them lessened. He shoved both hands through his hair. "They don't just hang around all the time, do they? Because they'd definitely curb a man's . . . appetite."

Hannah's lips twitched, a ghost of a smile spreading across her face. "Most of it was illusion, Jonas."

"Then how did four men just die? They did die, didn't they, they weren't an illusion?"

"They're dead," Sarah said.

"So where are their bodies? I'm not going to find them in the ocean, am I? And even if I took the house apart, I'm not going to find DNA in the wood. You don't find this just a little bit creepy?"

"I find men who want to kill my sister creepy," Joley said firmly. "I had no idea you were such a baby, Jonas. I'll bet you don't go to scary movies."

"I don't. There's nothing wrong with that."

Hannah wrapped her arms around him. "No, there's nothing at all wrong with it. I don't like scary movies either."

He was grateful for her support when the rest of her sisters were looking at him with wicked intent. He brought Hannah's fingers to his mouth. "I'm heading outside, baby, so get the house to calm down. I don't want to get thrown into the ocean."

Joley smirked at him. "It wouldn't hurt for you to go swimming."

"Joley," Hannah warned, "stop teasing him. You're perfectly safe outside."

Sarah glanced at Hannah, eyes somber, shadows lurking. "But Hannah isn't, is she? It isn't over, is it, Jonas? They really are after her."

"They. Who the hell are they?" Jonas asked. "That's the burning question, and all of you are going to have to consider this is being done by someone with power. We mentioned it, but all of you said the same thing. No surges, nothing to follow, but what would make a perfectly normal couple attempt murder if not under some kind of compulsion?"

"It isn't Ilya Prakenskii," Hannah said. "And he's the only one we know with that kind of power. I didn't feel it. I know I didn't. I would have automatically made a move to counter it."

"Then if not compulsion, you tell me. What would make someone do this?"

"I don't think the men attacking tonight were under compulsion," Kate said. "They might have been following orders, but there were no countermeasures taken against illusion and that would be the first thing we would have done if we were manipulating someone and they ran into trouble. If someone is directing them, and he knows how to manipulate energy, he would have aided them."

The women all nodded. Jonas sighed and climbed to his feet, careful of the candles. "I'm going to take a look around outside."

"While we're here," Libby said, "and there's so much power to draw on, I'd like to do another healing session for Hannah."

Hannah shook her head. "You're already exhausted, Libby, all of you are."

"Look around you, honey," Libby suggested, "you can feel the energy. I'm feeling invigorated, not exhausted."

Jonas moved out of the circle, shaking his head. "Invigorated" wasn't the word he'd use. Creeped out. Skin crawling. He didn't even know what he was dealing with anymore — and at this point he didn't want to know.

He stepped outside into the cool night air warily, hand on the butt of his gun, not that it would do any good if the house suddenly came alive and heaved him into the ocean. He'd always, *always,* thought of it as home. He had climbed the tree a dozen times, the one that had thrown one of the intruders into the ocean. He'd swung from the branches and leapt to the balcony. When his mother was in so much pain he couldn't shut out the moans and cries, when things were particularly bad, he'd crawled through that same kitchen window and had taken refuge inside, listening to the Drakes' laughter and silently praying he would be part of it someday.

He had wished for a family and now he had one — strange as they were. He had to find a way to keep them all safe. Originally, when he saw Hannah packing a bag, he'd thought it was a good thing, that he'd move her away from the others and narrow down the risk of someone else accidentally getting hurt, but after seeing what the house could do, he changed his mind. As long as she was inside, no one was going to get to her.

The fog was back, thick and gray and wet, surrounding the house and grounds and spreading across the highway, muffling sound and obscuring sight. Still, Jonas knew he wasn't alone. He whistled softly, a short, one-two note, that cut through the night. He wasn't in the least surprised when an answering whistle came back to him. He made his way down the slope until he saw Jackson.

"Hell of a show," Jackson greeted him.

"You saw that? I thought maybe I was hallucinating." Jonas wiped his brow again and shook his head. "Makes me wonder what I'm getting myself into."

Jackson's eyebrow went up slightly. "You got yourself into it a long time ago."

"True. Nasty thing, watching a house swallow a man and spit him back out."

"I've got to agree with you there." Jackson peered through the wisps of fog at the walls, where foot- and handprints were burned into the wood. "Do you suppose we can take that in as evidence? We could cut out the sections."

Jonas snorted. "You can try taking a saw to that house, but personally, I'm not about to get anywhere near it with anything resembling a weapon."

"You have any enemies in the crime lab?"

Jonas grinned at him. "Jackson, you're such a mean son of a bitch."

"Yeah, well. I try." He glanced at Jonas. "Hannah all right?"

"She will be. She's scared and worried about her sisters. Jackson, you were there, in the hospital when the wife made her try at Hannah. Did you feel anything? Could you tell if she was under some kind of compulsion?"

"You're asking me if Prakenskii could have been directing the attack."

"I like him. I don't know why. He's a killer. I can see it in his eyes, but I like him and that doesn't make sense. I have problems when things don't make sense."

Jackson sent him another look, one Jonas preferred not to interpret.

Light was beginning to streak across the sky, turning the dark of night to a softer charcoal gray. Mist continued to creep in, long bony fingers of fog, stretching out over the ocean and land, moving inland. The men approached the side of the house cautiously, studying the surrounding ground before they took each step. There wasn't a single yawning crack anywhere near the house itself. The balconies appeared intact and completely stable. There was no blood spatter, in fact the entire area looked pristine, with the exception of the blackened hand and boot prints burned into the side of the house.

"Do you have a camera?" Jackson asked. "We could get some pictures and maybe take a print or two if we're lucky."

Jonas shook his head. "We'd probably get a bunch of ghosts and that would just freak me out."

Jackson sent him a faint grin. "You're safe. They're fading already."

The blackened marks grew fainter, beginning to diminish as the sky lightened, gradually losing color until finally they simply disappeared altogether.

"There goes the last of our evidence. There aren't even any shells left behind. Guns, bodies, blood and prints, all absorbed. What does that, Jackson?"

The deputy shrugged and reached inside his jacket to pull out a pack of cigarettes. "This is a hell of a mess, Jonas." He glanced up at the house, his gaze touching on each window before bending his head to the match cupped in his hands.

There was a faint glow coming from inside the house and Jonas knew the Drake sisters were holding another healing session for

Hannah. Between the plastic surgeon and Libby, Hannah's physical body was going to be fine. Jonas wasn't as certain about her emotional state.

"It isn't Prakenskii. I'm certain of that, but what of Sergei Nikitin? Would Prakenskii know if his boss had the same abilities? We thought the Drakes were unique. Then Prakenskii came along. Why not another? Nikitin is cunning, street smart and violent, but smooth enough to cover his tracks so that he's accepted, and that's damned hard to do. Nikitin might have psychic ability."

Jonas held out his hand for the cigarette. "Would Prakenskii tell us if Nikitin did?" When Jackson passed it to him, he took a slow, satisfying drag. He rarely smoked, but once in a while, like now, when his world had been shaken, his woman nearly killed in front of his eyes, and he'd watched a house consume a man and spit him out, he figured a drag or two were appropriate.

"Who knows? Prakenskii tends to play everything close to his chest. He lives in the shadows and men like that don't trust anyone." Jackson took the cigarette back.

Jonas refrained from pointing out Jackson tended to be the same way. Instead he walked to the edge of the bluff and looked down into the crashing waves. It didn't surprise him that there were no bodies. He hadn't expected to find any. But someone would be looking . . .

He turned back to Jackson. "Someone lost four men tonight. There aren't any bodies and they aren't going to believe the one that got away. What's he going to say to his boss? The house came alive and ate his friends? They're going to be looking and that means they'll leave tracks. Get the word out that we want to hear of anyone asking about disappearances or strange occurrences. Maybe earthquakes or anything they can tell themselves would be a reasonable explanation."

Jackson exhaled a thin column of smoke and nodded. "Who would hate Hannah this much? Someone has made this very personal, Jonas."

"Venturi was here, bringing her flowers. And the Reverend is in town with his band of bodyguards. Let's see if they're all accounted for. Maybe you could pay a visit to them nice and early and see if they're all in their beds."

"No problem." Jackson went to take another heavy drag from the cigarette when it flared bright red in his hand and disintegrated into ash. He dropped it, shaking his hand from the sting of the burn and cursed, glaring at the house. "Mind your own business," he snapped under his breath.

Instantly the wind rose to a wild, outraged shriek, tugging at his jacket, exposing the pack of cigarettes, catching it with a burst of speed before Jackson could grab the box. "Theft. Pickpocketing," he yelled. "Back off, Elle." He managed to get his fingertips on the pack, juggled a moment fighting to keep it, and then the wind whisked it away, out over the sea. "That's littering," he called out, "and I can arrest you for that."

The box flared into flames, the ash falling into the water.

The window slid open and Elle stuck her head out, long red hair cascading like a waterfall of silk. "I'm so sorry, Jackson. Smoking always kicks off my asthma and I reacted without thinking."

"I'll just bet you did. I'm outside and you're inside with the window closed." He glared at her. "Asthma my ass."

"I'm sensitive. And Jonas, Hannah would like a word with you." Elle smiled sweetly and disappeared again, slamming the window closed.

"Oh hell." Jonas sighed. "Hannah must have eyes in the back of her head."

Jackson kept watching the window where Elle had disappeared. "The wind talks to her, Jonas, and everything, voices, scents, information of all kinds are carried on the wind. You aren't going to get away with much with that woman, if that's what you're thinking."

"What about Elle? Hannah tells me she has all the talents."

"Elle is going to have to come to terms with me sooner or later. She's choosing later, but I'm running out of patience."

Jackson *was* patient, unlike Jonas. It was one of the things that made him so good at his former job as an Army Ranger. Jackson had it bad, which was odd, because half the time, Jonas didn't think he felt much emotion. He was loyal to the few people he called friends, but nothing much rocked him. Like the house. He'd seen what the house had done, but he just shrugged his shoulders and took it in stride. Jonas, however, was going to have a few nightmares.

Something — some instinct — made him turn his head and he saw Hannah slip out of the house. Everything inside him stilled as he watched her come toward him. She moved with the wind, elegant and graceful, her famous hair, spirals of platinum, silver and gold, hanging well past her waist and enveloping her slender shoulders, flowing like a silken cape around her body. In the dawn, she looked a dream, moving through the mist.

"She's so fucking beautiful," he whispered aloud, pressing his hand hard over his heart. It wasn't about what others saw, not for him, it never had been. She stole his breath with her smile, the way her eyes lit up, the flash of temper — he loved that flash of temper — he found it sexy as hell.

"Hannah," Jackson greeted her. "You look as if you're feeling a little better."

"I am, Jackson, and thank you for looking out for us. Elle said you were outside."

"She warned me not to come onto the property," he said.

Jonas scowled at him. He knew Jackson and Elle had a strange relationship and could communicate, but they rarely admitted it — and Jackson hadn't said a word to him about Elle warning him off.

"There really isn't much to write up in my report, Jonas. I'm not going to say the house swallowed a man, if that's what you're thinking. I don't need to go in for any more psych tests," Jackson said decisively. He touched the back of Hannah's hand, a rare gesture of affection. "You need anything, just call."

"I will," Hannah assured him.

Jonas knew her so well, knew what it cost her to look straight at Jackson, to let him see the slash marks on her face. They were less raw, less red, already beginning to heal with the continuing aid from her sisters, but it was difficult to let anyone see her wounds. He was proud of her courage, the way she stood straight and tall, so slim she appeared fragile. Her lips trembled, but her gaze never wavered.

"I'll see you both later," Jackson said. "I need to catch some sleep."

"Were you here all night?" Hannah asked.

"No, I didn't see them arrive and I never did catch a glimpse of the car. They had some sophisticated equipment, though. They used earpieces to keep track of each other and the one that got away called in a ride from somewhere close by. I couldn't get into position to even get a make on the vehicle."

He lifted a hand and turned to walk away. The mist swallowed him until there wasn't even the sound of footsteps.

Jonas stood for a moment just looking at Hannah because it gave him so much pleasure. "You're being very brave coming out here. The photographers are still everywhere, although I doubt they can penetrate this fog."

She smiled at him and stepped closer. "I came for you."

"Me? Are you all right?"

"Yes, but you aren't. I can feel that you're . . ." She paused to search for the right word. "Distressed," she finally settled.

The knots in his stomach began their familiar tightening. "I'm worried about you, Hannah. I knew it wasn't over. It doesn't come as a shock to either of us, but I still can't help being angry."

"Anger isn't the same thing as distress, Jonas. You may be angry on some level on my behalf, but this is different, not about me at all." She frowned and lifted her face to the wind, let it play over her skin and through her hair while she waited for him to tell her the truth.

Jonas looked down at his hands. There was no use in trying to hide anything from Hannah anymore. He had built solid shields over the years, but one night together and she seemed to have knocked a few holes in the wall. "All right, yes, it's upsetting to me. I can't figure out who is after you without knowing who they are. And . . ." He shook his head, reluctant to admit the truth out loud, even to himself.

Hannah reached for his hands and brought them to her heart. "And?" she prompted.

He sighed, feeling foolish. Feeling like a traitor. "I can't stop thinking those men have families, a parent or sibling at least, someone who cares. That person will spend the rest of their life wondering what happened to the one they loved." He pulled one hand away and shoved it through his hair, unable to meet the intensity of her blue eyes. He was worried about the families of men who had tried to kill her. What did that say about him?

The silence lengthened and stretched for what seemed an eternity. Finally he looked down into her upturned face — met her gaze and was instantly held there — made captive by the love he saw. "You're a good man, Jonas. It isn't a weakness to have compassion for others."

He didn't pull her close, simply leaned down and kissed her, his lips slanting over hers — gently — tenderly. "And you came out here in the cold just to tell me that?"

"That's exactly why I came out."

14

"The natural fog isn't quite this thick and to keep it around the house is dangerous and tiring, but I hate the thought of going in. I feel a little bit trapped and claustrophobic," Hannah said.

After he saw what the house could do, Jonas wanted her in it, safe, where no one could get to her. He ran the pad of his finger down the side of her face, skimming over the slash marks and trailing to her throat, where the cuts were deeper. The attacker had started with light slashes, cutting across her body, back and forth. He had been whispering to her that he was sorry. Maybe he hadn't wanted to destroy her looks. Maybe it had been something altogether different.

Jonas slid his palm down her slender arm, feeling the defensive wounds, remembering how she lifted her hands, a slim protection against the vicious assault. His fingers tangled with hers and he tugged her forward. "The fog is still naturally thick along the beach right below your house. We can walk there. You and your sisters can easily take care of any cameras with zoom lenses, can't you?"

A smile flitted across her face. "I think that will be easy enough."

They went down the stairs leading to the beach in silence. Hannah shivered a little. She was wearing a short, denim jacket, but it obviously wasn't keeping out the chill coming in from the ocean. When they reached the sand, she kicked off her shoes and waited while he removed his.

Jonas shrugged out of his heavier coat. "Take this, it will keep you warm."

Hannah shook her head. "I'm used to the weather. I'm always sitting outside, remember? I don't want you to get cold."

"It's my chance to show you how manly I am after I looked wussy."

She let him enfold her in the warmth of his jacket. "Wussy? When did you look like a wuss?"

"You know how horror movies make my stomach turn. The house gave me that same creepy feeling and your sisters picked up on it. Your manly man looked like a baby. It was humiliating. I've got to find a way to redeem myself."

She laughed softly, the sound floating over the endless waves. Ripples appeared in the water as if sea creatures responded below. She tucked her hand in the crook of his arm, her blue eyes bright with amusement. For Jonas, Hannah created a magical world around her, and she always brought him into it. There was such beauty in the world, and when he was with her, he could see it so clearly.

"Any man who's been shot as many times as you have should never worry about anyone calling him a wuss," she pointed out.

"Getting shot means I'm slow, not brave."

"You're brave. I don't like horror movies either. They give me nightmares. Joley's even worse. If she watches a scary movie, she has to sleep with the lights on and most of the time she won't sleep alone."

"Then why do you watch them?"

"Joley likes to be scared, and she can't watch them alone."

"I don't know how you can make that sound perfectly logical."

Her laughter brought streaks of silver flashing to the surface of the water. White foam curled along the edges of the waves as they curled back under. Spray leapt up around the rocks and burst through holes formed centuries earlier by the wash of the sea. Jonas inhaled it all and felt at peace.

"You know what it is, Hannah? I have some kind of balance when I'm with you. My mind can slow down and enjoy the world around me. I realized it when I was a kid and things were so bad with my mom. I'd hear her crying — never in front of me — but in the night and when her door was closed. I couldn't do a thing — nothing at all — God — it made me feel so fucking helpless, and I'd come to your house. I'd go through every room until I found you. You didn't have to talk to me, but as long as you were there, my mind would quiet down and the rage that was burning a hole in my gut would subside."

She slipped her hand into his, entwined their fingers together. "I'm surprised it wasn't Libby, but I'm grateful it was me."

"It was definitely you. In those days, I didn't think about the whys, I was so confused. I didn't want Mom to die, I wanted her with me all the time, but she was in so much pain that I knew I was being selfish and that I should be able to find the strength to tell her it was okay if she let go."

"Jonas." Hannah touched his face with gentle fingers. "She wanted to be with you.

I know she did. I was over there a lot with my mother and her will was absolute."

He drew her fingertips into his mouth and then kissed them, before letting her go. "That's why even when you make me crazy, I can still feel this . . . this . . ." "Peace" was the only word he could think of and she was staring up at him with stars in her eyes and all he wanted to do was kiss her.

"Marry me, Hannah."

She blinked up at him, shock driving the color from her face. "Jonas . . ."

"No, Hannah, don't think. Just say it. Say you want to be my wife. You want my children. You want me to come home to you every night. Say it so I don't have to keep thinking if I say or do the wrong thing, I'm going to lose you." He shoved his hand through his hair, leaving it rumpled and in complete disarray. "Hell. I'm walking on eggshells with you."

"You are? I hadn't noticed."

"Do you want those things? Do you want to go to bed with me at night? Wake up with me in the morning? Drive me crazy looking all sexy and drowsy over your tea? Spend your life with me, Hannah. Grow old with me. We can sit on the porch in our rockers and I swear, baby, at the end of it all, you'll know no one could have loved you more or better. I can give that to you. I swear I can, baby. Love me back, Hannah."

Jonas had never looked so vulnerable or so heart-breaking. He made her want to melt into his arms, get lost in his eyes, press close to the shelter of his body. She took a deep breath and let it out. "I love you with every single cell in my body, Jonas. With my heart and my soul. I want all those things with you, I do, but not right now. It can't be right now. I'm barely hanging on to my sanity and I have to know I'm going to be able to come to you whole."

She reached up with both hands to frame his face. "I need you to understand this and have patience with me. There will never be another man for me. It's always been you, but I have to figure out why I worked at a job I hated for years. I have to find out why I can't see what everyone else sees in me. I don't feel beautiful. When I look in the mirror, I never saw beautiful. For this to happen to someone like me, it's devastating, Jonas. I don't want you to think it's vanity, it isn't. I can't see me and I need to be able to do that. I need to find out what I'm like and what I want. I have to be comfortable in my own skin before I can be in a relationship the way you want."

His breath stilled in his lungs. He couldn't

look at her, not when she was handing him back his heart. His jaw tightened and he swallowed the sudden lump in his throat.

"Don't." Hannah pressed her fingertips over his mouth. "You don't understand what I'm saying. Yes, I want to marry you. Absolutely. But just . . . not now."

Jonas backed up a couple of steps to keep from dragging her to him. Hannah was so elusive, like water slipping through his fingers. He had wanted her for so long, had her for a night, and now she was gone again. "I want to understand, Hannah, but it seems to me you're making this complicated when it's really simple. I love you. I want you. If you feel the same way, we should be together."

"I couldn't make love to you. I know I couldn't. I'd want to, Jonas, but . . ."

"You aren't always going to be in pain, Hannah, and that's not what's important."

She sighed, wanting desperately to say the right thing even at the expense of her pride. "You knew I had trouble with my body image before this ever happened." Embarrassed, she looked out over the ocean, watching the rise of the waves. As always, the motion and sound and beauty of it soothed her and gave her courage. "I can't even look in a mirror, Jonas, let alone think about you looking at me."

"I did look at you, Hannah, before and after. You're the most beautiful, sexy woman I've ever seen. Yeah, the wounds are fresh, but they're already healing and they'll fade. They don't take away from who and what you are. Not to me, never to me."

"But they do to *me.* I need to feel beautiful and sexy, not ugly and disgusting."

Jonas scowled at her. "Hannah, my God, you don't really feel that way about yourself? The wounds are going to fade. The plastic surgeon was one of the best in the country and your sisters . . ."

She stepped closer to him. Waves of distress poured off him, not distress for himself — but for her. Not pity, she realized with relief, but genuine concern for her. "I know my face and body will eventually recover, but right now, I don't want you looking at me."

"You don't have to be perfect for me, Hannah." His voice was low and furious. "That fucker Simpson did this to you. He made you think you had flaws and that you weren't good enough. I heard him yelling at you to lose weight and that your breasts were too big. Screw him. And screw that damned job. You're beautiful. Hell, baby, you stop traffic. You always have."

"Whatever the problem, Jonas, it's something I have to deal with."

He opened his mouth to argue with her some more, to persuade her that he was right and she should just be with him. Abruptly he closed it, swallowing the demand. He loved her and he needed to understand her. He wasn't the best at expressing himself, but he had to think of a way to say the right words for her.

He was silent a moment, staring down at her face, the skin that was so flawless it begged to be felt, even with the wounds stretched across her cheek and chin. So what exactly did he want from her? He'd always wanted her to stand up for herself, to choose what she wanted to do, whom she wanted to be with — but what had he really been saying? He wanted her choice to be him, to stay home and have his children and be his best friend and lover.

Jonas sighed. He was proud of her for being courageous enough to look at herself and want to find her own strength. And he loved her with everything in him, so that meant, if Hannah wanted and needed time, he'd give it to her. Besides, her admission left a lot of interesting loopholes for him to explore.

He ran his finger from her eyebrow to the

corner of her mouth. "So what you're saying is, you love me, there's no other man, but you don't think you could make love to me right now because you feel ugly. Am I getting this?"

"It's certainly part of the problem." Her stomach began to settle. He wasn't angry with her, or hurt anymore, he was struggling to understand and that's all she could ask. "It's hard to feel desire when you don't feel desirable, Jonas."

The pad of his finger slid over her mouth, rubbing back and forth along her full lower lip before sliding over the curve of her chin to shape her neck. His fingers curled, the palm resting lightly against her throat. "So you don't really want me physically right now, but you think that might come later, when you're feeling better about yourself?"

His touch was electric, sending small currents leaping through her veins. She didn't feel desirable, but Jonas, up close and touching her so possessively, could still produce desire. How insane was that? She'd just been thinking how impossible it would be to take off her clothes and let him see the wounds again, but now, with his palm against her and the pads of his fingers caressing her skin seductively, her body was stirring to life.

"I couldn't give you anything but chaos and emotion with me falling apart every few minutes, and you deserve better than that, Jonas." She ignored the wild yearning his voice, his hands and the look on his face produced.

He tucked a spiral curl behind her ear, his hand sliding to the nape of her neck to hold her in place. "If you fall apart, I can be there for you."

"That's not how I want us to be. I don't want you to have to pick up the pieces." Now she knew exactly what she did want to say. "I want to find out what I want."

Jonas's gaze went dark and hot, dropping to her lips. Her stomach flipped. Searing heat spread through her lower body. "I don't mind helping you figure out what you want, Hannah. You can . . . talk . . . to me all you want."

The blatant suggestion in his voice curled her toes in the sand. His palm cradled the nape of her neck, gentle and warm, yet effectively holding her in front of him. All of a sudden he was close. She knew he moved, shifted. She hadn't seen it, but suddenly he was there, his body a mere inch from hers. She could feel the heat from his body, the powerful muscles in his thighs and chest, yet they weren't touching other than his hand curled around the back of her neck. The whisper of his breath slid over her, into her. She felt them breathe together.

"Jonas." She tried to put warning — censure — into her voice, but it was impossible, not when his eyes were so dark with hunger.

He didn't bother to disguise it or wrap it up into something pretty for her. He let her see the stark need in him, the heavy bulge in the front of his jeans, the race of his pulse and the cocky, sexy smile as his hot gaze drifted over her face. She touched her tongue to her lower lip and instantly his attention was riveted there.

"You aren't going to seduce me." She held up her hand in warning, torn between wanting to run, wanting to laugh and wanting to throw herself into his arms.

"I'm not? You're certain about that?" His thumb slid over her pounding pulse.

"You're distracting me, Jonas. I can't keep the fog hanging low if I'm distracted and I wanted to walk on the beach." There was desperation in her voice; she couldn't help it, she felt desperate. If he kissed her, she wasn't going to be strong. She would cave. She could already taste him in her mouth, wild and crazy and masculine. Jonas could make her come apart in his arms whether or not she felt beautiful and that wasn't the point. She wanted to come to him whole, not broken. She was so broken, and yet, she'd been given a second chance to do things right. More than anything, she wanted her relationship with Jonas to be right.

He bent his head and brushed his lips gently across hers. "I'm going to love you, Hannah. Forever. For always. Sex is part of that so you can expect to handle a little seduction now and again. I have no doubt in my mind that I can make you feel beautiful. And I can make you want me. And I can make you scream my name and forget everything but pleasure. I may not be good at a lot of things, but I can give that to you."

She cupped his face in her hand, her thumb sliding along his shadowed jaw. "I want that from you. Just give me a little time."

His eyes searched hers, evidently saw what he needed, and he bent down to brush a butterfly-soft kiss across her lips before releasing her. "Whatever you need, baby, I'm your man." He began walking down the beach, a small, satisfied smile on his face.

Hannah tucked her fingers into his back pocket and walked beside him, the crushing weight that seemed to be ever present in her chest easing. He was her man, and even though she wasn't stupid and knew he was saying much more than on the surface, Jonas was willing to wait for her to figure her life out and that meant everything.

Gulls cried out and the water rushed toward shore, slamming into rocks to spray white droplets into the air. Water foamed and sizzled, leaving tiny holes in the sand as the waves retreated. They sauntered in companionable silence until Hannah glanced back at their footprints in the wet sand.

"You have big feet, Jonas."

He glanced down at her, straight faced. "I have big everything."

She rolled her eyes and laughed, unable to help herself. It felt good to laugh. "I walked into that one, didn't I?"

"Yep. So I've been thinking about this situation."

"Oh, Lord, that's scary. What situation?"

"Us. You and me. We're together, right? Solid. But basically we can't have sex unless I catch you off guard."

He had to quit saying "sex" or even thinking about it. She detested her body. She sure didn't want him looking at it, but every single time his eyes slid over her with that possessive *hungry* look, each time he spoke in his low, I'm-ravenous-and-going-to-eat-you-for-dinner voice, she melted. If she melted any more, she'd be a puddle at his feet. He would never take her seriously and she absolutely needed time to figure things out.

"You aren't going to catch me off guard, Jonas, so don't even go there. I might want to . . ." She trailed off, color rising.

"Have sex. Make love," he supplied, amusement tingeing his voice.

She scowled at him, although it was impossible to intimidate Jonas. "Yes. That. But in the end, I'd have to take my clothes off and I'd be self-conscious and it would be awful and you'd be frustrated and mad at me. So it's best just not to go there."

His grin widened enough to make her breath hitch in her lungs. He didn't have to be so good looking or sexy. And he didn't have to have that look on his face, the one that said he was a predator about to pounce and gobble her up. "I can think of quite a few ways to make love without removing all your clothes. The more I think about it, the more erotic it is, you with a nice long skirt and no panties. Or panties I can rip off. No, let's say you don't have any on and I just happen to slide my hand over your sexy little ass. Just because you look good enough to eat."

His hand cupped her body through the denim of her jeans, and made a leisurely slide as if searching for panty lines. Color crept into her face and damp heat curled deep inside her.

"No panty line. I'd say you were wearing a thong. Yeah, baby, that's sexy, but under this nice long mythical skirt, you aren't wearing anything but bare skin." His hand slid to her hips and then up her waist, under her blouse. His fingers skimmed gently, careful not to touch anywhere that could hurt. He cupped her breast, resting the weight in his palm. "And you wouldn't even be wearing this lacy little thing you call a bra. So when I bent my head like this . . ." His mouth closed over her breast right through her shirt, suckling gently through the material, his teeth tugging at her nipple, sending a flash fire sizzling through her body.

Her eyes went opaque, glazed, her breath catching in her lungs. Jonas was careful to ignore his own needs, forcing his mind away from the almost painful hardness between his legs. Hannah was all that counted to him. She had to know she was a beautiful, desirable woman and had needs of her own.

The knowing would be enough for both of them for now. He pulled back, breathed warm air over the small wet spot, teeth lingering for just a moment on her nipple before releasing her.

"So when I bent my head like that, I could just shove the shirt, that lacy little peasant thing you wear that drives me crazy, right out of the way."

She didn't know her lacy peasant blouse drove him crazy. His mouth and hands did it for her. She stayed quiet wanting more of his fantasy, knowing that she was skimming the line of danger with him, but wanting it to go on a little longer, before she had to go back and face reality. She ached for him and it made her feel alive. She might be hyper-aware of the cuts on her face, throat and body, but Jonas managed to make her feel as if her face — her skin — was flawless when he looked at her.

"I love that look on your face, dreamy and sexy and a little bit mischievous. I have no idea how you can look seductive and in-nocent at the same time."

"I wish I could see myself through your eyes." He certainly made her feel beautiful, even if she couldn't see it for herself.

He tugged at her hand and they began walking again, leaving prints side by side in the wet sand, stepping around kelp and several small jellyfish to round the cove where the tide pools were. The tide was in, so they skirted the rocks and stayed up on the beach, watching the waves crash against the barnacle-encrusted caves and boulders. Birds flapped their wings impatiently, waiting for the sun to break free of the fog before launching into the air for breakfast.

"When I take you out, Hannah, wear that long flowing skirt that moves with every step you take. It's light blue with swirls of darker blue and goes with your lacy blouse."

She couldn't help being pleased that he could describe one of her favorite outfits. "I wish you could risk taking me out. I feel like I'm locked up and someone's thrown away the key. And now that I know the danger is still present, I'm going to be sitting in my room forever."

"You can't let this make you a prisoner. We just have to be a little inventive. We could go to my house tomorrow evening, or maybe the lighthouse. Inez has the keys."

"How would Inez get the keys to the lighthouse? She runs the grocery store."

"Inez has the keys to the entire town. How do I know how she got them? We could have a private picnic there, at the lighthouse. No one would know. It's easily defensible. And you don't have to pack your bags and run away."

She was a little ashamed of that. Of course the house had protected them, she'd heard it for years growing up, but she'd never actually seen it. She'd even had a little doubt, but she wasn't going to admit it out loud. "You want to take me to the lighthouse on a picnic with people trying to kill me?"

"It's that or sit in your room, and Hannah, another day or two and you're going to be climbing down the side of the house, trying to escape. We can sneak away. Your sisters can distract everyone and we'll slip out in the dark."

She was touched that he'd suggested it. She was already going stir-crazy, but with the reporters, and now with the knowledge that whoever wanted her dead was somewhere close, directing assassins, leaving the protection of the house seemed terrifying. She didn't want to go anywhere alone.

Jonas caught her around the waist and lifted her over a wide channel of cold water streaming across the sand toward the sea. She rested her hands on his shoulders, feeling the muscles bunch. It seemed so effortless for him to swing her over the distance. It was a little like flying, yet she was safely anchored. He set her on her feet and kept walking away from the house.

"The fog bank isn't going to hold forever, Jonas," she reminded him.

"No, but you and your sisters can handle a few photographers."

She squared her shoulders. It was true. Why had she been so afraid? Jonas was so sure of her. He believed in her and it was difficult not to believe in herself when he had such absolute conviction. "So if I was wearing my blue skirt and peasant blouse, and we went to the lighthouse, what exactly would we do?"

"I'd bring music so we could dance."

She knew he was a wonderful dancer. It had been one of the things about him that set him apart in school. He had danced with the Drakes, learning every type of dance from ballroom to salsa, and it had made him a hit at every school dance. She loved to dance and Jonas knew it. Even as a child she'd floated around the house, pretending to be everything from a ballerina to a ballroom competition dancer. Jonas had even done the Lindy and jitterbug with her.

"This picnic is starting to sound tempting."

"Strawberry Italian soda," he bribed, knowing her weakness. "And French bread." Two of her favorite things.

The lighthouse would be deserted and it would be easy enough for Jonas to get permission to go there. If they could really sneak away, it would be such a relief to have a few hours when she wasn't feeling trapped. And she loved being with Jonas. It was really that simple. She needed time to sort herself out, but she loved every moment in his company. "Do you think we could really get away with it?"

There was hope in her voice. Jonas flashed her another cocky grin. "Tomorrow night I'll sneak you out," he promised.

"Sarah will have a fit," Hannah warned.

"No she won't. She knows you can't stay cooped up in the house and you can't go in public, so this is the next best thing. No one will think of looking for you there. You'll be safe, Sarah will approve, and I'll get to wonder whether or not you're wearing thong underwear or nothing at all."

"You're awfully obsessed with my underwear," she teased.

"Or lack of," he admitted. "I think about it more than I should."

She glanced up at the honesty in his voice. How in the world could that simple admission make her hot all over? "Let me assure you, I almost always wear underwear." She had to clench her teeth together to keep from laughing at his expression.

"Almost always? That's just wrong, Hannah. Now I'm never going to have a moment's peace around you."

She looked smug. "I know."

Jonas laughed, the sound deep and real, filled with amusement and making her heart soar. She did a small dance pattern in the sand, throwing out her arms, for a moment forgetting entirely she was disfigured and someone hated her enough to kill her. She glanced at the sky. "We could probably build a sand castle before the fog is gone."

"We don't have any tools."

"Tools?" She gave a sniff of disdain. "Amateur."

"You did not just call me an amateur."

"I did. You build your sand castle over there. You have twelve minutes. That's it and we have to go."

He was already crouching down, digging for wetter sand. She was on her knees doing the same. A few minutes later, when Jonas glanced over at her, she was cheating, directing little wind flurries to etch out the castle walls. He opened his mouth to call her on it, but she looked so absorbed, a child playing, carefree and happy, and he wasn't about to interrupt even to tease her.

Hannah dug her hands into the sand,

absently guiding small bursts of wind to carve the castle. The sand felt good, earthy and grainy, the castle taking shape quickly. She formed a bridge over her moat by sending a spear of wind blasting a tunnel through the sand. It burst out the other side, spraying Jonas hard enough to sting him.

She covered her mouth, muffling her laughter when he whirled around so fast he lost his balance and fell into the wet sand which he'd been carefully avoiding. "Poor baby. And your sand castle looks a little anemic." She leaned over to push her finger into the sloping side where the sand kept caving in. "You have to pack it solid, Jonas."

He caught her arms and tugged until she lost her balance and fell across him. He took both wet, sandy hands and rubbed them dry on her denim-clad butt, leaving smears all over her bottom. "You deserve that for cheating."

"I didn't cheat."

"You used the wind."

"I can't help it if it likes me and not you." She stayed sprawled across him, lifting herself up to look down into his eyes. "You're a beautiful man, Jonas Harrington. You really are." She brushed the hair from where it spilled across his forehead.

"I'm glad you think so, Miss Drake."

"If I kiss you after all, will you think I've lost my mind?"

"Kissing doesn't mean we're going to have sex, Hannah."

"I know, but you've given me . . ." She broke off. *Hope.* The word shimmered in her mind and she sent it to his. *Laughter.* She bent to brush a kiss on his chin. *My life back.* She kissed the corner of his mouth, rubbed her lips over his. *I felt broken, Jonas, and you make me feel whole.*

She settled her lips over his, sliding her tongue shyly along the seam of his mouth, uncaring that he was seeing her face in the early dawn. She needed to kiss him, to find a way to show him she loved him. Because she did. Bone deep. Her entire heart. Even her soul. She poured her love into her kiss, opening her mind a little, wanting him to feel what he meant to her. Wanting him to know what he did for her. She could face her future. And she could be strong even when she felt as if she wanted to crawl into a hole.

"You gave me that," she murmured against his mouth. "Thank you."

He reached up to cradle her head, holding her to him. "I love you, Hannah. Whatever you need, I'll be it for you."

She smiled into his eyes. "So the whole

bossy thing was just an act?"

"Of course, to impress you. And it worked." He lifted his head to cover the few inches separating them and captured her lower lip with his teeth, tugging gently. "Kiss me again."

He didn't wait for her, taking the initiative, sliding his mouth over hers, gentle, tender, small kisses, like butterfly wings, over and over, rubbing her lips with his, teasing the corners of her mouth with his tongue, savoring her taste, slow and languid, taking his time, taking her with him on a journey of texture and taste. Of melting heat that began as a slow burn but grew hotter degree by deliberate degree.

His fingers tangled in her hair, held her in place while he took her over, letting passion slip slowly past control into desire-laced love. When she didn't pull away, he pressed further, his mouth hot and demanding, deepening the kiss, storming her every defense. He had waited so long to claim her. She'd been too young, then he'd been gone, then he'd been too hard and wild, and then he'd made too many enemies. But he'd dreamt of her, his body aching, starving for just this — the taste of her on his tongue, the feel of her silken skin beneath his hands, her body soft and pliant and belonging to him.

She smelled like heaven to him, and she felt even better, with her breasts pressed tightly against his chest and his erection, thick and hard and so filled with need of her, pushing against her soft belly. Need was dark and hot, rushing through him like a tidal wave. Her mouth was velvet soft, just as hot and dark as his need. The edges of reason were beginning to blur. He let one hand drift down her face to her breast and his mouth followed. She flinched when he dragged his teeth across her breast.

Instantly he pulled back, slamming the back of his head into the sand. "I'm sorry, baby. I got carried away and didn't think. What an ass."

She framed his face with her hands and leaned down to brush a kiss across his lips. "You know something, Jonas? I forgot, too. For one moment, I was completely whole. You gave me a perfect moment. Thank you."

He couldn't answer her. His body still throbbed with need and he was cursing himself for being an insensitive, selfish idiot. Her generosity was nearly his undoing.

Hannah rolled over to lie in the sand beside him, breathing deep, her hand finding his. Trying to think of something safe to say, she stared up at the mist hanging thickly over their heads, trying valiantly to give them privacy. "What are you going to be doing today?"

"Jackson and I are going to be checking to see if anyone filed a missing persons report. We'll take a boat out and look for bodies. He's trying to get evidence off the house and fence to see if we can identify anyone who was here last night. We'll do a sweep of the neighborhood. Damon and Sarah are your closest neighbors. Sarah was here and Damon said he was asleep, so no witnesses."

"It's just as well. We don't really have the powers to make people forget what they see. I know you hated that last night."

"It felt wrong."

"Better you shoot them than the grounds and house protect us?"

He frowned. "I don't like to call what you do magic. You're magical, but the rest — you have gifts. And you all try to use the gifts for good, but last night, it felt like magic. And the spirits in the house . . . we're never making love in there again. What if one of them was floating around?"

She pressed her lips together tightly to keep from smiling. "It really did freak you out, didn't it?"

"Give me a nice clean bullet anytime." He was silent a moment. "On the other hand, I never thought about the receiving end when you sent the wind to help me out when I was in San Francisco. I would have died in that alley without you. I was so focused on moving, staying on my feet and not making poor Jackson carry me, that I didn't think beyond that."

"Neither did I. Someone was trying to kill you, Jonas, and I did whatever it took to protect you. Last night, you would have done whatever it took to protect us. And the house, and our ancestors, did whatever it took to make certain our lineage continues."

"I know, baby." He gave a small sigh and sat up, climbing to his feet with his fluid grace and tugging her hand to help her.

"Does it bother you what I can do?" The tinge of fear she felt showed on her face. She didn't bother to try to hide her feelings from Jonas. He always found out anyway.

He leaned down to brush another kiss across her mouth. "It's so much a part of you, a part of your family, that there's no separating one from the other, Hannah. That's who you are. Believe me, sweetheart, I don't mind taking advantage when the bullets are flying."

Hannah dusted the sand from his back and bottom and then turned to let him do the same. His hands lingered a little too long, shaping her butt, massaging when he could have just smacked the sand off. Just when she thought she'd have to object, when her body was reacting with a little too much heat, his hands slid away and he tucked her hair behind her ear, looking innocent.

She shook her head. "I hope you enjoyed yourself."

"Very much, thank you. Need any help with the front?" He'd been careful to keep the sand away from her wounds. "Maybe I should do an inspection."

"Maybe you should start considering how we're going to get up the stairs to the house without a hundred zoom lenses taking shots of us." She pulled his jacket closer around her for protection.

"That's your department, Hannah." He slid his arm around her shoulders and drew her to him as they began to walk back toward the house. "I could throw you over my shoulder in a fireman's carry and make a run for it, but they'd take pictures of your cute butt and plaster it from here to hell and back. That would make me angry and then I'd go punch one of them and lose my job, so I'm guessing you'll just have to do your thing, woman, and get us out of it."

"Lose your job?" She grinned at him. "I wouldn't have to worry about you getting shot at ever again."

"But then we'd starve."

"Jonas, I made a pretty good living and most of it is in the bank or invested in very safe stocks. We aren't going to starve."

"You're giving me a stomachache. I don't want to know that you have more money than me."

She slapped his ribs hard. "You're such a chauvinist."

"Absolutely. I'm supporting you while you stay home and raise our children. I don't want some stranger raising them. And I don't want them going to school at some obnoxious age just because they're smart. We're keeping them home and looking after them ourselves."

"Is that what we're doing?"

He glanced down at her. "Yes. Unless you have a better idea?"

"That *was* my idea. I told you so when I was eight. You ignored me for that awful little Sherrie Rider. Thank God she moved away when she was ten. And she burped all the time. I have no idea why you found her interesting."

"She played sports, Hannah. And you wanted to play dolls or something. Geez. Basketball or Barbies, come on."

Her laughter flowed over him again, making him want to smile. "We're in the danger zone and your sisters are waiting for us. Are you ready, baby? Because I will carry you even if it means I have to share your butt with the photographers."

"My hero. It won't be necessary, though." She lifted her arms toward the sky and began to move her hands in flowing patterns.

He heard feminine voices in the wind as it rushed in off the ocean, driving the thick band of fog before it toward the surrounding bluffs. Birds took to the air, flying inland, swarming toward the cliffs and trees as Hannah and Jonas, hand in hand, sprinted up the stairs leading to the Drake home.

15

"Hannah, would you mind coming downstairs," Sarah called. "We'd like to do another healing session on you. Libby's feeling great. Jonas isn't here and the house is in protection mode, so we should have a few hours with no interruptions."

Hannah closed her eyes briefly and tugged the blanket closer around her. Jonas had been gone all day, and why that depressed her, she didn't know. She'd detested being cooped up in her room, but where else could she go? If she went downstairs, everyone spoke in the hushed tones she'd come to despise. She couldn't say anything because she didn't want to hurt anyone's feelings. So she was holding a first-class pity party in her room and waiting for Jonas to come back and treat her normally again.

"Hannah!" This time Sarah's voice was sharp and imperious, as only an eldest sister could manage. "Come down here."

Hannah made a face at the door, feeling childish. Sarah could reduce them all to children when she was on a roll. It was easier just to go along with what she wanted than to try to argue. Hannah tossed her blanket on the bed and reluctantly opened the door of her bedroom. At once, familiar scents filled the air. The tea kettle whistled merrily and Joley's contagious laughter mingled with Libby's. Hannah stood in the hall for a long moment, breathing it all in. She loved them all so much — her sisters — even when they were killing her with kindness. And no one laughed like Joley. She could light up an entire city, let alone a room.

Hannah descended the spiral stairs and discovered the lower story was lit only with candles. The scent of cinnamon and apple potpourri filled the air. The flickering light threw dancing shadows on the walls. She hoped that the candlelight also softened the effect of the wounds on her face.

Already, her body was healing. Her sisters gathered twice a day, pushing themselves in order to boost her body's ability to recover. The wounds had closed and this afternoon she'd noticed the raw redness was already fading. Unfortunately, the healing sessions had little effect on the trauma. With Jonas next to her, she could sleep a little, but alone, she was terrified to close her eyes.

Sometimes she tried to recapture the moment of the attack in an effort to give Jonas more details, but her mind didn't cope well with the trauma and steadfastly refused to provide anything else that might help him. The only thing she remembered with any certainty was the shocking slash of the knife. Although it made no sense, she could have sworn she remembered her attacker whispering an apology as he drove the knife into her again and again.

Her sisters were gathered in the large living room, where they usually met in the evenings when they all came home. Most no longer resided full time in the family home. Sarah lived next door with Damon, and Kate and Matt had a house on the bluff by the old mill. Abbey and Aleksandr were purchasing a large two-story home overlooking the sea a mile down from the Drake house, and Tyson and Libby had an extraordinary home he had found for her up on a bluff surrounded by acres of private land. Only Hannah, Joley and Elle still used the family home as a permanent base when they weren't traveling.

Hannah waved her hand at the fireplace and flames leapt to life. "I should have baked cookies earlier, but I didn't think about it," she greeted her sisters, forcing a cheerful smile.

"That's okay," Kate said. "I made some myself." She arched a look over her shoulder at Joley. "*All* by myself."

"Hey!" Joley objected. "I started the first batch and you kicked me out of the kitchen."

"She set the oven on fire," Sarah explained.

"It wasn't my fault," Joley said. "I put the cookies in the oven and just forgot I was baking. Did you know that cookies can turn to charcoal if they're in the oven long enough? And then they can actually catch on fire."

"You caught the cookies on fire, Joley?" Hannah covered her mouth to smother a laugh, and looked away from her younger sister. For the first time since the accident, she felt more comfortable with her sisters, and she realized she couldn't feel overwhelming pity from them. If they felt it, they were careful to shield her from their emotions. They were acting much more normally, and teasing Joley was habitual. She just gave them so many opportunities.

"Yes, actually I did, and they were surprisingly resistant to being fixed."

Alarm spread. "You used magic to fix them?" Hannah cast a mock-terrified look around. "No one has eaten them, have they?"

Her sisters shook their heads. Joley put her hands on her hips. "I'm not feeling the love here. I went to a great deal of trouble to try to fix those cookies; the least you could do is try one. What a bunch of chickens."

"Joley, you can't fix burnt cookies with magic," Hannah said. "What spell did you use?"

"I countered it," Elle said. "Sorry, Joley, but it was the only safe thing to do. Considering the mood you were in and the way you were muttering about Prakenskii, I was afraid your spell might take a wrong twist and turn the things into bombs or something."

"It's okay, sweetie," Libby said, wrapping her arm around Joley. "At least your heart was in the right place."

The girls tossed pillows on the floor and sank down in their familiar circle.

"Speaking of Prakenskii, what's going on with you and him?" Hannah asked. "He asked me if you were a spell-singer. I didn't like that he might even know what that meant."

There was a small silence while they all exchanged anxious looks.

"He was almost possessive with you," Sarah added. "And to use up a personal favor just to get the name of the man you supposedly were photographed in a compromising position with in a tabloid, that's just plain crazy."

Joley swept her hand through her hair. It was a bit shorter and a new color, not dark like Libby's anymore, but rich bands of red and dark brown with streaks of gold. Hannah touched her own hair, so difficult to work with, heavy enough to give her headaches, and wished she had the courage to do whatever she wanted with it the way Joley did. It was just that everyone loved her hair. It was so unusual, so beautiful, but then no one else had to cope with the tangles and weight of it.

She leaned toward her younger sister. "If you don't want to answer, Joley, you don't have to. I'm just worried."

Joley sighed heavily. "I don't know how to answer. I think he put a spell on me or something."

The Drake sisters gasped audibly, almost in stereo. Joley held up her hand. "Wait. I don't mean literally. I think I'd know if he

413

really did. I think you'd know. Wouldn't you?"

Hannah reached out, but didn't touch her arm. "May I?" Because she wasn't going to invade her sister's privacy ever again without permission. None of the Drakes liked their privacy invaded and she wasn't going to push beyond Joley's boundaries.

Joley nodded. "I want to find out."

"Then let Elle as well. She's strong in different ways, and between the two of us, if he's there, we'll find him," Hannah said. "Are you ready?"

Joley compressed her lips. "Yes. Ignore anything you see about how I feel about him, because it's crazy."

Hannah and Elle reached for her at the same time and energy immediately crackled in the air, manifesting itself as tiny white arcs and zigzagging streaks between the three girls. There was a small silence broken only by the sizzling of electricity and then Hannah and Elle dropped their hand from Joley's arms. They looked at one another over her head.

"He's all over you, Joley," Hannah said. "And it's consensual. You let him get inside you."

"I didn't, though. Not really. He just kept whispering to me, night and day, and his voice was so — *sexy* — God, not even that, more than sexy. Mesmerizing." She rubbed her palm back and forth on her thigh without being aware she did so. "I just couldn't resist him anymore. I wanted to see him, really see him. I thought I would be stronger and I could force him to go away, but he . . ." She broke off shaking her head. "I'm so worn out. He was so enraged with me over the tabloid thing."

"Why didn't you just tell him the truth?" Hannah asked gently.

"Because he makes me so angry. If someone with magical skills manipulated the attack on you, Hannah, it wasn't him. I would know. I know it isn't him."

"What does he want?" Kate asked.

"Me. He wants me," Joley admitted. "I told him I don't date criminals and he said he doesn't date. I don't dare ever be alone with him. I can't seem to resist him for very long. I've gotten good at surrounding myself with people when I know he's in the area, but . . ." Again she broke off.

"Tell him you don't want anything to do with him, that you're not attracted," Abbey suggested.

"I have told him to stay away, but he knows I'm physically attracted. I can't hide it from him, not when he's in my head. It's

415

horrible, like one of those moth-to-the-flame, stupid-idiot attractions. I know better. I never — *never* — meet him alone, face to face."

"All right, honey," Hannah said, "don't panic. You should have come to us a long time ago, before he was able to get a real foothold in you. Tonight, we're doing a healing session for you instead of for me. I'm strong enough now and the wounds are healing nicely. A session or two with all of us will give you some breathing room and I'll do a little research and see what's in the books to combat this."

Hannah looked around her at the circle of faces. They were all being matter-of-fact with her, treating her normally, rather than overwhelming her with sympathy. She could breathe again. Let her guard down a little. If felt good to have them all back — even if it was just for the moment.

"No, no, you can't do that, Hannah. Tonight is all about you. We planned it," Joley said, "and it's important to me — to all of us — that you have this night. We need to tell you something — show you something." She looked around the circle at her sisters. "I'm going first since I spoke out of turn."

Hannah pulled back suspiciously. "What

is this? Have I been ambushed?"

"You'll like it," Joley promised. She waited until the scrapbook Sarah pulled out was handed to Hannah and flipped open. "This is the page I made for you. I wrote you a letter, put a couple of my favorite pictures of us together, and I also wrote a song for you. It's not entirely finished. I'll tweak it before I record it, but it's from me to you."

Hannah pulled the book closer so she could read the letter penned in Joley's scrawling cursive.

Hey baby girl,

How are you doing? I really hope that you are good. I've been thinking back over our lives, Hannah, and there are so many amazing things we've done together. You and I were — and are — best of friends and that will never change, no matter what.

You truly are an amazing person, Hannah. Everything inside of you is so beautiful. You are one of the strongest people I've ever come across to give up so much just for your family. I've never taken the opportunity to really show my love and feelings for you, and I should apologize for that. I've always looked up to you. You were always my role model.

You are always kind and gentle to everyone, yet so fun and exciting to be with. I always have the best of times with you, whether it be dancing around the house singing at the top of our lungs, or sun bathing on the beach and checking out the hot surfers.

You've always been there for me and I'll always be here for you. Nothing can ever change my love for you. I care about our relationship so much and I hope you see that I'll always be here for you. The song I've written for you is titled "All of Time." I hope you like it, because it's how I really feel.

Love always,
Joley

Hannah looked up at her sister and then around at the circle of faces. Tears shimmered in all of their eyes. "Joley, this is beautiful. Really, it isn't any of you. It isn't. I'm struggling, but I love you all and I'm just trying to find a way to work things out, and I will. I'm sorry I've been so difficult."

"Don't, Hannah," Sarah said. "We're the ones apologizing and for a very good reason. Joley, show her my page."

Joley leaned over and turned back the pages until she came to the first one. There were pictures of Sarah and Hannah at various ages, all evoking memories of Sarah carefully brushing out the terrible tangles the tight spiral curls always caused, and wiping away tears when someone called her a poodle. There was even one of all the girls in poodle skirts with their hair teased into fluffy curls because Hannah had been so upset that she couldn't straighten her hair.

The memories brought a tightness to Hannah's chest. Sarah had always been so good to her, watching over her when she went to school early and helping her to keep from stuttering in front of others. She pressed the scrapbook to her breast and fought against the lump in her throat threatening to choke her.

"You have to read my letter, honey," Sarah encouraged.

"I don't think I can. It will make me cry," Hannah said.

"It's supposed to make you feel better," Sarah pointed out. "It comes from my heart."

"I'll read it, but if you make me cry, I'm going to turn you into a toad," Hannah promised. "And who's supposed to be making the tea?"

"You always make it," Kate said. "You know everyone's favorite and no one else can make it taste the way you do. I've never figured out what you do to it."

"She adds love," Elle said. "That's always been Hannah's secret."

To give herself a moment, Hannah waved her hand toward the kitchen and at once the tea kettle began to whistle. Her hands followed a familiar, graceful pattern as she wove a spell that would bring each of her sisters their favorite tea. Only when the mugs were floating out on a tray, and her sisters had chosen their brew, did Hannah look down at the bold, precise and very honest writing that could only be Sarah's.

Dearest Hannah,

From the time you were born and I first held you in my arms, it was apparent that your soul was as old as time and that your very essence put forth a calm healing light that drew all who looked upon you. Yes, on the outside, you always looked like a golden goddess. However, dearest sister, it has always been your inner beauty and light that has drawn and kept us close to you.

You are my sister and I love you dearly, but you know me. I have never put much store into exterior looks or beauty, because some of the most beautiful people have the ugliest of souls and intentions. You need to know I am proud of you and that as your big sister I put great store into who you are as a person. It has always been so hard for you to be out there in the world, and the people who meet you have no idea how hard it is for you to be there, but there you are and you always manage to come through for us all. No matter what the cost is to you.

Not one of those pushy photographers have ever taken the time to know you, let alone what your life costs you, or how much you would rather be curled up at home in an armchair enjoying a hot cup of tea surrounded by the people and things that you love. Rather than feeling awkward, shy and ready to crawl out of your skin and ready to run away and hide.

Perhaps, dear sister, we too have failed you, we always thought that letting you know how beautiful you were and how amazing you looked was important to you. We always thought that you wanted to travel, that you wanted to be in the forefront and that you were happy in your career even though it cost you emotionally. We just didn't see the bigger picture, let alone know how much we had set up the playing field and how hard we had made things for you. Know this, Hannah, whatever you want to be in life, wherever you want to go, is just fine by us. We love you and completely support your decisions whatever they may be. I am just so sorry that it has taken me this long to figure out you were doing all these things for us and not for yourself. Please forgive us for our ignorance and know that we love you unconditionally with all of our hearts.

Love you, as always,

Sarah

"Okay, now you've really made me cry," Hannah accused, brushing at the tears running down her face. "You have to know you don't owe me an apology. I should have told you how I felt. I really should have, Sarah."

"Why didn't you?" Sarah asked, leaning forward.

"I just hate letting down the people I love most. I didn't even talk to you about it. As many times as we all sat here together, I never once told you how unhappy I was."

"Jonas saw it when none of us did," Sarah said. "We got into an argument about it and then suddenly I could see what he was saying so clearly and I was ashamed of myself. I'm your sister and I should have seen how unhappy you were."

Hannah shook her head. "No, Sarah, it was my life, and my decision to make. I should have told all of you. Please don't take responsibility for my mistakes. If one good thing comes out of this, it's that I'm determined to make decisions based on what I really want."

"Is Jonas what you really want?" Libby asked. "The two of you did a lot of yelling yesterday, but today things seem better."

Hannah bit down on her lower lip. "Actually I love him with my entire heart and soul. I should have told him a long time ago."

Joley and Elle exchanged a quick look of alarm while Sarah and Kate smirked and Libby mouthed I-told-you-so to Abbey.

"Don't you think he's a little bossy?" Joley asked hopefully. "I mean, really, Hannah, how are you going to put up with him?"

"Don't listen to her," Abbey said. "She's thinking of her own skin. If you fall, she's next on the list."

"Don't even go there." Joley shuddered visibly. "I'm not dating ever again, just so there's no way I'll get caught. Can you imagine me trying to live my life with one of the wack jobs I'm attracted to? I've got loser stamped in neon letters across my forehead. If they're big and bad, and hotter than hell, I'm their girl. Then they open their mouth and annoy me and it's over." She sighed. "I'll be the old lady with the cats."

Kate waved toward the kitchen and a plate of cookies floated out. Hannah waited until everyone had one before she turned the page to Abigail's entry. Pictures of the ocean and long-haired girls running hand in hand over the sand brought back memories of laughter.

Abigail leaned over and pointed to one with her arms around Hannah when she was about thirteen. "That one is my favorite. See the light spilling around you? That's the way I always see you, shining from the inside out."

Hannah ducked her head, taking a slow sip of tea. For a moment she felt nearly overwhelmed with love. She'd always known she was lucky. All of them were. Good times or bad, they banded together and shared. She took a breath and let it out before looking at Abbey's letter.

Dear Hannah,
I just wanted you to know how much I

love and admire you. You are always so strong and there for everybody, even when it is so hard for you. You never complain and are the first one to jump in and help out.

I wanted to remind you of something you did for me that was special to me but I just can't narrow it down to one thing. You have always been my support and I don't know what I ever would have done without you. When I was being silly or rash, you helped me through it. When my temper (the one I still say I don't have) rears its ugly head, you are there to bring me back to a simmer.

Growing up, when I got hurt, you were always the one who would hug me tight and take the pain away. If somebody picked on me at school, you were there before I ever had to ask. More than one time somebody that was picking on me mysteriously got sick. You always said it was not you doing anything but I was sure it was just you protecting me.

I guess what I am trying to say is you are perfect in my eyes and someday I can't wait to have my little Hannah running around protecting her older sister no matter the problem. I can't imagine anything more promising than that in life. I want you to know that I love you unconditionally and no matter what you do in your life I will always love and support you. You have my shoulder, just as I have always had yours.

I love you,
Abbey

Hannah swallowed the lump in her throat. "I'm very, very lucky to have all of you. You always make me feel so loved and so special. I don't know what I was thinking, afraid you couldn't accept me because I'm not a model anymore."

"Did you really think that, hon?" Libby asked gently, "or did you have trouble accepting yourself?"

There was a small silence. Hannah took another sip of her tea. Honey and milk combined with the tea to soothe her throat. "Of course I have trouble accepting me. Look at me, Libby. I already look at myself and see every flaw, real or imagined. Part of me wanted to crawl into a hole and never come out." She frowned, trying to really analyze her feelings. "Part of me was terrified and sickened that someone would want to do this to me, but there is a tiny part that felt free. I felt if I could focus on that small triumph instead of the wreck of my face and body, I might find a way to emerge victorious. I'm really sorry I shut you all out."

"Don't be," Sarah said. "It was good for us to have to figure out what we were doing wrong. Jonas said something the other day that made a lot of sense. He said when Damon and I have a fight, he doesn't interfere. I really thought about that. Jonas has always been protective of us, and he never once interfered with any of our men when we argue. He must want to — maybe even need to — but he doesn't because it would be wrong. And it was wrong for us to try to run your life for you, even if our intentions were good."

Hannah looked around at the faces smiling at her. Acceptance. It was what made them all so close. Joley, as wild as she could be; Elle, so quiet and with fire simmering beneath the surface; Abbey, more at home in the sea; and Libby, without a mean bone in her body. Sarah, organized and reliable; and dear sweet Kate, whom everyone had to love. "You're all pretty great sisters," Hannah said, trying not to cry.

Kate bit into her cookie. "Of course we are. When you were a little girl, you were very angry with us because it was time for school and you didn't want to go. How old was she, Sarah? You remember when I'm talking about."

"Oh, don't tell this story," Hannah said and put her head down on the crook of her arm, laughing. "Joley and Elle don't know and you just can't tell them."

" 'Cuz we think she's so perfect and would never do anything bad," Joley said. "Spill it, Kate."

"How old was she, Sarah? You remember the time we were hurrying, trying to get ready for school, and she decided she absolutely wasn't going to go?"

"Six," Sarah supplied. "She was only six."

Hannah groaned and took another sip of tea. "You're both going to be sorry for telling this story."

"It will be well worth it," Kate said. "She sat on the stairs with her arms crossed, glaring at us, and if we touched her, we'd get zapped."

"An electrical shock," Sarah added, "a real jolt. She zapped us all — including Mom and Dad. At six she was already making up spells."

There was a small silence. Joley sat up straighter. "I'm seeing you with new eyes, Hannah. You're a goddess. You really zapped Dad? I wish I had known that spell. He caught me going out the window one night and, well — let's just say I could have used something."

They all burst out laughing. When they sobered, Libby took the book and a little shyly opened it to her page. The pictures were all taken of a day they'd been walking together in the forest. Hannah remembered the day because it had been so perfect — everything from the weather to the company.

"This was one of my favorite times with you," Libby said. "We talked about everything and I was so distressed. I was in med school and the hours were killer. I was younger than everyone else and some of the other students weren't very nice. You made that day so wonderful, Hannah. I knew, after that walk, that I could face everyone and do what I wanted to do and still be me. You gave me hope." She pointed to her letter. "I'm not very eloquent, but it's from the heart."

Hannah dropped her gaze to the scrawl that was Libby's.

Hannah,
I need to tell you just how much you mean to me. You are so very special and a large part of my heart belongs to only you.

We have shared so many laughs and

tears through the years and have made enough memories together to last forever. I still get a smile on my face every time I remember the time we were playing cards and were hysterical with laughter when the phone rang. We couldn't answer because we couldn't stop laughing and when you did finally answer it was a wrong number which only sent us back into another round of laughing until our stomachs actually hurt.

My life would not be what it is today had you not been a big part of it. You were always there for me with your love and support, and often your protection. Many times, I've seen you step out of your comfort zone to help me as well as many others. You are one of the most loving and giving persons I've ever known.

Dear sweet Hannah, there is nothing you could ever do or say that would change my feelings for you. You are a huge part of my life, and I love you just because you are YOU!

Your loving sister,
Libby

Hannah closed the book with a small snap. "Now you've got me crying."

"Just drink more tea," Elle suggested. "That's what I do."

The door banged open and Jonas hurried in, the wind and mist coming in behind him. "It's getting cold out there," he greeted them, striding into the room and stopping abruptly. He frowned. "You're not having one of your girlie things, are you, with everyone crying and being all mushy?"

"That's exactly what we're doing," Joley said cheerfully. "Come on and sit down and join us."

Hannah felt pleasure bursting through her. It had been this way for so long. The seven sisters and Jonas. He'd always been in the circle with them. He complained, of course, and sometimes rolled his eyes and sneered, but he always flopped on the floor and became a part of who and what they were. She watched him as he took his place between her and Joley, wedging his thigh against hers and sliding his arm around her waist, fingers at the nape of her neck, slowly massaging.

"Did anyone bother to cook dinner? I'm starving."

There was another burst of laughter. He scowled at them. "What?"

"You *always* ask that, every single time,"

Hannah explained. "You're always hungry, Jonas."

He bent down and skimmed a kiss down Hannah's cheek, right over the fading wounds as if they weren't there. His kiss ended at the corner of her mouth. "They're being mean to me, baby. Can't you turn them all into toads or something?"

"Yeah, now you want her casting, now that she's on your side," Joley said.

"Don't worry, Joley," Jonas said as he snagged a mug of tea floating by and scooped up a handful of cookies from the plate. "She really just wants sex. The minute she gets what she wants and I start bossing her around, it'll be back to the seven of you against one lone man."

Hannah choked on her tea and had to have Jonas whack her on the back.

"He's right, you know," Elle piped up. "Think about that, Hannah, before you do anything stupid. Sex is great and all that, but he's going to be so bossy. Do you really want to put up with that night and day?"

Jonas grabbed Elle in a headlock and rubbed his knuckles over the top of her head. "I already boss all of you night and day, you little wildcat. Someone has to, or you'd all be out of control." He let go of her, ignoring the punch on his thigh. "So are all the letters read?"

"You knew about this?" Hannah asked.

"I know all," Jonas replied, expanding his chest.

"She's turning to my page now," Kate said a little shyly. "Please remember, Hannah, I'm better at fiction than reality. I have such a difficult time expressing myself."

"Not with Matt," Jonas said. "You're all over him."

Kate gave him an undignified smack on his arm while Hannah looked through the pictures. They were of a shoot Hannah had done. First she looked glamorous in several gowns and then she was laughing, in her jeans and sweater, hair piled on her head, making faces at them. "I love those, because they show what a real person you are underneath all that glam."

Hannah took a deep breath to still the overwhelming love she felt for her family so she could read what Kate had written to her.

Dearest Hannah,
When I think of love, of family, of the way sisters should be, I think of you. When I think of courage, of incredible personal strength, it's your face I see. Though you may never have realized it,

you are the strongest, the bravest, of us all.

I know what you suffer when you go out in public. We're both so alike in that respect. To be surrounded by strangers, to be the center of attention, to feel emotions beating at you: I could never do it. I've always clung to the shadows, to the security of solitude, but you never have. I can't tell you how much I've always admired you for that.

I realize now that your bravery has always been for our benefit, not for your own, and that must stop. I love you, Hannah. What I want for you is all I've ever wanted: your happiness. So be brave for yourself, not for us. Live your life the way you want to, seek out the happiness waiting for you. And let us love the sister you are, not the sister you think we want you to be.

Love forever,
Kate

"Thank you, Katie," Hannah said simply and leaned over to kiss her. "I don't know what I'd do without all of you. I really don't."

"Fortunately we don't have to find out," Kate agreed. "You scared us all, Hannah.

Really, really scared us. I couldn't think or breathe. When you went down, you took all of us with you, and for one terrible moment, we knew what life without you would be like." She glanced at Joley. "I know Prakenskii is dangerous. All of us touched his mind, and we could catch glimpses of a very scary man, but I'll always be grateful for what he did, whatever his motives. He saved your life. He kept you alive for us and it took a huge toll on him. He knew it would make him vulnerable to our magic, but he still kept you safe for us. I pray every single day for his health and happiness."

"Pray for his health, Kate, but leave off the happiness part," Joley muttered.

Jonas threw a brotherly arm around her. "If he was your man, I wouldn't have to worry about you so much. He'd scare everyone off. Maybe I ought to bribe him."

Joley pinched him hard and shoved a cookie in his mouth. "You're such a joker, Jonas. Ha, ha, ha. Very funny."

Hannah leaned back into Jonas and instantly his arms came around her. His chin nuzzled the top of her head.

"What else is in that scrapbook?" he asked.

"My page," Elle said, shyness in her voice. "The first pictures are of you directing the wind. I love to see the power in you, your hair blowing and your arms outstretched to the sky. You glow, Hannah, and you look so feminine. Nothing makes me prouder than to see you that way. And the others are of you in the kitchen. When I come home and I'm so tired and . . ." She broke off, looked around at her sisters' faces and then down at her hands. "When I feel so weary that I don't think I can go on, there you are. The moment I see you, I know I'm home. That's what you represent to me, Hannah. Home. Safety. Love and acceptance."

Hannah turned her face into Jonas's chest for just a moment to brush aside the emotional tears. Elle was so quiet and rarely talked about herself or her feelings, and when she did, Hannah felt privileged. "That's such a beautiful thing to say, Elle. Thank you."

"It's the truth," Elle replied simply.

There were nods all around. "She's right, Hannah. Now that Elle brought it up, you do represent home and family for all of us," Sarah agreed.

Hannah couldn't talk so she read the letter instead.

Hannah,
Hey Goldie-locks, though I'm no writer like Kate and I sure don't have the Joley

touch, I can't let another day pass without telling you how much I love you. And what you've meant to my life.

Did you know that one of my first memories is of jumping in my crib chanting Hann, Hann, Hann and knowing that you'd come running? You'd pull me up over the rails and out of the crib, hug me close and dance me around the room. When I was crying you tickled me and made me laugh. Hey, I still have the tiny penguin you gave me when I was five. It's a treasure I keep in my purse and pull out when I'm a little sad or lonely, and need a reminder of how much I'm loved. Who could forget our penguin walk and laughing until we cried? And my prom date . . . when I wrecked my dress and Joley fried my hair . . . remember how you held me tight, reassuring me that it wasn't the end of the world? Like always, you dried my tears and fixed everything better than new. You made me look like a fairytale — even though my date turned out to be a frog and not Prince Charming. Somehow you even made me laugh over that disaster. I always think of you on the catwalk, twirling under the wind and rain and night sky . . . you were the one who showed me the stars.

Hannah, I always knew you were there for me and more importantly that you'd understand how I was feeling. Through all these years you've been the one to help lighten the load when I started feeling the pressure of being the seventh of seven. You'd tease me and make me laugh and remind me that we're all in this together . . . sisters forever. Did you know that your sweet smile has always been one of the brightest spots of my life? You're brave and courageous and one of the most giving people I've ever had the privilege to know. Maybe you've never realized — I'm sorry I've never told you before how much I've always looked up to you (in every way — all puns intended) and how much your mischievous ways bring me real joy and make me laugh out loud in a world that's sometimes pretty sad. You've always been there for us, being what we needed you to be, keeping the smile strong in our hearts. Now it's your turn. Please be brave and strong just for you this time. You deserve everything good and wonderful. I love you so much.

Love,

your baby sis, Elle

Now Hannah was crying in earnest. "Elle, I love you, too. Thank you all. This was the sweetest, most thoughtful thing you could have done. I'll treasure these pages for the rest of my life." She hugged the scrapbook to her tightly.

"You're not finished," Jonas said. "I made you a page, too. This book is about things we love about you. Don't worry, I didn't put in any embarrassing pictures, because I didn't have any."

"You really made me a page?" She turned her face up to his, her heart lurching.

"Of course I did. I put a mixture of my favorite pictures up, there's one or two that really matter, but mostly there're ones with animals. I know you love dogs, even though you don't have one of your own."

"It wouldn't be fair. I'm never home long enough to spend time with a pet. Sarah's dogs love me, though."

She opened the scrapbook to Jonas's page. There was a small silence as she stared at the series of pictures of Hannah and Jeanette Harrington dressed in 1920 vintage clothes. She recalled that afternoon vividly. She'd been invited for tea and Hannah had found a closet filled with spectacular clothes. She looked at the pictures, trying to see through the tears in her eyes. She was so little with curls everywhere, wrapped in a too-long coat with a band and peacock feathers on her head. She was holding Mrs. Harrington's hand.

She blinked rapidly to clear the tears, focused on the masculine scrawl on the next page, and in spite of the lump in her throat, burst out laughing. " 'Reasons Why Hannah Should Marry Jonas,' " she read the title out loud.

"I've listed them all." He pointed to the long column. "Joley made me put reasons why you shouldn't, and as you can see, there're very few and they're lame."

"Lame?" Joley echoed. She jabbed her finger at the first one. "That's reason enough. I'm next in line for the big fall and it's your duty to protect me by staying unmarried forever. And . . ." She glared at Jonas. "I put stars by the next one and three exclamation points."

Jonas peered over Hannah's shoulder. "She did that after I was finished, the little sneak. I am *not* arrogant and bossy. I am charming."

Hannah choked and her sisters whooped with laughter. Joley and Elle fell over holding their stomachs. Libby tried to maintain her composure, but even she succumbed, laughing with her sisters.

"You've all lost your minds," he said with great dignity. "Not that I was ever certain you had minds in the first place." He grabbed another handful of cookies for comfort, and when Hannah doubled over laughing, he leaned down, swept her hair out of the way and attacked her neck in retaliation, leaving a very large red mark. Satisfied, he went into the kitchen looking for something more substantial to eat, leaving the women to sober up.

16

"Jonas! Jonas, come down here," Sarah called from just outside the door.

Jonas muttered an insulting protest loud enough for her to quit knocking. When he heard Sarah's footsteps fading down the hall, he rolled over, taking most of the covers with him, groaning as the sun hit his face through the French doors. "Baby, we're being summoned."

"You're being summoned, not me," Hannah said. "I'm still asleep." Not that she'd gotten any sleep with Jonas stroking little caresses down her spine all night.

Lying in bed beside Jonas without touching him had been a lesson in frustration. He'd certainly taken every opportunity to touch her, leaving her mood edgy and her body hypersensitive. She couldn't count how many times his hands had slid over her bottom. His pillow had somehow managed to be the exact height as her breasts, so he'd spent a great deal of time breathing warm air over her nipples, his mouth inches from her straining flesh.

In desperation, and to keep from begging, she'd turned over, keeping her back to him, and he'd immediately curled his body around hers, pressing his thick erection tightly against her butt while his hand tucked very naturally right beneath her breast. Just as she thought she might drift off, his hand would move, his knuckles skimming the underside of her breast, and a jolt of lightning would sizzle through her entire system and her muscles would clench. She had never felt so wound up, pulsing with heat and desire, in her life.

It was enough to make any woman crabby and Hannah was no saint. She lifted her head to look at him. "Go away and let me sleep." She hadn't slept for ten minutes. "You were supposed to be restful and hold the nightmares at bay."

His grin was slow and sexy. He leaned over and brushed kisses back and forth over her lips. "Then I did my job. You didn't have nightmares. Don't forget we're going to sneak out tonight. I've got to go to the office and do a little work. I'm running the tapes again of the crowd. Jackson's trying to find out if anyone's turned up missing."

"Just a regular day on the job. Find out who's trying to kill your girlfriend." She tasted the word and it felt strange. *Girlfriend.* She'd never been anyone's girlfriend. "Does that make you my *boy*friend?" She laughed softly at his expression.

"I'm no boy, Hannah, I'm a *manly* man."

Her laughter bumped up a notch. "A *charming* manly man."

"Laugh away, baby." He rolled on top of her, capturing both wrists and slamming them to the mattress on either side of her head. "But I'm going to remember and take my retribution."

At his suddenly aggressive action, her heart beat triple time and her entire body sang. He had her so primed with his all-night touching that her blood was pounding in her veins and pooling low and wicked in her body. His legs nudged hers aside so that his hips fit between her thighs. He tugged at her earlobe with his teeth, licked the pulse beating in her neck and kissed the very bright strawberry mark he'd left there the night before.

She could almost see the electricity arcing between them. She certainly felt it. She stared up at his hot, seductive mouth and felt weak just looking at him. Incredibly, she could taste him and all he was doing was looking at her, his hungry gaze drifting possessively over her face. A rush of liquid heat pooled low and wicked in her body in response. When his sinful mouth settled on hers, she forgot all about body image and the reasons why she wasn't going to make love with Jonas Harrington.

She wrapped her arms around him, her lips melting under his, her hands finding his hair and dragging him closer. Flashes of fire whipped through her body, as his tongue stroked along hers with demand. Sexually, there was nothing hesitant about Jonas. He took what he wanted and he made certain she wanted it, too.

"Good morning," he murmured.

She swallowed hard, absorbing the dark lust in his voice. There was something intoxicating about the sound, rough and husky and seductive, that crawled down her spine, made her breasts ache and sent muscles, already slick and hot, clenching with need. She could barely breathe through the arousal, her inner thighs so sensitive that when he moved, she felt the walls of her most feminine core begin to pulse and ripple in response.

"Jonas, really, I'm sorry to bother you, but you have a phone call. Pick up," Sarah insisted.

He'd been so far gone he hadn't even heard the telephone ring. Still lying over her, he reached lazily for the phone. "Harrington."

"Duncan Gray, Jonas. This is a secure line. I wanted to keep you informed that Boris Tarasov tried to rescue his brother two nights ago. They knew where he was being held and when we were transferring him. In the gun battle, he was shot and is in critical condition."

"The traitor?"

"Not yet, but I'm narrowing it down."

"Thanks for the information, Duncan."

Hannah blinked up at him as he hung up the phone. "What was that all about?"

"An old case, nothing important." He trailed kisses down the side of her face to the corner of her mouth.

"Are you sure? Your worry lines are back."

"Are they? Not over that case. The perp's in custody and it has nothing to do with me anymore. I'm out of that line of work for good." And he was. For the first time he realized hearing Duncan Gray's voice hadn't made him feel guilty. Hadn't made him feel as if he needed to go out and rid the world of evil. He was a man with a woman he treasured, and being with her, making certain she was safe, his family was safe, was enough for him. He could be the sheriff and come home at night and be satisfied.

He grinned at Hannah. "I'm happy, baby, and you did that all by yourself."

Sarah thumped on the door again. "Jonas! Jackson's already here to pick you up. He says you've got some big meeting you're late for." She gave the door one more hard smack. "And I'm not coming back up here. I'm not your messenger."

Jonas sighed, brushed another kiss over Hannah's trembling lips, his teeth tugging at her intriguing lower lip. "Thanks, Sarah. I'll be right there." He pushed up into a sitting position, the muscles on his back rippling beneath his skin. "I'll be home this evening to pick you up, baby. I'll sneak you out of here and we'll have a good time. Don't think about things too much. Just rest. Libby said you need lots of rest."

Without warning he turned back to her, pushed up her tank top, exposing her soft stomach and the crisscrossing lines made by the knife, bent his head and pressed a kiss just below her belly button. His tongue felt like a velvet rasp as he traced one of the lines leading downward into the pajama bottoms riding low on her hips.

Hannah gasped, her stomach muscles bunching, and between her thighs, the damp heat sizzled and sparked, demanding satisfaction.

His smile was sheer confidence, his eyes intense with desire, his mouth touched with a dark lust. "I'll see you tonight, baby." There was seduction in his voice, a rough promise of excitement.

Hannah rolled over, taking the covers with her, hiding her head and trying to slow her breathing as his footsteps faded away. Jonas Harrington could stir up more passion in her in three seconds than any other man could take a night doing. Hannah groaned and sat up, her body humming, her breasts too sensitive, and the ache between her legs growing stronger as she thought about him. So, okay. She might have to revise her thinking a little.

Downstairs she could hear her sisters moving around and she squared her shoulders. Today was going to be different. Today she was going to act normal and make good decisions based on what she wanted to do, not what she thought everyone wanted from her. Today was going to be the start of the new Hannah Drake.

Hannah spent the better part of the morning and afternoon assuring her sisters she was capable of doing housework and cooking. She found that Libby was right in that she seemed to have less energy and often had to rest, but as soon as she could, she got back up and did normal household chores, interacting with her sisters as much as possible.

She planned dinner for her siblings, even though she knew Jonas was taking her on an evening picnic. Most of the day she managed to keep from thinking constantly about the attack. Before it had consumed her every waking thought, but she was happy that she managed to replace the dread and fear with anticipation of seeing Jonas and the idea that she might actually be brave enough to seduce him.

All the while, she was aware the reporters and the crowd hadn't gone away. It was a little thinner, she thought, but she could hear Reverend RJ shouting and once, when she glanced out the window, she saw that he'd climbed on a small step stool and was waving his arms around as he delivered his sermon in his theatrical voice.

"Hey, woman, you're mooning around again," Joley said. "You're looking lovesick and that's just wrong. I can't take it, Hannah." She made a face at the contents of the refrigerator. "If you actually fall madly in love with Jonas, what's going to happen to me? And Elle? You said you weren't about to fall like our older sisters. We made a pact, remember?"

"Get out of the fridge. I'm making you dinner." Hannah closed the heavy door and leaned against it. "I did make the pact with you and Elle, but I didn't think I had a chance with Jonas. I didn't think he was interested."

Joley rolled her eyes. "I love you, Hannah, but when it comes to men, you don't know a thing."

"And you do?"

"I know enough to stay away from them. What in the heck is all that racket outside?" She was already heading for the living room, where she could peer out the large picture window.

Sarah glanced up from the magazine she was reading. "Come away from there, you don't want to give any of them the satisfaction."

"That horrible man, the Reverend something, is out there in front of the cameras again, Sarah," Joley hissed, her teeth clenched. "Can't Jonas have him arrested?"

"For what? Preaching? That would look lovely on the news. He'd lose his job, the Reverend would sue and get even more publicity. Right now he's just soaking up the press and they're so bored out there they'll do anything at all for a story."

Joley's eyebrow shot up. "You think?"

"I know." Sarah lowered her magazine when Joley's tone got through to her. "What are you thinking, Joley? Don't do anything crazy." When Joley ignored her and continued to look out the window, Sarah put the magazine on the table beside her tea, really alarmed. "Hannah," she called, sticking her head in the kitchen. "Joley's up to something and you're going to have to stop her. She never listens to anyone else."

Hannah dried her hands on a towel and followed Sarah. "What's wrong, hon? And come away from the window before a photographer gets a picture of you."

Joley shrugged. "What's one more photograph? At least this time it will be for a good cause. That idiot Reverend is out there using the attack on you to preach to everyone about the consequences of sin."

Hannah went still. "He's talking about me? Are you sure? Where's Jonas?"

Sarah wrapped her arm around Hannah's slender waist. "There's no need to worry. He doesn't appear to be interested in coming in here to talk to any of us. He wants his moment in the sun with the television cameras and the press."

Hannah moistened her lower lip with her tongue. "He's slime, Joley, not a real preacher. He started his own church for the purpose of conning people out of their money and sleeping with every woman in his sick little flock. He's disgusting. I know, because I touched him. I felt dirty for a week. You stay away from him, Joley."

"Is Jonas aware of what the Reverend is like?" Sarah asked.

"Yes, we've had a couple of conversations about him."

"And the Reverend, is he aware of your knowledge, Hannah?" Sarah asked, suspicion in her voice.

Hannah crossed to the window and, standing to one side, took a quick look out. The Reverend was surrounded and he was booming out his sermon, his voice thundering over the crowd extolling the merits of seeking forgiveness on one's knees and avoiding the harlots of the world.

"He's so clichéd," she hissed. "I should just go out there and tell the world what he's really like."

"Hannah, don't you dare. For one thing, you have no proof. He could sue you for making those kinds of allegations."

"They're true."

"True or not, you have to have proof."

"So he likes women, does he?" Joley ventured and turned away before Hannah could say anything else. She raced up the stairs.

"Hannah," Sarah persisted, before she could follow Joley. "Did you confront the Reverend? You did, didn't you?"

"He was protesting at every single shoot I went on. If not the Reverend personally, he has four or five men who travel with him and they protested. It wasn't directed at a designer, or even furs, but at me personally. My agent was afraid we'd lose assignments if he kept causing negative publicity. So yes, I went to see him with the idea that once he met me, he'd see I wasn't the devil's daughter."

"And?" Sarah prompted, pressing her lips together tightly.

Hannah sighed. The lip thing was always a bad sign with Sarah. "Well, in the end I think I just proved to him I was the devil's daughter, by reading his mind and letting him know I was disgusted by him." She glanced up as Joley came running back down the stairs and went straight to the front door. "Oh, no. Sarah. Stop her."

Joley was dressed in slim vintage blue jeans, riding low on her hips and highlighting the shape of her butt very lovingly. Her tight pink tank top hugged the full curve of her breasts and stopped short of her waist, showing an intriguing strip of her flat belly. A golden chain glittered just below her waist and above her jeans. The way she moved screamed sex. Her hair was wild, her full, pouting lips a dark siren red. She didn't just walk, she flowed, all soft lush curves and windblown hair. She was temptation wrapped in casual elegance.

The crowd at the fence went crazy, yelling and waving. Cameras turned away from the Reverend and focused on her.

Joley waved and sauntered down toward them, her every step an answer to the wickedest erotic dreams.

Hannah clutched Sarah's hand. "She's going to start a riot out there. Where are the security people? Matt isn't here and neither is Aleksandr or Damon."

"Joley can handle a crowd," Sarah reassured her, silently praying it was true.

The Reverend RJ, realizing he was losing his audience, lifted his hands to the sky and called louder for the Lord to forgive the sins of Hannah Drake, parading her body, strutting around deliberately tempting men to be sinners and leading other women to wear the clothes of the temptress.

Joley went right up to him, looking every

inch of sex and sin, her fragrance enveloping him in deliberate enticement. She flashed her perfect white teeth and batted her long lashes. "Reverend RJ? I'm Joley, Hannah's sister." She offered her hand, her voice pitched low, the rhythm hypnotic — mesmerizing even. It dropped another octave so that she sounded sultry and tempting. "It's so sweet of you to pray for her soul."

The Reverend opened his mouth, but nothing came out. Joley often had that effect on men. He slipped his hand into hers and she ran the pad of her thumb over the back of his hand, reading him, reading his perverted thoughts and his darkest secrets, even as she gave him a thrill.

Joley ignored the rush of memories and concentrated on his perverted thoughts. He couldn't stop thinking about her breasts and he loved the chain. Mostly his thoughts were all about what he'd like to do to her. She gave him a slow, seductive smile that had his body reacting and his mind racing.

"You're so caring to worry about my sister's soul." She moved, a soft undulation of her body, enough to show off her lush curves without seeming to do a thing. It was easy enough to boost the microphones when the Reverend talked, and interfere when she did so the broadcast would only hear him — the lust and excitement in his voice.

She smiled at him, her sultry come-on smile. "It's too bad you don't like women, you're a good-looking man and we could . . ." She shrugged, letting her body just barely slide against his, her fingers slipping away from his almost reluctantly. Before he could respond to her allegation, she stepped even closer so that her breath warmed his ear. "You look like you could save even me."

He reacted visibly, a shiver of excitement going through his body. She tilted her head, her gaze holding his so for a moment they were the only two people there. Her voice was a soft whisper. "I like games, do you?" He was imagining her at his mercy, tied up and taking whatever he gave her, while he preached that it was for her own good. She heightened his imagination, letting him taste the power he'd have over her.

He licked his lips and the bulge in his trousers grew. "We could explore possibilities if you want to be saved."

"Do you think you could save me? I've — done things." Her voice was pitched low and implied all sorts of sinful, wicked and very sexual things.

The Reverend swallowed several times. "I

could save you, child."

This time when she stepped close, her breasts brushed his chest and then she slid away again, her lips in a seductive pout. "What would you do? Tell me. Tell me right now." Her hand slid down his chest and belly, stopped just short of the front of his trousers, her fingers tapping and then sliding away.

He swallowed hard, the images in his head overcoming everything else. He reached for her, his hands settling around her arms, fingers digging deep. "I would have to tie you down to keep the devil from getting you. He'll fight me for you. You see how necessary it is."

She blinked up at him, her face innocent, her eyes hot with desire — for him. He could taste her, feel her already. The Reverend was oblivious to his men, trying to pull him away from the cameras. There was assent in her eyes, need. She would let him because he had the power.

"Flogging is beautiful on a woman and sometimes it's the only way."

"I have a lot of sins," she said. Her hand trailed up his chest, eyes still locked with his. "Will I feel you deep inside me?" She ignored his bodyguards just as he did.

"Oh yes." He nodded, barely able to

breathe with wanting her. "I'll fuck you blind. I'll make you scream. You'll be lovely with blood running down your back and breasts and buttocks." He was so mesmerized, he was completely unaware of speaking out loud.

Joley chose that moment to step aside so the cameras could pick up the perfect image of a very perverted man lusting after a woman. "You talk a lot of crap, Rev, but inside you're a sick bastard. So basically, you're saying to save my soul, you have to strip me naked, tie me up, flog me and then do me? Wow. Kinky. But no thanks."

Still half under the spell of her voice and body, the Reverend looked up at the cameras blinking, his hand reaching for her as she stepped away.

Joley brushed him off, rubbing her hands down her thighs. "You disgust me. You're after sex, pure and simple, and you like to hurt women. You get off on that, don't you? Hurting women? You know why? You can't get it up any other way."

The tallest bodyguard slammed her back with a hand to her chest as they grabbed the Reverend, pulling him away from her mesmerizing voice, protectively shoving him behind them.

Joley staggered and nearly went down, but

she caught herself. Deliberately running her tongue along her lips, she sent the Reverend another seductive smile. "You think my sister is the devil? You got the wrong one."

"You bitch." The tallest of the Reverend's bodyguards came at her again. Joley waited, on the balls of her feet, for the blow. She wanted the man to assault her. It would look so wonderful for the cameras and do even more harm to the Reverend's already severely damaged reputation.

Before his fist could land, Ilya Prakenskii stepped between them, a flow of muscle and coordination, his hand catching the fist in midair and stopping the forward momentum. The man went to his knees, agony on his face.

Joley stepped back, one hand going to her throat in a defensive gesture as she felt the buildup of energy — red-hot and black with anger, pulsing in the air. "Don't kill him," she whispered. "Ilya. Don't."

The Russian turned his head, his smoldering gaze meeting hers. "Go into the house now." He bit the command out between clenched teeth.

Every vestige of color drained from Joley's face, but she turned and hurried back into the house, straight into Hannah's arms.

"It's all right, baby, I'm here," Hannah assured.

"I feel so dirty. That man is so sick and then Ilya came. I didn't know he was there. I didn't feel him, and he saw the whole thing — what I did." Joley, who never cried, burst into tears. "Someone had to stop that horrible man."

The door burst open and Ilya Prakenskii stood framed there, his wide shoulders filling the space. The room pulsed with black rage. He took two long strides in and waved his hand behind him. The door slammed closed.

"Are you deliberately trying to get yourself killed?" Ignoring Hannah and Sarah, he yanked Joley out of Hannah's arms and spun her around to face him. "Because that man isn't just a pervert, he's dangerous, and you must have known that the moment you touched him. You just destroyed him on live television. What the hell were you thinking?"

Joley bit her lip hard to try to stop crying. It was humiliating to have Prakenskii catch her in such a weak moment. He punctuated each word with a hard shake and she wanted to break free and spit in his face, but he was right. He was so right and she had touched a monster and it sickened her.

"Nikitin saw the entire thing. He's fixated

on you, too. What do you think the first order he's going to give me will be when we're alone? He's going to want the son of a bitch who hit you taken out. Damn it, Joley. Don't you ever think before you act?"

"She did it for me," Hannah said, stepping close to her younger sister. "She was protecting me."

"She used her voice and her body on him. He'll be obsessed and it won't go away." Ilya released Joley after one more, hard, frustrated shake and stepped away from her, one hand scrubbing over his face. "If your voice was picked up by the microphone, you'll have more than one man obsessed with you. What the hell is wrong with you?"

"Maybe it was a little rash," Hannah defended, "but her heart was in the right place."

"Just like it was when she pretended to be Libby? Half the world thinks she's into sex orgies and kink and the other half is so obsessed with her, they're dangerous."

Joley swiped at her eyes and lifted her chin, her expression stubborn, defiant. "Maybe I am into kink and orgies. It's no one's business if I am."

His breath hissed out. "Don't push me right now, little girl. You'll find yourself over my knee right in front of your sisters. I'm furious with you."

"You wouldn't dare. I'd have you arrested."

"No, Joley, you wouldn't. We both know that, so just back off and let me rant about this as you deserve. But I'm warning you." He stepped closer to her. "The next time you do something so foolish, so dangerous, I'm going to give you a lesson you will never forget."

He swung away, paced the length of the room like a restless tiger, visibly pulling back and regaining control. When he turned around, he was no less furious, no less frightening, but this time his rage was icy. "And what's the matter with all of you?"

The other Drakes had drifted into the room, one by one, all standing in a loose circle watching him with wary eyes.

"Do you honestly believe she's that tough? That strong? What's wrong that you don't look after your younger sister?"

Joley's swift intake of air was audible. "I am that tough and you'd better not threaten my sisters or you'll find out just how tough I really am."

Hannah's head was pounding, the emotions swinging out of control, beating at her. This was her fault. Joley's exposing herself to danger was her fault. As much as she might detest Prakenskii's manner, he was right. Joley was rash and she did act without thought for her own safety when she was protecting her family. Was it possible that whoever hated Hannah that much would turn that hatred on Joley?

"You're right," she said, her voice strangled with tears. "You're right. Joley, honey, you have to be more careful. You're out there, all over the news, and the wrong people are watching."

The knock at the door jarred her nerves. She pressed her fingers tightly against her lips and turned away to try to keep the others from seeing how distressed she was. Just like that it had all come back. The knife. The pain. The utter horror of it. And now she had to worry about someone doing the same thing to Joley.

Ilya held up his hand when Sarah made a move to the door. "It's Nikitin," he said. "Tread softly. He knows nothing of your capabilities."

Elle moved close to Hannah and circled her waist with one arm, positioning her body just a little in front of her sister. Hannah frowned. Elle was the youngest, the quietist, and definitely the most lethal. Hannah didn't want Elle's protection anymore. If anything, it should be the other way around, but already her heart was pounding, lungs burning, and she could barely think with the buzzing in her head. A full-blown panic attack was setting in.

"Joley, take Hannah upstairs," Ilya commanded. "Hurry."

Joley glanced from him to Hannah's pale face. Without protesting, she grabbed Hannah's hand and took her out of the room, up the stairs. Behind them, she could hear Prakenskii opening the front door to let the mobster in.

"I-I c-can't breathe," Hannah stammered, her breath coming in long wheezes.

"Yes you can, honey," Joley said. "You'll be safe in your room."

"Outside." Hannah indicated the balcony. She could breathe outside. She was safe with the wind and the sea. She groped her way along the walls to the French doors and threw them open, stepping with relief onto the tiled balcony.

"Better?" Joley asked, pulling Hannah's chair closer.

"Yes. I'm sorry, Joley, and I'm sorry you felt you had to go out there and protect me from that slimebag pervert. You're an amazing sister."

"People like that make me so angry, Hannah." She was silent a moment, her hand shaking as she pushed back her hair. "I hate it that Ilya saw me like that. It made me feel cheap and dirty."

"Oh, Joley." Distressed, Hannah reached out to her. "He didn't look at you as if you were cheap or dirty, he looked concerned and upset, and afraid for you. He made me afraid for you."

"And I hate that he was right. It was a stupid thing to do, but I'm still glad I did it. Very few people are going to follow the Reverend after his little display."

"Be careful, Joley. Be very careful from now on. You've made an enemy." Hannah rocked herself back and forth, trying to find balance again.

"Jonas is going to be really upset with me, too." She brightened. "But you're going out with him tonight and that ought to mellow him right out."

"Maybe I shouldn't go with him. I don't want him to love me like this. I want to be whole for him. Strong for him."

"Jonas has loved you forever, Hannah, you're the only one who didn't know. He isn't going to stop loving you because you tell him to."

"Then you think I should go?" It was a commitment if she went. She understood that, and more, she understood that if she went with him, she was going to seduce him and that would be binding as far as Jonas was concerned. Was she ready? She honestly didn't know.

"Do you love him, Hannah? Really love him?" Joley asked.

"With every breath in my body. Bone deep. All the way."

"Why? Why do you love him so much, Hannah?"

Hannah sank into the chair and put her feet on the railing, the tension slipping from her body. "He makes me feel alive. He sees me. I can't hide from him. He sees me and he loves me anyway. He makes me feel beautiful when nothing else makes me feel that way. I can see myself in his eyes and he makes me a better person than I am."

"What else?"

"He knows how to have fun and he's okay with me having fun. He doesn't care if I'm rich or famous. He doesn't care if I'm a huge success out in the world. He makes me feel as if the things I want to do, stay home, cook and be a wife and mother, are just as important as saving the world."

"And?" Joley prompted with a small grin.

Hannah grinned back. "And he's hot in bed."

Joley laughed. "Then I say, you have your

answer. The rest of it will all fall into place. Let yourself be happy, Hannah."

"What about my panic attacks? They aren't going away."

"You deserve to have a few panic attacks after some nutcase tried to carve you up with a knife. Jonas doesn't care. We don't care. Why should you? Be happy."

Hannah nodded. "You're right. How'd you get to be so smart? I'm going to take my bath and get ready and then will you come in and help me with something else, something important to me?"

"Sure. I'll be back with the 411 from whatever's happening downstairs." Joley winked and left her alone.

Hannah went back into her room, carefully closing the French doors and drawing the blinds. She stood in her room waiting for her heart to stop pounding. Hadn't she promised she would be true to herself? What did she want to happen tonight with Jonas? She was the one trying to hold off being with him physically because she was ashamed of her body, yet she wanted him with such intensity it shook her. As night fell, the tightness in her body seemed only to increase. She wanted to be lying under him, over him, with him, his body taking hers over and over. And God help her, she wanted to see that fierce, possessive look on his face again and again.

Every single thing she had said to Joley was the truth. She loved Jonas. There had been no one before him and there would be no one after him. If she wanted him, she needed to stand up and take him.

She walked slowly to the mirror and stared at her face. To her, the injuries were all she could see, her face carved into a wreck, pieces, like Frankenstein, but when she took a deep breath and forced herself to analyze her wounds, it was clear they were already well past the raw stage and into fading. The lines were red, but not inflamed. The skin looked healthy and soft again. The bruising and swelling was long gone. Her sisters really had accomplished a miracle, along with a brilliant plastic surgeon who had taken his time to ensure that he had meticulously seamed her face back together.

Slowly, Hannah removed her clothes, still staring at the mirror. Her throat, breasts and ribs looked far better, just as her face did. The deeper injuries were a little redder, but still, even those had healed so much faster, thanks to her sisters. She frowned as she tried to see what others saw — what Jonas saw. Was she beautiful like everyone said? She wanted to be for Jonas. And maybe in the end, all that mattered was the way he saw her. If Jonas thought her body was beautiful and he enjoyed it . . .

She blushed, thinking of how much he had enjoyed touching her. He took command of her, almost as if he meant it when he said her body belonged to him. She filled the bathtub and poured scented salts into it, wanting to give him more pleasure than he'd ever known. She wanted her body to belong to him, she wanted to see that same look of absolute possession and fierce hunger on his face and in his eyes.

Hannah took special care with her appearance, soaking herself in her favorite fragrance so her skin would have the light scent of peaches. She used lotion to make her skin soft and washed her hair with the same scented shampoo. Her makeup was applied with care, a professional's touch — using just enough to enhance her natural looks, play up her eyes and mouth without overdoing it.

She stood for a long time in her underwear, a lacy bra and matching thong of shimmering blue. What had been his fantasy? She reached for the flowing skirt, the soft sea blue swirled with midnight, and sprinkled with silver stars. She loved the feel of the soft, sensual material sliding over her hips and brushing her ankles. She wrapped a chain of silver stars around her left ankle and another around her hips. Staring into the bathroom mirror, she cursed herself for breaking her full-length one. She wanted to see if she could get away with no panties.

Her breath caught in her throat and her heart thundered at the idea of being so daring. Just to see how it would feel, Hannah slipped off her underwear and walked across the room. Only she would know. She'd be so aware that she was naked and ready for him. Would he see it in her eyes? She made a small twirl and watched her skirt flow out. There was no hint, not even when she walked and the folds settled along the vee at the junction of her legs, but she felt sexy.

She reached up and unhooked her bra. In the mirror, she caught sight of her bare breasts swaying as she turned slowly around. Dragging the peasant blouse Jonas loved so much over her full breasts, she took another look. She was covered completely, no hint that she was bare beneath her clothes, waiting for his touch.

"Hannah?" Joley stuck her head into the room. "Elle gave me this file for you. She said it's the one you asked for on all the nutcases writing to you. Are you certain you want to read it?"

She had been certain when she'd first woken up in the morning, but now she was not so sure. "Just put it on the dresser. I'll think about it."

"Well? Are you going to turn around so I can see you?"

Hannah nodded, holding her breath as she did so, waiting to see if Joley noticed anything different about her.

"You look beautiful. Jonas will love that outfit."

No sly teasing. Only Hannah was aware of her own daring. For some reason, that secret knowledge gave her courage. She picked up the scissors she'd set out and extended them toward her sister. "I want you to cut my hair."

Joley stared at the scissors without moving. "What are you talking about?"

"I want to cut my hair."

"You have beautiful hair, Hannah."

"Everyone else loves my hair, but I don't. I want you to cut it. You do all kinds of things to your hair. I'm not asking you to dye it pink or anything, just to cut it."

Joley took the scissors reluctantly. "Are you certain?"

"Absolutely. And while you're at it, tell me what happened when Nikitin showed up." She led the way to the balcony. The birds would appreciate her hair for their nests.

"Sarah said Nikitin really turned on the charm. He asked about you and said how sorry he was about what happened. He said he was glad he and Ilya were on hand to stop the madman."

"Ilya did the stopping. Was Nikitin anywhere close?"

"I'm just repeating what Sarah said. He wanted to see me. Libby told him I was resting, that I was shaken up by what had happened."

"Did he buy that?"

"I don't think he had a choice. He told Sarah that he wanted me to be careful because the coast was filling up with Russians."

"What does that mean?"

"I have no idea, neither did Sarah. Apparently Prakenskii didn't say one word with Nikitin in the room. At least now I know how to shut him up. If I have to talk to him, I'll make sure his boss is around." She stepped back to admire her work. "This is really sexy. Sexy and sassy and more you than ever. Check it out in the mirror. See if you like the way I shaped it."

Hannah held her breath until she looked.

The heavy fall of hair was gone, leaving her curls falling to her shoulder and feathering around her face. It felt light and Joley was right. She did look different and she felt different, too.

"I love it, thanks, Joley."

"Well, I'm heading downstairs to eat. Jonas should be here any minute," Joley said as Hannah trailed her to the door to take the scissors. "Sarah thinks she's going to put me on restriction or something. She's afraid for me to go out for a while until we know the Reverend's reaction."

Hannah stiffened, one hand on the closed door as she stared down at the sharp scissors in her hand. *Someone hated her enough to try to destroy her.* The realization hit her hard and she felt sick — panicked — her newfound courage turning to dust. She swallowed hard and looked over at the file sitting on her dresser. It was a lot thicker than she had ever conceived it of being. Did all those people hate her and want her dead? How could she have ignored it all the years she'd modeled? How many were there? And what had she done to make them feel that way about her?

17

Someone hated her enough to want to kill her. They had already made three attempts and would make another. What had she ever done to make someone loathe her so much?

Hannah shivered, feeling the black hatred sliding into her room. Desperate to get outside, where the wind would protect her, would wrap her up and keep her safe, she snatched up her blanket, drew it around her and hurried out to the balcony to sit in her chair. She'd have to refuse to go with poor Jonas. Oh, Lord, what had she done? She was naked under her skirt and blouse and she'd cut off her hair. She was an absolute idiot to think she could blithely go out for the evening and seduce Jonas. She felt like a fool. Thank God he didn't know what she'd been thinking all evening, getting ready for him. If he saw her in her skirt and blouse, he'd know what had been on her mind. It would be so humiliating to have to refuse him and . . . She buried her face in her hands. He'd know she was falling apart again.

Jonas swore and stared for a moment at the locked door. He'd spent hours going through suspect files and working to find out who was trying to harm Hannah. All day he'd thought about nothing else but getting back to Hannah. He'd worked out the steps of escaping safely with her, paying attention to the smallest detail so she wouldn't have to feel a prisoner in her own home — so she could be empowered. And now — once again — she'd locked him out.

The sweep of anger shaking him was definitely out of proportion, but he'd had enough of locked doors. Hannah knew him better than that. Resisting the idea of breaking it down, he picked the lock and let himself in.

The French doors leading to the balcony overlooking the sea were open as usual. White lacy drapes billowed into the room, bringing in the mist and tang of sea salt. She was wrapped in a blanket and sitting in a chair, staring down at the turbulent water, stubbornly refusing to look at him. He leaned one hip lazily against the doorjamb and studied her averted face.

The blanket slipped as she leaned forward to throw something over the railing. The wind blew some of it back toward him. A long spiral curl landed on his chest.

"What the hell, Hannah?" he demanded, balancing a mug of tea in one hand and catching platinum strands in the other. "What have you done?"

She jumped, a small squeak of fear tangling in her throat. She drew the blanket closer around her like a hood, covering most of her face. "A locked door usually means someone wants to be alone." Her voice was that husky whisper of sound he found sexy as hell. It played up and down his spine and gave him one hell of a hard-on. He shifted a little to try to ease the continual ache centered in his groin.

"I don't like being locked out."

She flinched under his steady gaze. "It's called privacy."

"You've had enough of privacy. You can be angry with me, Hannah, and yell and tell me to go to hell, but you don't fucking lock the door against me. It just pisses me off more. If you're having a difficult time, say so."

"Locking the door *is* saying so."

"It's the two of us together, not you alone anymore. We aren't going to have one of those lame, half-assed relationships."

She frowned. "What exactly does that mean?"

"It means you don't lock the damn door on me."

"Sheesh. All right. Fine." She sighed and capitulated. "In all honesty, I didn't realize the door was locked."

"Then why didn't you just say so?"

"Because you yelled at me."

"Well, just don't lock the door again." He handed her the mug of tea and snagged another chair, dragging it beside hers.

She immediately wrapped her hands around the warmth of the cup. "Thanks, Jonas."

"You're welcome. I put honey in it for you. Are you ready to go?" She didn't look ready, not the way she was clutching the blanket so desperately and hiding in its folds. He couldn't see her hair, but there were several long strands on the balcony floor.

She started to speak, to tell him she wasn't going, he was certain, but she stopped and took a small sip of tea as if gathering courage. When the silence stretched, she sighed. "I want to go, Jonas. It's just that . . ." She trailed off.

"Baby." He said it softly. "Let's just get it

over. Let me see your hair."

Her long lashes fluttered. She reached up a hand and touched the springy curls beneath the blanket. "I did it for me."

He let his breath out. "That's good, honey. Let me see."

She glanced at him as if trying to gauge his true emotion. "I have so much hair and it weighs on me, you know? I just wanted to get rid of some of the weight. And it was such a burden to always be so perfect."

His answering laughter was soft. "People always did write about your perfect hair," he agreed.

"They're not the ones who had to put a zillion gallons of product in it to keep it from poofing out everywhere. I wanted to do something that was my decision alone." She wanted him to understand. And she wanted him to like it, not to be disappointed.

"Has anyone seen it?" He knew the answer before she said it.

"Joley did it for me, but she promised not to tell."

"She didn't dye it some outrageous color, did she? You don't have purple curls under the blanket, do you?" He reached over and took the mug out of her hand, taking a drink, allowing the liquid to warm his insides.

A small smile curved her soft mouth, drawing attention to her full lower lip. He wanted to spend some time nibbling at her lip again, but Hannah wasn't giving him any help.

"No color. Joley says the style is sassy and sexy. But everything is sexy to her."

"Are you going to let me see or do I have to wrestle the blanket off of you?"

"A couple of reporters hired boats and tried to get pictures this afternoon while you were gone. And Joley went crazy and confronted the Reverend. She basically had him confessing his sins on national television."

"So I heard. It was a crazy thing to do." She was stalling. He knew she was and considered calling her on it, but there was more going on here than a new shorter hairstyle. He needed to let her work her way around to telling him the real problem.

Hannah took the tea back, swallowing hard, once again not looking at him. "I thought this story would just die down and everyone would go away, but it isn't going to happen, is it?"

"Not for a while."

"And Joley could have made herself a

target as well, right?"

She looked young and vulnerable and so fragile he ached for her. "I'm sorry, baby, I want to tell you different, but the truth is, Joley made herself a target a long time ago just by stepping out into the public eye."

His voice was gentle and grief hit her hard, making her throat raw and her chest tight. "Like I did." She swallowed hard and shook her head, tears spilling over when she'd tried so hard to hold them back. "Jonas." She couldn't say anything else. As it was, his name was choked out of her, ripped from somewhere so deep it left an open wound. "Why do they hate me so much?"

"I don't know, baby." He pulled her into his arms, holding her as tight as he could, pressing her face into his chest, wanting to smash something, anything, to relieve the fierce frustration and helplessness he felt. "It's going to be all right, Hannah. I'm going to find them."

"I don't even know how to hate someone that much," she said, her voice muffled.

He did. Whoever had ordered the hit on her needed to die. Jonas could hate and he had a very long memory. He held her as close as possible, while she clung to him, listening to her cry as though her heart was broken, and deep inside, a monster grew stronger. He finally lifted her and sank back into her chair, rocking gently back and forth, murmuring reassurances, feathering kisses over the blanket and down the side of her face where her skin peeked out of the cover.

"I'm sorry. I'm sorry, Jonas. I thought I was over this. I don't know why it hit me so hard all over again."

She was careful to keep her face turned toward the sea, but he felt the wash of tears. Jonas let his breath out slowly to stay in control. She was everything to him, and seeing her so torn up, so frightened and fragile, destroyed him. He rubbed his face over hers, skin to skin, trying to show her what was inside him — that she had him always — *always* — and he would stand for her.

"After you left this morning, I asked Elle to get the file from Jackson, the one with all the people who have written threatening me. Joley handed me the scissors to put away and I just flashed on the knife. I couldn't help it. The file was sitting on the dresser and I thought it might give me some answers. But all those people, Jonas . . ." She drew back and looked at him then, her eyes wide and hurt. "There are so many of them. I had no idea there would be so many."

He leaned back in the chair, pulling her close again. "Listen to me, Hannah. Those people have nothing to do with you. They're sick — disturbed. Mentally ill. Yes, there are plenty of them fixating on you, but most are just harmless. Jackson should never have given the file to Elle. You didn't need to see those letters."

"I needed to see them. This is about me, and I needed to see them."

He let her slip out of his arms and watched as she paced restlessly across the balcony, one hand holding the blanket closed, the other wiping at tears on her face. Finally she picked up the mug of tea he'd set on the railing and took a sip before handing it to him, watching his strong fingers settle around the handle. "I wish I were more like you. I feel so afraid now, and sometimes I look in the mirror and I don't know who I am."

He made a faint sound of disbelief. "You know exactly who you are, who you've always been. You're not Hannah Drake the model, she's a small part of you, that's not who you are at all. It never was you."

"You're always so sure of yourself, Jonas."

He shook his head. "I'm sure of you. I

know exactly who Hannah Drake is. That streak of stubborn, the one of wild. The crazy sense of humor. You never wanted to go out looking into the world for other things and other people. You wanted to stay home and just be the barefoot girl running on the beach in her rolled-up jeans."

Hannah blinked back tears again. "I cry a lot. I think I'm okay and then I fall apart again."

"You suffered trauma, baby, it's normal. If you didn't cry, that's when you can worry about having a problem."

"I was so ready to go out with you tonight. I was feeling strong and happy about making my own decisions, and the next thing I knew, I was terrified, angry and weepy, all rolled into one. I'm a mess."

"You're as normal as a Drake can possibly get." He tugged at the cover. "Now lose the blanket and let me see your hair."

"What if you don't like it?" She put a hand on top of her head in a defensive gesture. He could still see the faint wounds running up and down her arms and palms. Defensive wounds. The knots in his belly hardened into lethal lumps.

"Do you like it?"

She nodded slowly, then with more conviction. "Yes."

"Then I'll like it, too. Ditch the blanket."

With a show of reluctance, Hannah lowered the blanket to her shoulders, her gaze suddenly shy. She looked more vulnerable than ever. The spiral curls were as thick as ever, but much shorter, framing her face and nestling along her neck and skimming her shoulders. He had always loved her naturally curly hair; it was thick and rich and uniquely Hannah. As long as it had been, well past her waist when wet, the spirals were so tight, the hair had still pulled up around the middle of her back.

Without all the extra weight, her new shortened curls were even tighter, but the cut suited her face, emphasizing her delicate bone structure and incredible large eyes. He reached out and tugged at a silky spiral. "Joley's right. It's very sassy and sexy — and it suits you." His voice had gone rough and husky.

She was wearing her peasant blouse, the one he loved. His mouth went dry at the sight. She wasn't wearing a bra. In the cold her nipples had hardened into two tight peaks. The sight ignited him like a flashfire, burning instantly hot and nearly out of control. He took a deep breath and battled back the urge to slam her against the wall and bury himself deep and hard over and over.

"It does suit me, doesn't it?" Hannah flashed the smallest of smiles, but the shyness refused to fade from her eyes as she flipped the blanket back over her head.

"Are you thinking of spending the rest of your life inside that blanket?" He had to be careful, he couldn't lose her. She'd made up her mind to give herself to him — before she panicked — she'd deliberately dressed for him — wanted him.

She frowned, lips pursing as she contemplated. Finally she nodded. "Actually, yes, I think I like the idea." Because if she didn't cover up, then he'd notice her outfit, and being Jonas, he'd realize exactly why she'd dressed the way she had.

"We have our getaway planned." He struggled to keep his voice neutral, but it was harsh with need. "Your sisters are bringing in the fog. Jackson is dressed like me and will be taking my car about half an hour after we slip away, so if someone is following me thinking I might lead them to you, Jackson will lead them to the sheriff's office."

She looked up at him with both longing and tears. "I tried today, Jonas. I really wanted it to be a good day."

"I know you did." He tugged her to her feet. "Get your coat and let's just go for a drive and see how you feel getting out of here. The crowd's gone — the night got a little too cold and the wind was howling and blowing sea spray all over them."

"That would be courtesy of either Joley or Elle."

"I think Joley's retired to her room for the night."

"Aren't you going to rant about Joley putting herself in danger?"

"I'm all out of rants tonight." He couldn't think of anything but dragging her into his arms, holding her and kissing her and doing every single one of the things he'd fantasized about for years to her. All night long. He wanted her all night.

He sounded different, almost harsh. Hannah immediately looked up at his face and noted the shadows there. He looked older, lines etched into his face, and his gaze was locked on her, intense, focused, almost hungry. Her heart lurched. "I think a quiet drive together is just what I need, Jonas." Maybe it was true, she didn't honestly know, but it was true for Jonas. He needed — loving.

Hannah kept the blanket around her until she disappeared into her closet and pulled out her long coat. There was no chance to grab a bra and panties from her drawer unless she blatantly did it in front of him, and she hadn't worked up the courage to do it. Strangely, as she drew her coat around herself, heat slid into her body. There was something delicious and decadent about wearing her long, flowing skirt, standing innocently beside Jonas, and knowing she was wearing nothing but skin beneath the thin material of her clothes.

One moment she had been scared and crying, now excitement sizzled in her veins just at the thought of sitting beside Jonas and knowing she was dressed exactly as she had been in his fantasy. Looking at him sent a shiver of anticipation down her spine. She took the hand he held out and followed him down the stairs.

They escaped into the thick mist, moving like shadows, hand in hand, Elle helping to blur their figures as they ran to the far end of the property, using the grove of trees for cover. As they neared Jackson's truck, the fog was even thicker.

With every step Jonas took, he ached for her. The heat grew and spread until his cock was near bursting. He needed to touch her. It was no longer wanting. He needed. Knowing she was inexperienced and a little shy, yet she'd dressed for him in the fantasy clothes he'd asked for, was almost more than he could deal with.

Jonas placed a hand low on her back, guiding her quickly toward the truck, but once there, he suddenly turned her, pushing her against the door and trapping her there with his larger body. "I thought I was protecting you all those years and I wasted them. So many damn long years."

His voice was low, rough and tormented, penetrating right through her skin straight to her heart.

"I was so stupid, Hannah. I deprived us both for what?"

"I wasn't ready, Jonas." She ran her fingertips down his face, trying to soothe the frown lines, the desperate longing mixed so clearly with desire.

"Are you now, baby?" His voice was a harsh rasp of sound. "Are you ready for me now, because all I can think about is burying myself in you, over and over until you're screaming for mercy and I can't move."

He pushed his heavy erection tightly against her soft mound, even as his hands framed her face, holding her still so he could bend his head and sink his tongue into the dark velvet mystery of her mouth. He groaned, the vibration traveling through his body — her body — so that she wrapped her arms tightly around him and gave herself up to the sinful pleasure of his hot, hungry mouth.

He was ravenous for her, his need so urgent, his skin too hot, too tight, his groin well past pleasure and into pain. He needed the relief of her silken channel, tight and hot, gripping him like a fist, or the velvet pleasure of her hot, sweet mouth. He groaned again and their tongues tangled and dueled, until he thought his erection might rip right through his jeans. "I need you more than I need to breathe right now, Hannah."

He licked his way down her neck as her head fell back, teeth grazing and nipping, until he found the swell of her bare breasts beneath the neckline of her peasant blouse. Her hands fisted in his hair and she held him to her, arching her body closer to his.

He dragged his head back and looked at her, his blue eyes stormy, his breathing ragged. "Are you afraid, Hannah?"

She nodded, truthful. "Yes. That I might not be able to please you. That I'm too inexperienced for you. That you'll look at me and see what I see."

"I look at you and see a miracle, Hannah." He kissed his way right past the elastic neckline, his hands catching the hem and tugging slowly. Jonas nearly stopped breathing as the elastic at the neckline stretched and slid over the full curves of her breasts and popped underneath them, leaving him staring at her incredible creamy flesh and tight nipples.

Her coat framed her figure and she stood there, pressed up against the truck, leaning slightly back so that her breasts were thrust toward him in invitation. She looked so damned sexy he nearly lost control right there. His cock jerked and wept in anticipation. He didn't dare bend down and lick and suck the way he wanted to. He wouldn't have the ability to stop.

"Get in the truck." He pulled her coat around her body. "Just like that, Hannah. Don't cover up with your blouse." His breath came in a harsh gasp. "I may not survive."

She wasn't sure she would survive, but for certain, Jonas Harrington made her feel beautiful and sexy and loved. It was an amazing, daring feeling to stand there with her coat brushing her bare breasts and know the ragged breath Jonas drew into his lungs was on her account.

He jerked open the door and caught her around the waist, tossing her onto the seat and slamming the door closed after. She watched him walk around to the driver's side, and if the bulge in the front of his jeans was anything to go by, he really wanted her.

She sat demurely while he slid behind the wheel, closed his eyes for a moment and adjusted his jeans to ease the ache between his legs. "Where are we going? Last chance, Hannah. You tell me."

"Your house." Her voice shook a little, but her answer was immediate.

Jonas sent her a single burning look, his face lined with sensual intent. Her breath caught in her lungs and her inner thighs pulsed with awareness.

She ducked down, and as Jonas started Jackson's truck in the heavier fog, back up at the house, Jackson stood on the porch in plain sight with much lighter mist surrounding him, wearing Jonas's familiar coat and hat, talking with Sarah, who called him Jonas loud enough for anyone lurking near the property to hear.

"We're clear, honey, slide back up here. Are you cold?" He turned the heater up a notch.

"No. My coat is warm." But she was nervous. She didn't know the first thing about seduction. She might be scared, but if there was one thing she knew for absolute certain, she knew she wanted to belong to him and have him belong to her.

"We're going to be okay, honey. We can take it slow tonight." It would kill him, but for her, he could do anything.

Hannah wasn't certain she wanted slow, and if the low growl to his voice meant what she thought it did, neither did he. She could feel waves of lust and love, desire so hot and deep, coming off him in waves. As they drove through the streets, her body tightened in anticipation. Her inner muscles clenched and she shifted, afraid she might have an orgasm just listening to Jonas breathe that ragged, rough way.

He suddenly reached over, slid his hand inside her coat and stroked her soft breast. He cupped the soft, creamy mound in his hand, thumb sliding back and forth over her exposed nipple. Each caress sent streaks of fire straight to her hot feminine core.

"Keep your hands on the seat for me, baby," he instructed softly.

She realized she was clutching his arm, preventing him from full access. Hannah dropped her palms to the seat, fingers bunching the material of her skirt in her fists. His hand stroked and her heart accelerated, and the flames turned into a slow burn that just kept getting hotter. She thought she might have an orgasm right there when all he was doing was touching her breast.

She moistened her lips. "You are paying attention to the road, aren't you?"

He flashed a small grin at her, cocky, sexy, and filled with confidence. "You think I'm too distracted to drive?" He glanced down at her skirt. "You aren't wearing a bra. What else aren't you wearing?"

"Get me to your house and find out," Hannah said bravely.

His long, warm fingers continued to stroke her breast, and with every touch, nerve endings deep inside her sizzled with reaction. He groaned, a harsh rasping sound that thrilled her.

"God, baby, you're fucking naked under that skirt, aren't you? And I'm driving. You're killing me here." He took a deep breath. His cock was so swollen he was straining the material of his jeans to the breaking point. "And you're doing it on purpose."

"I'm not telling you. Just get us to your house. And pay attention to the road."

He drove the narrow winding highway with one hand on the wheel and the other stroking her breast. All the while he kept casting little glances toward her skirt. Just seeing that she could make him crazy with desire sent heat coursing through her body and made her feel daring and sexy. His gaze was hot, his fingers possessive.

"Pull it up."

"No."

His hand dropped down to her thigh. "I swear, baby, I can feel your heat. Pull it up for me." His voice was hoarse.

"You'll wreck."

"No I won't. I'm keeping my eyes on the road."

"Put both hands on the wheel."

When he obeyed, she sent him a siren's smile and began to slowly bunch the flowing skirt inch by slow inch up her bare thighs.

Jonas nearly stopped breathing as her soft white inner thighs came into view. "Higher, baby, a little higher." He could just make out the lips of her sex and tiny blond curls. Moisture glistened invitingly. His hands tightened on the steering wheel until his knuckles turned white. He'd never wanted a woman more. He was almost insane with desire. "Spread your legs a little more. Just a little, Hannah. You're the sexiest woman I've ever seen in my life."

She could see the effect she was having on him. His breathing, his voice, the dark lust in his eyes, the bulge in his jeans; all sent waves of need crashing through her system. Feeling powerful, beautiful and sensual was an aphrodisiac she hadn't expected. She widened her legs and gave the smallest of tugs to her skirt, allowing it to ride up just a little more.

Jonas turned off the road onto his long drive and slowed the truck. He dropped one hand onto the seat between her legs and caressed her hot, wet entrance with his knuckles, over and over, each time putting a little more pressure on her. Hannah's breath came out in a sob. Her body shook, breasts swollen and aching, her stomach bunching in knots. She caught his thick wrist with both hands, afraid of what was going to happen if she let him continue. She'd started it, but her body was already flaring out of her control, too hot too fast, the heat building and building until she was afraid she was going to be burned alive.

He parked the truck one-handed, refusing to give in to her tugging. "Ssh, baby, easy now. What do you think is going to happen? I'm just going to make you feel good."

"It's too much. You've barely touched me."

"Take your hands and put them around my neck."

Their gazes locked. She swallowed hard.

"Do it now, Hannah. Put your hands around my neck and hold on." He refused to let her look away from him, keeping his voice low and commanding. "Trust me, honey."

She did trust him. She just didn't trust herself. She had no idea she was such a sexual person. She'd gone years without too much interest. Even when Joley pointed out hot man after hot man, she didn't get all that excited — unless Jonas walked into the room. She'd secretly lusted after him for years. She dreamt about him, fantasized about him. But in all that time, she'd never realized that one smoldering look, a stroke or caress, would send her careening over the edge. "I don't want you to think I'm . . ."

"That you love sharing sex with me? That you enjoy my body and love having me enjoy yours? That's a good thing, baby. What we do is between us. Private. Intimate. Not wrong. It's out of love, sharing our bodies with one another out of love. I need to bring you pleasure. I don't just want to, I *need* to be able to have you shatter under me." His knuckles brushed her entrance again and he watched the rich need darken her eyes. "Put your arms around my neck and hang on."

She linked her hands together behind his

neck and pressed her brow to his, gasping as his finger slid over her and into her, instantly twisting the knot of nerves into a fiery bundle of streaking electric currents that sizzled through her body, destroying any semblance of control she thought she might still have.

"Jonas." His name came out in a ragged gasp.

"I'm going to love teaching you all sorts of wonderful new things, Hannah." Most of all, he was determined to show her how beautiful she really was. Beautiful and sexy and his. If he gave her nothing else, he wanted that for her.

He stroked a second time, gently, sending shivers through her body. Without warning, his fingers plunged deep and she cried out, throwing her head back. His thumb found her most responsive spot and raked over the hypersensitive nub. Her body just seemed to melt, to come apart. A small whimper escaped, torn from her throat as she pushed against his hand. The sound went straight to his groin. He felt himself swell, jerk, his balls tighten. He had to get out of his clothes or he wasn't going to survive.

"I need to get you inside, Hannah, or I'll be taking you right here like some eager teenager."

She looked up at him in a kind of mindless daze, the look so sexy he nearly lost control right then, but he wasn't going to jerk his cock out of his pants and take her in a damned truck. He wanted to ride her, hot and fierce, but not like this. He took a deep breath for control, pulled her skirt down and opened her door.

"No lights, Jonas. Keep the lights off."

"We'll do whatever you're comfortable with, baby." But he was going to make her so damned crazy she wasn't going to think about anything else but him and what his hands and his mouth and his body could do to hers.

Knees shaking, legs weak, Hannah didn't wait for him to come around and help her out, but preceded him up the front steps to his home. She craved him. Was obsessed with him. She wanted Jonas to replace her innocence with experience, and was determined to have him teach her how to please him. She wanted to learn every way they could pleasure each other. Most of all, she wanted Jonas Harrington for herself, and for the first time in her life, she was fully taking what she wanted.

Jonas reached around her and unlocked the door. Hannah stepped inside and he grabbed her, kicking the door closed and yanking the coat from her shoulders. He dropped it on the floor and dragged her back against him, hands cupping her breasts, chin resting on her shoulder. His breath came in hard gasps as he pressed his erection tightly against the curve of her bottom, so only the denim covering him and the thin material of her skirt separated them.

"I'm going to eat you alive, Hannah." He bit down on the side of her neck. "You're so soft, how the hell do you get so soft?"

She was afraid she might fall right to the floor. His hands were all over her breasts as he stepped back, forcing her body to bow and give him even better access. One hand slid over her hip and around her body, tugging at her skirt. Her hands automatically flew to his. "Just pull it up," she said hesitantly.

"It's dark in here, baby. Let's be skin to skin. Right here, right now."

He spun her around and found her mouth with his, tongue plunging deep, stroking along hers, devouring her just as he said he would, not giving her time to think. He'd always loved the shape of her mouth, the full lower lip, how soft and perfect it was. He bit at it, teased and tugged and went back to kissing. He craved the taste of her, sweet and hot and addicting, and he kissed her over and over until she gave herself up to him, her body molding to his and her arms stealing around his neck.

He tugged her skirt from her hips, allowing the material to pool around her feet. Jonas broke the kiss, skimmed his hands down her breasts, and then leaned forward to replace his hands with his mouth. A choking cry broke free, her body shuddering as he licked and sucked until she was writhing against him. His teeth bit gently down on her nipple and heat rockets flared, streaking straight to her thighs.

Jonas tore his shirt off and yanked hers over her head, tossing it aside, before backing her up to the wall. He caught both wrists and drew her hands over her head, pinning her there with one of his, while his mouth ravaged hers and his free hand tugged at her nipples and slid down her belly to her damp, heated entrance. "Oh, baby, you're so ready for me. I've waited so long for you."

Hannah couldn't talk. Couldn't even plead. She was nearly blind with want. He had driven her body to such a fever pitch of excitement, she couldn't think clearly. Then he dropped her hands and his mouth was skimming down her body as he went to his knees. He widened her thighs and clamped his mouth on her, his tongue plunging deep, stroking hard, then alternating with suckling.

She screamed, her legs going out from under her, her hands gripping his shoulder for support, the only thing holding her up as he devoured her. Her body spasmed, her stomach, her thighs, her buttocks, even her breasts, as lightning streaked through her. His mouth was merciless, driving her up and up, so that her inner muscles rippled and clenched and waves of sensation burst through her. It wouldn't stop, not even long enough for her to catch her breath. He was eating her alive, making her his, leaving his brand on her.

Hannah gave herself up to him, letting him have her completely, her body no longer her own. Jonas stood up, lifting her into his arms, shoving her against the wall.

"Wrap your legs around me, Hannah." His voice was a harsh rasp in her ear.

She circled his neck with her arms, and his waist with her legs, feeling the broad head of his erection poised at her entrance. And then he dropped her body over his, locking them together. She heard her own shattered cry as he filled her, driving through her ultrasensitive folds. He was so thick, almost too big for her, the friction hot and tight and dragging over the fiery knot of nerves so that it threw her into another shocking orgasm.

She looked at his face, the glitter in his eyes, the harsh intensity of his desire written into every line of his face. Her breath stilled. Her mind. Everything in her went quiet for just one moment of realization. That was love in his eyes — for her. If he owned her body and soul, she owned him right back. And then the moment was gone because he was holding her hips still and lodging so deep inside her she felt him bump hard against her womb. Once again she was drowning, going under as waves of sheer ecstasy washed over and through her.

He began to thrust hard, pumping into her, her channel hot silk, muscles swollen and gripping him tightly as he drove into her, his mind coming apart as he felt the climaxes building and tearing through her over and over. Her body fit his perfectly, squeezing like a fist, sending fiery streaks rushing through him from his toes to his head. His body strained, muscles locking as his own climax ripped through him like a firestorm, his heart thundering in his ears, pounding against hers as he fought for air.

They collapsed against the wall, arms holding one another up, until, shaky, he allowed his body to slip from hers and they sank onto the floor. "Give me a minute, Hannah, and I'll carry you to bed."

She curled her fingers around his arm, wanting to hold on to him. "We can just sleep here."

"You'll get too cold," he protested. "Besides, I want to make love to you in my bed so I can wake up with your scent on my sheets."

"We can't possibly again."

He reached for her, his smile slow and sensual. "Anything is possible, baby."

18

Jonas woke with his heart pounding and sweat beading on his body, the echo of his nightmare still ringing in his ears. He dragged in air and turned his head to look at Hannah. She was lying facedown beside him. Soft morning sunlight spilled through the window, bathing her in celestial light, so that her skin seemed luminous. The contour of her bottom was heart-stopping, nearly driving the nightmare from his head. He slid his hand possessively down her long back, noting he was shaking as he traced the long, beautiful line of her. He touched the dimples on either side of her spine, and then ran his hand over the enticing curve joining her back to bottom.

She looked tired, sprawled out, one arm flung wide, hair spilling everywhere. Tired — and vulnerable. He'd made love to her over and over, pushing her beyond her comfort zone more than once, but she'd gone with him and they'd exploded together often, like rockets going off on the Fourth of July. He'd never experienced sex the way it was with her and he could only conclude that loving a woman wholly, with every breath in a man's body, took mere sex into a whole different realm. He didn't want to wake her just because he was so needy with nightmares crowding close, but he considered it. His body was already reacting to the sight and scent of her.

He tried to recall the dream that had awoken him. He'd been back in the alley, watching the Russian mobsters, hiding like a coward in the shadows while one of them had put a bullet in an undercover agent's head. Terry, the driver, had run to him, begging for help, and he'd calmly continued to film as Karl Tarasov walked up behind him and shot him. And then Hannah was there, smiling at Tarasov, and he leaned down to kiss her, only a knife was clutched in his hand. He lifted it and the world turned red.

Jonas rolled over with a small groan, taking the sheets with him, flinging one arm over his eyes, trying to stop his mind from replaying the attack on her over and over. Beside him, Hannah stirred. She turned slightly toward him, a leisurely, slow movement of her body, drawing his immediate attention. Her lips were full and soft, sending an electrical charge through his body when she leaned close and kissed his navel. He felt the slide of her new, short curls over his thickened cock. Every nerve ending leapt to life. The sweep of her soft breasts contracted his muscles and brought him to full alert.

What could be more beautiful than Hannah sliding over his body, naked and willing, with the smile of a temptress and the promise of heaven in her eyes?

"You look like a fairy tale lying in my bed. Goldilocks with her hair spread across my pillow."

She lifted her head just enough to flash another smile at him — teasing — mischievous. "You had fantasies about Goldilocks?"

Now he could see the curve of one breast, full and tempting, adding to the allure of her curved bottom. "Hell yes I did. A very naughty woman with golden curls just waiting naked in my bed, knowing she deserves punishment and I'm the one going to give it to her." He caught her hair in his fist and lifted the mass from her neck so he could lean in and taste her skin. Deliberately he scraped his teeth down to her shoulder, tongue swirling as he found every intriguing dip.

"So you're a bad bear."

"When I have to be." His hands slid down her back and cupped her buttocks, kneading the firm muscles and pressing her closer to him. "Are you going to give me my fantasy just like you did the last one?"

She leaned closer to him, brushing the corner of his mouth with hers, trailing kisses along his jaw to his neck. He closed his eyes, feeling the small velvet rasp, the stinging nip of playful teeth, and then her lips were moving over his shoulder. The perfect way to start a morning. "I'll give you any fantasy you want, Jonas." She rubbed her face against him like a purring cat. "As long as you give me mine."

He opened his eyes and looked at her, feeling lazy and aroused, a slow burn moving through his body, as if he had all the time in the world to enjoy her. Hannah. His. He slid his hand down her spine to her lower back, making lazy circles. "You have fantasies about me?"

She gave him a wicked smirk, lowered her mouth to his shoulder and bit him gently. "I said I have fantasies, I didn't say about you."

He narrowed his eyes at her, his hand moving over the rounded curve of her bottom in warning. "I'm a jealous man, Hannah. Your fantasies need to be about me."

She laughed softly, the sound sliding through his body, fanning the slow burn into something altogether different. She sounded happy and relaxed, and when she looked at him, he saw love in her eyes. His heart stumbled. It was damned scary how she could turn him inside out with just one look. He would never understand how he managed to get so lucky, he sure as hell didn't deserve her, but he wasn't ever going to be stupid enough to lose her.

When she moved, her hair slid in a caress over her skin, hiding her generous breasts from him one moment. The next — he'd catch a glimpse of the lush curve and tight bud of a nipple. She was inches from his mouth — tempting candy — so sweet.

Looking at her hurt. Taking her over and over through the night hadn't changed that at all. He would think he was fully sated, his body completely satisfied, and then she'd move, with her sexy, flowing grace, brush her skin against his, or do that little pouty thing with her mouth and he'd be hard as a rock again. Worse, deep down, in some hidden core where no one else could see or ever know, he turned to mush — melted — and knew with a certainty that he was lost forever — caught in her spell.

"I love you, Hannah." His throat hurt he felt so raw with love.

In answer, she shifted, an erotic flow of muscle beneath skin, sliding over his body, her head on his chest, her breasts soft and full along his belly, her long, beautiful legs nudging his apart so she could settle comfortably into him. His body temperature spiked as she began a leisurely slide down him, pressing little kisses over his chest and belly. Her tongue felt like velvet as she gave small little flicks along his ribs.

His heart jumped and began to race. Hannah surprised him with her playful nips and her gliding tongue. Blood surged hotly in his veins.

"I love this, knowing I can touch you like this."

Her breath whispered over his skin, hot, erotic, making his body tighten, harden, nearly burst with the anticipation. She left a sensual trail of dampness along his thigh as she continued to move lower still, sliding her soft wet mound deliberately over his leg. He was going to lose his mind before she was through, but he'd make the sacrifice.

There was nothing hurried or frenzied about her exploration. Her hands were slow, shaping his muscles, tracing over his ribs. She teased and flicked his flat nipples, and all the while, her mouth did that slow, lazy burn down his body. Although he had made love to her most of the night, it felt like the first time all over again — the breathless expectation, the raging assault on his senses, the fire burning through his groin until he wanted to scream with the pleasure-pain of it.

Hannah had no idea what she was doing, but it was fun. Jonas's body was sprawled out, completely open to her — her private playground — and she wanted to play. She wanted to know every intimate detail about him. He knew her body, knew exactly how to make her shatter and come apart for him, she wanted the same knowledge of him. Jonas made her feel confident in herself, in her body, in her sexuality.

She pressed kisses down his belly, enjoying the feel of his muscles bunching beneath her lips. The texture of his skin was amazing, hot and firm and soft yet unyielding. His body was taut, hips restless, but for her, he tried to be still and let her do as she wanted. It wasn't easy for him. His body trembled and she knew he was naturally dominant, but he twisted his fists in the sheets and held himself still for her. When he did lift a hand to slide it over the curve of her back, she lifted her head in warning.

"Keep your hands on the mattress, Jonas."

He grinned at her, but his eyes were hot. "My little dominatrix, sexy as hell."

"It's my turn. You spent all night exploring my body, and I want to have my chance with yours. It's only fair." She slipped a little lower still and blew warm air over the broad, flared head of his straining erection. "You're a little intimidating."

He tried not to come off the mattress. "But I make you feel so good."

"True." She blew more air and watched his body jerk, and his hips buck toward her waiting mouth. Eyes locked with his, she experimentally flicked her tongue out to taste him.

"Son of a bitch, Hannah." The words broke from him, a curse — a prayer. His voice was harsh, broken.

"Well, I've never done this. I might need a little instruction."

When she spoke, her lips brushed the sensitive head and her tongue glided over him in hot rasping strokes, punctuating each word.

He closed his eyes briefly, but couldn't stop looking at the erotic sight she made. "Wrap your hand tight around the base, baby." His breath hissed out of his lungs as she complied. Her hand was small, delicate even, circling as close to the base as possible. "Tighter, honey. Don't be afraid. When I'm inside you, you're so damn tight you're strangling me." He groaned in sudden pleasure. "That's it, that's what I need."

She smiled at him and lowered her head again, her tongue gliding over him, curling under the broad head to stroke fire along his most sensitive spot. She'd never felt more powerful than at that moment. He looked as if she could destroy him, his blue eyes so dark they were almost black, his breathing harsh and his pulsing flesh so hard and thick it felt like velvet over steel.

Locking her gaze with his, she parted her lips and, with slow deliberation, encased the hot, engorged head of his cock in the moist heat of her mouth. His entire body jerked and his hands flew up to catch her hair in two tight fists. He let out a strangled gasp, said something rough and low that made her body throb and weep with excitement.

She wanted to devour him the way he had her, take him apart, piece by piece, until he was writhing in ecstasy. He had already taught her what a lover could do with a masterful mouth and she wanted to learn everything. More than anything, she wanted to bring him the kind of pleasure he'd given her. A gift — a loving. The benefit was the thrill, the heat in his eyes, the total joy of giving that brought her own body to a fever pitch.

Jonas groaned, working to keep control, to keep his thrusts shallow and hold back when he wanted to slide down her throat. She was just too damned sexy, looking both shy and sensuous rolled into one. She *wanted* to bring him pleasure — wanted to know his body. It showed in her eyes, in her touch, in her sinful, wicked mouth as she wrecked him slowly and with purposeful intent. "Right there, baby, with your tongue."

She was good at following instructions — too good. He would whisper hoarsely — sometimes crudely — and she would find the exact spot, the right suction, her tongue so devilish he was sure she would destroy him with pure mind-numbing pleasure. She watched him, looking for signals from him, to see what tightened his body, made his temperature soar and the muscles contract. When she sucked hard, her mouth a silken trap of molten heat, she turned him into a lust-filled maniac, guttural growls rumbling from his throat, and when she flattened her tongue and slid it under the flared sensitive tip, rubbing hard, hitting the spot that sent him into orbit, he couldn't stop the rough cry torn from his throat or the automatic thrust of his hips to deepen his stroke.

She nearly pulled away, but he held her with both hands. "That's it, Hannah. Deeper, take me a little deeper, relax your throat for me, baby." Another hoarse cry escaped as she obeyed him, her throat closing around him, squeezing hot, living flesh to the exploding point.

The savage intensity burning in his eyes would have been encouragement enough, but her own body had gone into meltdown. Pleasing him was an aphrodisiac in itself. She could feel fire racing through her bloodstream and flames over her skin, her body burning with incredible need. Deep inside, her body was already melting, rippling and fiercely needy. She wanted more from him, all of him. She kept her eyes locked with his and deliberately drew him nearly out of her mouth, so that he shuddered, his chest rising and falling, his eyes a glittering blue. He trembled. His hands tightened in her hair, locking on her head as if he needed an anchor. Then she took him deep, nearly swallowing him, her mouth deliberately tight and so hot she knew she was melting him. He was pulsing now, his flesh a steel rod. Harsh lines etched into his face as he gasped for air and struggled for control.

Jonas threw his head back and fought to keep from ravaging her soft, hot mouth. No woman had ever driven him to the very edge as Hannah was doing, untutored, inexperienced, but so willing to please him. The joy on her face, the desire, the sheer sensual image ripped through him, a torrent of need rushing through with a destructive force. "Harder, baby, give me more."

He could feel his body swell. And he could feel his hands in her hair, controlling her head, her movements taking over when he wanted the control to be all hers. It was just so good, so perfect. A moment in time he would never forget.

He was burning alive, so far gone, he was thrusting helplessly into her mouth, quick and hard and deeper than he should have been going. She choked. Coughed. Brought him to his senses. His hands stilled her head and he forced his body to quit bucking. "I'm sorry, Hannah, you're making me crazy and I'm out of control."

He closed his eyes when her tongue curled around him.

"I want you crazy and out of control."

He shook his head. "We'll save the rest for another day." Because if they didn't, Hannah was going to learn about love mixed with lust in one catastrophic explosion.

"Come up here. Straddle me, honey. I can already feel how ready you are for me, hot and wet and so damned perfect. Come here."

She started to move, sliding up his body, her breasts leaving twin streaks of fire where her nipples dragged over him. For the first time she hesitated. He saw her gaze shift from him to her surroundings. The glazed excitement glittering in her eyes faded, and one hand went up to her face and dropped to her breasts.

It was morning. She'd been so wrapped up in him she hadn't really noticed the daylight. Satisfaction curved his mouth and settled in his stomach. He could make her forget to hide herself with his hands and mouth and body.

Jonas reached down and framed her face with his hands. "I have to see you, just for a moment. I love your breasts, so soft, baby, so perfect for me. I spent half the night waking you up by sucking on them." He rubbed at a strawberry mark he'd put on one creamy mound. "That's mine. You're mine. And I love you more than life."

"But the scars, Jonas." It was hard to think of anything but the pulsing desire hot between her legs where she was achingly empty and desperate to be filled. And his gaze was burning over her, so possessive, that she nearly climaxed from the look on his face.

"Did you hear me, Hannah? I *have* to see you. Sit up for me, straddle me. Let me have you." He put just the edge of command in his voice, rough with need, dominating with desire.

She moistened her lips, took a breath and then slowly complied. Hannah straddled him, shaking her hair back so it was wild, framing her face in shimmering spirals of gold and platinum, as she sat up with languid grace. She looked a sultry temptress with her perfect breasts and her glowing skin.

There was a moment of silence followed by the sound of the harsh rasp of his breath. She covered her breasts with her hands, an automatic gesture, but he captured her wrists and pulled them down, holding her there so he could look his fill. "Stay like that for me, honey. I just need to . . . I just *need.*"

Releasing her, Jonas slid his palms up her flat stomach, traced her ribs and came up under her breasts, cupping the soft offerings in his hands. His thumbs slid across her nipples and he felt her answering shiver, the rush of heat and moisture as she shifted slightly. He loved watching her face as he leaned forward. The nerves. The arousal. The anticipation. She was so responsive to him. Her nipples tightened before he even got there and he felt the wash of hot liquid on his belly where she straddled him. His cock rested against her soft buttocks, pressing eagerly, wanting to drive home.

He drew one breast in his mouth and caught the other nipple in his fingers, tugging and flicking while he suckled her. She gave a little gasping cry, her body trembling as she pushed closer to him. He took his time, not giving in to the urgent demands of either of their bodies, forcing her to climb higher, licking and sucking, teeth scraping and tongue flicking, tormenting her until she was writhing, her body pulsing sensually. Her stomach muscles bunched into knots. The junction at her legs grew hotter than anything he'd experienced, wet and ready for him. And she wasn't thinking about anything but Jonas — he was certain of that.

He bit down gently, forcing her once more out of her comfort zone and into another realm, the little bites causing flares of heat and arrows of darting pleasure snaking hungrily through her body. Her thighs tightened around him and her hips began a helpless bucking.

He caught her around the waist and lifted her. "Slow this time, Hannah. Slide down slow and ride me." He refused to let her impale herself hard and fast as she wanted to — drawing out the pleasure, forcing her to go slow.

"Jonas. Please."

The soft pleading filled his already full cock with pounding hot blood. He felt every silken muscle as he pushed with torturous slowness into her fiery folds. She was so tight she had him gasping, the shock waves riding his body, ripping through him, demanding release, but he held her hips, lifting her with exquisite care and moving in her with an almost languid pace until she was sobbing his name, begging him for more.

"Tell me what you want, baby," he whispered. "You like this, I know you do. You want something else?"

Oh, God. She *needed.* Needed him wild. Slamming into her, pounding into her until he drove her up and over the edge. She needed release and each slow stroke sent whips of lightning streaking through her body, every nerve ending singed and scorched and desperate for more. "Please, Jonas, I can't take any more. I can't." Because she might go up in flames before she had a chance to actually shatter. Or she'd shatter before she went up in flames. Either way, she had to have release.

Without warning, he rolled them over, sliding her under him, easily, smoothly, dragging her legs over his shoulders, hands on her hips to hold her still. The first thrust was a streak of sheer fire, his cock steel hard, ramming through her swollen, sensitive folds, driving deep, so deep she was afraid he would land in her womb. She heard herself scream, a ragged gasping cry, but he was already withdrawing and slamming home again.

There was no way to control the pleasure, she felt insane with it, giving herself up to it as he pumped into her body with hard, desperate strokes. He pushed her knees back, pulling her hips closer under him, giving him a better angle to go even deeper, driving over knots of nerves screaming with fiery sensations. She writhed under him, her hips bucking, her head thrashing, her muscles tightening around him, gripping him hard.

He whispered against her neck, his mouth skimming down her soft skin, his voice a rough rasp that washed more heat over her. The tension in her built and built, and still he drove into her, taking her on an endless flight. She thrashed, nails biting deep into his shoulder, her small cries turning frantic. He was relentless, driving her up but never over, bringing her to the edge until she was clawing at him, pleading again.

Jonas could barely hold on with her sheath pulsing around him, so tight and so slick, he felt he was moving in a fiery bed of silk. She was strangling him, so hot he was melting, but he wouldn't stop, wouldn't take her over until she knew — until she was certain.

"Who do you . . ." He gasped. Clenched his teeth as her body clamped down on his. "Belong to? Say it, Hannah. Tell me you're mine."

"Jonas." His name came out a wail. She tried to lift her hips to meet his, but his hands held her tightly, keeping her pinned while his body tortured hers with pleasure. "You. You idiot. There's never been anyone else." Her hand curled around his neck. "Oh, please, Jonas, I don't think I'm going to survive."

The sheer lust in her voice, the pleading cries, drove him so far past control he couldn't have held back if he wanted to. He shifted subtly, the movement rocking her, as his cock filled her, burying deep, swelling, the friction increasing to the point that she simply fragmented, her body coming apart under him. His own body jerked hard, the pleasure bordering on pain as he washed her in his release. Still her muscles wouldn't let go, wouldn't stop clasping him, wringing the last drop from him.

He collapsed over her, burying his face in her neck, his hands finding hers and holding them to the mattress on either side of her head.

"I love you, Hannah. I'm not going to be able to come home at night without having you in my bed." He rubbed his face over her breasts, nuzzled a nipple and drew it into his mouth, feeling her body spasm around his. He licked, watching her face, watching the pleasure wash over her. "I want this. I want you. It's been so damn long, baby, empty nights without you, long years waiting to have you. I don't want to wait any longer."

It was difficult to think clearly when his body was so deep in hers and his mouth was on her breast, sending streaks of fire from her nipples to her groin. She would give him anything, do anything. He had to know that. Why didn't he know that?

"I want to be with you, too, Jonas. Everything is mixed up right now, but . . ."

"There isn't going to be a 'but,' Hannah." Jonas sucked at the tender mound at the curve, just above her nipple.

"What are you doing?" She tried to lift her head to see, but he was holding her down and her body was too relaxed to move. More than anything she didn't want to dislodge him, loving the feel of him buried inside her. She narrowed her eyes suspiciously. "You'd better not be putting another mark on me."

He kissed her lips, spearing his tongue into her mouth. "I hate to be the one to tell you, baby, but you have marks all over you. My fingerprints and my mouth are on the inside of your thighs as well as on your breasts, and your belly." He kissed her again. "Mine."

"You're so possessive." She kissed him back. Bit his lower lip. "I left a few marks of my own, to show who you belong to."

He flashed a small grin and rolled off her onto his back, retaining possession of her hand. He brought it to his mouth and nibbled at her fingertips. "I don't want a big fancy wedding like your sisters are planning. I want to do it fast, right away, without the newspapers and magazines hanging around."

She turned her head to look at him, her heart pounding hard. "You think I'm going to marry you?"

"Damn straight you are. I'm not some little play toy, Hannah."

She burst out laughing at his arrogant tone. "And here I thought I was going to have so much fun." She leaned over and nipped his earlobe. "Most men ask."

"You'd just say no. You already did say no."

"I did not. I said later; that's not the same thing." She rolled onto her side and pushed her fingers through his hair. "When I came here to your house and played dress-up, your mother and I talked about weddings. Little girls love weddings and I was no exception. She said, if you ever got married, she'd have it here, at this house, and everyone would come dressed like the 1920s. She'd have a speakeasy dance hall for the reception in your ballroom. She showed me the flapper clothes and then we got dressed up and had tea. We should do that."

His heart nearly stopped. "Have the wedding here?"

"Wouldn't you like that? Dress like she wanted and have the ceremony here? It would be such fun. Joley would love it."

"I would, too, but would you?" His eyes searched hers.

She smiled. "Absolutely. I think it sounds perfect." She grinned at him. "If we're going to get married, I mean."

He kissed her nose. "Oh, we're getting married, baby. You don't want ten kids running around without my ring on your finger. Your father would make you a widow before you ever became a wife."

She laughed and rolled over, wincing. "Wow! I guess I am sore. I must be out of shape."

"I don't know, Hannah, you outlasted me. Come on. I'm going to run you a bath." He jumped up, uncaring that he was naked, went into the connecting bathroom and turned on the faucet. He stuck his head out the door when she didn't move. "You coming?"

"No. I can't walk. I'm going to stay right here all day." She pulled the sheet over her.

"No, baby, you need to soak in a tub, you really won't be able to walk. As it is, you're going to be sore. I don't have any bath salts, or crystals or whatever it is you girls all use, but I lit some of the candles Sarah gave me last Christmas. Don't tell her I said this, but they're soothing."

She laughed. "You're so funny, Jonas, not wanting to admit candles and crystals have healing powers." She rolled onto her side and propped her head in one hand, elbow on the mattress, studying him. He was completely at ease in his nudity.

"I admit it. It's just that you all think I need those things for protection." He glanced into the bathroom to check the water level in the tub.

"You do need them, silly. In our own way, we try to shield you the way you do us. You matter to all of us . . ."

He swung around. "You're mine, Hannah. It's no longer a family thing." There was finality in his voice.

Hannah frowned. He'd always enjoyed the relationship he had with the Drake sisters. He knew he was family to them. He loved them. She couldn't imagine why what she'd said would irritate him. "What's this sudden driving need to establish dominance, Jonas? What's wrong?"

He sighed. "Come here." He crooked his little finger at her.

Hannah rose, wrapping herself in the sheet, trying not to be annoyed that he always made everything sound like an order. "I'm here. Tell me what's wrong."

"Lose the sheet first."

Just like that, as tired and as sore as she was, her body responded. Her breasts tightened, her womb clenched and a frisson of excitement skittered down her spine. "I want you, Jonas, I swear I do, but I think if you make love to me again, you'll kill me."

A reluctant grin curved his mouth. "It would be a nice way to go, locked to you forever. Inside of you. Deep. Right where I belong." He tugged at the sheet.

Hannah let it drop to the floor.

"I like looking at you. Don't hide from me." He caught her chin and leaned down to kiss her. "Not me. Not ever."

"Jonas . . ."

He simply picked her up, carried her to the bath and set her in the steamy water.

"I can't go home with that skirt and blouse and nothing else." The water felt so good. She could just stay there all day, forget the bed. She rested her head against the lip of the tub.

"I'll find you an old pair of my jeans and a shirt. I have to have something around here that will fit you."

"You didn't tell me what's bothering you."

He stood watching her, his expression grim. "You didn't say you loved me, Hannah. I know you want me, but you didn't say you loved me."

"I said it a million ways. Do you think I'd let another man touch me the way you did? Or put his mouth on me? His tongue *in* me? Jonas, don't be an idiot. If you know me at all, you'd never doubt for one moment that

I love you with everything in me. And I have told you before. On the beach I told you."

"That isn't the same as when we're making love. I told you a dozen times last night. You never said it."

"I thought I was saying it, over and over." She hid a smile. Jonas was so big and bad, but underneath it, he was as vulnerable as she was. "I love you, Jonas Harrington. And I trust you not to forget it."

He grinned at her, that same cocky, satisfied grin he often wore, the one that always made her heart melt. "Have your bath, baby. I'll be back with some clothes for you in a sec."

Jonas rarely threw anything away and he rummaged through his drawers in the hopes of finding clothes small enough for her. Tucked away in a box in his closet, he found a pair of jeans from years earlier. He thumbed through the shirts and found his favorite old plaid. As he started out of the room, he glanced at the dresser. The pictures he kept there were all facedown. He'd bumped it when he'd gotten a little wild with Hannah. Smiling, he lifted the middle one and set it upright.

It was one of his favorites of Hannah, with the sun shining on her hair and a dreamy expression on her face. He kissed his fingertips and brushed it across the glass just as the phone rang.

"I'm tossing the clothes in, Hannah."

"Don't throw them in the water!" Hannah stood up to catch the jeans and shirt as they sailed into the bathroom.

The shirt was far too big, but it covered everything, and the jeans were old and faded and snug on her. As she pulled them up over her hips, she saw Jonas on the phone. He went suddenly still, the expression on his face harsh as he reached out and snagged his jeans, putting them on one-handed.

Something was wrong. Really wrong. "What is it?" Hannah asked, anxiety creeping into her voice as she observed his murderous expression and the uneasy glances he sent her way. "Are my sisters all right?" But she would know if one of them was in trouble. She always knew.

Jonas put down the phone, his hand going to the nape of her neck. "Early this morning, when Jackson was heading into the office, someone tried to run him off the road. He was in my car and still using my jacket. I have his."

"Oh no. Was he hurt?"

"The car is totaled and he's got a few scrapes and bruises, but he's alive." He grabbed a shirt and shrugged into it. "Jackson's been with me through more nasty battles with the bullets flying and neither of us thinking we were going to get out than I care to remember. I don't like that he took another hit for me." He paced across the floor, too restless to stay still when he was puzzling it all out.

"This doesn't make sense. They had to have thought it was me driving the car, but clearly you weren't in the car. Why would they make me a target?"

Hannah slid down the wall to the floor, crossed her arms over her breasts and drew up her knees, making herself smaller, huddling in the corner. This was her fault. Someone had tried to kill Jonas and poor Jackson had gotten in the way. Anything that happened to him had been because of her. Why? She didn't understand what she could have done to make someone hate her so much. Her sisters were in danger, and so were Jackson and Jonas. She closed her eyes on the tears burning so close.

Jonas glanced at her white, pale face and instantly knelt down beside her. "It's okay, baby. It's going to be okay. Jackson is all right."

She shook her head, rocking back and forth. "Where can I go that I won't take the chance that someone I love is going to be hurt?" She looked up at him with sorrow and shock in her eyes. "Who could possibly hate me so much they not only want to destroy me, but everyone I love? What could I have done to cause this?"

Jonas had seen victims of crimes, hundreds of them. He'd reassured them, soothed them, broken bad news and good news, but it had never been personal. Her emotion choked him, strangled him, made him feel helpless and racked with fury that someone could put that look on her face. "Nothing, Hannah. You didn't do anything at all. People who choose this kind of madness are ill. A slight can be imagined, fantasized. It isn't really about you. It's about them and their self-absorbed hatred, an all-consuming destructive emotion. It isn't someone you know. No one who knows you could ever do this to you."

"I don't know what to do."

"I do, sweetheart. This is what I do. I'm taking you back to your house . . ."

She shook her head. "I don't want them going after my sisters."

Jonas framed her face with his large hands. "Baby, you're not thinking clearly. Your house eats people for snacks. Your trees throw them into the ocean. Your balcony comes alive and your windows repair themselves. You and your sisters are damned safe in that house, which, by the way, I'm never going to look at in the same way again."

She almost managed a smile as she allowed him to pull her up. "All right. I'll go home with them, but you'd better stay in the house as well. I mean it, Jonas. Whoever is doing this is obviously trying to kill you now."

He looked around, found their shoes in the living room and handed her sandals to her. She flushed, seeing her skirt, blouse and coat right at the entrance to the doorway.

"We didn't get far, did we?"

He grinned at her. "Best night of my life, Hannah. Thank you." He leaned over, kissed her and pulled on his shoes. "Let's get out of here. Let me go first, just in case. Get right into the truck."

She nodded and waited for him to take the lead. He stopped long enough to lock the door behind him, and hurried to the truck, his gaze quartering the area around them, looking for anything suspicious.

Hannah settled in the truck, drew her seatbelt across her and drummed her fingers on the seat in apprehension while he shoved the key into the ignition.

Jonas reached for her hand, his fingers running over hers in a little caress before he picked up her hand and brought it to the warmth of his mouth. "It's going to be all right, baby. It won't be much longer before we figure this out." He nibbled on the tips of her fingers and turned the key.

The engine whined, but refused to turn over. Jonas swore under his breath.

"Maybe we should talk to Abbey. She hates using her abilities, but she can determine truth," Hannah said hesitantly.

"I don't think we have anyone she can question yet." There was something worrying at the back of his mind, something just out of reach, if he'd just remember it. He turned the key again and the motor made the same noise, refusing to start.

Jonas snapped his teeth together and grabbed the key, impatient, but suddenly he went still. His alarms were screaming at him, his stomach burning with knots, he just had been too absorbed in Hannah to focus on it. Jackson's truck was always — *always* — in perfect running condition.

Hannah frowned, the sudden stillness in him sending her natural alarms shrieking. "What is it, Jonas?"

He reached down and unsnapped Hannah's seatbelt. "Get out of the truck. Get out now, Hannah. Hurry, damn it."

She reacted to the urgency in his voice, the fear. She tried to push open the door, remembered it was locked and reached for the handle.

"Run for the trees, away from the house. Run fast, baby, I'll be right behind you."

Hannah slid out. "Tell me."

"There's a bomb in the truck." His voice was calm, but his eyes were savage. "Get the hell out of here, Hannah — now."

19

Hannah didn't wait to ask questions. She took off running away from the house toward the trees to the back of Jonas's property, her heart thundering in her ears. She glanced over her shoulder, to reassure herself Jonas was coming. He was right behind her, his body squarely between hers and the truck.

"Go!" he said urgently, one hand on her back, pushing her forward.

Hannah ran until her lungs burned and her legs ached, stumbling across the uneven ground. She felt the blast before she heard it, the buildup in the air, the smashing concussion that lifted them both and flung them like paper dolls through the air. She landed hard, the wind knocked out of her, body sore and bruised, the world silent as her ears protested the violation of sound.

Around them the wind rose, leaves and twigs whirling in the air along with the debris from the truck. Orange-red flames mixed with black smoke, burning hot and bright, billowing high into the air. Blackened parts of the truck were scattered across the wide expanse of lawn leading down toward the trees and a door lay in the bushes near the front steps of the house.

Frantically she crawled to where Jonas lay just a few feet from her. *Jonas!* She didn't speak aloud, there was no point until their ears settled from the terrifying blast. For one heart-stopping moment she thought he was dead. He lay still, his face pale, his chest not moving. Her world came to an end, crashing down around her so that she sank onto the ground beside him, her trembling hand sliding over his skin to find his pulse. *Oh, God, please, Jonas, be alive.* She'd know if he were dead, she was certain, but still, until she found his pulse, her mind screamed and screamed.

He drew in a gasping breath and his eyes flew open, hands coming up to capture her wrist in a viselike grip, and drag his gun from his shoulder harness. His eyes were savage, his face grim. Hannah's heart stopped as the gun swept across her. His gaze found her face and he visibly settled, then began running his hands over her looking for injuries.

I'm all right, she assured him. *What about you?*

Good. I'm good. He looked at the towering inferno. *Jackson's truck is toast.* Sitting up, he looked warily around him, indicating the trees again. *We're too exposed here.*

My sisters will know and they'll send help. Already the wind was picking up around them. A ringing in her head began to grow. Something flew by her ear with an angry buzz.

Jonas slammed into her hard, rolling her over in the dew-wet grass. They continued rolling along the slope and then he was dragging her up. "Run, damn it, zigzag and get into the cover of the trees."

His gun was up and he squeezed the trigger, aiming back toward the house. Four bullets rang out in rapid succession, even as his other hand shoved at her back.

Hannah ran. Her breath came in sobs, but she forced her mind to find calm. She had to help Jonas. More than one person was shooting at them.

Bullets hit in front of them, effectively halting their progress. Jonas threw her to the ground again, trying to find a target to give her a chance. She knew saving her was the only thing on his mind. They were caught out in the open on the rolling expanse of lawn that led to the edge of the forest surrounding three sides of the property. They were hemmed in. The barrage of bullets came from various directions, trapping them.

"Listen, baby, they could kill us right now if they wanted. Whatever they have in store for us is worse than taking a bullet. We have to get out of here. I'm going to lay down cover, and you start running. Just keep going and don't look back."

She caught his arm and shook her head, staring at the flames bursting up into the sky in one big conflagration. "Fire. We have fire, Jonas, one of the five elements. They started it, but it's mine to use."

She knelt up slowly, her hands already flowing in the air, weaving a complicated pattern, and she lifted her face to the sky, her voice soft and melodious. He couldn't catch the words but power shimmered in the air.

The enemy closed in, ringing them, still a distance away, confident they'd run their prey to ground. Hannah never looked at them, never acknowledged they were even there. She looked like an ancient goddess as she called on the universe for protection.

The blackened carnage of the truck shook violently. A stream of orange and red sparklers rocketed into the sky, racing forty — fifty feet straight at the clouds. Abruptly the flames stopped, hovered overhead briefly in a fantastic display of flame and light, then shot across the sky in a fireball, leaving a trail of fire raining down on the heads of the men standing between Jonas and Hannah and the forest.

For a moment no one moved. The first fireball struck one man's shoulder, driving him to the ground. His clothes went up in flames. He screamed and rolled frantically on the ground. And then it was raining fire, flames hurtling out of the sky, sending their attackers running for cover.

Jonas dragged Hannah to her feet. "Run! Get to the trees."

She knew Jonas's property fairly well. He owned sixty acres, most of it forest which backed up to a state park. She made for the trail that took them into the thickest grove of trees, bursting through the underbrush guarding the parameter and then into the forest itself. The canopy overhead darkened the interior. Branches lay on the ground where they'd snapped off, and moss clung to tree trunks and branches, turning some of the trees a brilliant green.

Jonas caught her hand and signaled to take the narrow animal path to his left, away from the wider trail for his Jeep. Hannah moved through the narrow tunnel of broken branches, the brush scraping her arms and shoulders right through her shirt. Jonas's breath was harsh against her neck, but his hand was steady on her back.

The fireworks had given them breathing room and they headed deep into the interior of the forest, where the trees gave them cover and the brush was thicker, making it much more difficult for anyone to find them.

The buzzing in her ears had settled to an annoying hum. "Do you think they'll follow us?"

"It's hard to tell. Your sisters will send help, but it's going to take a few minutes. Who are these guys? I didn't get close enough to recognize anyone."

"Me either." Hannah looked around her. It was difficult walking over the uneven ground in sandals. She glanced up at Jonas's face. It was difficult to remember sometimes, that he hadn't always been a part of their family and that his estate was so large. "I'd forgotten how beautiful it is here."

His hand guided her along the narrow trail, steering to the left where he had played as a child. He knew vines hung there and the brush was thick and tangled. "Go this way, baby. I used to build forts out of the downed branches and formed tunnels from the foliage. There'll be more cover along this path." He'd crawled like a soldier through the animal trails on his belly back then, never knowing he'd be doing it for real in an effort to save Hannah's life. At the time it had been an imaginary game, pretending to attack the "germ" soldiers killing his mother. Now he had real enemies after them.

Hannah reached back and took his hand, knowing he was suddenly thinking of his mother. These were the woods his mother loved so much. She'd enjoyed the sea, the sight and sound of it, but the forest was her first love and her husband had bought the estate with the beautiful home and acres of mixed forest where one could stand in any room on the main floor and just look right over the trees to the ocean.

"No harm will come to us here," she murmured, wanting it to be the truth. Not in his mother's beloved woods.

They turned along a path that followed a stream. Wild turkeys burst out of the huge ferns growing along the winding creek and up the slope. The huge birds called to one another in alarm, flapping wings and rushing up the hill to another path, two of them taking to the air in agitation.

Jonas swore and caught her shoulder. "There's no way they didn't hear that. If they lost our trail, they'll be on it now. I should have hunted those idiot treacherous turkeys a long time ago."

"You don't hunt."

"I'm going to start." He'd never really hunt the turkeys. His mother had watched them every morning from her window. She would count the toms, even name them. She knew which trees the turkeys preferred roosting in at night. The hens would sometimes shelter the chicks under the deck during the day, or lead them down to the stream in the thickest part of the ferns, just at the edge of the forest where Jonas kept the weeds cleared so she could always see. The wild turkeys had brought pleasure and, in a way, relief to his mother. They would always be safe from hunters on his property.

Jonas never hunted animals. Not the deer or bear or bobcat, not even those damned wild turkeys his mother had loved so much. He hunted men and he was damned good at it. He wasn't so good at running from them. "I could find a safe place to stash you, Hannah, and double back."

She stopped so abruptly he ran into her. "You aren't stashing me, Jonas. We're in this together." Her hand gripped his harder. "I can't lose you. Not now. Not like this. And you're a crazy man when you get angry. You're angry now, I can feel it."

He was shaking with fury, a fierce warrior trapped and unable to fight his way out. His instinct was to turn the tables on them and go hunting, but he refused to put Hannah in more danger. She knew that. Understood it. But she wasn't willing to let him separate them.

The sound of gunfire reached them a split second before the bullet. It hit the tree closest to them, spraying bark all around them. Instantly a shower of bullets zinged into the trunks around them, thunking into wood and sending splinters and bark over them. Jonas pulled her down, his body covering hers as he cautiously lifted his head to peer through the leaves.

"Can you see them?" she whispered.

Jonas glanced down at her. Beneath him, her body was trembling, but despite her stark white skin and enormous eyes, Hannah's mouth was firm and her gaze steady.

"If you can give me a direction, I can slow them down or maybe, if I'm lucky, pin them down until help arrives."

She took a long sweeping look at the trees around them. The forest here was full of old growth, the trees tall, many of their lower branches cracked and hanging.

"Lure them in, Jonas. Bring them to us. If we fall back and let them have this spot, I think I can stop them right here."

"You move quietly, Hannah, stay low to the ground. Go deeper into the forest, we may need an escape route." His ears had stopped ringing and he could hear voices shouting back and forth. "Can you hear that?"

"Just barely."

"That's not English. You know languages. What are they speaking?"

Her small teeth bit at her lower lip as she concentrated. "The accents are very heavy. They're speaking Russian, Jonas." She let her breath out slowly. "They have to be Nikitin's men."

Jonas frowned. "Why would Prakenskii save your life if Nikitin wanted you dead? He's definitely Nikitin's man."

Hannah's shirt caught on a splintered branch and jerked her to a halt. Jonas reached down to pull it carefully loose.

"Is he?" Hannah asked. "Are you sure? Because he wanted Joley to go upstairs with me when Nikitin came to our house. He warned us to be careful of using our powers and said Nikitin didn't know about or suspect us."

"I'll admit we can't get much on him. We've asked Interpol and every other source we could tap. There are rumors. They say Prakenskii was trained from childhood as an agent. He was raised learning how to make killing an art form."

"How awful for him." Hannah went down on her knees to maneuver through a particularly low tunnel of debris.

Jonas followed, his shoulders catching on the network of old downed branches and leaves forming the game tunnel. "It's too much of a coincidence for me to buy. Prakenskii right there to save you. Nikitin chased you through the damn room. What the hell are they up to?"

Hannah frowned. "I just can't imagine that Prakenskii could be in the same room with me — with Joley — with all of my sisters — and not one of us pick up on his guilt. It's too big of a secret to hide. If his intentions are to harm me, and why would that be his ultimate goal . . ." She broke off with a little gasp as her hair caught in the low, sharp, very brittle foliage.

Jonas felt his heart leap. "Hannah." His voice was a soft hiss of reprimand. "We're not out here for a Sunday stroll. I'll get it, stop pulling. You're shaking the brush around us."

Hannah tried to stay still, her heart slamming hard against her chest. The dead network of branches felt like she'd run into a thorn bush. Her scalp, owing to her naturally curly hair, was very tender. Between the branch and Jonas yanking on it, tears swam in her eyes.

A barrage of bullets had Jonas slamming her to the ground hard enough to knock the wind out of her. Her head throbbed where she was certain a patch of hair had been yanked out.

"Scoot through the vegetation on your stomach," Jonas whispered.

Hannah tried not to be a priss. They were about to be shot. She shouldn't be worried about ticks and spiders, but she could think of little else as they eased their bodies forward, trying to find cover.

Sarah had better get her ass in gear and send us some help. Jonas swore crudely under his breath as a bullet hit the ground close to them. To her credit, Hannah made no sound, but it was enough to fuel the already murderous anger in him. He resisted the urge to leap up and fire back. He had to stay hidden. The enemy wasn't certain yet exactly where they were. All he could do was to try to keep his body positioned in front of Hannah's and protect her until help arrived.

Sarah knows. They've sent Jackson and the others by now and they're out on the captain's walk waiting to send aid. I can feel them, the power gathering in the air waiting for me. Just get those men to come in the forest. I can do the rest.

He stopped her with a hand to her shoulder and leaned over her to put his lips against her ear, not wanting any mistakes. "You want me to draw them to us?"

She nodded. Her mouth was dry, but this was what she was born to do and she was confident in her ability.

"Keep moving back, baby," Jonas cautioned and fired several rounds, more to give away their position and draw the attackers in than to hit someone. He snapped another clip in his gun and continued pushing her forward. "Watch the stream, Hannah. There's a narrow strip of land with a downed log over it. Use that to cross."

That would put the stream between them and their attackers. Ferns grew large and thick on either side of the stream going up the slope leading to the stands of trees. He followed Hannah through the plants, noting where the ground dipped down and where their attackers would have the best cover.

"Here. I can use the water. Find us a place to wait for them, Jonas."

He made a careful sweep with cool, assessing eyes. He'd spent hundreds of hours in this place. It was his childhood playground and he knew every single square inch of ground. He nudged her to the left. "Make for that little slope. Use the ferns for cover, but you can't brush them with your body, Hannah."

Her skin itched and prickled as if a million bugs crawled over her. She was terrified there were ticks in her hair. The ground close to the stream was marshy and wet. She didn't want to think about that as she slid along, using her elbows to propel her. And she hated the fact that any of that was in her mind when they had men chasing them with guns. She glanced at Jonas.

Harsh lines were carved into his grim face. His jaw was set in that stubborn look she knew so well and his eyes were alive with fury. She wanted to be like him. He wasn't worrying about bugs and filth, he was bent on destroying the danger to them — to her. Pride welled up in her.

"There's no one else like you in the world, Jonas," she said softly.

He glanced down at her, his gaze holding on hers. At once his face softened. "I love you, Hannah. I always have."

Her heart gave a funny little flip and her stomach took a dive. "I love you, too." She couldn't believe she was with him. In spite of the danger, there was exhilaration in the moment. She'd spent her life afraid. Stammering. Consumed by panic attacks. Yet she was hiding in the woods, killers on her heels, crawling on her stomach with snakes and bugs like some wild soldier, and she felt strangely elated. And very much loved by Jonas Harrington.

They found a depression in the soft ground right behind several large wide trees. It was a natural fortress camouflaged on three sides by the brush and fallen leaves and twigs around them. Jonas arranged several dead branches with drooping leaves over them so anyone would really have to look closely before spotting them.

"No matter what, Hannah, you keep down." His hand pressing on the nape of her neck made it impossible to do anything else. His voice held a whip of fury.

She was scared, no doubt about it, but Jonas was in full-blown protector mode and the familiarity of it made her feel confident of her own abilities. Jonas had always been there, fighting at the side of her family since they were children, and he was very good at it. She liked the feeling of being partners with him — of belonging.

"You're going to have to let me up long enough to call the elements in, Jonas. We'll need rain to put the fire out so it doesn't get out of hand. And we need the wind and then maybe the fog. I can manipulate the ground and the water if I have to."

He could hear them coming now and the thought of letting her, even for a moment, risk her life was abhorrent to him, but at the same time, he'd be stupid not to give her the best chance. Hannah was her own best chance.

"I'll be careful," Hannah assured him. She raised her head cautiously and peered through the heavy brush. "Can you give us a taller screen? I have to use my hands."

Biting back a protest, Jonas snagged two of the larger fallen branches, both with sweeping fans of needles. He added them to the existing brush around them, making certain the dead limbs looked as if they had fallen there naturally.

Hannah lifted her hands toward the sky, weaving a graceful pattern in the air as she called on the elements to assist her.

Jonas watched her, and even surrounded as they were by danger, or maybe because of it, pride in her swelled in him. He'd always loved to see the natural elegance of her slender body. Her face was devoid of makeup and she looked impossibly young but breathtakingly beautiful and completely unaware of it. As she wove her magic, she was wholly focused on her task, murmuring softly as she moved her hands.

He scanned the surrounding area again. What he wanted to do was crawl out from under cover and hunt the bastards down one by one and shoot them. Another minute — another turn of the key in the ignition — and Hannah would have been killed.

"They're coming in, baby." He shifted subtly, ensuring his body was slightly in front of hers and that he could drop on her if necessary. "Hurry."

She didn't acknowledge him, or shift her attention even for a moment. As always, when Hannah used her gifts, he could feel the subtle buildup of energy. It started as an electrical current around them. The hair on his arms stood up. His ears buzzed with the crackle of power in the air. The tops of the trees swayed gently, a subtle change as the breeze shifted.

He felt it on his face then, a soft touch of fingers, heard feminine voices chanting in the distance, and his mouth curved in satisfaction. Mess with the Drakes and life could get rough.

The splash of water got his attention. If the enemy came in by the strip of water, they might have a chance of spotting them as only the large ferns provided cover.

He sank lower, pressing his hand onto the small of her back and exerting pressure, silently telling her to drop down. "In the stream, Hannah." He sank onto his belly and thrust the gun forward, waiting.

She allowed him to bring her down to her stomach, but she propped herself up on her elbows in order to use her hands as she turned her attention to the long ribbon of stream she could see. The water began to bubble and then slosh back and forth, each wave growing in strength and intensity until the water was rocking well above the sides of the stream. Back and forth, it rushed, gathering strength and power, feeding itself as the speed increased.

Overhead, dark clouds gathered ominously. Veins of lightning edged the clouds, glittering angrily. Thunder rumbled and the morning sky darkened. All the while the water in the stream sloshed back and forth, growing in height with each new wave. The men walking in the creek rounded the corner.

Jonas could see their faces clearly. The

shock. The horror. The utter terror. They stood frozen as the wall of water raced toward them, a tower now. The one in the lead yelled something in raw fear and turned, using his shoulder as a battering ram to take out the man behind him. The water hit them full on, slapping them hard, driving them to the rocky streambed, tumbling them with the force of a mini-tsunami.

At the exact same moment, the clouds burst and dumped the pounding rain. It fell so hard and fast it stung, and reduced visibility to zero. Jonas shifted until his upper body protected her head and shoulders, all the while his restless gaze sought targets.

There was quiet as the rain pelted down and the waves in the stream began to ease without Hannah feeding them power.

"We've got to go now before they recover. We're just playing hide and seek until the others get here." He kept his hand on her lower back, urging her to back out of the depression and move around the thick network of tree roots. "I'm sorry, baby, I should never have brought you out of your house where you could be in this kind of danger. I had no idea we were facing this kind of adversary, but I should have."

Hannah would rather have continued to face them than to run, especially when they were back to crawling. "Why? Whoever this is has manpower and tenacity. He isn't giving up. It isn't a regular hit where they just send one killer." Every time she thought about someone hating her that much, she felt sick to her stomach. "None of this makes sense to me."

"Me either," he admitted. "You just aren't the kind of woman to inspire this kind of hatred. Fantasies maybe. Sick ones even, but not this kind of thing. Now Joley . . ."

"Don't you say a single bad word about Joley!" Her defense of her sister was swift and furious. "She's a wonderful person."

"Honey, she took down the Reverend on national television. Do you honestly think that his followers, the men surrounding him that benefit from his scam, and the Reverend himself, don't have a hate as big as Texas for Joley right now? She's rash and she's too honest. She says what she thinks. It doesn't matter if she's right. She's like an avenging angel. Put that together with her sexy image and you've got trouble."

He held a low-hanging branch out of the way so she could gain her feet. "Take the right-hand path. That curves back around and starts leading up toward the house. We go up over the slope and then follow the stream back downhill. We'll be able to hear when the rescue squad gets here."

"Tell me about Nikitin. What do you know about him?" Hannah asked. "I wish I could figure out just what his interest in Joley really is. And why won't Prakenskii say?"

"Prakenskii has his own interest in Joley, Hannah, and it has nothing whatsoever to do with work and everything to do with being a man."

Hannah pushed aside several cracked branches, remembering at the last moment, before releasing them, that the movement could give away their position. She stood bent over, feeling helpless and stupid until Jonas took control of the foliage and waved her on.

"The Russians have always had a problem with violent mobsters. They're highly organized, international and very bloody. Along with the Colombians and the Italian mobsters, the Russians are considered the most powerful criminals in the world. You name it, they're into it. And where they really shine is in laundering money. They can take dirty money and make it clean like no one else. Where other organizations have rules about killing cops and families, they don't. They could care less."

"Why is Nikitin rubbing shoulders with celebrities and politicians?"

"He has a clean image. Interpol, hell, every cop from here to Europe and back, knows he's dirty, but no one can get anything on him. He's good at what he does and he likes the image of being a good guy, so he works at it. Boris Tarasov, one of his greatest rivals, wants the fear from everyone more than the celebrity image. We're talking billions of dollars, Hannah. That kind of money buys you a lot of protection. They buy police, government officials, customs, you name it, they have someone in their pocket."

"I don't understand how we ended up getting mobsters after our family. Joley would have said if she'd had a run-in with one of them."

His hand on her shoulder stopped her and she sank down into the cradle of the earth, surrounded by roots and thicker tree trunks for protection. Her heart began to thump hard again. She could hear the approach of the men following them, the whispered voices with their heavy accents.

"You're going to be all right, baby," he whispered against her ear, his lips brushing over the thin lines on her face where the knife had slashed her. "Jackson and the others will be here soon."

"I know." She couldn't tell him she was

more worried about him than herself.

Jonas was a man of strong emotions with an equally strong need to protect. Most of the time, Jonas shielded her automatically from his feelings. He'd been doing it for so many years, he didn't think about it. But there were occasions, like now, when his mind was totally focused somewhere else and she was swamped with the sheer intensity of his fury.

There was no other word for it but rage. It rolled off him in waves. His face was a grim mask, his eyes glittered dangerously, and although he sent her a small smile of reassurance when she reached up to try to ease the frown on his lips, it was far from the real thing.

"Jonas, we really are going to be okay," she said. "I know we are."

His dangerous blue eyes settled on her face. Immediately the flow of emotion stopped. "Sorry, Hannah. I wasn't thinking, I should have been more careful." He brushed a gentle kiss on the top of her head. "I know we will be."

"But?" she prompted.

"But they came after you and they're still coming and that's not acceptable to me. At least I know where to go looking now."

The rain slowed to a steady drizzle. Three

men moved toward them at a right angle, carefully avoiding the stream, obviously unaware of their exact position, but making a sweep to find them. Jonas extended his gun.

"I'm still feeling strong, Jonas," Hannah said. "The others are feeding me their power. I might collapse after, but right now, let me hold them off as long as I can. We'll save ammunition and they won't know exactly where we are. With any luck, they'll be superstitious."

Jonas shifted again and allowed her to slide out from under him. They moved with care to keep from shaking the brush around them. With the rain falling, it helped to cover any soft sound, but it also muffled the approach of the enemy.

"How many?" Hannah asked.

Jonas shrugged. "More than five. Seven maybe." And that worried him. They wanted Hannah bad. Why? The question nagged at him. Who could hate Hannah? It didn't seem possible to him, but the answer was right there — just out of his reach. He could practically taste it in his mouth, but couldn't quite spit it out. His brain worked fast at computing data, and along with his highly developed intuition, that was the reason he was good at his job. Now, when he needed his ability to process data fast, it seemed to be failing him.

The men were moving through the brush and trees, inching their way, guns drawn. Hannah's hands began their graceful motion, her melody changing, the tone much more earthy. Near the redwood trees, just in front of their enemies, the ground rippled, moving leaves and redwood needles along with fallen vegetation in a gentle rolling swell.

The men stopped their approach abruptly. They spoke rapidly in another language.

"They think they're feeling an earthquake," Hannah interpreted, her voice distracted. "That the stream acted the way it did because of . . ." She trailed off.

Jonas glanced down at Hannah. Her concentration was once again completely focused on the soil and vegetation where the enemy huddled whispering together. The rolling swells spread out, reaching toward the group, the waves rising and falling with gathering speed. Above them, the trees shook, and as they looked up, brittle branches cracked and splintered, falling from above them to drive like spears into the ground. The thick branches fell with enough force that they drove deep into the soil. Standing upright, each branch formed a piece of fence so that it ringed the men as the ground continued to pitch and roll.

"I hear sirens," Jonas said. "Another couple of minutes and the troops will arrive." He wasn't good at hiding. He wanted to stand up, and blast away at the men who wanted Hannah dead.

She suddenly leaned into him, her head lolling back on his chest as his arm came up around her waist to support her. Jonas swore softly and began to ease her to the ground. She clutched his wrist.

"Not yet. Wait. Tell me if they come at us again."

Jonas saw the men breaking through the wall of branches, stumbling back away from the area. The swells followed them, but much more gentle now with Hannah's power waning. He sighed. They were going to make one more fast try. He could feel it more than see it.

The men formed a loose semicircle and began spraying the forest with bullets. He flattened Hannah instantly, swearing as the bullets penetrated into their space, digging into trees and the ground around them. He heard Hannah's soft voice. Melodious this time, the notes familiar. Her affinity with the wind was legendary within the family. And the wind answered immediately, leaves rustling as the breeze grew stronger, branches swaying, trunks of trees bending.

Sharp needles shot from the redwood trees, swarming like angry bees, the sound an ominous buzz as they hurtled through the air at Hannah's enemies. The needles penetrated skin, spearing deep, the stings of hundreds of insects on every inch of exposed skin. The enemy turned and fled, running from the forest as if demons were behind them.

Hannah turned her face into Jonas's chest and went limp, her body slumping against his, all energy drained out of it. He sat in the midst of brush and trees, Hannah in his arms, listening to cars start up and the rain fall down. She hadn't panicked. She hadn't fallen apart and clung to him in terror, although he could see it in her eyes. She had fought by his side courageously. The next time she called herself a coward, he was going to shake some sense into her.

Tires screamed on the asphalt drive up by his house and he heard the sound of running. "Jonas! Hannah!"

20

"The women need strong, sweet tea," Ilya Prakenskii greeted Jonas as he entered the kitchen. His cool, appraising gaze ran over Jonas, noting the smears of dirt and scratches, the evidence of the explosion. "I felt the surge in power and knew they'd need help. Is Hannah all right?"

Jonas watched him gather mugs onto a tray. "She's fine. A little shaken up."

Ilya rested his hip against the counter. "You have something on your mind."

"The attack on Hannah by the Werners could have been directed by someone with your abilities."

"I considered that as well, but I was close to the man. I would have felt it." Ilya shrugged his shoulders. "Unless you're implying I was the one directing him."

"The girls say no and I don't think so either." Jonas rubbed his shadowed jaw. "Is it possible Nikitin has that kind of power?"

"Absolutely not." Prakenskii added a powder to the tea.

"That could just be an act."

"He has no power. He would laugh if you told him anyone had the ability to manipulate energy. I would have known. There's a charge in the air, much like an electrical current, when the elements are being manipulated. You've probably felt it. You have your own talent. It's the only reason I'm allowed into this home. You'd have shot me and asked questions later if you believed for one moment that I could have orchestrated the attack on Hannah."

Prakenskii had read him correctly, Jonas couldn't very well deny the charge. He'd considered the possibility because he had to, but he knew Ilya Prakenskii had saved Hannah's life, not tried to take it.

"What did you put in their tea?"

"Vitamins. A healing compound. All natural and nothing illegal."

Jonas held out his hand for one of the mugs. Ilya handed him one and took one himself. Both drank.

"I'll give this one to Hannah." Jonas watched Prakenskii arrange cups on a tray and carry it toward the living room. "Why aren't you floating it in like the girls do?"

Prakenskii shrugged. "Even small things

are a drain on energy and I prefer to reserve mine for what lies ahead."

"And what would that be?" Jonas asked, gliding easily in front of the man, blocking his way to the door.

Prakenskii glanced at him. "Hunting, Mr. Harrington. I will be going hunting very shortly and I'll need every ounce of energy I can muster."

Jonas studied his expressionless face. "You aren't what they say."

"I'm exactly what they say. I do the job nobody else wants."

Jonas continued to lock gazes. "Maybe you do, but the real question is not what you do, but who you work for."

Ilya Prakenskii didn't so much as blink, but Jonas knew, in the strange way he often knew things, that he had hit a target.

"I work for Sergei Nikitin."

"Is he the mark?"

"Think what you like." Prakenskii stood waiting for Jonas to get out of his way.

Jonas shook his head. "You can't have her, Prakenskii, not if you're what you want the world to believe, and I think you know that."

Ilya didn't bother to pretend not to understand. "My relationship with Joley Drake is not your business."

"Actually, it is. The Drakes are my family

and I look after my own."

"Is that what you're doing?"

Jonas stepped back, allowing Ilya to take the tray into the living room, where the Drake sisters sat, or lay, on the chairs, couches and floor, the drain of energy after helping Hannah taking a toll.

Jonas narrowed his eyes, watching as Ilya carefully handed each woman a mug of tea, giving Joley the one he'd sipped from. He opened his mouth, but a cough instead of words came out, and Joley frowned, looking up at him as she sipped, and then at Ilya.

"What did you do?" she demanded, her voice husky. "I felt that small flare."

Jackson crossed the room to touch Elle's cheek, placing his body carefully between her and the Russian. Jonas knew him well enough to know he had put himself in a position to get a clear shot if necessary.

Ilya appeared not to notice, but when he moved away from the sisters, he settled with his back to the wall, directly facing Jackson and the other fiancés of the Drake sisters. "I put natural vitamins in your tea. Nothing poisonous."

Hannah took another swallow. "You'll have to tell me how you make it. I can feel the difference already."

"Jonas," Sarah called him to attention.

"There's a message for you from a man named Duncan Gray." She straightened in the chair and pushed back her dark hair. "He said to tell you Petr Tarasov died a few hours ago from injuries sustained during the attempt to break him out of custody. He also said the agent he told you about has been identified."

"Who is Duncan Gray?" Libby asked. "Why is that name so familiar?"

"Jonas worked for Gray when he first got out of the Rangers," Sarah said. "Why would he suddenly be calling you now, Jonas? Is this anything to worry about?"

"Who is Petr Tarasov?" Joley asked.

"Petr Tarasov is the brother of Boris Tarasov, one of the most violent mobsters alive today," Elle answered. "Boris Tarasov is wanted around the world for just about everything from fraud to murder. Word had it that the defense department arrested Petr for murdering one of their agents, and was holding him in an unknown location. A few days ago, an attempt was made by Boris's organization to get him free."

"What else do you know, Elle?" Jonas demanded.

"Petr was shot and again taken to an undisclosed location for treatment." She looked directly at Jonas. "There must have been someone in the defense department feeding Boris information for him to find both locations, and if I'm not mistaken, the cryptic message to Jonas was to tell him the traitor has been identified and is now deceased."

"How the hell would you know all that?" Jackson demanded.

Elle lifted an eyebrow at him and took a drink of tea to avoid answering.

Jackson took a step toward, going from protective to menacing in a heartbeat. "We had a talk about this, Elle. I told you to quit."

She stood up, her dark eyes flashing fire at him that fast. "You tell me a lot of things. I told you to quit and I see you're still a deputy." She glanced at Prakenskii. "Giving me orders doesn't work, Jackson, so back off. And now isn't the time for this anyway."

"This isn't over, Elle," Jackson said.

"It is for me," she replied.

Jonas held up his hand for peace, looking around the room at the women he called family. They were tired and pale, but the tea was helping. "Let's just put this aside for now. We're all tired and upset."

"I have a bit of news that may interest you," Ilya said, watching him closely. "There is a rumor going around that four of Boris

Tarasov's crew went missing and when the fifth delivered the news, telling an outrageous tale of a house eating a man, trees coming to life and windows shattering and repairing themselves, Boris put a gun to his head and shot him."

Jonas went absolutely still. Everything in him froze. The news was a sucker punch to his gut. Hard. Out of nowhere. Completely debilitating. For a moment he couldn't think or move, his mind screaming a denial. It was impossible for Boris Tarasov to connect him with Petr's arrest. *Impossible.* That sneak and peek in the alley had been completely off the books. Gray had picked Jackson and Jonas up himself. No one else knew they had been there except Gray, and Jonas trusted him implicitly.

The silence stretched. The tension in the room climbing.

Had someone seen him? Recognized him? No one in San Francisco would know who he was. A stranger brought in, no name, no connection. He'd gone to the clinic, but hadn't used his own name. They'd been careful to give no ID, careful of touching anything in the room. No one could identify them.

His gaze jumped to Hannah. He loved her with every breath in his body. He couldn't be responsible for the attack. He couldn't be responsible . . .

The attack. The pain. The terror. Her life destroyed because of him.

His eyes met hers across the room in sudden knowledge — in complete and utter despair. "The picture." His lungs burned. "God. Oh, God. The fucking picture, Hannah."

He couldn't look at her — at any of them. Without a word he turned and walked out of the room, slamming the kitchen door closed with such force it shook the house. A chair hit the door with an ominous crack and the sound of glass shattering followed.

Jackson started toward the kitchen. The Drake sisters pushed out of their chairs. Their fiancés followed them. Hannah beat them all to the door and stood in front of it, blocking the way.

"No. Leave him alone. Everyone. Leave him." Her blue eyes glittered with real menace, backing them all up. "This is mine. No matter what, you stay out." She decreed it, facing them down, knowing whatever was wrong, Jonas would never want them to see him so completely out of control.

Sarah nodded and waved her sisters back into the living room. She waited for the men to reluctantly follow before she squeezed

Hannah's hand and left her alone.

Hannah took a deep breath and cautiously opened the door. Slipping inside, she turned the lock and took a look around the room. The chairs were turned over, one was broken. Plates lay smashed on the floor. Jonas was across the room, his arm and shoulders moving rhythmically as he hit the wall with his fist. With every strike, blood sprayed and he swore obscenely. His face was a mask of fury, the punching merciless.

Hannah stepped carefully around the broken glass, deliberately moving into his view. "Jonas. Stop. Whatever this is, whatever happened, we can deal with it."

He turned to her, his eyes alive with pain. "Can we, Hannah?" He shook his head. "There's no dealing with this one. Not now, not ever."

She reached out to him and he jumped out from under her fingers, denying physical contact. "Tell me then. Just say it."

"It was the picture." His lungs burned. "Hannah, I'm so fucking sorry. They found the picture at the hospital. It was there, in my shirt pocket, and they cut my shirt off of me. I just left it there on the floor when we went out the window. It was my mistake. *Mine.*"

He sank to the floor, his legs turning to

rubber. "It was in my shirt pocket," he repeated, rubbing his hands down his face. "I did this."

"I don't understand, Jonas. What did you do?" Hannah's voice was gentle, compassionate, loving.

He couldn't bear for her to be loving. Or understanding. He wanted to put a bullet in his fucking head.

"Which picture, Jonas? Start there."

"The one of you Sarah took outside in the backyard. You were surrounded by flowers and you were laughing. I was looking down at you. Sarah gave it to me and I kept it with me all the time." He looked up at her in complete despair. "I should have known. It was in the back of my head when I saw the picture on my dresser. For a moment it was there and I lost it again. I didn't want to know." He slammed the back of his head against the wall. "Damn it. Just damn it."

She eased her body down next to his, thigh to thigh, not touching, but close, so close she could feel his heat — and the jumble of emotions so intense they swamped the room. She was careful to allow them to wash over her and not let them in to affect her own emotions. Jonas needed her steady, not reacting.

"I loved the way you look, but . . ." He bit

off a curse. "Anyone looking at the picture would know I'm in love with you."

Hannah tried not to fixate on the blood dripping steadily from his knuckles but the sight of his mashed and bleeding flesh made her slightly queasy. She wanted to put her arms around him and comfort him, but he was ramrod stiff. She let the silence stretch out, forcing herself to allow him to tell her at his own pace.

"You're a supermodel, Hannah. No one knows who the hell I am, but your face is everywhere. They took one look at that picture and they knew just how to get to me. The fucking bastard is going to die for this."

She was beginning to comprehend. Maybe she'd known from the moment he'd gotten that look on his face, the dawning horror. She twisted her fingers together to keep from touching her face. In a way, it was a relief to know. She could never imagine why someone would hate her so much, but it wasn't about her. It had never been about her.

"Boris Tarasov did this to me because he was trying to get to you?"

"I should have known when there was no magic involved. It was too brutal. The killers were amateurs and both were reluctant.

He must have threatened their child. And he would have done it quite brutally. Tarasov has a certain reputation for bloody vengeance. He probably made them believe that if they didn't carry out the attack exactly as he instructed, he would chop their little girl into pieces and send her back to them one piece at a time. That's the kind of thing he's famous for."

Jonas looked at her then — at the scars on her face and throat. "I spent my life trying to take care of my mother and then all of you. I wanted you more than anything, Hannah, but my old job was so dangerous, and I was afraid I'd bring that danger on you and your sisters. So I stayed away. When I took the job with the sheriff's department, I thought we might have a chance. It was so much safer than what I had been doing." He dropped his face in his hands. "All those years of being careful, and in the end, I still brought the violence straight to you."

Hannah looked into his eyes — his gorgeous, dangerous eyes — and saw such misery, such rage and hopelessness. She forced her brain to slow down, not react, but to think. Jonas spent his life trying to save people. He put himself in harm's way every single day in order to help others and it had cost him far more than he realized.

He hadn't done this. He could never be responsible for what another human being chose to do and somehow she had to find a way to make him understand that.

"No, Jonas. You didn't put that knife in my attacker's hands. You didn't force him to use it. Boris Tarasov did. He's the one responsible, not you." She put her hand over his knuckles, pushing healing energy to take the sting away.

"Don't!" he said sharply. "This is . . . *unacceptable*, Hannah. You're my damn world and to have someone try to destroy you over something I did . . ."

"*You* don't," she answered with equal sharpness. "Don't you dare! I mean it, Jonas. This isn't about you and don't try to make it that way. Your mother's illness wasn't about you either. You take on too much, you always have."

"She was over forty when she had me. She was too frail to have a child and she never recovered." He shoved both hands several times through his hair, needing to hit something again. "Her immune system shut down after I was born."

"She wanted you more than anything else in the world. Both your mother and father did. You have no right to take that away from them. It was their *choice* and one they never regretted."

"She suffered, Hannah. Every damn day. She suffered."

"She was very strong, not frail, and she fought it long and hard because it was her decision to stay with you. I'm an empath. I went with my family to see your mother. I knew what she wanted, and it wasn't death. Not even to escape the pain. She wanted every single minute she could have with you." She took his hand again, linked their fingers together. "And that's what I want, Jonas. Every single minute I can have with you."

"Look what happened to you, Hannah."

"It happened. It was frightening and horrible and we both wish it hadn't happened, but it did. And something good came of it. In a way, Jonas, I found my strength. I know who I am and what I want. I gained my freedom."

"Damned hard way to get your freedom, baby. And you're going to have nightmares for the rest of your life."

"So I'll have nightmares. Don't we all? Don't you?" She framed his face with her hands because everything she said was true. She was stronger and she did know what she wanted. "We're partners. Now. Forever. You can't shield everyone you love from bad things, Jonas. They're going to happen. When they do, we'll handle them together."

Jonas stared into her eyes for a long time, searching for the truth. "I don't know if I can forgive myself."

"Have you heard a word I've said? Jonas, if we're going to make it together, if I'm as important to you as you say I am, then you have to listen to me. I want all of you. Every single bit of you. I won't accept a man who is afraid to love me with his entire heart and soul and body. If I can't have all of you, then there's no point in this. You can't control the world, Jonas, and you can't continue to blame yourself for things beyond your control. I never asked you to be different. Yes, you scare me sometimes, but I'll take fear over you trying to be someone you're not."

Jonas opened his mouth and then closed it. If he had remembered the picture, then Tarasov would never have connected Hannah to him. He wouldn't have destroyed an entire family . . . He groaned. He couldn't take that on, too. The couple had choices. They could have gone to the cops, put their daughter into protective custody, but they'd elected to murder an innocent woman to protect their own. That was on them. He rubbed his hands over his face and looked down into Hannah's face.

"I'm not going to tell you that you're right."

"But I am."

His eyes softened. A small smile tugged at his mouth. "Hannah. You didn't stammer. Not once — not even when you were putting me in my place."

He leaned in to kiss her. Gentle. Tender. So sweet it brought tears to her eyes.

"Are we good?" she asked.

"We're good," he answered. He'd live with what happened because he had no other choice. He'd made a mistake and she was right, there was no going back. He wasn't about to lose her over it. If she could look him straight in the eye, then he was man enough to do the same.

He looked slowly around the room. "I don't suppose the house repairs furniture and dishes?"

Hannah laughed. "No such luck. But if you notice, there's no hole in the wall. Next time you decide to go crazy and punch the wall, you might remember, this house could protest and just lock your fist inside, and then where would you be?"

He narrowed his eyes and looked warily at the wall. "This place is definitely creepy." He kissed her again. "I suppose I'm going to have to face everyone. I hate telling your sisters that I put you — and maybe them — in danger."

"It isn't like we haven't been in danger before, Jonas," Hannah reminded him.

The truth was, he could barely stand the idea that he had exposed his family to a madman like Boris Tarasov. The Russian was brutal and vengeful, his reputation scared even seasoned investigators. With a small sigh, he stood up and reached down to take her hand, pulling her to her feet.

"I guess I have to get it over with." But instead of going into the living room, he wrapped his arms around Hannah and held her against him, his hands sliding down her jeans to cup her bottom and bring her tight against him. "Thank you."

"I love you, Jonas."

"Thank you for not telling me what an ass I am for tearing up the kitchen. Sometimes I have so much anger in me," he confessed in a whisper against her ear, "so much rage, it scares the hell out of me."

She pressed her mouth to his throat, remembering very vividly the day, long ago, he had come into their house so angry he couldn't stand still. Waves of grief poured off him and mixed with impotent rage. He'd torn up the kitchen then, too. Her mother had taken Libby and had gone to do what they could to ease Jeanette Harrington's suffering. Mrs. Drake had never chastised Jonas, but she had handed him a broom.

"It doesn't scare me, Jonas," Hannah said. She kissed him again. "But after we're married, if you break my dishes, be prepared to clean up the mess and then go out and get me new ones immediately." She reached back, tugged at his hand until she had possession of it and brought his injured knuckles once more to her mouth. "Let's go. I can feel how worried the others are about you."

The moment they entered the living room, he was swarmed by Hannah's sisters — his sisters. They crowded around him, their hands soothing, bringing peace, healing his knuckles — healing his soul. Sending him waves of love and support. He went from wanting to viciously beat something with his bare hands, to being choked up. The Drake sisters. His family. Hannah. The love of his life. Who could be luckier?

"Are you all right?" Sarah asked gently.

He nodded, wanting to ease the concern on their faces. "I lost it there for a minute." He glanced back toward the kitchen. "I made a mess, Sarah, I'm sorry."

"Tell us what's upset you."

"Boris Tarasov went after Hannah to draw me out. I'm the real target. He'll try to kill her because she matters to me. He might try to kill all of you."

Joley frowned. "I don't understand. Why would a Russian mobster want to kill you? That doesn't make any sense, Jonas."

"Duncan Gray is my old boss and he asked me to do a little job for him, nothing dangerous, or at least I didn't think it would be, but we caught Petr Tarasov on tape murdering an undercover agent."

Ilya Prakenskii made a small noise at the back of his throat. There was silence, as if by that one small sound, everyone instantly understood the chilling repercussions.

"I was shot in the ensuing battle and went to a clinic. I had a picture of Hannah and me, one I always carried with me. Tarasov's crew must have found the picture, and in order to bring me out into the open, they attacked Hannah using an innocent family to do so. My guess is, we'll find that the mother has ties to Russia and that's how he chose her. She would know his reputation and believe absolutely that he would kill her daughter if they didn't do what he said."

Joley's hand moved defensively to her throat. "Is that true, Ilya? Would someone be so convinced they'd kill another human being?"

Ilya stroked a caress down her hair, a gesture of comfort. "Unfortunately men like this exist, Joley, very evil, and yes, those who know of him would do whatever they could to spare their loved ones the brutality of his chosen executions."

"Then you have to stop him, Jonas," Sarah said. "We all do."

"Do you know where this man is?" Joley asked Prakenskii.

Rare expression rippled across Prakenskii's face. "Joley, these people . . ."

"Want to kill my sister, Jonas and possibly us. Do you know where they are?"

He pushed away from the wall. "I'll take care of it."

Jonas shook his head. "This is my fight, Prakenskii. He did this to my woman, not yours. Where is he?"

Prakenskii swore in Russian. "You cannot arrest such a man, Harrington."

Jonas lifted an eyebrow and remained silent.

Prakenskii swore again. "He's on a yacht with several of his crew."

Jonas nodded. "We'll need Duncan to get the necessary warrant to board. We'll have to strike fast before he has a chance to launch another attack. Can you girls give us the weather we'll need and help from here?"

"Of course, Jonas, tell us what you need," Hannah said.

Prakenskii shook his head and walked out. Jackson hesitated a moment and then followed.

The Drake sisters may have overdone the fog, Jonas decided as he approached the boat where Duncan's grim-faced men waited.

"These people play for keeps, Jonas," Jackson warned softly. "If you leave Tarasov alive, he'll keep coming at you — even from jail."

"I heard Prakenskii, same as you," Jonas snapped. "Where the hell is he, anyway? You'd think he'd want in on this."

"He didn't show, but then, with Duncan Gray running the operation, I can't blame him too much." Jackson flashed a small grin. "Gray thinks Prakenskii's both a spy as well as the world's best hit man." The smile faded. "You know Duncan's going to want to take Boris into custody. It would be the biggest international arrest of the decade. It isn't going to matter that Boris is after you and your family. We have to get to him first."

"I know." Jonas leaned down to examine his gun for the hundredth time to avoid looking at Jackson.

"I'll take him out, Jonas," Jackson said.

Jonas shook his head. "It's my responsibility, Jackson, I'm not laying it on you."

Jackson didn't bother replying. He'd already had a long conversation with Prakenskii — well, as long a conversation as two men like Ilya Prakenskii and Jackson Deveau needed when protecting a friend. Jonas had the courage to charge hell with a bucket of water, and he never walked away from a fight or a fallen comrade, but he didn't have the makeup for the kind of extermination job they needed to do. Jonas had been raised to revere life, in the same way the Drakes had been raised, and had far too much compassion in him to live comfortably with what needed to be done. He'd do the job, but it would haunt him. Jackson wasn't going to let that happen.

"The girls will be waiting in case we need them. Already they've got the fog thick and still, so we'll have plenty of cover going in," Jonas said. He stepped aside to allow Jackson to enter the boat with Gray and the rest of his team.

Gray barely looked up from studying the yacht's layout for the millionth time. "Our information says Tarasov's got fifteen men aboard the yacht and no civilians. All of his men are armed and will cut you down without thought. These four are the most dangerous. Don't get close to them for any reason. Don't try to cuff them. Don't try to disarm them. They know more ways to kill a man than you could possibly imagine. Contain them and wait for my team to apprehend. This is our target." Gray passed around photographs.

Jonas found himself staring at Boris Tarasov. The man was short and stocky, with a shock of gray hair and bushy eyebrows. He had heavy features and mean, bullish eyes. The second picture was of the captain. He was taller with an athletic build, a very handsome man.

"That's Karl Tarasov, Petr's son. He's been the number one hit man for his family for years. He's ruthless and bloody and doesn't mind killing women and children," Gray continued. "No one has ever come up against him and lived. He'll do anything to protect his uncle."

"If we don't arrest them, Jonas, you and the Drakes are never going to be safe."

That was a blatant lie and it twisted Jonas's gut into knots. Gray knew as long as any of the Tarasovs were alive, Hannah would never be safe. *Never.* And that meant they had no choice but to see to it that each of them were executed. He sighed and rubbed his temples where the beginning of a headache was throbbing. He thought he was long out of that business.

"How do they let someone like that into the country?" Jonas asked, disgusted.

"We didn't know he was anywhere near the area," Gray said, "not until you brought us the information about the yacht. Our last information was that he left the country after Petr was arrested. You're absolutely certain of your informant?"

Jonas wasn't going to give up Ilya Prakenskii, not to Gray. Duncan was ambitious, and if he arrested Prakenskii or Tarasov or even Nikitin, his political career would be made. Whatever Prakenskii was, he'd saved Hannah's life and Jonas wouldn't betray him. "Yeah, I'm sure."

"The other two I'm really interested in are known for their extreme violence. Yegor and Viktor Gadiyan are brothers. Yegor was married to Boris and Petr's sister, Irina. She died some years ago, but the Gadiyan brothers continued to work for Boris."

"Great family business."

"It was Yegor and Viktor who tried to kill Sergei Nikitin some years ago. The other

Russian families stepped in when Nikitin brought in Ilya Prakenskii as his bodyguard. I don't think any of the families wanted to chance having Prakenskii come after them."

Jonas studiously avoided looking at Jackson. "It's funny how these men have such badass reputations, but no cop in Europe or here can pin a thing on them."

"This cop is going to," Gray said. "We can't waste any more time. The fog being so thick is a huge asset but it can't last. We've got to move now."

The men were grim-faced and silent as they approached the yacht, moving through the rippling water, their boats climbing waves and slapping down with enough force to shake their teeth, yet there was absolutely no sound. Jonas knew the Drake sisters were controlling the air around them, but he wondered what Duncan's men were thinking. It was eerie to move over the choppy surface surrounded as they were by dense gray fog. Within the fog bank, darker colors swirled and moved, but the heavy mist layers were thick and still, stubbornly holding position for several miles in either direction around where the yacht lay stationary. Waves slapped the sides of the ship while men patrolled the deck, peering through the fog in an effort to see.

It was imperative that Jonas and Jackson reach Tarasov first. If Gray did, he would do everything to keep the mobster alive. It had taken effort and a lot of persuasion to get Gray to agree to allow Jonas and Jackson to slip aboard first. Fortunately, they'd always held that position when they'd worked for Gray, so in the end, he'd agreed it was best for them to do what they knew.

Jonas and Jackson slipped into the cold water, some distance from the yacht, pushing their waterproof gear ahead of them while they swam toward it. Jonas felt a nudge against his body as a gray shape slid soundlessly past him. His heart jumped and he whipped his head around, trying to peer through the water to see what was coming up below him. Beside him, Jackson pulled his spear gun out, but it was impossible with the combination of fog and darkness to see anything around them.

Voices rose and fell in the fog, soft and melodious, feminine. The voices sang of dolphins, sea creatures aiding sailors. The notes danced in the mist and slid easily into their minds. Both men relaxed, and when the dolphins pushed beneath their hands, they caught hold of the offered fins and accepted the ride.

As they neared the large bulk sitting in the water, Jackson caught Jonas by the arm and pointed at the splash of red on the side, down near the water line. The dolphin pulling Jonas suddenly abandoned him, diving deep, straight down. Jonas moved closer to examine the red smears.

"Fresh blood, Jackson, and a lot of it."

Jonas took a slow look around him. Waves slapped his face as the dolphin returned to the surface towing something behind him. Jonas saw the hand first, fingers outstretched and reaching up through the dark water. It seemed to come out of the fog and water, detached, a gruesome macabre sight. The knuckles had a tattoo across it, much like the one Rudy Venturi had described. Jonas reached to snag the sleeve and pulled hard. The dolphin let go, but the body seemed weighed down, too heavy to keep on the surface for more than a few moments.

Jackson reached over to help, tugging the arm out of the water. Shoulders and chest followed, and then the face with the heavy, handsome features and the gaping wound circling his throat from ear to ear like a ghoulish smile. Karl Tarasov had died hard. His eyes were dull and glassy, his face a mask of horror. He wore the coat of a captain, and beneath it, Jonas could make out the shoulder harness with the gun still in the holster. Jackson indicated something under the body weighting it down and Jonas nodded his understanding before allowing the body to drop away, back under the sea.

Jonas boarded first, moving as soundlessly as possible, trying to puzzle out the implications of Karl Tarasov's execution. He gained the deck and lay flat, waiting for his heart to stop pounding as he oriented himself to the surroundings. Jackson slid into position beside him and they pulled their gear from their waterproof bags and readied themselves for war. Jackson fit the radio piece into his ear and gave Gray instructions for his men. Two guards patrolled the deck. They would take them out as quietly as possible to allow Gray to get his men onboard.

Jonas signaled Jackson forward and he moved in the opposite direction, circling around to get in position to take out the guard as he came back around. He drew his knife and waited, heart pounding, a bad taste in his mouth. This day would haunt him. He knew it had to be done, and he was more than willing to kill these men to keep the Drakes safe, but that wouldn't make killing any easier. He just wasn't wired that way. His mother — and the Drakes — had seen to that.

The guard loomed out of the fog, his footsteps muffled, merging with the sound of water slapping the sides of the yacht and the occasional cry of a bird overhead. Jonas let the man go past him and stepped in, arm whipping up fast, knife sinking deep. He let out his breath, holding the guard while the life drained out of him before easing him to the deck. He asked the universe for forgiveness even as he was making his way down to the next level, seeking Boris Tarasov with every intention of ending his life — and wasn't that irony? Sometimes he made himself sick.

Jonas heard Jackson whispering through the earpiece. "I'm looking at Karl Tarasov alive and well. He's talking to two of the guards in front of the master state room."

Jonas frowned. There was no doubt in his mind that Karl was anchored at the bottom of the sea. "Are you sure?"

"It's him. He just patted a guard on the back. They laughed together and he went into the stateroom. The guards definitely think it's him."

"One at the helm," Jonas said. "He's got a bird's eye view, Gray, get one of your best on him." He made his way slowly down the stairs, hugging the wall, careful to make no sound as he eased each foot forward.

Someone laughed as he passed the salon. Jonas crouched down, making himself small as he studied the layout. The rooms were spacious, but there weren't a lot of places to hide. Movement attracted his attention. Karl Tarasov came out of the master stateroom, clapped a hand on the guard's shoulder and gave him orders. The guard snapped to attention. Jonas studied the Russian captain. He was tall and broad-shouldered. His uniform jacket was immaculate, not a wrinkle, the same with his pressed trousers. The shoes were polished and every hair in place. He walked down the hall to the salon and disappeared inside. Only then did Jonas realize he was wearing thin black gloves over his hands.

Jonas swore under his breath and lifted the gun, silencer in place. Before he could pull the trigger, both guards went down almost simultaneously, a crimson hole blossoming in each forehead. Jackson moved past them, kicking the guns out of the way and reaching for the door.

"Damn it, Jackson." Jonas had no choice but to cover him.

Jackson slipped inside the master stateroom, Jonas right behind him. Boris Tarasov lay on the bed. His eyes were wide open, staring and glassy. The bed beneath him was soaked red and around his throat was an obscene smile.

"Son of a bitch," Jonas said, and then spoke into his radio. "Gray. Tarasov is dead. I repeat, dead. It looks like Karl Tarasov killed him before we got here. I saw him coming out of the room just before we entered." He hesitated a moment before tossing in the red herring. "I think we stumbled into a power play, a takeover, going on here."

Gray swore softly in his ear. "Ben reported seeing Karl go toward the salon where the Gadiyan brothers were last seen. Everyone be damn careful, and for God's sake, keep the son of a bitch alive. We need one of the major players talking."

Jonas shook his head. If that was the real Karl Tarasov, then who was in the water? And if it was Karl, he would never be taken alive, Gray should know that. He was handicapping his team, sending them against a lethal killer and ordering them not to fire. They moved in tandem, Jackson point man, clearing the hall, and Jonas sweeping each room as they passed, then guarding their backs. Gunfire erupted in the vicinity of the helm.

Jackson let out a sigh. "There goes any advantage we might have had."

More gunfire burst out on the deck, this time a volley answered by another volley.

The doors to the salon burst open and bullets sprayed the hall, slamming into the walls and shattering glass, tearing up everything in their path. Two men stood side by side, automatic weapons blasting as they hurtled themselves out of the salon toward the stairs. Gray's men returned fire. One agent screamed and lay writhing on the floor, another was flung backward into the wall.

Jonas felt the familiar rage welling up and forced it down, taking careful aim, taking his time, making the shot count. Yegor Gadiyan went down without a sound. Viktor Gadiyan reached with one hand to try to grab his brother's collar and drag him even as he continued to spray the hall in a systematic and very thorough sweep. The noise in the small confines of space was deafening as well as frightening. Jonas stayed crouched low in the tiny alcove, sweating, pinned down, and waiting for an angry bullet to strike him.

Off to his left, Jackson signaled him, putting three fingers up, one by one indicating in three seconds Jonas needed to draw Gadiyan's fire. Jonas closed his eyes and sent up a silent prayer. He counted to three and allowed the edge of his shoulder to show for half a second and jerked back into cover. Bullets thudded all around him, spitting splinters into his face and shoulders. He heard the single shot Jackson squeezed off followed by a heavy body hitting the floor and then absolute silence.

Jonas looked at the wall around him. Bullets had smashed into the wood in every conceivable spot without hitting him. Some higher power was working to save him, but he didn't believe it could have been the Drakes this time. He allowed himself a moment to slump against the wall in relief. Viktor Gadiyan would have killed him given another few moments. He saluted Jackson, who was already checking the bodies.

Once more they began the dangerous task of clearing rooms. Overhead they could hear the firefight continue as Tarasov's men fought Gray's unit.

The earpiece erupted with a burst of chatter. "Karl Tarasov is trapped on the upper deck!"

Gray began snapping orders and both Jackson and Jonas took the stairs quickly, racing to try to intercept Gray's men. Jackson circled to the left and Jonas went right. Tarasov's back was to Jonas. The Russian snapped off an occasional shot to keep the agents away from him as he made his way to the railing. The agents were trying to surround him and take him alive. Jonas silently slipped into position behind him, cutting off his escape.

The fog thickened, swirling in and around the yacht, closing them into a gray, wet world, muffling sounds and cutting visibility nearly to zero. Karl Tarasov turned and ran right into Jonas.

The two locked wrists as Tarasov brought up a knife in one hand and a gun in the other. Jonas drove him back toward the railing as they thrashed around, his body between Tarasov and the agents, preventing them from a clear shot. Jackson twice brought up his weapon and dropped it, when Jonas was thrown into the line of fire, unable to see through the blurring action and the thick veil that shrouded the yacht.

Jonas slammed Tarasov hard against the rail, still struggling to control the weapons. The gun dropped into the sea. Tarasov, in a sudden burst of strength, threw Jonas back a step and smashed his fist hard into Jonas's jaw. Jonas staggered and the Russian turned and dove into the churning water. Duncan Gray ran to the edge of the railing and peered over.

"Damn it. Just damn it." He pounded the

railing with his fist. The water was choppy and dark, the fog making it worse to see. "He can't survive in that. It's too cold. He doesn't have a wetsuit on and we're too far from shore for him to swim. Get out there and look for him. He's got to surface."

Jackson reached Jonas and whipped him around, examining him for injuries. He pulled his earpiece free. "You hurt? That had to be Prakenskii."

"I recognized his eyes," Jonas agreed as he pulled off his own radio and slipped it into his gear bag. He rubbed his jaw. "He enjoyed that just a little too much," he said. "I'm going to have a whale of a bruise."

"Quit belly-aching. Those women have made you go soft. Two minutes after you hit the front door, they'll be all over you." He pitched his voice higher. "Oh, Jonas, darling, does it hurt? Let me make it all better for you."

Jonas shot him a glare. "You're just jealous because they don't fuss over you."

Jackson watched the boats searching the water in a grid pattern. "He's long gone, Jonas, they'll never find him."

"That was always the point, wasn't it?" Jonas felt inexplicably tired, weariness setting in all the way to the bone.

Jackson surveyed the damage. "I'm just

glad this is over. Let's get home."

"Sounds good to me." More than anything else, he wanted to be with Hannah, because wherever she was, that was home to him.

21

Jonas stood in his mother's bedroom and inhaled the faint scent of jasmine. He knew it grew just outside the window, climbing two stories on a trellis he'd put up himself when he was fourteen. He'd opened the window every day for years to allow the scent into the room because his mother had loved it, and now, smelling the fragrance gave him the illusion that she was there with him.

"Today's my wedding day, Mom," he said softly aloud. "I'm marrying the woman I always told you I would someday." He was silent a moment, listening to the echo of his voice in the room.

He'd read a thousand books here, even more poetry. He'd slept in a chair and later a small cot. There had been love in this room. Hannah was so right. It had been a tragedy for a young boy, but it hadn't been all bad, there had been wonderful times.

Laughter and whispers of secrets — like marrying Hannah Drake. He told his mother often and she never told a soul, encouraging him to follow his dreams, and assuring him that young Hannah would grow up into a wonderful woman someday.

"You would love her if you knew her now, all grown up, Mom. We both wanted the wedding here so you could be with us. If you look out the window, you'll be able to watch the ceremony and reception. The day turned out to be beautiful, although honestly, I don't know if the Drake sisters are keeping the fog and mist at bay, or whether it's natural." He ran his finger along the windowsill. "I wish you were here. You would love this. All these people. The clothes. Hannah made me dress up in this white zoot suit. We're doing a black-and-white-themed wedding. Nineteen twenties for you and Dad."

He stood for a few minutes again in silence. Voices drifted up from outside, where most of Sea Haven had gathered. There was no such thing as a small wedding, even if you were having a private, intimate gathering, not in Sea Haven. The Drake family alone comprised well over a hundred easily. Anyone growing up in Sea Haven had to invite everyone from the town, as they were considered more family than friends. He found himself smiling as laughter reached him from the lawns below.

"I did exactly what you said. I found a woman who will always be my best friend. She's so beautiful, Mom, and she overlooks those little flaws you were telling me about. She has a way of looking at me that makes me feel — makes me know — that I'm the luckiest man in the world."

He stood at the window taking in the semichaotic scene below. He'd always felt part of the Drake family, but now, when he was officially joining his life to Hannah's, he felt joy and an overwhelming happiness. "We're going to use this room as the nursery. I want our babies to feel your presence from the moment they're born. We plan on filling the house up with children and laughter, the way you always wanted it to be, and we're counting on you to help us look after them."

Jonas walked around the empty room. He'd long ago taken the bed out. He'd hated that bed, knowing his mother had felt a prisoner in it. Her things had been carefully packed, her most favorite possessions sentimentally kept in a glass cabinet in his den. He missed her, especially now, on this day, the one she'd so looked forward to.

A light knock had him turning. Jackson stuck his head in the room. "It's time, Jonas. You don't want to give Hannah time to rethink this."

Jonas smiled, saluted his absent mother and followed his best friend down the stairs. "I don't think she's going to run out on me." It amazed him how utterly confident he felt in her. Hannah was his best friend, his confidante and an amazing lover. From the moment he'd first set eyes on her, a part of him had known that this day was inevitable.

"You're already thinking about having children, aren't you?" Jackson said.

Jonas's gaze flicked to his friend. For the first time in his memory, he observed that Jackson looked uncomfortable.

"Hannah and I talked about it. We want a houseful. She's a homebody, Jackson. We have the money for her to be able to stay home and raise our kids. The house is enormous and the town is the perfect place to raise children."

"The thought of having kids doesn't scare you?"

"I grew up around the Drakes. For me, a big family seems natural and right. It's what my mother always wanted and it's what Hannah had. I can't imagine her without her sisters, or me without them either." He knew his eyes went a little steely. "Does the thought of children bother you?"

Jackson frowned. " 'Bother' isn't the right word. I've never been around children. I can't imagine being a father. I know I'll never be anyone's idea of an average dad."

"You've been around the Drakes long enough to know what a family is — what it should be. It's your choice whether or not you want it. Me? I'm grabbing it with both hands and hanging on tight."

Jonas walked with Jackson and the other groomsmen, down the long outdoor aisle between rows of chairs on the rolling lawn, surrounded by his family and friends. He looked around him and realized what he had. These people made up his life. And it was a good life. He had everything he needed right here, in this place, to be happy.

The music started and he turned to watch her come toward him. She was so beautiful she robbed him of breath as she stepped out of the authentic 1920s car and looked at him. Her smile lit her face as her gaze met his.

Hannah. I love you. Always. Always I'll love you. He meant it. Knew it, in his heart and soul.

I love you, Jonas. I want this more than

anything, to be your wife and have your children. I always have.

Her sisters came up the aisle dressed in vintage wear from the era, the dresses clingy with dropped waists. They looked beautiful, happy for him and Hannah. Pride swelled. This was his family and he mattered to them every bit as much as they did to him. Jackson had called it right on the yacht. The moment he'd returned, walking through the door, they had swarmed around him, hands brushing to make certain he was uninjured, lightening his heavy heart for the kill shots he'd taken, and removing the bruise on his jaw.

His throat closed as the music changed and everyone rose. Hannah Drake flowed up the aisle with her famous walk. Her blue eyes were vivid and bright, sparkling like the jewels on her wedding gown. The scars on her face and throat had faded to faint white lines, barely discernable, but it wouldn't have mattered if they hadn't. To him, she was the most beautiful woman in the world. Her father put her hand in his and Jonas closed his fingers tightly around hers, drawing her close to him. Emotional or not, he was damned if he was going to cry — Jackson would never let him hear the end of it — but he knew that moment would be forever in his mind. Hannah joining her life to his. So fine, his eyes burned and filled up, but really, who gave a damn? Hannah was finally his.

All of his life, Jonas had tried to be careful to keep her from feeling the emotions that often dominated his existence. Not today. Today he wanted to share every feeling — the rich fullness — the overflowing happiness. She had been there through his mother's illness and death and when he'd been shot. Through some of the darkest moments in his life. Now he wanted to share the best moment with her. He could never express in words what she meant to him, but Hannah was an empath and she could feel it.

She looked up at him and her eyes were swimming with tears. *I love you, too.*

Jonas listened to the ceremony, every sacred word, but all he could see was Hannah. The sun shone on her, colors danced around her, even her aura was present, a prism that glowed around her in rainbow colors.

Baby, did you know that you can taste happiness?

She blinked up at him, a slow smile curving her mouth. *Can you? What does it taste like?*

You. All hot and sweet and exciting. Mysteri-

ous. A combination of flavors.

She glanced at the minister and murmured an appropriate response, even as color swept up her neck and into her face. *You're trying to make me hot and bothered.*

He grinned at her. *I wasn't, but now that you mention it, just what are you wearing under that dress? I don't see a panty line.*

She nearly choked, covered it with a cough.

And then he was sliding his ring on her finger. Saying the words to make her his wife. Meaning them. The ring on his finger, a never-ending circle, felt solid and right. His heart jumped in his chest when the minister pronounced them man and wife.

Jonas turned to her, looked down at her, his hands framing her face so he could look into her eyes. "Forever, Hannah. For always." He bent his head slowly to hers, forgetting everyone, everything around him. His entire world narrowed to one woman. Hannah Drake Harrington. His lips moved over hers, feather-light. Seduction in its most elegant form. His kiss was gentle, tender, infinitely loving.

They turned toward their family and friends, sharing their happiness. The applause rang out, music blared and the party started.

Jonas greeted a hundred people, accepting congratulations, all the while keeping Hannah close to him. She smiled and murmured softly in response, appearing gracious and relaxed, but he was very aware how difficult it was for her. Often his hand moved up to the nape of her neck, easing the tension out of her with a slow massage. He bent his head to brush a kiss across the top of her head.

"Congratulations," a male voice repeated, drawing his attention back to the waiting line.

Jonas automatically shook hands, but then gripped Ilya Prakenskii's hand before he could let go. "You have a lot of nerve showing up here. There's law enforcement everywhere. Are you looking to get arrested?"

Prakenskii's eyebrow shot up. "For what? They're welcome to take me in, but they have no proof of any wrongdoing."

Jonas glanced around and lowered his voice. "You were on that yacht. You got there before us and somehow managed to kill Karl Tarasov and take his place. You were the one who killed Boris and you did it so I wouldn't."

"Did I? I have no recollection of this event," Prakenskii said.

"I looked into your eyes, Ilya. Straight into

them. I've heard of your ability to become a chameleon, to be anyone, but you can't hide your eyes. Color maybe, but not that intensity. And, you son of a bitch, you hit me." Jonas rubbed his jaw.

A hint of amusement crossed the Russian's face. "If such a thing had occurred, I'm certain the women in your family would give you adequate sympathy. Congratulations on your marriage. I must go annoy the sister of your bride by forcing her to dance with me once before I leave. I wish you long life and much happiness."

"Be careful, Prakenskii. Whatever you're into, it's very dangerous. Nikitin acts like a lamb, but I've done a little digging and the man is every bit as bloody and violent as Tarasov was, but then you already know that. I'm betting you know more about Nikitin than any other law enforcement officer in the world."

There was a small silence. Prakenskii didn't rise to the bait. Jonas sighed. "With Tarasov's territory wide open, Nikitin will be that much more powerful. You and I both know he'll take over most of Tarasov's operations."

"Since I work for the man, that just gives me job security."

Jonas shook his head. "You have to trust

somebody someday. Our family is indebted to you. You need help, you call." Because he didn't believe for one moment that Ilya Prakenskii was what the world believed him to be.

Prakenskii gave him a small salute and disappeared into the crowd.

Jonas found Hannah dancing with her sisters and pulled her into his arms. "Dance with me, baby."

Hannah slid into his arms, up against his body, as if made for him. The Drakes often had magic in their lives, and for Jonas, this entire day was his magical moment. She fit so perfectly. He swept her around the dance floor, the music heating his blood and singing in his veins.

"Do you remember last Christmas when I wished on the snowglobe, Hannah? You were so upset with me, and I wouldn't tell you what I wished for." He pressed his lips to her temple. "I wished for you." He spun her out and brought her back into him.

Her heart leapt, flying right along with her body as they moved together in perfect rhythm around the room. Everyone around them faded away until there was only Jonas. She felt his joy and knew he'd never been happier. She realized, in that perfect moment, that she was doing exactly what she wanted — what she was born to do. She was Jonas Harrington's wife. Complete. Committed. And happy beyond anything she'd ever dreamed.

She would always have the occasional panic attacks. And she would never believe she was as beautiful as so many people seemed to think she was, but she had come out of a terrible storm, emerging stronger and victorious. And happier than she'd ever dreamed she could be.

She stopped. Right there on the dance floor, her fingers linking behind the nape of his neck. All around her, her family danced and laughed, and filled the room with warmth and happiness. But this man in her arms, he filled her every empty place with strength and love. She met his gaze, saw the love shining there, and her heart jumped hard in her chest, her stomach did that funny little flip and deep down, where it mattered, she melted, just as she was supposed to.

"I love you, Jonas Harrington. With my heart and soul, I love you."

"I love you, Hannah Drake Harrington. With everything I am."

And that would always — *always* — be enough for both of them.

CHRISTINE FEEHAN

I live in the beautiful mountains of Lake County, California. I have always loved hiking, camping, rafting, and being outdoors. I've also been involved in the martial arts for years — I hold a third-degree black belt, instruct in a Korean karate system, and have taught self-defense. I am happily married to a romantic man who often inspires me with his thoughtfulness. We have a yours, mine, and ours family, claiming eleven children as our own. I have always written books, forcing my ten sisters to read every word, and now my daughters read and help me edit my manuscripts. It is fun to take all the research I have done on wild animals, raptors, vampires, weather, and volcanoes and put it together with romance. Please visit my website at www.christinefeehan.com.

The employees of Thorndike Press hope you have enjoyed this Large Print book. All our Thorndike and Wheeler Large Print titles are designed for easy reading, and all our books are made to last. Other Thorndike Press Large Print books are available at your library, through selected bookstores, or directly from us.

For information about titles, please call:
(800) 223-1244

or visit our Web site at:
www.gale.com/thorndike
www.gale.com/wheeler

To share your comments, please write:
Publisher
Thorndike Press
295 Kennedy Memorial Drive
Waterville, ME 04901